THE PLACE CALLED SKULL

William J. O'Malley

When they reached the place called Skull, they crucified him there and the two criminals also, one on the right, the other on the left. Jesus said, "Father, forgive them. They do not know what they are doing." Then they cast lots to share out his clothing.

—Luke 23:33-34

D1713635

Cover by Richard Moon
Moon Brand
Rochester, N.Y.

First published by Dog Ear Publishing
4010 W. 86th Street, Ste H
Indianapolis, IN 46268
www.dogearpublishing.net

ISBN: 978-1-4575-0943-8

This book is printed on acid-free paper.

This book is a work of fiction. Places, events, and situations in this book are historically
true and some characters have been embellished or conflated, but the people were
real.

Printed in the United States of America

This book is for

JACK E. POST

and

THE JESUITS OF LE MOYNE COLLEGE.

Muenschener Nueesten Nachrichten

Camp for Enemies of the State

On Wednesday, March 22, 1933, the first concentration camp will be opened in the vicinity of Dachau. It can accommodate 5,000 people. We have adopted this measure, undeterred by paltry scruples, in the conviction that our action will help to restore calm to our country and is in the best interests of the people.

Heinrich Himmler
Commissioner of Police
City of Munich

Prologue

1939

Monday, 21 August 1939 - Saint Blasien Sanitorium

From his sanatorium window Paul Reiser looked down the long valley to the domed church of the old Benedictine Abbey, across orange roofs to rolling hills furred with Black Forest evergreens.

The face reflected in the windowpane wasn't the face Lisl had always said was so "perfect." Lines around the hazel eyes, sockets blue-grey as old bruises. The once chiseled cheeks looked gouged, and the yellow hair she'd said "squiggled, like a hyacinth," was beginning to recede. Good for him. Dose of full-strength humility. He'd always been vain about his body. His face. Now, at twenty-three, he no longer looked the perfect Aryan they'd told him he was six months ago. And all the years before. Some getting used to. Not being perfect anymore.

Back in March, Paul had been in the *Priester Seminar* in Muenster, trying to study sacraments before his ordination as a priest next Christmas, after six years. Since his kneepants days, he'd always been first or second in his class, and in the seminary you either immersed yourself in the books, or went mad, or left. He had forged a Buddhist concentration. Yet when the bell rang, he could snap it off like a lightswitch and explode out into games, picnics, working with kids. Then within less than a month, the jolly giant began to metamorphose into a dithery old man.

His persistent cough got on everybody's nerves. In the library someone was always whispering, "Wake Reiser up, for God's sake. He's a bitch when he misses study time." When he was able to get home from the seminary for dinner, his usually easygoing mother fretted about how thin and pale he was. Finally, his father had asked to see Bishop von Galen. Before the week was out, Paul had been in a clinic in Berlin, hearing the head doctor say, "Tuberculosis."

Paul had sat forward across the desk at the pained, soft face. He shook his head. "No, no. *Herr Doktor*, there's some mistake," he laughed, lamely. "I've been a gymnast all my life. I'm only twenty-three. I never smoked. I thinned out, but...I've put in six *years* studying to be a priest. It's like...like pulling out three paces from the tape! Are you *sure*? X-rays. They get mixed up, yes?"

"Rarely," the doctor said with a wan smile, "and you hardly needed a team of experts, son. Any first-year resident could have seen. Why didn't you go to your doctor at the seminary?"

"I've been busy. Classes. Work with the boys." He tensed, trying to make space for this. "Look at me, *Doktor*," Paul said, twisting between laughter and tears. "A young ox. A bit run down, but I can still...I can still out-run, out-swim, out-climb anybody in that seminary. It *has* to be...."

"Paul, right now, you couldn't out-run a crippled child. We're certain. The right lung is heavily infected, the left seriously threatened. When you worked the swamps during Labor Service, you must have contracted pleurisy. But you do have the body of a fine athlete, and you're resolute. Enough to help you kid yourself a long time. But not with all the strain you kept putting your mind and body through. They've been telling you something for over a year. You wouldn't listen."

Paul fell back and put his palms over his face. "And now?"

"Saint Blasien. The only hope is rest. Good food. Sunshine. You have to live like a plant."

Paul's stomach plummeted. "Doktor, I'm to be ordained at Christmas. Seven months and twenty-two days. Couldn't I wait? Just that long? If I rested every day? The Dean would postpone some courses. I'll stop the boys' group for awhile." Tears burned. "I've waited so long."

The doctor shook his head slowly. "Son, unless you do as we suggest, you won't live seven months and twenty-two days."

The first months, once he'd surrendered, were like a drugged dream. Then he had begun to get restless, which the doctors said was a good sign, but he had to go slowly, slowly. He asked for something to read, but they would give him only magazines and detective stories. After an initial, priggish disdain, he finally picked one up, flittered the pages, and at last succumbed.

There were about a hundred patients in the men's wing, a motley group-slack-jawed and empty-eyed old men, boys whose sunken cheeks made their eyes seem the size of Easter eggs. One could diagnose by their pace. Some shuffled along like unwinding toys; others, healing, began to move into a brisker step, their voices thickening, coughing less often into their handkerchiefs.

The air was charged with talk of war.

In the evening, Paul sat in the dayroom playing chess with Heinrich Boell, a straight- backed Muenchener with falcon eyes. He had almost graduated from a military school when he had been diagnosed consumptive. Like most men in this dayroom, he was close to cured. Boell had little taste for priests, but Paul was the only one he couldn't beat at chess in five moves.

Others sat reading or working jigsaw puzzles. The radio played *"Eine kleine Nachtmusik,"* softly, and toothless old Spath leaned with his eyes closed, hand cupped to his ear, smiling.

Two men hovered above the chessboard. Auwi Saukel was a young apprentice bricklayer from Saalfelden who fretted that his girl, who wrote him once a day, was losing interest. Auwi always seemed to be dancing in place, as if there were a radio speaker implanted in his uncluttered mind. Max Fellgiebel was older, a waiter from Bad Reichenhall. Once portly, he now looked as if someone sacked him into a bigger man's skin by mistake. Round, black-rimmed glasses perched on his nubbin nose over a toothbrush moustache and gapped teeth. Max had been a Party member long before it was fashionable and had once served the Fuehrer himself at the Thalfried Cafe.

"I could sure use a smoke." Auwi looked at Spath mooning with his Mozart. "Can't he get nothing better than that," he said, snapping his fingers edgily, "something with a beat?"

"Decadent," Boell said, not taking his eyes off the board.

"What's that mean?" Saukel frowned.

"Jazz. Nigger music. Corrupts the soul," Boell said and took Paul's bishop with his knight.

"Hah!" Saukel sneered. "We're all gonna be dead in Poland 'fore the year's out."

"Auwi," Max prissed, "Poland won't last long enough for the Reich to conscript a man with a lung full of ping-pong balls."

"Who gives a shit for Poland?" Auwi winced. "And shut up about my ping-pong balls."

"It is *not* Poland, my young friend," Max said with a sour patient smile. "It never was. It's Germany. Until the War, the corridor between Germany and East Prussia was Germany. It still is Germany. Surely you can see that. You did go to school."

"So? They give that strip to the Poles to get to the sea. After the War. I learned that."

Max closed his eyes a moment. "But it's not *theirs*, Saukel. We have a *right* to take back a German city like Danzig."

Paul moved a castle to protect his queen. "And a right to take a Czech city like Prague and an Austrian city like Vienna?"

Boell looked up from the board at him. Fellgiebel looked down with a furry scowl.

"Yeah," Saukel said. "Listen to this man. Practically a priest, an' he oughtta know, right?"

Boell's eyes narrowed. "Are you implying the Poles have a right to Danzig?"

"If they've been living there for twenty years."

"Squatters," Max sniffed.

"But put yourself in a Pole's shoes."

"I'd die first," Max said, eyes rolling back into his head.

"It belonged to the Poles *before* we took it, no? We asked for the Austrian Germans back, right? We got them. And then the rest of Austria, for good measure. We asked for the Sudetenland back, right? We got that back. And then the rest of Czechoslovakia, for good measure."

Boell frowned at Paul, rolling the captured bishop round and round on its pointed head against the tabletop. Saukel pondered the whole thing, rocking his head from side to side.

"But those people *begged* us to rescue them," Max huffed.

Paul leaned down and concentrated on the game. "Look, we're not getting anywhere, right? Let's get back to the game. I've got an invasion of my own on my hands."

Suddenly, the music stopped. Old Spath still had his ear cupped toward the big box, his memory continuing the music. A loud, serious voice came on, and the old man jumped, bug-eyed.

"We interrupt this program for a special announcement. Word has just been received that the Reich and the Soviet Union have agreed to conclude a pact of nonaggression. Herr von Ribbentrop, will arrive in Moscow on Wednesday, 23 August, for the conclusion of negotiations."

The music seeped back into the room, and old Spath returned to his interrupted reverie.

Boell's face was beaming. He clapped his hands together. "What a union! With the Russians at the back door, the Poles won't dare invade us. And the British and the French will mind their own business now. No two-front war like the last time."

Max smiled down at Paul's immobile face. "What's the matter, Beauty? Hardly the response to such a historic moment."

"Rather not discuss it, Max. You're the politician."

Boell looked at him. "You smug bastard."

Paul leaned back, frowning. "Doesn't it strike you as odd?"

Boell sniggered. "Odd? To checkmate the drooling Poles? No, I don't find that odd at all."

"Don't you feel a kind of...grinding of gears?"

Max pursed up his mouth. "Can't you talk plainly?"

"Look," Paul paused, doubting if it was worth it. "As long as you can remember, who's been the enemy? The Communists, right? And the Jews. Would it make any of you even a bit uneasy if that radio said the Fuehrer had signed a mutual defense treaty with the Head Rabbi of Berlin?"

"That's the stupidest thing I ever heard," Max sneered.

"I thought it might be."

"But this is Russia!" Max said. "The Head Rabbi of Berlin isn't going to keep out the Poles."

Paul chuckled. "Keeping the three little pigs out of the wolf's house."

Max's eyes rolled. "Will you for once say what you mean, straight out? Fucking priests."

"The Fuehrer says Poles are illiterate children. Why should the great Third Reich be afraid?"

Max bustled over and picked up a newspaper. "Read this. *Berliner Zeitung.*" He slapped the blaring headlines, but before Paul could read, Max snapped it back. "Listen to this: 'Chaos in Poland. One and a half *million* Polish troops mobilized on the German frontier. Three German *passenger* planes fired on by Poles.' If those illiterate children roll down the autobahn in tanks, I by God want Joe Stalin on my side. If he was the devil himself." Max huffed and started to cough.

"Don't get so excited, Max," Paul said. "It's not good for you. And it's not worth it."

Auwi nodded, sadly. "My mother says our bombers go over every day. And rationing. Worse than the end of the War, she says. And they pulled up all the iron fences in the parks."

Paul heaved to his feet. "Bed time." He clapped Auwi Saukel on his thin shoulder. "Cheer up, Auwi. With Mother Russia growling at the Poles' back door, it'll be a short war. The Great Man won't have to get down to drafting hackers and hawkers like us from a TB sanatorium."

"Reiser," Boell said, looking up to him, razor-eyed, "are you mocking Adolf Hitler?"

"Not at all, Heinrich," Paul smiled. "I called him 'The Great Man.' He *is* a great man. You have to be a great man to control a whole country, no? Joe Stalin is also probably a great man. Even...as Max says...if he's the devil himself."

Boell's eyes narrowed. "You'll bear watching, Reiser."

"Don't bother yourself, Heinrich," Paul said. He patted Boell's shoulder, and Boell pulled away with a frown. "God watches over me."

"No trouble, Reiser," Boell said, putting the chessmen into the cigar box. "No trouble at all."

* * * * *

Wednesday, 9 November 1939 - St. Blasien

"Ha-*ha*" Max snorted triumphantly, and threw the last five trump onto the card table. "Last five are ours! Tot them up, Reiser. You and Auwi owe me and Boell a small fortune."

Paul added up the scores. "Thirteen pfennigs each," he said, and reached into the pocket of his robe for the coins. "There you go, Max. Now you can open your own hotel."

"Principle of the thing," Max pocketed the change. "Not how much, Beauty. Just that you *win*!" He jerked his head toward sad-eyed Martin Brandt nodding his head against the earpiece of the phone. "Our Martin looks like his broker's reading him the entire listings of the stock exchange."

Martin Brandt hooked the earpiece back and shuffled morosely over to the cardplayers. "My wife says she's worried about the kids," he said. "Only a pound of meat a week and a few pounds of bread. She says on One-Pot days the kids cry. Not screaming, she says, just kind of...mewing, you know? And no overshoes. They grow so fast. God, when will this war be over?"

Max raised his thin brows. "War? What war? We're at peace, friend Martin. All the Fuehrer can talk about is peace. Even the Russians are talking peace. It's over in Poland. So why should the British and French bother, eh? Can they honor a treaty with a country that doesn't exist anymore?"

Paul had been silent, but the itch that Max's courageous ignorance always ignited in his head was working. "Then why did we want to take over their country?"

Max eyed him over his glasses and pursed his mouth like a schoolmistress. "To give us room to *breathe*, for God's sake. Any *child* knows that, and you a learned priest? Place to park the goddamn Jews.

Don't think they'd let them into Palestine, do you? So park them in Poland."

"My brother-in-law died in Poland," Saukel said sadly, stacking the cards. "That's a war."

"Over for *weeks*, little Auwi," Max sneered. "No more Germans will die in a war. The Fuehrer's vowed it. Anybody fired a shot? Anybody dropped bombs? Leaflets! They drop *leaflets* on munitions plants, for God's sake. War? Hah! Sitzkrieg! We wait for the Frenchies to find a way to get out of the whole mess without looking like the perfect assholes they are."

Saukel scowled. "Then why don't they just leave us alone? Paper says Brits and Frogs got a hundred divisions other side of the Maginot. Are they just stubborn? Or stupid? Or cowards?"

"Yes," Max replied and began to buff his nails on the green felt table-top.

Boell took the cards from Saukel, riffled them, shuffled them, riffled them again. "The British and French aren't stupid," he said. "They're Aryans. And they know they'll get nothing from the Americans this time. Lindbergh's the conscience of...."

Suddenly the music stopped in mid-phrase. Old Spath's eyes popped open. He scowled at the radio and biffed it with the heel of his hand. It began a metronomic ticking, and the old man frowned at it as if it had turned into a time bomb.

"This is Rundfunk," the radio voice announced. "We interrupt this broadcast for a message."

"Turn it up, Spath!" Max shouted at the old man. But Spath had turned the dial, trying to get his program back. Max crossed to the radio, batting the old man's hand out of the way. "Get away from that, you old fool. They're probably going to announce a treaty."

The voice swam back, "...emphasize once again that the Fuehrer was completely unharmed."

"What?"

"Shut up! Turn it up, Max."

"Last night," the announcer continued, "our Fuehrer, Adolf Hitler, made an unexpected speech at the *Burgerbrau Keller* in Munich, part of the annual celebration of the 1923 putsch against the ill-fated republic. It was not thought the Fuehrer would speak this year to his fellow veterans of that campaign, owing to the pressures of his work in averting hostilities with our Western neighbors.

"After the brief speech, the Fuehrer left the hall to return to his struggle for peace. At precisely nine minutes after nine, a bomb concealed in a pillar below the stage exploded! Seven of the 1923 heroes were killed and sixty-three terribly wounded.

"It is a miracle our Leader's tireless efforts to secure peace drew him away when it did. Had he remained twelve minutes longer, he himself would almost certainly have been killed, as the bomb had been placed *directly* below the spot from which he had spoken only moments before!

"The police have apprehended a suspect: Georg Elser, a Munich Communist, a cabinet-maker and electrician. A search of his home showed all the makings of just such a bomb. Moreover, police found in the pockets of the suspect Elser a picture postcard of the *Burgerbrau*, with a large 'X' circled on the very pillar where the bomb had been placed! Police sources revealed that Elser was working as the tool of two British Secret Service agents arrested this morning at Venlo, on the Dutch border.

"We will interrupt broadcasts as further developments become available. But be assured that our Fuehrer is completely unharmed. We now return you to our regularly scheduled program."

The music swirled back. Spath settled back into his trance. Everyone else sat stunned.

"My God!" Martin Brandt breathed, wide-eyed.

"A miracle," Max sighed grimly. "An absolute miracle."

"Not a miracle," Heinrich Boell said. He pushed back his chair and stood solemnly. "His commitment to peace saved him." He took a few steps and stopped, turning to Paul. "Now what the hell are you grinning like an ape for, at a moment like this?"

"I was just thinking," Paul said.

"Thinking, thinking, thinking," Max scoffed.

"I was thinking that was one very dumb cabinet-maker."

Boell leaned on his knuckles across the table from him. "Dumb? Then how did he know that Hitler would speak last night? You heard. It was 'unexpected.' That very dumb carpenter had very inside information."

"I was wondering that, too. I guess he didn't have much time, did he? That's probably why they caught him so quickly. It's a wonder he didn't blow himself up, too."

"They've got new kinds of fuses," Max said. "You heard the radio. He got them from the British. Didn't I just *tell* you? They want to save face. Kill him, and they can call off the war."

"What puzzles me," Paul said, "is why the poor fool kept that postcard. Marked like that. Souvenir, maybe? For his grandchildren. He'd have been better off if he stayed with his bomb."

"What are you," Max sneered, "some kind of detective?"

"No. Just easily puzzled, I guess."

"Thank God he made such a short speech," Martin Brandt said and blessed himself.

"Yes," Paul grinned. "Providential. And not too typical."

"Now wait just a *minute*!" Boell straightened up and looked at Paul. "Are you trying to say this thing was a set-up? How do you know so goddamn much, huh?"

Paul was trying to hold onto his temper. "I don't know 'so goddamn much,' Heinrich. I was only wondering out loud."

"You goddamn smug bastard." Boell came around the table, pushing back the sleeves of his robe, and looked down at Paul, wild-eyed. "I've had about enough of your goddamn cynicism! You're a goddamn traitor to the Third Reich!"

Paul stood up slowly and looked at Boell, levelly, angrily. "Listen here, my friend," he said through clenched teeth. "I may be a bad Nazi, but I'm as loyal a German as any man in this room."

"Like *hell*!" Boell shouted, his face inches away from Paul's. "There's *no* difference between a good Nazi and a good German!"

"Oh, yes, there *is*, you thick-headed moron!"

"Traitor bastard! You're goddamn *sorry* the Fuehrer wasn't there when that bomb went off!"

"You're goddamn *right* I am!"

Dead silence. Both men breathed heavily. Paul looked around. He began to cough deeply.

"What I meant was...." He coughed. "What I meant was that the Fuehrer is a very charismatic man. If he'd stayed just a while longer...this Elser might have heard him talking about peace.... And all those men wouldn't have been...killed."

Boell was white with fury, his chest heaving. He looked for a moment longer at Paul, then Boell walked to the phone. He dialed, eyes riveted on Paul. No one moved or spoke or coughed.

"Yes," Boell said into the mouthpiece. "My name is Heinrich Boell. Saint Blasien. No. A patient. I want to report a traitor to the Reich. Reiser. Yes, a patient. I have reason to believe he is implicated in the plot to assassinate the Fuehrer. No, he won't leave. You can be sure of that."

Within an hour, the Gestapo arrived. Despite some nervous attempts by the administrator of the sanatorium to intervene, Paul Reiser was given a half-hour to pack his things and then hustled through the corridors and out into a waiting car. He was taken to the prison in Freiburg.

Finally, on Friday, December 1, he appeared before a People's Court for trial. The only witnesses called were Heinrich Boell, Max Fellgiebel, and Oberst Aloys Lange, head of Gestapo in Westphalia. Oberst Lange presented a thick sheaf of documents attesting to the defendant's anti-German activities: consorting with a Jewess, circulating propaganda, conducting meetings to corrupt the youth, possible homosexual activities. Less than an hour after the charges had been read, the head judge banged his gavel and said only five words, "Five years, hard labor. Next."

On Monday, December 4, 1939, exactly three weeks before the day he had hoped to be ordained a priest, Paul Reiser climbed into a truck with two dozen other condemned prisoners destined for *Konzentrationslager Sachsenhausen*.

I

THE ROAD

1933

Wednesday, 15 February 1933 - Muenster

Herr Stahl's classroom was as comfortably cluttered as an exclusive pawnshop. Under the anatomical charts at the front squatted a stuffed owl with big surprised eyes, an aquarium in which a tangle of grass snakes snoozed. In a tall glass case hung a white skeleton named Agrippina which Stahl insisted was the only mortal remains of an axe-murderess from Cologne of whom he had once had carnal knowledge so gratifying she had bequeathed her eggshell bones to him.

The professor himself hunkered momentarily on the edge of his desk. "All right, gentlemen, settle. Settle!" He stood, flapping the sides of his jacket like some genial bat and paced while the fourth-form boys took seats at their tables and arranged their books. He had the ruddy freckled face and squat body of a longtime country peddler, sly in the ways of rural persuasion.

"My little brothers," Stahl began, "there are three laws in nature's eternal struggle. First, heredity; second, self-preservation; third, survival of the fittest. Nature loves a winner.

"She rewards the strong and pitiless, not only with survival but children stronger than themselves. Therefore, stronger must *never* blend with weaker. Just suppose it really were possible for a lion to lie down with a lamb. There would be peace? No, no! Death, young worthies, because peace is death. What would the lion eat? Grass? What spindleshanks lamb-lions he'd produce, eh? *That* is the castrating effect of the so-called humanitarian philosophies: the degradation of power. Only one purpose for a lamb's existence: not to breed with the lion; to feed him.

"When the Aryans encountered lower beings, they saw them clearly as god-sent slaves, bred for menial tasks which had too long kept true men from tasks true men were born to do: expanding the horizons of their people. And the slaves were content; it's what they were *born* for.

"*But* then from the lazy Mediterranean countries came the poisonous message of mercy. Men became womanish, lamb-like. They pitied the mutant cubs, taught them language, lowered the natural barriers between master and servant. Then, the unthinkable. They *bred* with them.

"*The* Original Sin: bestiality. A world homogenized, bastardized, nig-gerized. Blood poison muddying the clear stream with browns and reds, turning sons of the hard-muscled warrior into simpering cowards. "It's in the new chancellor's book. Have you read *Mein Kampf*, Fuehlen?"

Kurt Fuehlen looked up from under a shock of sandy hair. A stallion with an impish white grin. "Well, uh, I've tried several times, Herr Stahl, but it must be...too profound for me."

Stahl tugged the forelock and grinned down at him. "Too sly by half, young Fuehlen. And when are you going to join the Hitler Youth, you great rascal?"

"I'm pretty occupied with the Catholic Youth, Herr Stahl."

"Hah!" Stahl looked around at all the scrubbed faces, most compla-cent, some quizzical, some grinding their jaws. "Questions?"

Herschel Gruenwald raised his hand, and Stahl nodded. Herschel's eyes were like ripe olives, but even when he smiled there was a down-curl to his pouty lips. At the moment, he was taking a risk. "Herr Stahl, what peoples interbred with the Aryans and...polluted their blood?"

"The pigmentation, young Gruenwald! At the extreme, black Africans and Orientals, then Arabs and Jews, then Slavs. As you move up the scale, you come closer to the human. Slavs, for instance, are burlap-colored, broad-headed, docile, like oxen. The very word 'Slav' means slave."

"But Aryans came from Asia. Isn't there a great deal of Slavic blood in the German people?"

"Quite correct. What's needed, then, is to gather the purest-blooded and allow them to breed only among themselves. That's the future, young Herschel. The Nazi Party."

"But Herr Stahl...," Gruenwald turned apprehensively toward Karl Hessemann, a beef-faced boy with the double-lightning Hitler Youth pin in his lapel. "Many Nazis seem pretty...brutal."

Hessemann curled his lip and muttered, "Watch yourself, kikey."

Stahl sidled between the tables to Hessemann. "Gruenwald is regrettably correct, young Hessemann. The National Socialist Party is a pyramid. The pinnacle is, for a time, forced to build itself upon a quite broad base. When enough pure Aryans are bred, we can purge the base-born. Where are the apes, eh? Now we go to the zoo to laugh at them while they play with themselves."

Hessemann's face purpled. "You said yourself Jews are even below Slavs."

"Quite right. But unlike the Slavs, the Jews are *not* broad-headed and docile, like oxen. The Jews are as wily as serpents. Now, even though I have a far higher nature than a cobra, I tend to show a great deal of respect in a cobra's presence, young Hessemann."

Paul Reiser raised his hand.

"Ah! The Golden Lion speaks," Stahl chuckled.

"Herr Stahl, if I look at the evidence, as you say, Jews I know are fine people. Mind their own business. Caring. Our family doctor's Jewish, and you couldn't ask for a kinder man."

"Of course!" Stahl bellowed. "What better way to assimilate and take over, young Reiser? Nothing to fear from the old rabbi hoarding shekels in a shoebox to vamoose to Jerusalem. I pray he prospers. I'll wave him *bon voyage*! Ah, but the ones who own the banks and news-papers!

"It's not the Zionists I fear but the assimilationists. I truly admire young Gruenwald here, as I would any clever chess-player. But if I had a daughter, I would *not* want young Gruenwald to marry her, nor would Papa Gruenwald! Herschel, would your father prefer Germany or Palestine?"

Gruenwald's face soured. "Palestine," he said.

"See, young Reiser?" He spread his palms like a magician, just fin-ished his trick.

Gruenwald put up his hand again. "Sir, in the last 25 years, ten Ger-man Jews have been awarded the Nobel Prize for sciences."

Stahl smiled again. "Which just proves my *point*-how successful, how serpentine! The Jew Einstein substituted nihilism for truth. If everything is relative, there is *no* truth, correct? The result? Utter chaos." He flashed a tobacco-stained grin. "A Jew like you, my Her-schel, can be such a seductive chessplayer. I take off my hat to you." He chuckled. "But not my head, Herschel.."

As if it had awaited Stahl's last word, the bell shrieked, and the boys clumped together books and papers, punching their arms into heavy coats and whipping long mufflers around their necks.

Paul Reiser walked shoulder to shoulder with Kurt Fuehlen, his face burning. "Can you *believe* what that man said?"

Kurt gave Paul's shoulders a shake. "Come on. You're just angry because Lisl's half-Jewish."

"One-quarter Jewish."

"So what does it matter. Ochre or olive or beige or tan. She's still lovely, isn't she?"

"Does she seem less human than...than an *ox?*"

"I think Herr Stahl said cobra."

Paul stopped dead in his tracks and turned to his friend, his jaw jutting and his fists clenched.

Kurt put up his open palms, "Just *kidding!* What are you getting upset about? I admit he was a bit...sweeping, but there was something to what he said, wasn't there? I mean if you take it-not about Lisl or Herschel, but at the extreme, where he was most of the time, you wouldn't marry a black African or an idiot out of pity and have children, would you? I mean you're hard up, but you wouldn't breed more idiots just to keep the idiots of the world from feeling inferior, would you?"

They crossed the rotunda toward the front door, shifting satchels from arm to arm as they wrestled into their coats.

"*You're* an idiot." Paul tried to make it sound like a growl.

"I know." Kurt swung open the heavy door and shoved Paul ahead onto the big porch, where beards of snow snaked across the stones. "But wasn't he right about aristocracy—in a way? If the illiterates outnumber people who study the issues, and each one has a vote... who wins? The loudest orator who promises everything and then reneges once he's in office. Who wins? Hitler wins."

"You're a foxy idiot. You've got promise."

"Stick with me, kid, and you'll be farting in fur. Oh-oh! Look over there."

At the base of the white slope of lawn, Herschel Gruenwald had turned to face four husky boys. One was Hessemann. Another was Dieter Lange, whose father headed the Muenster Gestapo, with Gerd Korman, a butcher's son, and Mueller, called "Ox," but only behind his enormous back.

Paul and Kurt could see the steam rising hotly from the sneering mouths. Herschel's eyes darted, and he backed slowly toward the iron fence. The wind whistled in the bare arms of the trees. "Brutes, eh?" Hessemann hissed. "But an ox can flatten a snake, no, pretty Jewboy?" He unclasped a shiny straight razor in his fat fist. "See my birthday present, Jewboy?"

A sour grin opened in Dieter Lange's roquefort face. "They cut off only a bitty part when you were born, Jewboy. We got a project for biology. See if worms really wiggle after they're cut in half. We're going for the Aryan Nobel prize."

Korman giggled, and picked his nose absently. Mueller merely grunted and flexed, waiting for the talking part to be over. Herschel stopped, his back against a brick pillar. His black eyes lanced at Hessemann, then to the slice of steel in his hand. "I warn you. I don't want to fight."

With the back of his hand Hessemann wiped the drip dangling from his spatulate nose and took a step toward the fence. But then he heard feet clomping behind him and turned to see Reiser and Fuehlen only a few yards away. As Hessemann turned to look, Herschel whipped his foot up square into the fat boy's crotch, and the razor dropped into the snow. As Hessemann bent to mother his throbbing genitals, Gruenwald brought his knee up into his chin and sent him flying backwards. Dieter Lange stood a moment open-mouthed, then turned to see Reiser and Fuehlen a few steps away and took to his heels along the fence toward the gate.

Kurt grabbed Korman by the lapel and began backhanding him across the face. The boy began to cry. Between his sobs, he choked, "They *made* me!" Disgusted as much with himself as with Korman, Kurt flung the boy away. He landed on his hands and knees and began crabbing away through the snow and brittle grass to the school gate. Hessemann, his face twisted and bloodied, one hand clutching a handful of testicular torment, clumped after him as fast as he could manage.

Paul had leaped onto the broad slab of Mueller's shoulders, and the Ox was whirling him around like a grizzly trying to unfang a wolf from his back. Gruenwald and Fuehlen circled the big whirligig, trying to find an opening, Reiser's legs flailing around and making them dodge and duck.

After a few moments, Mueller's dazed eyes betrayed a vague awareness of his own dizziness. He swayed drunkenly to a rocking stop, Paul dangling from his neck like an importunate damsel. At that moment, Herschel charged head-down into Mueller's belly, and he went back with an explosive "*Ooof!*" on top of Paul, whose eyes and mouth suddenly went mutely agape.

Mueller rolled painfully to his side, clutching his gut, and stumbled to his hands and knees. His whole bulge of brow seemed to cloud over his eyes, and he gargled, "You'll pay, Jewboys," and he stumbled across the brittle snow toward the gate, where his three pals huddled like refugees.

Kurt and Herschel turned to Paul, hunkering up dazedly onto his elbows.

"Hey," Kurt grinned, dusting the snow off, "you all right, Paulli?"

Paul smirked cockily. "You saw me take him down, right?"

"You? It was Herschel the Bull-Bull Ameer! Regular cossack!"

Herschel shrugged and blew the air from his bantam-rooster chest. "Whew! If you two hadn't come along, I'd have been a cossack eunuch. Thank you. Both of you."

Kurt hauled Paul to his feet and hooked his other arm through Herschel's. "Nonsense! All we did was send the gallowglasses off peeing in their pants. *You* were the one brought down Goliath! Let's get our books, and we'll stop off for cocoa at Koenig's to celebrate."

They trudged back to the porch, but Kurt felt Herschel tugging free. They pulled to a stop.

"What's wrong, Herschel? No worry about money. We haven't any, either. Grossmutter Koenig goes weak when Reiser comes in the shop. She'll give us sugar buns, too. You'll see. She's eighty-two, but when our Paulli walks in the shop, Strauss waltzes start up in her head."

"I can't."

"Why not?"

"I have...chores in the grocery. My father'll be angry."

"Half an hour. We have to celebrate! And he has lots of little Gruenwalds till you get there."

Herschel smiled weakly and turned away down the hill. But a few feet away he stopped and half-turned. "Thank you. You're good friends. But...but my father doesn't allow us to drink cocoa in Christian tearooms." He raised his arm and went on down the hill alone.

* * * * *

Saturday, 16 February 1933 - Muenster

Kurt Fuehlen's brother, Helmut, waited at the basement doorway behind the cathedral, stomping his feet and clomping his mittened hands against his beefy arms. His boxer's face burned with cold, and plumes of breath mushroomed from his bulldozer jaw into the early evening darkness. Inside, his brother Kurt and Paul Reiser were finishing up their weekly class with the *Bund Neudeutschland*, twelve-year-old boys they taught catechism every week, along with a bit of rough-and-tumble and a few roistering songs. Helmut stood guard against trouble from the Hitler Youth who were becoming more and more dangerous.

The door opened, and they came tumbling out, tussling and whipping scarves round their faces against the knifing wind.

"Have a good weekend, Tank," they called back at Helmut, fanning out across the square toward their own streets, biffing one another and shoving their pals into snowbanks.

The last two were Johann Schulle, a self-righteous sneer set between pudding cheeks, ahead of Josef Vogel, whippet-thin. "You slimy turd, Schulle!" Vogel snapped. "You puking snitch!"

"You drank Mass wine. I saw you. It's forbidden."

"I only took a sip, you fat pig. Sister Solana told me I'm gonna be an alcoholic!"

"Hey, hey," Helmut said, pulling Vogel's hand off Schulle's pudgy shoulder. He hunkered between them. "Look, Schulle. Every altar boy since the Last Supper stole a nip of wine once in awhile. And you know what? Peaching on a friend about something so silly is worse. Why fight with one another, huh? Now shake hands."

Vogel clamped his fists under his arms. "I'll die first."

It didn't matter. Schulle, chin out thrust, broke away and trotted off across the square.

Helmut turned to the little terrier. "You don't want to hear what I want to say," he said.

"Yes, I do, Tank. I *know* what you think about that rat."

"Then I don't have to say it, do I?" Helmut clapped the boy on his narrow shoulders.

"If Schulle's a Catholic, I don't know whether I want to be a Catholic."

"Come *on*, Vogel. Even Judas was a Catholic. For awhile." Helmut stopped, not sure where his improvising was leading.

"That's right, Tank," Vogel said, fighting against angry tears. "You wait. That fat turd'll sell us all out. You wait." He broke away and ran across the square. Helmut stood watching him.

Kurt and Paul emerged from the door and called goodbye to Sister Solana, the sacristan.

"All set, Helmut. Any problems?"

"Not from the Nazis. I had to pull that Vogel kid off whatsisname, the creampuffy one."

"Schulle? What was that all about?"

"Schulle turned Vogel in to Solana for copping a swig of Mass wine. Do you believe it? Let's get moving. I think all my toes have snapped off."

The three young men started off down the steps, heads hunkered against the wind.

"When we get to the river," Reiser huffed, "we could break a hole and take a little swim!"

"Hah," Kurt laughed, "like that stream when we hiked the Alps. I thought more than my toes were going to break off."

Helmut grunted. "You water lilies. That stream wasn't so cold."

"How could *you* tell," his brother threw a punch in Helmut's direction. "You were out and drying off before the nerves could send the message to your head through all that lard."

"All that lard gets frozen solid outside the church ready to save your tiny little tushie, little brother, and all the other little tushies like Vogel and whatsisname."

"Father Wolker says if the Brownshirts win big next election, they're bound to make any groups but the Hitler Youth illegal," Paul said, shivering against the wind. "What do we do then?"

"We go hiking," Kurt shouted. "Out in the woods, we have our catechism, sing a few songs, and if any of the little Brownies show up, we'll play cowboys and red Indians with them. Tank, you remember when you and Werner tied me up to that tree and didn't come back for an hour."

"And you sat there and cried the whole time."

"I was only four, for heaven's sake. I also peed my pants."

"And we had to tell Fraulein Nolte you'd been trapped in a cave by a bear."

The small shops were closed and lights were on in the apartments above them, people settling down for supper. At times it sounded as if somewhere someone were playing a radio very loudly, but they couldn't make it out, hunched into their collars out of the whine of the wind. As they turned onto Frauenstrasse the tall houses gave some protection, and they could finally catch their breaths. Suddenly Helmut stopped. "Well, I'll be damned. Look at that, will you."

Ahead of them the lamplighter was going from light to light, pulling the little lever up inside the glass globe with a hooked stick, lighting the gas. As each lamp blossomed, it bathed a large red banner with a white circle and a black swastika whipping in the wind on the lamppost.

"They weren't there when we came," Paul frowned. "They move in fast, eh?" The three began to walk along the empty, bannered street, like soldiers who missed the parade. Now they heard the sound they thought was a radio, coming from somewhere up ahead near the police station.

"People of Germany," the tinny voice blared, "we are on the edge of a great new leap into the future. For fifteen years we bore the burden of a Depression brought upon us by traitors and fumblers. Ask as you sit at your tables this evening: Is this the Germany Providence intended?

"People of Germany! Where is the leader who can give a decent job to the honest worker? Who can wipe out the decadence in our society? Who can restore honor to our Fatherland?

"People of Germany! *One* man sent by Providence can lead us into a future where hard work receives its reward-in Deutschmarks worth more than newspaper! *One* man to make our streets safe for our wives and daughters! *One* man to lead our Fatherland to prosperity, to justice, to a place where our sons stand tall with manly dignity and proclaim to the world, '*I* am a son of *Germany*!'

"People of Germany! That man of destiny is Reichschancellor Adolf Hitler! Support National Socialist candidates who will guarantee Adolf Hitler the support he needs to bring us into the New Era. Drive from the Reichstag the jackals of defeatism, compromise, and half-heartedness! Sunday is the day Germany will throw off her chains! Adolf Hitler! Adolf Hitler! Adolf Hitler!"

They turned onto Judefelderstrasse and saw the sound truck pulling away from the front of the police station. The three boys slowed. On the steps, flanked by two burly Storm Troopers, Aloys Lange, the new Muenster Gestapo chief, was beginning to move toward his car, apparently to follow the sound truck to its next location and assure there were no "difficulties." One of the troopers got in the driver's seat, as the other held the rear door for his chief. As he bent to get in the door, Lange turned his head and saw the three onlookers. He withdrew his foot from the running board, said something inaudible to the two troopers, and began slowly to walk toward the boys.

He was a tall, colorless, stoop-shouldered man, cinched in a long black leather trenchcoat, a dark fedora pulled tightly onto his head against the cold. His crooked nose shone red out of once pitted cheeks which had smoothed somewhat as he aged. His eyes, the color of dark mustard, squinted from behind thin glasses misted from his breath.

"Well, well, well," he said in a moist, friendly baritone, looking painstakingly through his wafer lenses from one face to the other, as if memorizing each detail, "the Pope's bullyboys, eh? Up to some mischief? Prowling for kikey schatzies? Or is it pretty little Jew*boys* you diddle? That's it, isn't it? I hear you like dimply little Jewboys. Heshie Gruenwald, for instance."

"Rather breezy, isn't it, Aloys," Kurt grinned amiably.

10

"*Herr* Lange to you," Lange hissed, "I'd watch that mouth, considering where it's been."

"Ah, forgive me!" Kurt's face became almost genuinely contrite. "It'd slipped my mind completely that you've had a meteoric rise, *Herr* Lange. I was still thinking of you mucking out my father's kennels for him and cleaning up the afterbirth from cows."

"Yes, *sir*," Paul's square jaw stiffened with conviction, "that is one meteoric rise, like a phoenix skyrocketing right out of the dog-...."

Lange grabbed the lapel of Kurt's jacket with one hand and Paul's with the other. He pulled their faces so close they smelled his breath. A bit of the shiny arrogance vanished from their eyes.

"Listen to me, bastards. You're three big boys. But do you see those men in that car? They are very big *men*. And they like to hurt people. They wet their pants when they can hurt people. Sometime very soon, if you don't watch your mouths, if you don't pull back into line, I'm going to let them hurt the three of you. I'm going to let them hurt you very bad. Understand?"

He turned toward the car. The trooper at the wheel gunned the engine, and the one at the door held it open. As he bent to get in beside Lange, the other trooper turned to the three boys and grinned sourly. The car ground into gear and sped noisily off down the Judefelderstrasse.

Helmut grumbled. "You two are going to dig your own graves with those big mouths."

* * * * *

Tuesday, 28 February 1933 - Muenster

"Gretel, hold still while I tie this bow." Elly Reiser was annoyed. Not at her infuriatingly patient ten-year-old daughter, blondly prettier than an Infant of Prague, but at herself. Paul's birthday party. She knew her sister-in-law, Marta Reiser Weider, and her Prussian general husband would smile through the whole affair with enough patrician tolerance to set a saint's teeth on edge.

Somehow Paul had escaped that Reiser quality bred, surely, into the genes after all those generations of professional Reiser diplomats. Paul retained a certain feisty irreverence, thanks to the fact his father had married, happily, far below his parents' expectations. Elly's father had been a farmer with six sons and one daughter, able to give her a dowry substantial enough to take the starch out of Willi Reiser's stiff Junker father. But Elly felt far more at home in the hearty give-and-take of the

Fuehlen boys—even though, as a veterinarian, Kurt's father was socially far below even her husband's civil service status. Then what would it be like tonight when the Herr General Weider and his Marta swept into the Fuehlen's lowly home? Something unredeemed in her relished the prospect.

It was all silly. Elly found no serenity in the damask and fragile bric-a-brac of Marta Weider's home. And she knew she herself was too earthy by an acre for the Herr General. Marta Weider was a true saint, of course, but Elly Reiser would have been more comfortable running a general store in the African outback than attending one of her sister-in-law's teas.

Gretel, though, was a Reiser to the toes of her mary-janes, and her pale blonde beauty would be a mixed blessing to her parents in five years. Or sooner. Thank God the Reiser coloring was one thing Paul had, too, she thought, not this horsehair of mine. Papa had always said some desolatingly handsome and swarthy gypsy had pitched camp one spring in some great-grandmother's knickers.

"Mama," Gretel groaned, "that's so tight it will cut me in half if I bend over! Aunt Marta will think I'm a scarecrow."

Oh, you're a Reiser, all right, my beautiful late-life doll, Elly moaned silently back at her daughter and began to untie and re-tie the bow.

"In class today we learned about aristocrats, Mama."

"Oh, my God."

"We're aristocrats, aren't we, Mama? We're not Jews, are we?"

"No, dear, we're not Jews. Your Papa and Aunt Marta and Uncle Ludwig are most *definitely* aristocrats. Which makes me an accessory, I guess." She reached for a brush from the dressing table to fluff those long waves. She was always off schedule; she got lost in the touch of things.

"Fraulein Inge told us in school today about aristocrats and Jews. Like the wicked witches are jealous of the beautiful Aryan prince and princess. The Jews get together in dark caves, like the witches, and make plans to take away the prince and princess's gold, so they can take over the Fatherland. That's why we have to drive them out and never buy anything at a Jewish store. You can brush harder, Mama. She showed pictures, and they were *terrible*! They gave me shivers. They have big hook noses, like witches' with warts on the end, and big thick glasses like dragon eyes, and these awful dirty braids coming down out of big black hats on either side of their heads right here."

Elly Reiser stopped brushing her daughter's hair and set the brush back on the table. She turned the little girl around and looked straight into her pale blue eyes. "Gretel, Doctor Weiss is a Jew. Hasn't he always been kind? He helped Mama bring you into the world. Would someone wicked give Papa and me such a lovely gift, the way Fraulein Inge said? After Paul, Mama lost several babies, and if it weren't for Doctor Weiss, we wouldn't have you. He's a Jew, Gretel, and a good, kind man."

"It's all a trick, don't you see, Mama? Like the witches. That's why we must never go to Doctor Weiss's office again. The Jews put on these disguises to cover up their big hook noses and those dirty braids. They pretend to be nice to put us all to sleep, like the princess, and while we're asleep they'll take over the Fatherland. Then when we wake up, we'll be slaves and have to clean the Jews' bathrooms. With our *hair*! That's what Fraulein Inge said. Isn't that awful?"

"Yes, Gretel, it's awful. But, darling, it's awful because it just isn't true."

"Oh, it is, Mama. Fraulein Inge told us."

"Gretel, if Mama says something *isn't* true, and Fraulein Inge says it *is* true, who do you think would be right?"

"Fraulein Inge, Mama. You see, you're just a mama, but Fraulein Inge's a teacher."

"Oh, my God."

"I'm going to be a teacher. Now we're ten, we can join the Jungvolk, and go camping and have games and gymnastics like Paul. Then we can join the Hitler Youth and work on farms with cows and chickens. And the very best will be chosen to join the Youth Elite and fight for the Fatherland, like Saint Joan of Arc, except she was French and we hate the French."

Elly sat looking at her child as if she had suddenly become a changeling, transformed by a witch named Inge into a child she no longer knew and could not reach. "Gretel,..."

"Elly, we have to leave soon, dear." Her husband stood at the bedroom door. Willi was tall, angular, slim except for a slight swell of paunch. The planes of his gentle face were creased with deep smile and frown lines, framed by a thicket of hair the color of golden smoke. "Ah, look at them! My Snow White and Rose Red!"

"Oh, Papa! You tease all the time. Like Paul."

"I mean it. No man ever lived with such ravishing beauties in his home. Except maybe Zeus." He planted a kiss on each of their upraised foreheads. "But come along now."

Gretel scampered out of the room to the stairs, and her parents descended the narrow staircase, flanked by pictures of high-collared

Prussians and easy, big-jawed farm boys. It was the nearest any of them had been to one another since the wedding.

"Has Gretel said anything to you about this Fraulein Inge, her teacher?" Elly asked.

"Enough to make me suspect the woman's a veritable Valkyrie."

"The woman's an ignorant bigot! Filling the children's heads with stories of fanged Jews plotting to steal away the country from the lily-white Aryans."

"Surely you're exaggerating. Or Gretel is."

"If what she says is true, we ought to complain. Or put her in another school. She's a very susceptible little girl, Willi. And she's starting to talk like a little Nazi. I'm frightened."

Willi took his wife's hands into both of his and looked at her. "I'm frightened, too, Elly. Things have only begun. As of today, they can shut up anyone they choose to, even the papers. They can read our mail, listen in on our telephone, search our home and take away anything they have a mind to take. And this election Sunday will validate it. If anything should happen to Hindenburg, I think this little fool in Berlin is going to push us to the brink. And beyond."

"But what can we do, Willi? They're taking our little girl away from us. I can just feel it. This woman Inge is a menace to the children. What can we do?"

"I don't know, my dear. What do you do when a pack of mad dogs takes over the town. Shoot them, one by one? Move to another town? Wait till they get caught out-or restless and move on? I just don't know. But even if they can only make a compromise, they've won."

* * * * *

"Herr General Weider, Frau General Weider," Jakob Fuehlen, bald and tun-bellied, beamed and raised his glass of raw schnaps, "you do my house honor!" He tossed his glass back at a shot, and the General, after a moment's reflection, did the same; Frau Weider let the liquor touch the edge of her smile, then let it slide back. The General began to cough, and big Werner Fuehlen clapped him heartily on the back, which set him coughing again. Fraulein Nolte, the housekeeper, came terrified from the kitchen, wiping her hands on her apron, little Rudi Fuehlen peeping red-haired and wide-eyed from behind her left shoulder.

"Is everything all right," Noddy gasped, moaning inwardly at the thought of all the food that would now surely have to be abandoned.

"Wrong throat," Werner smiled, thumping the General's back like a chef tenderizing beef.

"No, no," the General panted. "My fault. Quite out of practice."

General Weider sat up straight, patted Werner's great paw in the hopes of stilling its ministrations, and took a deep breath. "There, now. Thank you, Werner. A great help." He wiped tears from his eyes, and grinned, "I haven't drunk schnaps like that in...twenty years!"

Jakob Fuehlen began to refill his glass. "Now, slowly this time. For the friendship in it."

General Weider looked up at this smiling bear and thought of a sergeant-nurse he had known in the hospital near Ypres, Emil Knutschweil, "The Teddy Bear." Emil had been a growler with a great heart. Jakob Fuehlen and his sons were men like that. Perhaps it was the massive infusion of schnaps, but God, how he missed the war! The brotherhood that knows no castes.

"Thank you, Herr Fuehlen. Prost!" But this time he took only a small pull on the glass.

"What could have detained the Reisers," Frau Weider asked of no one. "And Paul?"

"Oh, Kurt and Helmut are bringing Paul from the Catholic boys' meeting," Werner said. "He doesn't know. He's to stop here for cocoa on his way home. To warm up." Werner smiled lamely. "Because of the cold."

"And Kurt and Helmut are also your sons, Herr Fuehlen?" Frau Weider asked, like an angler fly-casting at a distant teacup.

"Ah," Jakob Fuehlen beamed, "I have four sons, Frau General. Helmut is my ox. When a cow is having trouble with the birth, he can give her a big squeeze in the middle, and the calf comes out, zooop! Like a pea from a pod. And the mama smiles back at him."

Frau Weider smiled a bit wanly and reached for her schnaps.

"Werner is my poet, a bull with the soul of Rilke. Werner works at the library, putting books back in place but most of the time he reads. All my Werner's problems would be solved if only Marlene Dietrich would walk off the silver screen and become his patroness. Eh, Werner?"

Werner blushed and mumbled, "Papa!"

"Kurt. Kurt is my Mercury. As easy to put your thumb on as quick-silver. He'll be either a doctor, or a circus aerialist, or a priest. And my youngest, Rudi, my saint. Rudi is...at home."

"Oh, I haven't met Rudi," Frau Weider said with a smile that faded an instant later, as she realized too late there must be a reason.

"Rudi is 'special,' Frau Weider. He was born rickety. The palsy. But," Jakob rose from the upholstered chair with an air of indomitable pride, "you shall meet him." He went to the doorway of the kitchen and called, "Fraulein Nolte! Frau Weider would like to meet our Rudi."

After a moment, Noddy appeared in the doorway with Rudi in tow, flat-faced, scrubbed, and slicked down, but his big blue eyes fearful this might be the moment of his nightmares, the moment when the people he loved had enough of his foolishness. But the moment he entered the room, Frau Weider rose, her hand extended to meet him.

"Rudi," she said, taking both his limp hands, "my name is Frau Weider. But you can call me Marta, all right? Marta is an easier name. I'm so pleased to meet you. I'm Paul Reiser's aunt. You know Paul, don't you?"

Rudi blushed and smiled. "Paul'dth Kur'dth frendt. Heathe nydthe. Hea'dth beudeefull."

"Well, I surely agree, even if he is my own nephew. He's both nice and beautiful."

Jakob Fuehlen and Noddy exchanged surprised looks.

"And I'll let you in on a secret, Rudi. I think you're very nice, too. And handsome." She stroked his shining red hair.

Rudi hung his head and said, "Oh, Marda."

"He's bright, too, Frau Weider," Jakob said, putting his big palm on the boy's slender shoulders. "Just his body won't keep up with his mind. I think he knows more about animals than I do. I think it's because he looks at them. Really studies them, without having to worry about getting along to his next call. He has a kind of menagerie. We bring it into the basement in the winter." He winked. "You know, I think they talk to Rudi. They tell him about themselves."

Marta Weider's eyes caressed the broken boy, thinking of her own three stalwart sons, wondering how God passed around his gifts. "You know, Rudi, when I was a girl in Prussia, we had big barns on our estate, and my brothers and sisters and I used to set up a hospital every winter in a corner of one of the barns to take care of the broken animals we'd found in our park."

The General looked at his wife with a kind of quizzical pride. She'd never told him that.

Rudi tried to wrap his uncooperative mouth around the words and said, in his twisty, labored way, "That wa' berry widthe. Na boddees ob unther hammals kepp 'hem warm. 'Ey muss be kepp warm. 'Ey 'member na warm nength do neir mama's boddees."

Frau Weider reached out her hand to him. "Would you show me your animals, Rudi?"

Noddy's face collapsed into an ashen gape. "Oh, Frau General, no. It's too...."

But Rudi had already taken her hand and was dragging her into the kitchen to the cellar door, his small face hardly able to contain the hugeness of his grin. "Come, Marda."

Fraulein Nolte turned to her kitchen just as the doorbell rang.

"I'll get it, Noddy," Werner said, and she fled to the controllable challenge of sauerbraten.

"It's Ernst," the General said. "He stopped for Monsignor Lutz and Father Wolker."

The two priests entered the vestibule of the big house greeting Werner and shaking the snow off their hats and shoulders. General Weider and Herr Fuehlen moved to the open doorway to the vestibule and shook the priests' cold hands.

Ernst Weider, a pilot lieutenant, stepped into the room, dusting snowflakes from his thick dark hair, his dark blue eyes shone above a big grin. "We're safe now. I've brought the clergy."

"Welcome, fathers, welcome," Jakob Fuehlen bellowed, "and Leutnant Weider." Monsignor Lutz forced a hearty smile back at him. "Have a bit of schnaps to take the ice out of your bones. Werner, take the fathers' coats, and would you get some more glasses from the kitchen? A bit of schnaps will warm you all up."

But Monsignor Lutz pulled a paper sack from under his arm and handed it to him. "A bit of brandy. I wasn't able to buy a present for Paul, so I thought I might bring a present for the adults." He had been to the Fuehlen's before. Like the General he was unused to raw schnaps.

"Napoleon!" Jakob marveled as he opened the sack. "My house is too small to receive so many blessings at once. Two priests, a lieutenant, a general, and now Napoleon himself! I will get better glasses." And he disappeared into the kitchen leaving the strangers to seat themselves. The four men moved somewhat awkwardly to the gathering of unfamiliar chairs near the fire.

"Where's Mother, General?" Ernst Weider asked his father.

"On safari to darkest Africa, it would seem. Herr Fuehlen's youngest son, Rudi, has a menagerie of animals in the basement, and your mother couldn't wait to see it."

Ernst's looked skeptical. "I'd be as surprised if she'd rolled up her sleeves in the kitchen."

"See for yourself. Unbeknownst to me, your mother's been a Circe of sorts all along."

"Excuse me, would you, fathers-all three fathers. But it's difficult to resist," Ernst said, and moved toward the kitchen door. "Fraulein, might I take a look at the menagerie, too?"

Inside, Fraulein Nolte merely nodded, and pointed to the cellar. This was not the soiree she had planned. The world was at sixes and sevens when aristocrats began acting like people.

"General," Lutz said, "have you any news about this recent fuss?" He caressed the soft white hair feathered over his ears absently with his fingertips, like a white angora cat, preening.

Monsignor Johann Lutz was quite different from his horsefaced, rumpled clerical companion, Father Wolker, the supervisor of Muenster Catholic youth groups. He was the chancellor of the diocese, second only to the great Clemens August Graf von Galen himself. If Wolker "belonged" to the blue-collar Fuehlens, Lutz most definitely belonged to the aristocratic Weiders and Reisers. Had he decided on some other line of work, he surely would have been a minister of state or at least a matinee idol. He was not physically prepossessing, a man of average, well-fed girth and height, ramrod straight. What caught the eye was the luxuriance of prematurely white hair, carefully trimmed and swathed, framing a ruddy, chiseled face which served as the perfect setting for deep-set violet eyes. They were eyes which made women swear that, though no other had been worthy of him, they would have tried.

Before the General could answer, Jakob Fuehlen was back from the kitchen. "Forgive the delay, gentlemen. Fraulein Nolte insisted on a tray." He poured a hefty dollop of brandy in each glass and passed them round. "This, Herr General, is not down the hatch!"

"Indeed it is not." Ludwig Weider raised his glass. "If I may: to our host and his fine family, which is the heart of our Fatherland. May family and Fatherland prosper!"

"Hear, hear!" they said and sipped silently.

"You were asking of news, Monsignor Lutz," the General said. "I've heard little. Things are still precarious. Most of my army friends are sure that, sooner or later, there must be a confrontation between the Reischwehr and these secret Hitler paramilitary groups–SA, SS, SD, Gestapo. You simply can't have several armed groups each covering the whole country, at loggerheads with each other, not even talking to one another."

Lutz's face paled, and he set down his glass. "Surely you don't mean a civil war."

"There has to be some solution. These Brownshirts and Blackshirts can't keep roaming the streets bullying anyone they choose. The police don't know what to do. How can they arrest them when they are all working for the same government? But sooner or later, Hitler will have to choose. They can't coexist much longer, not if the Nazis get more brazen after Sunday's election."

"And the vote?"

"I think they're going to solidify power. Not a landslide, this time anyway. But all the little businessmen and workers are beginning to feel solid ground under their feet again. Or the hope of solid ground. Now this Communist threat? I'll wager he'll take half the vote."

Suddenly, the front door banged open, and through the frosted glass of the inner door, they could see the boys trooping into the vestibule, trailing veils of snow and stamping it from their boots. They leaned against the walls to wrestle off their overshoes.

"Ah, they're here!" Jakob went to the kitchen and whispered harshly to Fraulein Nolte, "They're here. Call them from the cellar. Rudi mustn't miss it."

The other men stood, smiling, as Rudi ran into the kitchen doorway and Marta Weider came up behind him and put her hands on his shoulders. Her son Ernst and Werner stood behind Noddy, whose face was close to a smile. Kurt opened the inside doorway and stepped back. Paul walked in and stopped. As his mouth worked from gape to puzzlement to smile, Helmut opened the outer door behind him to welcome Paul's parents and Gretel.

"Surprise!"

Rudi skipped in the doorway and Marta Weider grinned as she hugged him. Gretel threw her arms around her big brother's neck. Everyone beamed. And Noddy went back to her pots, more than a little relieved. Everything was just fine now. Everything was back in place again.

* * * * *

After the dinner dishes had been cleared, Paul had opened his presents. The party itself, of course, had been the present of the Fuehlens; Fraulein Nolte had knitted him a grey muffler; the Weiders had given him a new silver pocket watch; and his family had given him a pair of skis. Then Noddy brought out a great cake. Fifteen minutes later it was a memory of dark brown crumbs.

Jakob looked from the younger table to the people at his own table and smiled, "Ah," he said, "this is Germany, my friends! Good food and children laughing, the mothers, the servants, the workman, the civil servant, the clergy, the soldiers, sharing the food and laughter and a drink. And all in peace. All in peace. This is what Lord Jesus," he said, bowing his head at the name, "meant by the Kingdom of Heaven on earth."

"Jakob," the General said from the other end of the table, "I can't remember when I've had a more...a more fulfilling evening. Not in years. And I thank you for it."

All the adults raised their glasses to Jakob, and he bowed his head, warm with pride and thankful to a God who could give such gifts as these.

The doorbell rang.

"Good heavens," Fraulein Nolte said, "Nearly ten-thirty. Who could that be?"

"I'll get it, Noddy," Helmut said and strode through the parlor and peered out the glazed glass of the vestibule door. "It's...it's a chauffeur," he called back to them.

"It's Lisl," Paul jumped up. "Excuse me please!"

"Put on your...," Elly turned to call after him, but he was gone. "Ah, young love!" she sighed, with a kind of resigned and wistful shrug.

"Lisl?" Marta Weider asked from across the table. Everyone at both tables was all ears.

"Lisl Zalman. They've met at gymnastics competitions. Her father has the jewelry stores."

"Zalman?" Jakob asked.

"The father is half Jewish, the mother is Lutheran. I doubt he practices. Not seriously."

Monsignor Lutz sniffed.

"Monsignor, have another tot of your fine brandy," Jakob said quickly, and the Monsignor didn't mind if he did. "As Fraulein Nolte knows, with the exception of herself, I am not too keen on either Lutherans or Jews," Jakob laughed, "but I have no objections at all to jewelers!"

At the other table, Rudi's face contorted with a giggle, and he began to sing-song, "Pauldth godda gor-rul, Pauldth godda gorrul!"

Ernst wrapped his big arm around the boy and rocked him back and forth. "And how many hearts have you broken, you little carrot-top! Huh!"

Rudi giggled all the more, and Fraulein Nolte looked a bit apprehensive. Too much giggling had been known to have unhappy effects on Rudi's bladder. But how could an aristocrat be expected to know about such things?

* * * * *

In the back of the limousine, Lisl had drawn the center curtain so Weber wouldn't pry and tattle. Paul bundled quickly into the car, huddling to keep warm, and dusted the snow off the shoulders of his sweater. He slammed the door behind him.

"A night of surprises," he grinned and sat so he wouldn't wet the pearl-grey velour.

"Kurt told me. I couldn't let your birthday go by without giving you a present, could I, Viking?" Lisl beamed softly back at him. "Mama was having palpitations at how late it was, and made a few accusations just short of 'strumpet,' but Papa said, 'For heaven's sake, Magda, Weber will be with her. The man was an Olympic wrestler, for heaven's sake. It's not as if the girl were trotting up and down Pigalle, for heaven's sake.' Papa uses 'heaven' a lot to persuade Mama."

Her eyes were white-blue. The color of sapphires, he thought. Even in the winter, her satiny skin was tawny and blushed with summer, and her long raven hair was parted in the center, clasped at the crown with a bow the color of her eyes, and draped over the shoulders of her pale blue coat.

"You look like a sapphire shining in the shadows," he said, unable to look anywhere but deep into the grasp of those eyes.

"You didn't just think that up, did you?"

"I wrote it in my diary last night."

"You're a poet. And you're silly!" She lowered her eyes a moment, and a filigree of black lashes touched her cheeks. Then her eyes popped open again, "And I *love* it!"

With a twinkle of a laugh, she reached behind her back and pulled out a package wrapped in silver paper. Her hand lingered on his wrist. He made no move to open the package. He was hardly aware it was even in his hand. Just the warm weight of her hand and her eyes.

She edged closer and whispered, "If you don't open that package, we'll be here all night. And Weber will grow suspicious that you're doing highly naughty things to my perfect body with your perfect body. And he will come back and make you a cripple. And the man was an Olympic wrestler, for heaven's sake. And then I'll have to go into a convent."

Their noses were almost touching, and they could feel one another's breath on their lips. And Paul softly whispered, "Jewish Lutherans don't have convents, for heaven's sake."

She fell back and giggled, "Open the package, Paul. I hope you like it."

Paul tore the silver paper and found a large diary covered in soft, pale blue leather.

"Some day when we're both very, very famous, and they discover your diaries with all those poetic and passionate descriptions of me, I don't want that masterpiece to be found in a cardboard covered copybook. I have standards."

There were three polite but unmistakable raps on the glass behind the chauffeur's seat.

"I have to go." Lisl edged forward and laid her hand on Paul's knee. Her pale blue eyes locked on his, and they were both very still. "I'm glad you were born, my blond Viking."

Paul's heart quickened, as if it were beating not just in his chest but in the pit of his stomach and his loins. Waves of warmth spread along the heartbeat through his thighs. He could hear the short soft puffs of his own breath. Those lovely hypnotic eyes drew him closer, and his lips met hers. Her arms went around his neck and clasped the back of his curls. Paul felt he was drowning in a warm, pale-blue sea. Somewhere far above him voices were echoing, harsh and admonitory, but very far away. Then she opened her mouth, and her fingers moved along his thigh, and a voice inside him echoed, I don't care, I don't care!

The two of them fairly jumped out of their skins when there was a very definitive thump, thump, thump on the glass in front of them, and Weber ground on the ignition. They sighed and smiled softly at one another.

Lisl laid her soft hand against Paul's cheek. "You're the most beautiful human being who was ever born," she whispered.

"No," he whispered. "You are."

"No, you are."

They both laughed together.

"I have to go, Paul."

"So do I."

He leaned forward to kiss her once more, but she put her fingertips on his lips. "I'd go mad in the convent."

Instead he kissed the air between them and opened the door. As he was about to close it, he whispered, "I love you, Lisl."

He slammed the door, and the car sped down the dark street. As he sauntered, hands in his pockets, to the stoop of the big, brightly-lit house, Paul Reiser was completely unaware the temperature was well below freezing and his hair and shoulders were silting with soft snowflakes.

* * * * *

Saturday, 11 March 1933 - Muenster

The wet wood in the big cabin fireplace hissed and sputtered, and twenty school boys of Bund Neudeutschland sat Indian-style or propped or leaned or sprawled on wooden benches and picnic tables just inside the arc of warmth. Outside, snowflakes tiny as sun-motes sifted off the edges of the roof, swirling and dancing up and down in the light drafts of afternoon breeze. Kurt and Paul sat on stools at either side of the fire. Helmut, squatted on a keg by the window, his eyes on the woods that edged the big clearing. Paul clapped. "Problem," he said. "We haven't gotten the treatment yet, but other Catholic troops have. Only a matter of time. That's why we change meeting places like this. But I won't kid you. Our time'll definitely come.

"You're scared." He winked. "Psst! So am I. Oh, I'm not afraid of a fight. I'm afraid of you-being afraid. And I'm afraid fear'll make you knuckle under to the pressure and the threats. But each one of us knows he doesn't have to fight all by himself. Right?"

"Right!" But some were not so sure.

"Nothing wrong with being afraid, you know. Our Lord was so afraid he sweated blood. *But*, in the end, he said to his Father, 'All right. If you think I can, I'll try.' The only real courage is coward's courage; when you say, like Our Lord did, 'I *can't*...but I'll try.'

"So let's reach out our cowards' hands to one another, in one unbroken circle, and ask the Father we share with one another and with Jesus, our Brother, to give us coward's courage."

Together they began, "Our Father, who art in heaven...." Paul looked around at the faces. Some-Heinie Weygand, Paul Schmidt, doughy Johann Schulle-stared apprehensively into the fire, lips hardly moving. Others looked at the crucifix on the mantel over the fireplace. Josef Vogel sat taller than tall, eyes riveted on Paul, ready to die if he asked it. He'll do, Paul thought. But, God, give the others courage. Please. And while you're at it, I could use some myself.

When they'd finished, Paul clapped his palms on his thighs, and leaned over with a big white grin. "Now! As basic training for the battles ahead, *my* squad claims all the meadow to the right of the cabin door and challenges wimpy *Kurt's* squad to try to take it away from us!"

With a whoop and holler the boys scrambled over one another to get to their coats, boots, scarves, mittens, and jam through the door to the fray. Kurt ambled up beside Paul and put his hand on his shoulder. "Not bad, oaf. Not bad. If Monsignor Lutz hears you talk like that, you'll be packed off to the seminary in a wink."

"Hah! Fat chance! Meet me on the field of honor, poopface!"

Outside, to the left of the cabin, Vogel gave orders to the boys in Kurt's squad to reinforce a hummock flanked by two scrawny bushes. Several squatted like dogs and whipped the snow back between their legs to begin a battlement, nearly asphyxiating boys awaiting orders. Vogel shoved Schulle and several small boys behind the hummock to prepare an arsenal. On the right, Paul's squad was at sixes and sevens, bumping into one another wondering which direction to go.

Paul shouted as he leaped off the porch, "Consolidate! Consolidate! Follow me!" And he began to head toward the corner of the porch, directing the smaller boys to pile up ammunition as Vogel was doing. But just as he was about to turn the corner of the porch, where Helmut stood, watching the perimeter, a snowball caught him flat in the back of the head. He turned to see Vogel at the top of Fuehlen's hummock, dusting his hands and daring him to single combat.

"Varlet Vogel, I come for you!" Paul cried and set off at a run toward the hummock, where a lot of smaller boys were wondering whether they had coward's courage or not.

Vogel crouched and picked up another snowball from one of the smaller boys and winged it at Paul, who was dodging a hail of snowballs from the older boys of the Fuehlen pack.

"Aim just ahead of where you think he's going to turn!" Kurt hollered and lobbed a whopper that whipped off Paul's ski cap.

Vogel leaped from atop the hummock to challenge Paul man to man, Beowulf, fearless before Grendel. Then suddenly his wits got to his courage. He saw this big, rangy boy, with his doorway-wide shoulders, bearing down on him, and prudence or instinct got down to his feet. He took off giggling across the meadow, arms pumping, with the big Viking bearing down on him.

"I've got you, Vogel!" Paul panted, eating up the white space between them. "I've *got* you, Varlet Vogel!" He leaped and tackled Josef, and the two rolled around in the snow. Paul pinioned his arms with his knees. "*Now* Vogel! I will wash your satanic face with snow!"

The boy giggled and screamed, "Help!" as Paul ever so slowly lifted two big handfuls of snow and lowered them down toward Vogel's face. Behind him, Fuehlen's squad clumped to rescue their champion-followed by the Reiser squad, running full tilt and ready to leap.

Then suddenly they heard Helmut's voice, "*Kurt! Paul!*" and they wheezed to a halt, turning back toward the porch. Slowly, Paul got off Vogel's arms and helped him up.

"What?"

"To the right. Halfway to the gate. Just behind the trees."

Slowly the boys turned and their eyes swept the edge of the clearing from the cabin to the gate. At first there seemed nothing to see. Then, slowly, all their eyes focused on a stand of sumac between the porch and the gate.

"Somebody there," Schulle gasped and stumbled away a few steps.

"And down there, coming up the road to the gate," Heini Weigand moaned and promptly wet his pants. "Let's get into the cabin!" He started to run; Schulle started to follow him.

"No," Kurt shouted. "They'd have us bottled up in there. I wouldn't put it past that bunch to set the place on fire."

Schulle and Weigand stopped, considering the alternatives.

"Paul!" Josef Vogel grabbed Paul's arm and pointed back up the long slope behind the cabin. "They're back up there, too. Three of them. Ox Mueller and two others."

Paul looked back toward the gate. "Seven or eight down there. I can see that little rat Lange, but I can't tell who the others are." Then he raised his voice, turning full circle, wary as a panther. "All right, everybody. Calm! Ten or twelve of them and twenty-three of us. Bigger, but we outnumber them two to one. Just don't panic. Get into groups of five or six and stay *together*. Kurt's squad with him. My squad with me. Coward's courage. Coward's courage."

Slowly, Helmut came down the steps, looking right and left. "Paul," he yelled, not looking at him, "you and your kids take the bunch with Lange on the left, coming through the gate; Kurt, take the lot coming over the fence with Hessemann; leave the Ox and his pals to me."

"I'm staying with you, Paul," Vogel breathed at his side.

"No. Take Neuwirth, Klum, and Koehler and help Helmut. He'll take the Ox. You four keep the other two busy. Go."

Vogel took Paul's three biggest and turned slowly up the incline to join Helmut crouching behind the end of the porch. Paul was left with seven twelve-year-olds to face four fourth-form boys.

Ox Mueller and his friends trudged closer down the long hill toward the cabin, trying to cock their eyes around the corner. The two with him carried sticks; Mueller did not. Shielded by the edge of the cabin porch, Helmut squatted carefully, picked up a piece of firewood in one of his ham fists and side-mouthed to Vogel, "Keep back. They think it's only the bunch out on the lawn. You two take the one on the right; Vogel and you take the other. *Don't* fight fair. Go for the *nuts*. Grab the stick as it comes down. Let your hand move with it, and it won't hurt so bad."

From the stand of sumac midway along the fence, four big boys with swastika armbands over their heavy winter coats emerged and began moving out of the woods. Beef-faced Hessemann pointed to the rotting old fence and two booted it down. The four walked over the wreckage and onto the field, fanning out as they came, each carrying a big fallen branch.

Through the gate below them Dieter Lange, his pocked face set, eyes cold as a hawk's, led three more boys, all bigger than himself. They spread to their right so that the three groups of Hitler Youth could encircle the younger boys and close in.

"Little puppies!" Lange shouted. "Pissing their nappies! Here we come, pissies!"

"Your mamas aren't even going to recognize you when we finish, little Catholic shits," Hessemann called out hoarsely. "We're gonna initiate you. A new club. No pansies allowed."

"Steady!" Kurt whispered hoarsely to his trembling boys, crowded around him as if he were a tree. "Go for the crotches! Use your feet; use your knees. *Bite*. Don't get noble on us. Wait till I tell you, then break! Two to each of them."

The battle began as Ox Mueller rounded the corner of the porch and Helmut Fuehlen caught him square in the belly with his firewood club. Vogel and the three younger boys flew at the other two and tried to get hold of their sticks.

On the gate end of the field, one of the older boys with Lange caught one of Paul's boys on the side of the head with his stick, and the boy crumpled to the snow. Two of the smaller boys leaped on the attacker from each side and pulled him down. One of them grabbed the bigger boy's muffler and began to choke him with it. Paul clasped his hands together into a double fist and backhanded another Nazi boy in front of him with all his strength. The boy's pupils disappeared up into his head and his knees buckled. Paul turned and saw that Dieter Lange had struck two more small boys to his right and they were bent over in the snow, bleeding and crying.

"You scummy coward!" Paul shouted and went for Lange's throat. The two fell rolling and punching in the snow, but all the heavy clothing absorbed the blows on both sides. Finally, Paul rolled on top of the Gestapo chief's son and began back-handing him across the face. Next to him two of his boys had managed to wrestle the stick from their attacker and were chasing him out the gate with it. Paul got up from the bleeding Lange and pulled him to his feet. "Get out of here, you little rat," he gasped, "before I kill you." His nose gouting blood, Lange stumbled to his feet, cursing, and limped toward the gate.

Paul looked at three bleeding boys sitting in the snow to his left, whimpering softly, and decided they just had to wait. He went to the two boys sitting on the chest of one Hitler Youth tugging both ends of his muffler. The older boy's face was purple. Paul pulled them off. "Stop, or you'll kill him! You!" he said to the boy he'd knocked out, whose eyes were just beginning to focus again, "Get this *Dreck* out of here, or I'll turn these two little hellcats loose on you, too!"

The older boy lurched painfully up and struggled to get his gagging pal to his feet. Slowly they staggered toward the gate.

"All right," Paul said to the two garrotists, "get those three hurt boys over there into the cabin. Quick now. Clean them up as best you can with the canteens."

Near the broken fence, he could see that Kurt and his squad, with greater numbers, had had an easier time of it. Two or three of the kids sat plump in the snow, bleeding around the face, and grinning proudly; another six were all piled on the only boy who had not run, trying to get a punch in whenever a space opened up; and beyond the fence Kurt himself was running like an antelope through the brush toward the trees where Hessemann was blundering through the branches behind two of his friends. Paul could hear Kurt calling, "I'll get you, you sadistic shit!"

"Hey, you lot!" Paul called to the boys thumping Hessemann's only remaining man. "Let him go and two of you take those three there into the cabin. The rest of you come with me."

Paul turned toward the cabin just in time to see Ox Mueller fire a heavy fist into Helmut's chin that dropped the big Fuehlen face-down to the ground, and Paul set off at a clumsy run uphill through the snow, a pack of six or eight small boys behind him. Two of the boys he had sent with Vogel were stretched out on the snow. The other had his teeth sunk into the free hand of one of the Ox's boys and with the other held the stick at bay as well as he could. Vogel himself was trying to wrestle the club away from the other with both hands and taking the boy's awkward left-handed blows to the back of his head and shoulders.

Just as Mueller raised his club over Helmut's head, Paul and his boys fell onto the three of them like a pack of vampire bats. Paul grabbed Mueller's big arm and tried his best to hold back the blow but succeeded only in deflecting it onto his own left shoulder. He groaned with the pain but held onto the stick with his right hand. Meanwhile, one of the smallest boys, Gerd Anderson, no bigger than four feet tall, ran head-down, full tilt into Mueller's crotch. At the same moment, two other boys each fastened their arms around one of his legs and, between the three of them, managed to throw the big Ox unexpectedly off balance and brought him down. Paul, dumbfounded, realized he was standing over Mueller, who was momentarily immobilized under three boys, with Mueller's club in his hand. He stood there, dizzily, and looked to where the other two Hitler Youth had disappeared under two more piles of flailing arms and bodies.

"All *right*!" Paul cried. "Let them up!" The boys eased off and got to their feet, backing up, suddenly aware of what they had done. Their victims lay still, rolling their eyes to see what might be lurking either side of them. They were not about to get to their feet and find out.

Paul held the tip of the club between Mueller's eyes, the heel of his useless left hand poised at the stub of the stick near his throbbing shoulder, as if he could jam it downward.

"I'll put this through your empty skull if you don't *vow*, as you hope to see God, you'll never attack these boys again. *Swear* it, you tub of *Dreck*, or I'll jam your eyes out your asshole!"

Ox Mueller moaned under the weight of the three smaller boys and rocked back and forth on his hips. "All right, all right."

"*Swear* it!"

"I...I *swear* it!"

"As you hope to see God!"

"As I...as I...hope to see God!"

"Crawl out of here. *Now*!"

Mueller rolled to his stomach ready to lever himself up onto his hands and knees, but as he did, Paul put the heel of his boot on the back of Mueller's neck and pushed the big boy's face into the mucky snow. "And you will warn us when your friends are planning to attack us. *Swear* it!" Mueller's response was gurgled into the snow. Slowly, Paul took the club and forced the face out into the open. "Swear it."

"I can't. They'll *kill* me!"

"Vow it, or we'll make you walk back to town buck naked. I swear we will."

"I'll...I'll help you all I...all I can."

"Good enough. Now get out of here. All of you." The three Hitler Youth lay still a moment, as if they expected yet another attack by maniac dwarfs. Slowly, they ached to their elbows, then painfully sat up. They looked around again warily, then got to their feet and began to lumber downhill toward the gate.

The little boys, released suddenly from their fear, began to hoot hysterically after them, "Assholes! Cowards!"

"*Stop* that!" Paul shouted at them. "Don't do that. Please. Don't enjoy it." He put his hand protectively up to his throbbing shoulder. "You'll end up like them."

The boys hushed and turned to look up at him. He tried to smile. "We did all right with coward's courage, didn't we?"

For awhile, the cold and the exhilaration of their victory had made them unaware of the bruises they were going to be very much aware of next morning. They all grinned widely back at him. Helmut moaned, and they tried to pick him up, but he waved them off and rose clumsily to his feet. "Ready for the next round!" he mumbled, as if his mouth were full of marbles.

They propped the arms of the two hardly conscious boys and stumbled drunkenly back to the porch. As they rounded the corner, they could see Kurt trudging disconsolately up the incline.

"Got away, the swine," he growled. "Everybody all right?"

"More or less," Paul winced.

A ten-year-old opened the door and peered out like a frightened monkey. "Is it...over?"

"All over, Alfie. Everybody accounted for?"

The boy looked around, to be sure. "All but Weigand and Schulle. They...left."

Kurt ruffled the hair of the boy who stood leaning wearily against his hip. "Come on, warriors. Let's go in and see how they're doing in the field hospital."

But as they turned up the steps, they heard a car grinding through the gate and up the incline to the cabin. In the back sat Dieter Lange and his father, Aloys, head of Muenster Gestapo; in the front, two Storm Troopers. The car ground to a halt in front of the steps. Aloys Lange eased his thin length from the back seat and walked slowly toward the steps.

"Well, well, well," he said, looking carefully through his wafer lenses from one face to the other, as if he were memorizing each detail, "the Pope's bullyboys, eh? Up to some mischief? I thought the Gestapo had given the Catholics a warning."

Kurt smiled bitterly. "We didn't know you were going to send boys to carry it out."

"Oh, *no*, young Kurt Fuehlen. My son tells me he and his friends were having a peaceful meeting here in this cabin, and you and these ruffians came and drove them out."

"And you just happened to be cruising down the road as they limped away," Kurt sneered. "It was all planned, wasn't it?"

"Aloys...," Helmut came to the top of the steps..

"What did you say?" Lange's pitted cheeks puffed into a vinegar smile.

Helmut swallowed his gorge. "Herr Lange, your son and ten or twelve hoodlums-we can give you their names-busted in here and tried to maul a group of *children*, for God's sake!"

"The facts will not bear that out, Fuehlen."

"We signed out this cabin in the park office! Look it up!"

"The secretary who deals with such matters is willing to swear this location was signed out exclusively to a meeting of Hitler Youth this Saturday afternoon."

The older boys looked to one another with incredulity and then, reluctantly, resignation.

"Ah!" Lange smiled, "your faces acknowledge the truth, then. You are to report to the police station this evening with your *fathers* to answer to charges of assault and battery."

"Now wait a minute, Herr Lange," Paul said, reining in his temper. "You're the chief of the Gestapo. The Gestapo's part of a political party, not an arm of the government. You have no power to order us to report to the police station."

"Oh, you are uninformed, Reiser." Lange favored them with a crevice of smile. "This very day, Reinhold Gruber, Chief of Police of Muenster, announced his unexpected retirement. For reasons of health. Since I already have some experience in these matters, the city fathers begged me to take the job, temporarily. Until matters could be...made permanent. This evening. Eight o'clock would be about right, I think. With your fathers."

"I thought you were going to let your bullyboys 'hurt' us," Kurt snarled.

"*Kurt!*" Helmut growled at him from between his teeth.

"Oh, *no!* We are not savages, Kurt Fuehlen."

"Your son and his friends must be mutants, then."

"Kurt, shut your damn mouth," Helmut said. "You'll dig your grave."

"All right, Helmut." Kurt sank to the steps and stared helplessly at the torn up snow and grass. One by one, the boys sat, too. The door opened wider behind little Alfie, and the battered little boys peered out, wondering if perhaps one of their fathers had come to pick them all up.

"Eight o'clock, then. Looking forward to it," Lange said, and turned back to the car where his son huddled sneering in the back seat. Lange stopped a moment and looked at the arrangement of boys and young men sitting on the steps like a losing team. "I've got you now, you bastards." He got into the car. "Get us out of here." And the back door slammed.

The driver revved the engine, pulled forward, then shifted into reverse to turn down the slope. But the wheels ground into mud and slush. He spun the wheels again. And again. The rear tires dug themselves more and more deeply into the muck.

Kurt began to giggle behind his hand. Then Paul, holding his shoulder and wincing, began to guffaw. The boys started with snorts, then giggles, then howls. Finally, even Helmut couldn't hold back his laughter. "Come on, boys," he howled. "We've... we've got a long hike back to...," but he couldn't say any more and doubled up in laughter over his aching belly.

They filed past the grinding car, spurting gobbets of muck, and trekked toward the gate.

* * * * *

Herschel Gruenwald's family lived on the two floors above their grocery. On the top floor were three bedrooms, one for his parents, Tovah and Zindel; one for the three boys, one for the four girls. Zindel Gruenwald had come from Poland in 1911, at 25, and met Tovah through a marriage broker. They had married a year later, and Tovah had dutifully delivered a child about every year and a half. They were all good children and worked very hard.

Supper was over, and Shabbat drew to a close. The family stood around the candlelit table, women a pace behind the men; even Esther, who was sixteen, yielded to Judah, the baby. Zindel Gruenwald was finishing *zimmun*. "Shabbat has passed, and our travail commences again. May our toil one day bear fruit in the Land of our Fathers. May He who sets the holy and the ordinary apart protect us and keep us from the strangers' ways. Amen."

Zindel removed his black hat and smiled. "Time to begin again, children. Let us get the room back in order." As the boys began to rearrange the heavy furniture, Zindel beckoned to his eldest. "Herschel, a word with you, my son."

Herschel's face sagged like a melted doll's. Zindel put his hand on the boy's shoulder and led him to the window. They stood near the laddered drapes, the boy intent on the baseboard, the father intent on the secrets between the lines around his son's grim mouth.

"What is it, Herschel?"

"Nothing, Papa."

"It is nothing when my son looks like *zimmun* is Mourner's *Kaddish*? You are having trouble in school? Those boys?"

"No more than usual, Papa."

"What, then?"

"We pray to keep us from the strangers' ways. But I love the strangers' ways, Papa. I love Germany. The books and music and parks. We work like slaves to go to Palestine." The boy raised his dark eyes. "Papa, I don't *want* to go to Palestine. I'm a German, Papa."

Zindel's mouth disappeared inside the grizzled beard. "You are a Jew, Herschel. Before even you are a man, you are a Jew. You must *cling* to all that makes you a Jew-to Talmud, to the ways of our people, and above all to the dream! 'Next year in Jerusalem!' If we don't cling to those ways and that dream, we will be swallowed up into the nations. The Chosen will be gone."

"You sound like Stahl," the boy said and went back to studying the texture of the drapes.

"And who is Stahl?"

"Our biology teacher. A Nazi. He says the same thing. Go back where we belong."

"He speaks truth." Zindel's roughened hand turned the boy's face to his. "Don't you see the Lord is using these Nazis on our behalf, as he has always used our enemies?"

The boy tried to look away, but his father's hand held him. "We want to leave and they *want* us to leave! Already the Elders are negotiating. So the poorest Jew can leave, and the highway will be open to the *Judenstaat* we have dreamed of so long, to the new Zion!"

Herschel took his father's hand and held it, glaring back at him. "Father, you can't believe these Nazis are beating up old Jews and breaking shop windows for our *benefit*."

"Not willingly, my son. But the Lord is *using* them for our benefit. It is as with the Pharaoh. Soon, very soon, this Hitler will open the gates and say, 'Get up, you and the sons of Israel, and get away from my people!' And we will go. And the waters will open up before us again on the way to the Land of Promise. You must have faith, my son. You must have faith!"

Herschel bowed his head and said, "Yes, Father."

"That's good, my son. That's good. Now, let us get things ready for tomorrow. You'll see. Just have faith, my Herschel." Zindel patted his son's soft cheek and turned to go downstairs to the shop and arrange things for the morning.

Herschel stood looking at the lights cheering the dismal street. His stomach felt empty and his eyes filled. With a pang too painful to contain, Herschel Gruenwald suddenly realized that in the last few weeks, without his even being aware of misplacing it, he had lost his faith.

* * * * *

Aloys Lange lifted the wire bows of his thin lenses off his ears and painstakingly polished them with a handkerchief he made sure was clean before the interview began. Without spectacles, he squinted. But it was a way to pass the time without looking at the five standing before his desk. If he were to look directly at them, squirming like schoolboys, he would burst out laughing, which would spoil this delicious occasion.

Surely no pleasure like this pleasure, not even the sexual release. To sit polishing his glasses while his former employer, the quick-tempered veterinarian Fuehlen and his two sinewy sons, Kurt and Helmut, stood before him in infuriated silence! ("Aloys, you've let those dogs run all over the neighborhood! Is it so *hard* to learn something as simple as turning a *latch*!")

Jakob Fuehlen, bald and bellied like a monk, scowled right, then left, at Helmut and Kurt. His huffs seemed a kind of groping apology to his two big sons for his impotence.

It could not be better. Yet it was. Also the Reisers, golden Paul and his father, Willi, same family as the Reich's former ambassador to Havana, then Buenos Aires, and other ambassadors to Ottawa and to Rangoon. Lange had looked it all up before the meeting.

Aloys had been at cadet school with Reiser's nephew, Ernst Weider, son of a Wehrmacht general, aristocrat, head boy, able to do no wrong. Weider had been Lange's only competition as brightest boy in the school. Until that soul-crushing day when Weider summoned him to the commandant's office. His besotted father had begotten a child on a fifteen-year-old girl. It was all over the town. A mark on the school. "You must understand, Cadet Lange...." And when he stormed out of the office, strangling on tears, there was Weider saying, "Lange, I'm...I'm sorry." Arrogant swine. Now there was a new aristocracy. And Aloys Lange had a firm foothold in it.

Willi Reiser's scowl was more patrician than Jacob Fuelen's but no less fierce. As if the whole diplomatic corps stood to toast Aloys

Lange—factotum to this boor veterinarian, then door-to- door sales-man, bartender, street-sweeper, lifelong member of the Nazi party, dis-trict Gestapo chief, Police Chief! Oh, if his drunken cur of a father could see how he'd gotten it all back!

He put on his glasses carefully, and folded the clean handkerchief four times, and slipped it into his inside pocket.

"Aloys, how long...?"

"*Chief* Lange, Fuehlen. Is it so *hard* to learn something as simple as that? I have had to remind your sons of that, too, several times. Per-haps the mental weakness is hereditary."

"This is *iniquitous*," Willi Reiser rasped.

"Herr Reiser, you insisted on an attorney before you or your sons would say a word in this office. I believe I quote you correctly? Then, at your own request-no, at your own *demand*- you will stand there and keep your damn mouths *shut* until your lawyer arrives."

Lange steepled his fingers under his nose, pressing them hard against his lips to suppress the snigger. A rap on his door, and Spitzig, his young secretary, smiled at him.

"Advocate Karl Vorsicht to see you, Chief."

"Send him in, Spitzig," Lange snapped.

Karl Vorsicht entered in a flurry of overcoat, whipping his hat from his bald head, and going from one of the standing men to the other, shaking hands formally with each and clicking his heels, his strong palm cold and dry, his puffy, tired eyes trying to reassure them a competent servant of the law had finally arrived. Vorsicht seemed a student of lapels, chests, and chins. He rarely looked one in the eye, like an actor fearful of being distracted from his lines.

"I feared I was late. You must have just arrived yourselves."

"We've been here twenty minutes, Karl," Willi Reiser said.

"But why are you still standing? Sit down. Please, sit."

The five men sat on the wooden chairs facing the desk.

"May I remind you, Herr Vorsicht," Lange hissed at Vorsicht's back as the lawyer clumped hat, coat, and briefcase on a side table, "that this is not *your* office."

"No, it is not, Chief Lange," Vorsicht favored him with a frosty smile as he took a chair himself. "But you see, I have been *sitting* with clients in police stations for the last forty years. I recall sitting in that very room outside with your own father more than once. Poor psy-chology to allow the accused to stand and look *down* on you, Chief Lange. Quite poor psychology."

The older man rose with minimum motion, took two steps to the desk and leaned over it, looking expressionlessly down into the eyes of the Police Chief. He stood in silence a moment, and Lange shifted his position and laid damp palms on the desk blotter.

"You see?" Vorsicht smiled.

Lange saw quite clearly that this arrogant old ambulance chaser was cascading ice water all over his tryst with revenge. Vorsicht did not sit down, and there was no unclumsy way Lange could rise and retake command of his lost advantage.

Vorsicht turned to the fathers and their sons and bowed. "I apologize for my delay. I was detained first in the chambers of Judge Strassenberg obtaining a writ, then at the city department of parks. It seems the young lady, who was so willing to swear the Hitler Youth had signed for the cabin in question, was so intimidated just by the large gothic type on the writ that she dissolved in tears and quickly volunteered, in the presence of a notary, even more information than I would have needed." He shook his head. "Pity I wasted the time getting the actual writ. I could have shown her my university diploma and saved myself the time and fuss.

"So, Chief Lange," he turned back to the desk, "as you see, we have, on the one side, the testimony of twenty angel-faced small boys-who have a quite marvelous effect on judges-plus three young men of impeccable reputations, *plus* the sworn and notarized testimony of an independent witness that the cabin in question was signed out to the Catholic youth group. On the other side, we have the testimony of twelve boys, three of whom have already been up before a magistrate at least once. I have found over the years that the focus of the eyes of an entire courtroom invariably makes one of them break-if, perchance, they are not telling the truth.

"I am an old fool. Surely you must resent all this advice from a 'voice of experience,' but might I also add that it would probably be in your own best interests to drop these charges?"

The edges of Lange's high cheekbones were white. "I will consider it."

"Then I assume we are free to go. Thank you, Chief Lange. Gentlemen?" As he snatched up his coat and case and hustled them out, he turned again and bowed to the Police Chief. "Again, Herr Lange, thank you for your superlative...utilitarianism. Good evening."

When the pack of them had cleared out of the outer office, Lange sat fuming at the arrest papers Spitzig had typed up with such care that afternoon. He crumpled them furiously and hurled them at the wastebasket. "Spitzig! Come in here!"

The boy entered cautiously, having caught the acid edge to his chief's tone. "Sir?"

"Do you have any copies of that arrest report?"

"Of course, sir."

"Destroy them."

"Yes, sir." He stood irresolutely in the doorway. "Sir?"

"What?"

"I'm trying to learn, sir. Are the Catholic Youth like the Jews, sir?"

"Sit, Spitzig." Lange felt the knot unraveling. "You saw those boys with their fathers?"

"Yes, sir."

"Perfect specimens, Spitzig. Fair-haired, clear-eyed, heavy-muscled. Quite intelligent, too. Men of Adolf Hitler's dream. But do you know they're *infected*, Spitzig?"

"Sir?"

"With Catholicism, Spitzig. Inside each of those perfect bodies is the soul of a *girl*! It's the *priests* who pervert them, did you know that? As our Leader said, priests' training is so unnatural it makes them perverts. Recruit the handsomest. Their monasteries are whorehouses for queer priests. You didn't know that, did you? Well, they have to get it someplace, right? The ones who go for women go to places they call Carmelite convents when they need it."

Spitzig's wide blue eyes grew wider.

"You ask if Catholics are like Jews. Was Jesus Christ born in Berlin, Spitzig? No, he was a *Jew*! How do you raise up a nation of warriors from men who've had their balls cut off by 'Love your enemies,' eh? Spitzig, I have absolute *proof* those two big boys were cornholing a little *kike*! My son Dieter's seen them groping one another."

Spitzig gasped. "My father says be careful of Catholics, but I never dreamed....."

"I swear by *Christ* I'll get them, boy. I'll get them. Let the goddam aristocrats watch their steps. Because it's *our* turn now, Spitzig! *Our* turn! Goddamn Catholic fairies."

* * * * *

Wednesday, 10 May 1933 - Muenster

It was one of those pungent evenings when winter memories have been warmed away, and it has always been Spring. The window boxes of the faculty houses around the university square frothed with perky scarlet and white geraniums, and their sharp cinnamon scent spiked the air.

Paul Reiser came out onto the big granite porch of the library with a satchel of books in one hand and the lithe waist of Lisl Zalman in the other. His big hand spread wide to feel the miraculous pocket, where her strong gymnast's shoulders tapered to this slender firmness and then eased away into the sleek fullness of her hips. Ordinarily, when they walked together, he held his arm around her waist easily, companionably, a pleasant link between two heartbeats. But now there were no other messages coming into his mind but the messages from his fingers and palm.

What is it that the human soul does to flesh, he wondered, to make it so precious? So intriguingly lovely and dangerous? Since long before he was able to comprehend the words, every adult had managed one time or other to warn him how precious holy chastity was. He himself had talked so many times about it to the boys in *Bund Neudeutschland*, it had become a truth beyond question. But how could something so vague and abstract and thin as chastity be more important than this palpable beauty at his fingertips?

"You're quiet," Lisl said softly. "What are you thinking?"

"How many miracles you are?" he whispered, catching the softness of her cheek with his lips. They started down the broad steps between the soaring pillars, in no great hurry to lose the touch. "Good thing you made me sit at a separate table," he grinned down at her. "If we'd sat together, I wouldn't have gotten anything done. I'd have spent the whole time looking at you."

She gave his hand a squeeze with her arm but said nothing.

"We have telepathy. Every time I looked across at you, you were looking up at me."

"No big miracle there, Viking," she answered. "I was looking at you the whole time."

"Since seven o'clock? What could you see in two hours you couldn't see in five minutes?"

"Oh, how your hair squiggles. Like a hyacinth. How big your shoulders are. How everything fits." She was silent a moment. "About miracles, too, I guess."

"Lisl, what's wrong? You're sad about something."

She took her arm from around his waist and brushed back her long black hair, breaking her part of the contact. "Nothing. What were you studying so ferociously?"

"It's the classics paper for Doktor Heikel. Comparing what war meant in Thucydides' time and our time. Whenever we read Homer, war seems so...invigorating, as if peace were something women dreamed up to keep men from what they were born for. Then I read this book."

"What book?"

"It's called *All Quiet on the Western Front*. It says, well, that war is about old men making plans and young boys dying." Paul braked her with his hand. "Lisl, what's wrong?"

She looked up at the buds puffing out along the arms of the trees. "I told you. Nothing."

She began walking again toward the far side of the square.

"Oh, no you don't." He caught her waist tightly, leading her to sit on one of the benches that lined the square facing the big library building. "Sit. Talk."

She put her satchel next to her on the bench and sat, smoothing her long skirt over her knees, brushing away lint that wasn't there, examining her short glossy nails. Then she exhaled deeply and turned to him, her eyes brimming. "We're moving away, Paul."

"What?"

"Since they ordered everyone to boycott Jewish stores...."

"But you're only partly Jewish."

"Paul, partly Jewish now is like partly leper." She folded her arms tightly across her belly. Paul put his arm around her and pulled her to him. "Oh, Paul." The tears spilled softly.

"Shh. It'll be all right, Lisl." He kissed her forehead and rocked her slowly in his arms..

"No," she sniffed in a soft whisper. "It'll never be all right, Paul. I can't even tell you where. Father made me swear. At first, we were going to emigrate. But father has no money. Isn't that foolish? Two stores full of diamonds, and no money! And no one dares buy them. So he knows a judge who'll give us papers changing our names. And he'll join the Party, and no one will know." She sniffed again. "Streicher. Clever, isn't it? Who'd suspect anybody being a Jew with that man's name? And we're moving Saturday. Clever, too, don't you think? Paul?"

He held her tightly, her face fitting into the hard hollow of his neck and shoulder. "I'm... I'm not to see you anymore, Paul." She looked into his eyes again. "Papa's afraid...afraid I might tell you where. We can't keep anything that ties us to Muenster. Even the labels in our clothes. It's not just me and my parents. The judge, too. Papa says when we get to...where we're going, I must meet other boys. I...I mustn't write to you. We'd be caught. You can see that's wise, can't you? We're to forget one another, Paul. You do see, don't you? We must. We just...."

Paul's mouth covered hers, if only to silence her. Slowly she relaxed in his arms and returned his kiss, hungrily, her hand abrading his belly, as if her hand could carry away the feel of him. His big hand caressed her shoulder harshly, then moved and cupped her breast, first timidly, then almost in panic, trying to drive all unthinkables from their minds, no matter how.

Suddenly, there was a crash behind them.

They jumped apart, eyes wide, as if the noise had been made by their fathers. They saw boys with swastika armbands clomping across the little lawn, hurling chicken crates and boards at the base of the statue of Felix Mendelssohn which stood on a short pillar in the freshly turned flower beds. One of the boys held an old wooden sled over his head. More and more came from the side streets, laden with boxes, boxes of their parents' books. A handful had torches.

Paul and Lisl sat dumbfounded. Across the square, boys were coming down the broad grey steps of the library with other boxes, brimming with books. Some of the volumes tumbled out and sprawled where they fell, pages fluttering gently in the soft evening breeze. They came across the cobbles like boys readying for a summer campfire, and gleefully hurled the cartons of books on the pile from all sides, scattering them this way and that.

Standing beside an SS trooper, one of the Hitler Youth, hurled his torch into the pile and the others followed suit, running back and forth to be sure it had caught, like savages attempting to immolate the granite effigy of the Jew who had composed "The Reformation Symphony." As the pyre grew, more boxes came in safari from the library steps and onto the fire.

Numbly, Paul and Lisl moved toward the blaze. Boys were scurrying about retrieving scattered books for the oblation. Paul could see the spines of some: *A Death in Venice*, Einstein, Helen Keller, *On the Origin of Species*, Freud, Gide, *Remembrance of Things Past*.

Paul stooped to pick up two books that lay inert at his feet. *All Quiet on the Western Front. Huckleberry Finn.* His knees went weak. The heat sucked the air out of him.

Suddenly, the books were wrenched from his limp hands. He turned to Lisl standing next to him, the books in her hand, face contorted, eyes ablaze. "Are you going to *fight* them, Viking? Of course! Kurt and Helmut and all the *pure* Catholic Youth! Their strength is as the strength of ten! Their strength is *nothing*, Paul! The sewers are open, and no Pied Piper. Not even you! The rats have taken over Hamlin, Viking! If we're going to stay alive, we have to learn how to swim in filth. Well, here's to the rats!" And she threw the two volumes into the enormous blaze.

She walked back to Paul and reached up, softly, and touched his face. "The Zalmans are now Streichers, Viking. Or the next bonfire is for us. Goodbye, Paul."

She crossed the square, back straight, washed by the light of burning books. Paul's mouth opened to shout, but his chest was banded with hoops of steel. Gone forever.

From the library steps, Aloys Lange watched through his thin lenses the big blond boy walk slowly into the shadows beyond the fire. The Jewess Zalman, eh? And the boy, weeping, like a girl. And Lange allowed himself a smile of genuine pleasure.

* * * * *

Saturday, 8 July 1933 - Muenster

Paul loped along the path in the woods from the meeting at Weiders' summer house. He trotted toward town, glad to be alone, with time to work the kinks out of his mind and body. Even running in the hot July sun, the sweat shellacking his bare chest and legs and drawing whatever cool there was from the air, he felt uneasy, as if he were being followed.

Well, maybe that's just what he needed right now to take the edge off, a little dust-up with that blob Hessemann or that little turd, Dieter Lange. But not Ox Mueller. Ox had taken an oath. Probably not worth the bad breath it took to take it, he thought.

He was not going to think of Lisl Zalman. Streicher. Whoever she was now. Wherever she was. A convent school somewhere. Marching proudly in her white blouse, blue skirt, and cloddish boots with the *Deutschen Maedel*. A proud neo-Aryan. With her sapphire eyes.

So. Now that all groups but Hitler Youth were banned, they decided that on Monday he and Kurt would become undercover agents in a Hitler Youth summer camp. Leave it to Kurt to hatch such a wise-ass, perfect solution. Catholic kids would have protection from the bullies, someone to give them other ideas. In August: Fuehlen and Reiser, Nazi counselors. In the enemy camp. Maybe that was what knotted his gut. Not nerves. Fear.

Ahead was a footbridge over a creek. He could sense the water chuckling over the stones, not just with his ears but with his skin. God takes care of the feeble-minded, his salty mother had always told him. He grinned. Perfect timing, God.

Paul shimmied down the bank by the rickety bridge to a pebbled beach where the stream bellied out under willows. Made to order, he mused. Thank you again. Your usual fine service.

He kicked off his canvas shoes, untied his shirt sleeves from around his waist, shucked off his shorts and underwear, took a short run and dove into the clear, cold pool.

Ah! He broke the surface and spewed a plume of water into the air. Grinning foolishly, he rolled onto his back and floated, levitating in the coolness, staring up into the blue-white sky.

"Paul?"

Paul's heart jerked in his chest and he churned toward the bank, his feet feeling for purchase. He stood chest-deep in the water and saw Herschel Gruenwald squatting in the pebbles at the edge of the stream. The bridge shaded Herschel's face, but his left eye was an iridescent purple and yellow. Another blue bruise on his right cheek. The corner of his mouth was scabbed.

"My God, Herschel, what happened?" Paul sloshed toward the shore, his heart twisted at the battered face of his friend and at a kind of inner deadness he sensed behind the bruised eyes.

He squatted next to Herschel, taking his chin gently in his hand and turning it from side to side. "It was that bastard Hessemann, wasn't it? Is that why you left school? God, Herschel, you don't have to do that. Kurt and I'll take care of you. We'll set up a schedule so...."

"It wasn't Hessemann," Gruenwald scowled, brushing Paul's hand from his chin and turning his head away into the shade. "And it wasn't Lange or Mueller or Korman."

"Who, then? Not your father. I stopped this morning, and he hadn't seen you since...."

"Herr Doktor Stahl."

"What?"

Gruenwald sniffed and sat back onto the pebbles. He curled into himself, away from Paul.

Paul reached for Herschel's shoulder to turn him, but the boy pulled away from his hand. "Herschel, he can't get away with this. No teacher can do that to a student. Not even...."

"Yes, he *can*!" Herschel cried out, helpless. "*Not* because he's a Nazi. But because... because he knows what *I* am!"

"Herschel, no matter what he feels about Jews...."

"Oh, God, you're so goddam perfect-Aryan *stupid*!"

Paul sat back as if he'd been struck with a board. Pebbles dug sharply into his bare buttocks, but he stared at the boy he'd thought was his friend, unaware of any lesser discomfort.

Herschel wrenched around onto his knees and cupped his trembling hands into the cold stream and splashed water on his battered face, wincing. He shook the water from his hands and dried them against his shirt. He sat back again with a huff, cocooned in anaesthetizing bitterness.

"I'm sorry," he said dully, his eyes looking wearily into the sparkles of the creek. "I telephoned your house. They said you were at Weiders', so I walked out here and waited. I didn't want the others....I didn't want to explain. Except to you.

"On Tuesday Stahl came to the store and told me he wanted to speak with me. At his flat. He's always been polite to me. I thought some Jew-thing in the wind and he wanted to warn me." He exhaled heavily, like a high jumper committing himself to his final run. "So I went."

Herschel picked up pebbles one by one and plopped them into the stream. "He...he made advances. Said I was beautiful, my body was like a Donatello. I tried to tell him he was wrong. He said Dieter Lange had seen you and me doing it in the baths. He started to knock me around. He said, if I didn't let him, he'd turn me in to the Gestapo. Castrate me. Tell my father. So...."

"Oh, my God, Herschel."

Gruenwald sobbed into his hands. "I...I let him do it more than once. I...wanted it."

Paul's heart thumped in the emptiness of his chest. Oh, my God. He pulled his knees to his chest and crossed his arms across them, lowering his forehead to his forearms.

"No need to hide yourself," Herschel sighed bitterly. "I'd die first. I swear."

Paul stared at him in disbelief. "Herschel, I could almost thrash you myself," he said quietly.

Tears squeezed once again down Gruenwald's face, his mouth contorted with pain and shame. "Oh, Paul, I'm sorry. You see? There's nothing left anymore! Everything's.... I can't go back to school. Or home. I've lost my faith. My manhood. I'm a faithless Jew queer!"

The boy was wracked with sobs. Paul put his arm around his shoulder, and Herschel thrust his head under Paul's chin, sobbing. He braced his hand against Paul's bare thigh, and Paul's whole body went rigidly defensive. Herschel pulled away and looked at him through his swollen red eyes.

"You see?" he whispered. "I've lost you, too. I can't even have a good, clean friend. I'm twice a leper." He ground the heels of his hands into his sore eyes and raked his nose with his sleeve. His mouth twisted into a grin. "I can get a bell. I'll stand by the side of the road and...."

"*Stop* it, Herschel," Paul ground his teeth and stared at the pebbles. "Just stop it."

They sat a moment gripped in silence.

"Where will you go?" Paul said quietly.

"I don't know," Herschel answered dully. "What can I pass for on Stahl's pigment spectrum? Ochre? Olive? Italian, maybe. I'm pretty good in French. But I have no passport." He blew the air from his lungs. "I'll find something. I'm not ready to jump off a bridge yet. So I'll just go out on the highway and try to flag down some friendly farmer. After that? Who knows?"

He levered himself painfully to his knees. "Goodbye, Paul." He held out his hand and Paul took it in both his own.

"God go with you, Herschel."

"Perhaps I'll meet him when I get there. Wherever that is. If he wants to show up."

Herschel stood and turned to go up the steep embankment. Halfway up, his hand gripping the root of a tree, he stopped and said, over his shoulder, "I love you, Paul."

He clambered to the top without looking back. Paul heard his shoes creaking the old bridge. Then nothing but the gurgle of the stream, the buzz of insects, the whisper of the willows.

Paul sat on the painful stones, trying to find a foothold in a world gone mad, where he didn't even know what love meant anymore.

* * * * *

Friday, 4 August 1933 - On Eder Dam Lake

The Herbert Norkus Hitler Youth Camp was really four camps for young people, dotted like four Indian villages along the Eder-tal-Sperre. On the northeastern corner of the long reservoir, the camp for the Hitler Youth boys abutted the camp for the *Jungvolk* boys under fourteen, and across one of the deep streams which fed the reservoir clustered the cabins of the League of German Girls and their younger sisters, the *Jungmaedel*. Except for Saturday night folk dances, the two pairs of camps might have been in different galaxies.

At three in the afternoon, Paul knocked on the door of Commandant Von Schleich's cabin.

"Come!"

Paul slicked the cowlick in the crown of his tight blond cap of hair and opened the door.

"Come in, Reiser," the Commandant half-smiled from behind his desk. The room was bare as a monk's cell, the only adornment a gold-framed picture at the side of the desktop. "Sit down."

Paul felt as if he were going to confession. He sat on the edge of the chair and forced himself not to stare either at Von Schleich's eyepatch or the lightning streak of white through his dark hair. He looked at the picture. Men in flying gear lounging against an old biplane.

"Relax, young man. I'm not going to birch you and send you to bed without your supper."

Paul sat back into the wooden chair and found himself staring at the eyepatch again.

"And don't be nervous about staring at my war trophies," the side of his face edged up in a partial smile. "After fifteen years, I'm rather used to them. Women find them quite dashing. Now," he said, steepling his fingers, "I suspect you're wondering why I summoned you."

"I was hoping it might be about the request Kurt Fuehlen and I submitted to work with the younger boys, Herr Commandant."

"In a way. We need Hitler Youth leaders, Reiser, not just on the playground but in Berlin. In the last year we've grown from a hundred thousand to three and a half million young people."

"That's...understandable, Herr Commandant."

Von Schleich's face smeared again into ironic bemusement. "By the simple expedient of making membership in any other group illegal. Quite diplomatic, Reiser. Doubtless inherited."

"I'm surprised the Commandant knows about my family."

"Oh, we're very thorough, Reiser. But, to the point at issue. We presently have only about one youth leader to each fifteen *hundred*. So Berlin is quite distressed not only at the lack of direct supervisory personnel but also at the lack of people to generate all that unreadable paper.

"You have almost every quality necessary, Reiser, to become a very important figure in the youth movement. Manifestly unselfish, racially acceptable, insultingly good-looking, demonstrated leadership. If you are accepted into the leadership training program, you will transfer into the Party next March after your *Abitur*, a year Labor Service, then an Ordensburg, a kind of 'finishing school for the National Socialist elite.' No problems along the way, you could end up with Von Schirach's job."

He smiled. "I wouldn't mention that. The man's pathologically suspicious of anyone more talented than himself. Which means he distrusts everyone."

"You said 'almost every quality,' Herr Commandant. My...attitude?"

"Yes, your attitude is open to question. Oh, not your fisticuffs with young Lange or even your encounter with his lamentable father, the Muenster Police Chief. Don't look so surprised. As I said, we're very thorough."

"If I have to stop being a Catholic, Herr Commandant, that's unchangeable."

"Perhaps. A third of the Party is Catholic-as well as a third of the S.A. and Gestapo. Hitler Youth serve Mass in uniform. We have a Concordat with the Vatican. All I would ask you to do is look at this...this 'resistance' of yours with an open mind."

"I want to be fair, Herr Commandant."

"Good," Von Schleich said. "This evening I would like you to begin helping with the youngsters at the campfire and also starting tomorrow with sports. Afternoons, political instructions with your own Hitler Youth platoon. I think that will be all."

"And Kurt Fuehlen, sir?"

"Not at this time. And think about my proposal, Reiser."

"I will, Herr Commandant, but I'm pretty certain I might like to try something else."

"You may have no acceptable alternative. Good day, Reiser."

"Thank you, sir." Paul stood, fired out his right arm, and turned toward the door.

"Reiser."

Paul stopped and turned.

"You needn't say 'Heil Hitler' alone in this office. But I think that would be another thing to rethink, wisely. Oh, and speaking of wisdom. A word with Fuehlen? I was informed a few minutes ago he made inflammatory remarks about the Fuehrer's policy about...inferior races."

"I surely will, Herr Commandant." He put his hand on the doorknob.

"And, Reiser, have him tell two men in his platoon...their names are Vischer and Schlamm, from Berlin...it would be *quite* unwise, like lovesick Leanders, to swim the narrow Hellespont out there tonight and attempt to woo the German maidens down the reservoir. That will be all."

* * * * *

45

At eight that evening, in the gathering twilight, boys in black shorts, white shirts, and neckerchiefs happily trotted out of the woods from all directions, like a regiment of giggling ants, laden with big branches to hurl on the huge pyre at the center of the field. One fat little boy, sweating like a raspberry pudding, was trying manfully to haul an enormous log by its one gnouted arm. It kept catching him at the back of the heels and tripping him up, but each time, like a pudgy Sisyphus, he grunted to his feet and started again toward the big mound of wood.

Paul slid down the bank toward the clearing. Ahead of him a straight-backed young boy wrestled a fat log along the path. "Hey! Wait a minute. I'll give you a hand," Paul called to him.

The boy stopped and turned. It was Vogel, the terrier from the Bund Neudeutschland. His face erupted in a smile. "*Paul*! They said you were our new assistant! Great."

Paul bent over to take the end of the log. They began to move along the path toward the field. "How are things going for you, Varlet Vogel?"

"Mornings are fine. We do sports. Afternoons I spend most of the time thinking about the easiest ways to commit suicide."

Paul laughed. "The lectures, eh?"

"Like catechism! Memorizing passages from *Mein Kampf*, all the names from the Munich Putsch, all the verses of the 'Horst Wessel Song.' One day we measured one another's skulls with these caliper things to show who had the most Aryan head. Stupid, or what?"

Ahead, several boys threw torches into the hillock of wood and the flames whooshed up. There was no statue of Mendelson.

"Anyway," Vogel said, "to get our first dagger, we got to run sixty meters in twelve seconds, do a long jump and shotput and go on an overnight march. I've done all but the march. Wednesday we laid telephone wires. Today we had small arms drill."

"You're kidding. Thirteen-year-olds?"

"For when the Polacks swarm up Koenigsstrasse and take over the Muenster Post Office."

"The Frenchies are closer."

"Except for the catechism, I do okay. I don't think Schulle will make it though."

"Johann Schulle? Little puddy-bottom. It must be hell for him."

"His father's a super-Nazi now. Johann's got to perform so Papa won't be embarrassed. They got this thing called 'fagging' where older boys test your limit, like hazing? I got this Klausner from Bavaria who's more afraid of me than me of him, so I'm all right. But Schulle's the kind that...well, he almost *demands* to be persecuted. Like Francis of

46

THE PLACE CALLED SKULL

Assisi'd like to wipe that look off his face, know what I mean? And Schulle's got this boy assigned to him that says he used to set cats on fire. I used to hate Schulle, but now I almost feel sorry for the poor bastard."

"When did you start using the word 'bastard'?"

Vogel winked. "Talk tough, they think you are tough. Anyway, it's good you're with us. Schulle and I are in the same platoon. Maybe you can help him. If he fails here, they say he may not be able to get into a good school, and he's very smart, even if he is a pain in the ass."

Paul grinned. "Call him a 'hemorrhoid.' It's more elegant."

The boy beamed up at him. "Even if he is a hemorrhoid."

They heaved the log into the blaze. Vogel caught Paul's elbow and said, "Over here," and led him to his new platoon. He introduced him to the boys and finally came to Schulle who sat at the back, arms gripping his knees, face hidden behind them.

Vogel stood over him. "Schulle. It's Paul Reiser. Remember? He's gonna help with games and things." The fat boy did not look up. "Johann?" Vogel turned to Paul and whispered, "I think he's been crying, and he doesn't want anybody to see."

"Johann, do you mind if Vogel and I sit with you?"

The fat boy rolled his colorless head back and forth, as if trying to say he didn't mind.

"Johann, I want you to know if you ever need my help, you just let me know, all right?"

From the fat scuffed knees came a mumbled whine that sounded like "Thank you, Reiser."

A microphone squealed. "Comrades of Herbert Norkus *Jungvolk*, before we sing our '*Gute Nacht, Kameraden*,' a moment of silence to grasp—each comrade in his own heart—how fortunate we are to have one another, to grow as men of honor and purpose, ready to put the tragedies of the Great War and the Great Depression behind and open a new and glorious future."

A silence hovered over the hundred and fifty boys. The only sound the crackle and hiss of the great fire. Then, over the microphone, came the soft chording of a guitar and a voice began: "Good night, my comrades," and it sprouted up around the blaze-washed field. "Here rests our caravan. Three gifts God gives us: Youth, Folk, and Fatherland."

Paul Reiser looked to his left at Vogel, ramrod straight, then to his right. Schulle, squat and suet-faced, but a proud smile beaming under the castings of tearstains on his puffy cheeks.

Yes, Paul thought. Yes.

* * * * *

Saturday, 5 August 1933 - Herbert Norkus Camp

After evening mess, a ragged line of young men moved westward in twos and threes along the dirt road from the older boys' camp toward the German Girl's Camp. Self-conscious horseplay, whispering, sniggering. But with the officers' vigilance and with one's comrades' ever-watchful concern, the ribaldry was hardly likely to get beyond nervous talk.

Kurt and Paul loped along, matching one another's long elastic stride.

"So how did you find out who turned you in to Von Schleich?" Paul asked.

"He just came up and told me. He said it was for the honor of the platoon and the Volk. He did it for my own good, he said. He's a nice kid, really. Kristof Obenauer. His father's a violin maker in Munich, but the kid's more ambitious. When we conquer the world he wants to be the Gauleiter of some small but very rich country in Africa. So help me. He actually said that."

"And what did you say when he told you he fingered you?"

Kurt turned to Paul with a triumphant grin. "Thank you!"

"Go on!"

"I honestly did. I didn't even giggle."

"Mind-boggling."

"Thank you."

"And how was *your* day," Kurt giggled.

Paul's faced sobered. "Kind of scary. The gamesmaster used to be a train porter, and now the little bugger carries a *swagger* stick, if you can believe it. 'No pampering, Weiser!' This morning we were to teach kids who couldn't swim, and this guy's got a real shortcut. He takes them out in a rowboat, six at a time, fifty feet from the dock and just...tosses them overboard, one by one. 'Here we go, here we go!' like mail sacks at a station."

"The kids must have been terrified."

"Johann Schulle pooped his pants. I know because I had to jump in after him. At first he put a brave face on, but then when the others went over, one by one, his face sort of fell apart, and he started whimpering, 'My uncle's a *priest!*' Whatever good that was going to do him."

"You think you ought to tell Von Schleich?"

"I suppose I ought to. It seems his only job around here is to wait for people to come in and squeal on somebody. I bet you and I are the only ones who haven't sung for our supper yet."

"Wrong. I turned you in for being a virgin."

"And I told him you wanted to be a nun."

They walked under an iron grillwork gate proclaiming "Faith and Beauty." In the broad meadow at the foot of the hill a large open-air pavilion had been cleared, and a band of accordions and fiddles was warming up a schottische. No one had yet arisen to call the dancers, and the boys and girls huddled in their own groups, trying to catch appraising glimpses.

The girls' uniforms were exactly like the boys', except for the black pleated skirts and, instead of hobnailed boots, ponderously sensible shoes. Most wore braids, woven into a crown. For a girl to have an unnatural permanent wave was asking to have her head shaved.

"Be still my heart!" Kurt said, pinching Paul's arm.

He nodded toward a girl at the corner of the pavilion, her cheeks tanned and flushed. She held a wisp of myrtle, brushing it across her chin, looking out across the calm twilit lake.

"Pining for her prince, too long away at the wars," Kurt whispered. "Patience, my princess, your Lancelot will soon be at your side. See you back here at ten, Paulli. Duty calls."

"Randy cockerel!"

"Thank you." Kurt walked away in long strides to the girl.

Many, like Paul, wandered the meadow, walking unconsciously to the lilt of the music. Slowly the field began to buzz with forced conversations, chit chat, then laughter. Couples wandered together in the half-light spill from the pavilion.

Then Paul saw Lisl.

She was standing, half turned away, talking with forced politeness to a thin blond boy. Her black hair was shorter, tied up in a black ribbon and spilling to the nape of her neck. Lisl. His hands still remembered her. As he came up beside them, he could smell the soap on her skin.

"Lisl?"

She turned, evidently surprised a boy would know her name, and suddenly her eyes flashed wide. "Paul!" She threw her arms around him and kissed his cheek. "Oh God, *Paul.*"

Suddenly she backed away, wiping her hands on her dark skirt, her smile almost a simper.

"My, how good to see you, Paul. I...I had no idea you were...." She turned to the other boy. "This is my...my cousin from Muenster, Paul Reiser. I'm sorry, I don't recall your name."

"Erich Edelmann." He gave a short bow and reached out to shake Paul's hand. "Pleased to meet you." He looked hopefully back at Lisl, then more grimly at Paul. "Well, if you will excuse me. You will have many things to talk about. Fraulein Streicher. Reiser. Another time."

He walked away. Paul turned to her. "Lisl....?"

The girl side-mouthed a whisper. "Walk me over there, away from the light. No, don't take my arm. When I looked over your shoulder I saw a boy from Muenster. A skinny boy. I think he's the Gestapo man's son. Watching us with a funny look."

"Oh, God. How do you know Dieter Lange?"

"Smile. Impress me. Like we hardly know one another."

They moved further from the light, passing groups and couples.

"You cut your hair."

"Mother wanted to bleach it, but I said, 'Is Hitler blond?' I've missed you so much."

"Oh God, Lisl, I never thought I'd see you again."

"Do you see anyone watching?"

They turned and searched but no one seemed interested.

"All right," she said. "I'll walk away and slip into the woods. See that holly? After I'm gone, walk over there and stay a few moments, as if you're trying to find a place to go to the bathroom and slip through. I'll cut around and wait for you there. I know a place."

Before the last word was out of her mouth, her open palm caught him flat on his right cheek. Her pale blue eyes blazed, and she stalked away toward the woods at the dark end of the meadow. Tears came automatically to Paul's eyes, and he put his hand to the burning spot on his cheek. He stood a moment, genuinely stunned, then stumbled in the opposite direction from Lisl.

When he got to the holly, he looked around with unfeigned apprehension. Just fuzzy silhouettes against the pavilion lights. He took a deep breath and plunged through the bushes.

"Here," Lisl whispered, and he followed her voice in the dark. Finally, he made out her hand and took it. She tugged him along through brush, sideways up an incline. Then Paul felt pine needles under his feet. Lisl said, "Watch your step. It gets rocky."

After a few more minutes, she finally said, "This is it."

"I don't see anything at all. I hardly see you."

He heard a door creak and touched the edge of it. He followed her across the doorsill, and heard her creak the door shut.

"There. No one'll find us here. I almost missed it first time myself, even in daylight. It's all overgrown. I was out wandering around. Against the rules, of course. Maybe it's a shed from when they built the dam. Sit down here next to me on the floor."

He sat and put his arm around her shoulders. "I wish I could see you," he said.

He heard her soft gurgling laugh in the dark. "Viking, we're both risking our necks. We can't even strike a match. We can pretend we're two blind people. We...."

But his mouth silenced hers. He kissed her cheeks, her eyes, her throat. Their hands groped one another's bodies, trying to devour one another. Paul felt her breast against his heavy heartbeat, her hand on his thigh.

Suddenly he pulled away.

"Paul, what's wrong? Did you hear something?"

"No," he hissed heavily, "No, it's just that we...we can't."

"Paul, we may never see one another ever again!"

"But, Lisl, what if you...?"

"I won't, Paul. I won't. Mama had me...fitted with something. She was afraid. She'd heard stories about the League camps. Please, Paul."

"Oh, God, Lisl, I want to so badly. Even if it's...." He was almost crying.

"Paul."

And she came to him.

* * * * *

The following week, Paul moved in exultant delirium. Everything was charged with electricity. The little boys flocked around the exuberant golden boy and basked in his vibrance. One boy from Kurt's platoon, Tusk Vischer, a tough little Berliner, sidled up one day after the political harangue and whispered to him, wondering where Paul got the booze.

He mystified even Kurt. Paul had said he was late Saturday because he got lost exploring. Kurt was also crestfallen since the girl he had approached intended to be a nun. A sign from God.

And every night, there was Lisl.

Everything beautiful in the world all in one small, compact, effervescent place. To be with her was worth risking anything, even damnation—if God really could damn anyone for something so beautiful. Worth lying awake till the boys' breathing assured him they were all asleep. Even worth having to leave her after only an hour, so neither would be missed. The shortness of their times together made them all the more precious.

"Reiser, wait up." Tusk Vischer sashayed from the Richthofen barrack. "Looking for Kurt? Gone. No, just for the day. After that asshole excursion last night, he's up at eight-thirty! Him and five other pain-lovers took off to explore the goddamn reservoir. You believe that?"

Paul grinned at the little cock-o'-the-walk. "I can believe it, Tusk. He's worked me into the ground more than once."

"You gotta talk to him, though, Reiser. This morning he mouthed off again at that dung-brain Lange. Lange says the pope's a Jew who's related to some English fairy named Disraeli. At first Kurt just kinda took it, but then when Lange says the pope's queer himself, Kurt says if he don't shut up he's gonna break Lange's nose for him."

"They can't send him home for defending the pope, right?"

"Yeah, I suppose so. So tell me. Where d'ya get the stuff, eh? Come *on!* I ain't gonna squeal. Hell, even if I turned *myself* in, they wouldn't believe me. Tell me, huh? If I don't get a belt soon, I'm gonna start believing all this Nazi shit. Come on."

Paul raised his right hand. "So help me, Tusk, never had liquor in my life."

"Bull-*scheiss*!"

"So help me."

"You're high on something, Reiser. I'm an expert."

"Hey, Tusk! I'm high on *life*!"

Tusk looked Paul up and down like a salesman sizing him up for a suit. Then a big grin spread across his pug face. "Well, I'll be *damned*! You're *gettin'* some, aintcha!"

Paul's face went suddenly flat. His brows knitted. "Don't know what you're talking about, Tusk." He turned to go, but Tusk caught his elbow and trotted along next to him.

"A virgin? In my experience, virgins are a mixed blessing. On the one side, they got no idea what they're missing. On the other side, there's a lot of bawling and, God, the *blood*!"

"Don't know what you're talking about, Tusk."

"Give over. Why ya so pissed? Everybody does it. I won't squeal. My word on it."

Paul kept walking, his heart chugging. There had been no bawling. No blood.

* * * * *

She was late. The older girls always took much longer to get to sleep. He paced outside the shed, cursing Hitler, God, himself, Lisl. Rewriting the upcoming scene in his head, choosing the words like a duelist choosing swords, then rejecting them for better, then rejecting those.

Earlier he had lain on his cot in a whirlpool of nerves, waiting for the boys to settle into a deep sleep. Two or three tossed longer than usual, and Paul was ready to smother them. About ten-thirty when they all becalmed, Johann Schulle begun to whimper over some remembered humiliation. God, why didn't they send the poor fat little bastard home? Finally, he snored.

He slipped off the cot in his bare feet, checking each bunk. He didn't stop for his shirt, for fear the sound of the locker would wake someone. He eased open the door, slid out, and quietly latched it. He headed for the latrine, calmly as he could. There was a slender week-old moon.

He walked the length of the shed, past the rows of fetid holes, gaping like obscene mouths in the dark. He pulled himself up to the two-foot ventilation space. He pivoted and slid down easily into the grass. Then he pushed through the brush for the quick swim across the river.

Almost an hour ago. His nerves and his anger became more tangled and raw.

The brush rustled, and Lisl emerged in the thin moonlight, the sight of her like a stab.

"Sorry I was so long. One of the...." She stopped ten feet away. "What's wrong?"

"Who was the first?"

The smile went out, and she took a few steps closer to where he leaned against the shed. "What are you talking about, Paul?"

"Have there been many? I'm a novice. No way to tell, but you're an expert, aren't you?"

She folded her arms round her belly. "Paul, I don't understand what you're talking about?"

He pushed from the vine covered shed and took a few steps, his back to her. "I'm talking about making *love*, or when there's no love they call it 'screwing.' Which have we been doing?"

Tears rimmed her eyes. "Paul, why are you doing this?" Her voice choked. "I love you."

"Whores have been groaning that since the caves, Lisl. Then it's, 'Ten marks to the lady at the entrance, dearie.'"

She put out her chin defiantly. "Are you calling me a whore?"

"I'm simply stating a fact: I wasn't the first."

"Who says you had the *right* to be? I thought I'd never see you again. Yes, there have been other boys I've liked. I was uprooted, Paul. Lonely. Yes, I slept with them. I slept with you, too, didn't I? Which hardly qualifies you to get up on your puritan soapbox." She lowered her eyes. She spoke softly, almost a whisper. "It was far different with you, Paul. So *different*."

He rocked on his heels, arms clamped against his chest, grinning sourly. "Oh, yes. Right! I was different. It's the body, right? I guess I really never knew what I had."

"Of course, that was part of it, Paul. But so much more than that." She leaned her head on her arm against the wall of the shed. "Oh, God, who *cares* how many times? Why do you Catholics have to be such prudes about something so beautiful and *normal?*"

Paul turned, trembling. "Well, maybe it's normal for you *Jews* to spread your legs for any boy you '*like*,' but for us it's a *sin*."

She raised her head from her arm and turned her fierce, tear-streaked face slowly to him. "And what we did wasn't?"

He took a breath to speak. But he couldn't.

"Goodbye, Paul." She sighed deeply. "It all worked out for the best, didn't it? In two weeks it would all have been over anyway. They were right all along, eh? All the commandment-makers. They knew that people were never meant to be just...happy."

She turned to go.

"Lisl?"

"Goodbye, Paul. I did love you."

"Lisl, please."

"Goodbye, Paul." And she walked away into the darkness.

He wanted to follow her, to take her in his arms and beg her forgiveness. He wanted to love her again. But he couldn't. He crumbled to the ground and wept and wept.

* * * * *

He didn't know how long he had lain there. What did it matter? He had lost the most beautiful thing in his life. Because of his own priggish stupidity, jealousy, anger. He wished he were a child again, when he knew nothing of sex but only love. He wished he were home, with his mother to tell him all men are fools and make him laugh. He wanted to wash himself clean of his self-hatred and his loss and his sin.

When he came to the river he stopped and stood looking at it, serene, moon-flecked, clean. Then he plunged in and felt the cool water soothe away the fever from his skin. He took long stretching strokes, scooping the water to him and under him and away.

When he came to the shallows, he stood, panting and dripping, and began to feel his way across the painful stones to the shore. Suddenly he thought of Herschel, and somehow the memory eased the ache. His pain was not the only pain or the worst.

He eased the door open. The only sound in the dark was the heavy breathing of deep sleep and soft rattle of snoring. Paul lowered himself carefully onto his cot in his wet shorts and sat for a moment, his elbows on his knees, empty and weary.

Then he looked up and saw Johann Schulle, his eyes wide open, watching him.

Paul cleared his throat softly. "I couldn't sleep either," he whispered. "I went for a swim."

A smirk split Schulle's fat face.

"How long have you been awake, Johann?"

"I had to use the latrine. Right after you did. Hours ago."

Paul's heart stopped.

The smirk widened, like a fat cat licking mouse from its lips.

"I saw you last night, too."

* * * * *

"Then you refuse to divulge the young lady's name?" Ritter von Schleich leaned back in his desk chair, his index fingers bisecting his lips, as if he were actually counseling silence.

"With all respect, Herr Commandant, I haven't said there *was* a young lady." Paul tried to smile but the focus of his attention was on the sweat on his palms. He saw Von Schleich's eyes follow them as he blotted them against his shorts.

The summons had come just after lunch, when the little boys were on their way for their siesta. Schulle had been quick about it. But Paul could muster no anger. He himself was no stranger to weakness. At the moment, he was too tired to care.

The Commandant leaned on the desk, shoulders hunched like a wounded hawk. "Come, come, Reiser. You're a perfectly normal young man, and what you are alleged to have done is perfectly normal. But these are not normal times. We've discussed our thoroughness before.."

"Herr Commandant, even if I were guilty of something 'perfectly normal,' as you say, what right would the camp staff have to know about it? Or the government? Or the Gestapo?"

"The theory is that confession is not only good for the soul but essential for the trust the community can place in the individual. You've heard the political lectures."

"But, sir, if I were to sin, even my parents wouldn't have a right to know it, would they? Even the priest has to act as if he doesn't know. It would be between me and God."

55

Von Schleich leaned back again. "Reiser, you have come into your manhood, but you've done it in the Third Reich. Your personal acts affect not only yourself but a State which must rely on you." He paused and arched one eyebrow. "That troubles you?"

"I love my country, Herr Commandant. But you make it sound as if the government...and God were the same thing. That, if I sinned, I'd have to go to confession twice."

Von Schleich tapped his two forefingers together in front of his lips.

"And my freedom? To make mistakes and learn from them?"

"But wouldn't you take your mistakes to your father as well as to your confessor?"

"In most cases, yes."

"Then extend your idea of family to the whole German nation. The theory is that we can *all* profit by giving the father of the family the last word. The patriarch must know *all* strengths and weaknesses of those entrusted to him. Therefore, we must know all about Paul Reiser, who, as I said, can be an outstanding servant of the Reich. This is petty, Reiser. We both know that. But the theory is that he who can be trusted in small matters can be entrusted with greater."

"Sir, you have only the word of one little boy who's a pariah looking to buy protection."

Von Schleich's face went stern. "No. We have the statement of another person."

Paul sat up in his chair. Faces raced through his mind like a kaleidoscope. Edelmann? Mueller? Lange? Not Vogel. Oh, surely not Vogel. What difference did it make? He blew the air from his lungs and collapsed back into the chair.

"Herr Commandant," Paul said, his cheeks hot, completely alone, "if honor is loyalty, what about loyalty of one's comrades?"

The Commandant folded his arms and nodded. "You're right, of course." His eyes went to the picture of his squadron on his desk. He seemed suddenly very tired. "The theory is...."

"Sir, you keep saying 'the theory is.'"

One side of his mouth slowly raised to a smile. Then he leaned forward. "Well," he sighed, "you leave me no alternative." He looked up with his half-grin. "Or let us say 'the theory' leaves me no alternative. No public floggings here, no stripping off the insignia. Best thing to do is to send you home as quickly and quietly as possible, along with your friend, Fuehlen."

"Kurt?"

"Again a trivial matter, enlarged when seen against 'the greater background.' Apparently a boy in his platoon made some foolish and disparaging remarks about Pius the Eleventh. Loyally, your friend Fuehlen demanded that the boy stop. Unfortunately, he backed his request with a promise of bodily harm, in front of more than a few witnesses, who felt different loyalties. And the boy in question happens to be the son of a highly-placed Gestapo official.

So," he got painfully to his feet and reached for his cane. Paul stood. "Gather your gear. I'll arrange a car. Train at about 1600 hours." He reached out his hand. "Goodbye, Paul."

Paul shook the Commandant's hand. "Thank you, sir. To be honest...I want to go home."

The Commandant nodded. Paul turned to the door.

"Paul."

The boy stopped. Von Schleich limped slowly around the desk and put his hand on Paul's shoulder. "You're going to pay for your soul, son." He touched the boy's cheek. "Go with God."

Paul's eyes filled. He nodded, turned, and left the broken hero in the doorway, watching him cross the parade ground toward the *Jungvolk* cabins.

* * * * *

Sunday, 24 December 1933 - Muenster

Monsignor Johann Lutz, chancellor of the Muenster diocese, was understandably irritable. He angled his watch to catch light in the near-dark of the confessional. Eleven-thirty. Nearly time for midnight Mass; Bishop von Galen would already have arrived and vested. High in the baroque loft, the choir was already intoning Christmas chants, making hearing more difficult. Lutz would very much like a good cigar before the long Mass began, but that now looked quite impossible. He caressed the snow white wave of hair over his uncreased forehead and sighed.

He had been prisoned in the confessional since eight. Something one never got used to, nailed alive into a coffin and, moreover, forced during the entombment to listen without surcease to the failings and foibles of one's fellow sinners. Sharing their purgatory.

Tonight, on the verge of Christmas, many made their only confession of the year, bringing months' laundry to the scapegoat's coffin and dumping it, along with their breath and its burden of onions and wurst and schnaps. Quite necessary, of course. Wipe away the degrading adulteries and dalliances, the petty thieveries and deceptions, but quite distressing nonetheless. The only thing that kept Johann Lutz from bolting out of the box was the knowledge that he himself laid his own burdens each week at the feet of his own confessor.

The penitent to his left rasped out his Act of Contrition, swallowed up, symbolically, in the choir's rhapsodies to the Prince of Peace. Lutz absolved him and took the ugliness through the impenetrable mesh into his coffin, where he would bury it beneath even his own memory.

Lutz pushed back the slide, blocking the opening on his left, and slid open the one on his right. "May the Lord be in your heart and on your lips, that you may open your soul to his forgiveness," he said, cupping his hand to his temple to assure the penitent he was not watching.

Nothing. He reached for the purple stole. But no. The penitent cleared his throat.

"Yes?" Lutz was not only irritated but nervous. The deacon at Solemn High Mass couldn't rush out onto the altar, tripping all over his cincture like a newly-ordained country curate.

In the box to the priest's right, Paul Reiser knelt, rigid, sweating, throat so dry he was sure he couldn't speak. In the dim light spilling over the top of the box, he could see the gleam of Lutz's magnificent hair. Like God. At first, he had wanted to confess his sin to anyone. Even to Kurt. And then to no one. As if his sins had corroded everything inside him and left him dead.

"Please," from inside the box, "we really haven't much time. I must be vested for Mass."

"Bless me...." Paul cleared his throat again. "Bless me, Father, for I have sinned. It has been...five months since my last confession, and these are my sins."

When he had gotten home, he had thought of going to the seminary and asking for a priest he didn't know. But that was cowardly. It had to be to the harshest priest, the one he found least approachable. If he were to do it at all. And so, for five months, it was not at all. But now it was Christmas. There was no way he could avoid Mass with his family. And Communion.

"Please, my son." The voice was barbed.

"Father, I've missed Mass since last August. I lied to my parents and to one of my friends -every week to my parents and twice to my friend. I told them I went to Mass somewhere else."

Silence again. Lutz began to squirm. Eleven-forty. The voice sounded familiar, young, strong. He put that out of his mind, but he knew even before the boy spoke the reason for the lies and missing Mass. "Go on, my son. Please."

Paul's heart beat faster. "I...Father, I had sexual relations with a girl five times. I...I was too ashamed to confess. I was at a camp this summer. I was lonely. I'd known the girl before...."

"Intimately?"

"No, Father. Never. This was...the first time, Father. We met one night at a dance, and we went to a hut in the woods that she knew about, and...."

"There's no need to give me all the details, my son."

"Yes, Father."

"For your penance...."

"But there's more, Father. Something worse."

Paul saw the priest put his hand over his eyes. Oh, my God, he prayed, I'm so sorry.

"I blamed *her*, Father, as if it were her fault. I made her feel cheap. Because she was my first, and I ...and I wasn't her first. I was cruel. Because it was as much my fault as hers. More."

Silence, and Paul feared Lutz would shout his sin to the crowded church. "Of *course* it was your fault," the voice growled. "The woman is the weaker vessel. You are supposed to be her protector, not using her as an object for your lust. Just as if you had taken the host from the tabernacle and trampled it with your muddy boots."

Tears poured down Paul's cheeks. Every word was a lash. But he deserved it.

"But the worst sin was you doubted God's forgiveness. The loving Father who...." Paul saw him pull out his watch again. "Do you have a firm purpose of avoiding this sin in the future?"

"Father, I swear on my soul."

"No need for that. For your penance, say...five rosaries, and now make a good act of contrition. *Misereatur tui omnipotens*...."

"Father?"

"Yes." The word ground out by the priest's perfect white teeth.

"If I can't finish the rosaries by Communion, may I receive?"

"Of course. Now get on with your act of contrition."

As the priest droned the Latin absolution, and the boy spoke his contrition in tears, the choir surged into the climax of the Latin Martyrology: "... is born in Bethlehem of Judah of the Virgin Mary and made man. The Nativity of Our Lord Jesus Christ according to the flesh!"

Scrubbing the tears, Paul stepped outside the stuffy box into the packed cathedral. He sucked in breath, dizzy with relief. Over. As if someone had come to his wheelchair and said, "Stand up! Walk!" And he had stood. He had taken the first step to being healed and whole.

* * * * *

1934

Friday, 16 February 1934 - Muenster

Kurt Fuehlen pulled up his collar against the wind whistling along Alter Fischmarkt, slanting down the thin spires of St. Lambert's, waiting for Paul to finish up in the basement. The two now worked part-time at The Kaiser Friederich Halle, a restaurant owned by Otto Lechler, father of a boy from the old *Neudeutschland*. Since Gauleiter Kleist interdicted Catholic Youth groups from all but spiritual instruction, Paul's cousin, Ernst Weider had taken the few young men willing to risk it underground, figuratively and literally.

With Herr Lechler's reluctant consent, the Catholic Youth members had repaired an old printing press once used for menus in the restaurant basement. Every night a handful of young men turned out leaflets opposing virulent anti-Catholic campaigns in the weekly *Beobachter*, exhorting Catholics to remain faithful despite reported scandals of predator priests, despite threats and physical abuse. Each member took a dozen copies out under his shirt, passing them along to friends with the understanding they would pass them along again. Even though they had been in operation only a month, they were already attacked in the Party press, and the discovery of their traitorous operation was predicted only a matter of days away.

These threats were unnerving to Herr Lechler. Although he was counting on the Nazi regime to be short-lived, he was also counting on his own life being longer than the Nazi regime. But since each boy worked at least one of the evening hours to alibi his presence, that was ten man-hours each night, by scrupulously honest, hard-working-unpaid-young men. This latter motive had induced Lechler to continue "one more week," but only if the press operated during noisy rush hours upstairs and not a single handbill left anywhere on the premises.

Paul shuffled out the door, pulling on his ski cap and shouldering into his heavy coat. 'Onward, my manly minion, into the bitter Arctic cold!'"

They walked along Bogenstrasse toward the first of the bridges to the tiny island in the Aa River. The spires of the cathedral stood stark against the pale moonlit sky. They hunched into their collars, bumping against one another at odd moments to jog the circulation.

"Maybe you can talk to Vogel," Paul huffed. "He smokes like a dragon down there with all that paper and cusses like a sailor. He's gone from being a terrific kid to a sour little hood."

"I'll try. But you're the one on the pedestal."

"I don't smoke. And I don't swear that much, do I?"

"You're...pleasantly vulgar. He's just trying to do everything you do, but better."

"No, he's bitter, Kurt. Disillusioned."

They got to the first bridge, its lights spilling silver on the parapets, biscuited in soft snow.

"What's Vogel disillusioned with? You?"

"I think he's disillusioned with everything-with the helplessness of the whole thing. When the ship's going down, toss the rule book overboard and raise hell. Why not?"

Kurt eyed him over his collar. "You're not going to go black-moody on me again."

Paul chuckled. He'd gone in for some wicked penances after his confession, confided them all to Monsignor Lutz, who never suggested curtailing them, sure he had another Augustine in hand. Until Kurt had beaten some sense into him. "Me?," Paul said. "Hell, no. I'm just worried about what all this is doing to good kids like Vogel. No, I'm working on big plans."

"So, next month you get the highest *Abitur* grade in history, zip through university in, oh, say a month, and be the first twenty-year-old ambassador to America."

"Or maybe a film star."

"Maybe the pope."

"That's a real possibility."

"Not me. I'm doing my Labor Service and get it out of the way."

"Kurt, you're kidding."

"No, I talked it over with my father last night. All right, don't say it! I'm very smart. Maybe true. And I don't apply myself. *Certainly* true. Big question is why. I'd like to maybe work on a farm for a year. Got to do the Labor Service sometime."

They crossed the second bridge onto Rosenstrasse, the big wings of the Priester Seminar hulking ahead of them. They turned up Kreuzstrasse, the lights winking in the cold.

"It's just...," Paul hesitated. "I thought we'd be going into the seminary together."

Kurt stopped dead in his tracks. A frown crinkled his brow. "You're *kidding* me, right?"

Paul smiled. "No, Kurt. I'm not. I mean it."

"This isn't another crazy penance, is it?"

Paul started walking again, his shoulders bowed to cowl in the warmth. Kurt ran forward and fell into step again, looking over warily, as if in a moment the kaleidoscope might shift again.

"It's not a penance. Oh, when I was going crazy with Lutz's help, I thought I'd run off to some monastery. Then I thought I wasn't worthy even of that. They probably *would* have slammed the door in my face. Not because I was a sinner, but because I was such an idiot!"

"Well, you're still an idiot, but a nicer idiot."

"But now I know I've got something to offer, Kurt. Thanks to you. I couldn't see what all the penances were doing to you, my parents. Only thing mattered was little Paulli and his big sin." He punched Kurt's shoulder. "I'm not offering sacrifices to my sin anymore. I want to count, Kurt. I've been given a lot. I want to change things. I don't want to go on being helpless."

"And being a priest, you won't be helpless?"

"Bishop Von Galen's not helpless. They can't shut him up."

"So, in six years you're ordained. You get in a pulpit and say, 'My dear people, the Nazis are assholes.' They haul you off to a camp. Six years for one sermon. Doesn't make sense."

They turned onto the Muensterstrasse toward the Fuehlens'.

"Kurt, there'll always be somebody trying to take over people's minds. Maybe not a big difference, but a difference. I can preach, teach, maybe even write. At least I can try."

They came to the steps of Kurt's house.

"You want to come in for cocoa or something?"

"Thanks, but Mother'll think they hauled me off in a truck."

"You told them what we're doing at Lechler's?"

"I told my father. I was putting them in danger. So I really had to. He was worried maybe, but, you know, pretty proud. You?"

"I told my father, too. Same thing. Stronger maybe." He scowled. "After what they did to Rudi. Just because he's...."

"Damn Nazis. As if cerebral palsy was contagious. Is Rudi all right?"

Kurt wrapped his arms around his belly. His jaw clenched, and tears rimmed his eyes. "He's terrified of swastikas. Even at church, he hides his face. At first I thought, oh well, he won't understand what it means to be...neutered. But he knows about animals. And he's seen all of us boys naked. He understands." He started up the steps. "Better get a move on or freeze."

"See you tomorrow." Paul turned to go, but stopped. "Kurt?"

"Huh?"

"You haven't said you're happy for me."

Kurt came slowly off the steps toward the curb, scuffing mounds of snow into the gutter.

"I don't know Paul. Maybe because I wrestled with it, too. Maybe I envy you...being sure." He snorted. "Hell, maybe it's because we've been Siamese twins so long."

"You worried? That I might be making a mistake?"

"No. You can always come out. Not worried. Just...uneasy."

"Kurt, it's not rebounding from Lisl. That's what you were thinking, no?"

Kurt turned to him. "Yeah."

Paul laid his hand on his shoulder. The two locked eyes, standing in silence.

Then Paul said, quietly, "It's not Lisl, Kurt. Honest."

For a moment, they just looked at one another. Then Kurt put his arms around him and rocked him from side to side.

"I'm happy for you, Paulli. I'm happy."

* * * * *

Sunday, 5 June 1934 - Muenster

Elly Reiser stood at the high sink, her sleeves rolled up above the elbows, cracking lettuce. She liked the touch of it, stiff ruffled silk, cold water dotting it with pearls. Say one thing for the Nazis. Lettuce again. Strange, all you take for granted. Like her Paul.

What a miracle, and she had been too busy to notice–with diapers, miscarried hopes, badgering butchers. Like enjoying food only from the aftertaste. That tall, sinewy boy had once been small enough to carry inside her own body. Tiny enough to fit into the dishpan for his bath, when they had still lived on Hansa Platz after Willi had "come down" from the diplomatic corps.

Now Paul was a man. Leaving the nest. We spend our lives bathing, feeding, shaping a child-only to give him away. Was there ever a time she knew all children are only adopted? Loving is so irresistible, and foolish. To free him to love someone more than he loves you.

She almost wished it were a girl she was losing him to. It would be like having another daughter, bringing grandchildren so she could coo and hum to them in language one never learns or forgets. But God was another matter. He takes the whole man, like a sacrificial virgin.

She'd spoken to Monsignor Lutz about it. He'd upbraided her, asked if she understood the privilege of having a son a priest, told her to compare her own sacrifice to the Blessed Mother's. Pompous prig. Was it possible he'd ever loved anything and given it away? When you become a priest, do you have to stop loving, feeling affection, caressing? She chuckled. No, Lutz surely loves that gorgeous white hair. Like a fat angora cat, licking itself. What if it all fell out? Would his fine hand still stray to fondle the soft waves?

"I thought it was *tea* leaves gypsy fortune tellers use."

Elly turned and saw her son filling the doorway of the kitchen, fresh from his bath, clean and golden. It was an act of will to keep from running across the room and holding him.

"How long have you been standing there, you big oaf?" She ran water over the lettuce and dumped it onto a towel to dry it.

"Couple of minutes." He ambled over to the sink. "I didn't want to break the spell." He pulled a peeled carrot from a pot of water and began to munch it.

"Only one. You'll spoil your supper. Have you seen Gretel?"

"She's in Papa's study, pretty as a princess, working away at her Nazi coloring book."

"Oh, God, the world's gone mad."

"It's all right. She didn't have a pink crayon, so she colored Hitler's face red."

"Is your father in the tub?"

"He has to wait. Gretel and I took all the hot water."

"Where's your necktie?"

"Aw, Mama, why do I have to? It's only family and Kurt."

"*And* Monsignor Lutz, *and* I won't have the General and Frau General Weider think your gypsy mother was too busy mucking out the cowbarns to see her son dresses properly."

"You know they don't think that, Mama."

"If they don't, it's because I make you wear a necktie."

"Oh, you're a tough one, Frau Reiser. All right, I'll get it in a minute." He hiked his rump onto a stool, cracking the carrot in his teeth.

"Jackrabbit," she said, giving him a sidelong grin. "Who's going to keep up with that appetite over there in the seminary? I bet they eat mush three times a day. Where would nuns learn how to cook? You'll wither away to a pole."

"Not a chance. I'll scheme. I'll charm the cook."

"You will, you rascal."

He stood and came over to her. He wrapped his long arms around her waist from behind and rested his chin on her dark hair. "I've been charming the cook all my life, haven't I?"

Elly put her wet hand on his starched sleeve and leaned against him. Despite all her plans, a tear ran down her cheek.

Paul turned her around. "Hey, what's wrong?"

She smeared the tear with the heel of her hand and sniffed. "Oh, God, look what I've done to your shirt. You'll have to change it before they get here." She broke away from him and dropped the lettuce in a bowl. "Could you get the butter from the ice box, dear? To soften."

Paul took her hands from the bowl and sat her on one of the stools and sat next to her, her small hands wrapped in his. "Mama, aren't you happy about what I'm doing?"

"Of course I am, you big ninny." She sniffed again. "The only thing in the world I want is that you do what's going to make you happy. It just takes some getting used to, that's all."

"I won't be that far away. Not even a mile. Just across the street from the cathedral."

She patted her son's hands. "Different kind of distance, Paulli. Not like when you and Kurt would go tramp up and down the Rhine in the summers. Not even the same as when your father went off to the war. Those times you were both coming home."

"But I'll be home part of the summer, and Christmas."

"Not the same, son. We'll always be your family, but you have your own family now. As it should be. That's what life's all about." She smiled softly, stroking the back of his hand. "That's what the gypsy was thinking about when she was reading the lettuce leaves."

"I wish I could do it without hurting you."

She put her hand to his cheek. "Ah, Paul, if I'd wanted never to be hurt, I'd have stayed an old maid. That would have been *much* worse. When you take the chance of loving people, Paul, it fills you up. And when they go away, it leaves you empty. But it'll heal. It always has."

She rose and went to the wooden ice box, but she stopped and turned, her hand resting on the handle. "One thing I.... It's not easy for a woman to talk about, especially to her grown son. Your father's spoken to you about...about matters between a man and woman, and I know you understand, at least for now, what you're giving up. But...I know there's a great deal of passion in you, Paul. If...if you change your mind, your father and I will understand. Completely."

"I know, Mama. But I've got to give it a try. And I will. If I'm home before a year's over, you'll know they threw me out. I'll give it a year, full throttle. Then I'll decide."

"One thing truly worries me. That they'll...dry you up. I suppose a priest has to be more careful of passion than other men. But so many seem to have... smothered passion. Not just the passion between a man and a woman, but *any* kind of passion. They seem so...so juiceless."

"Old maids."

"Exactly." She cupped his face in her two hands. "And if your peasant Mama ever saw you starting to become like that, my Paulli, she'd come and haul you out of that seminary even if she had to get every gypsy in Europe to help kidnap you."

Paul took her two hands and kissed them. "Thank you, Mama."

The doorbell rang.

"Let Gretel get that. You go upstairs and fetch a necktie."

"Yes, Gypsy Mama."

"Scoot! And change your shirt."

He darted out, and she went to the ice box. But she'd forgotten what she had wanted.

*　*　*　*　*

1937

Angriff, Friday, 15 January 1937

EXTRADITION SOUGHT FOR PRIEST ACCUSED OF SODOMY, INCEST

Johann Schulle, 16, of Muenster, has accused his uncle, Fr. Heinz Werner of forcing the boy into orgies the pen refuses to describe. Young Schulle, a principal figure in the outlawed movement, Bund Neudeutschland, declared that he himself had aspired to the priesthood until this harrowing experience showed him the true nature of this unnatural vocation.

As our Fuehrer himself has written, "the education priests undergo makes them perverts." Readers will recall 170 Franciscans were arrested at Koblenz for corrupting youth and turning the monastery into a male brothel. It is well known these monasteries are incubators of unnatural acts. What parents can still entrust their children to an organization which possesses more than a <u>thousand</u> convicted and imprisoned sexual-criminal priests?

Our publisher, Reichsminister of Propaganda, Dr. Paul Josef Goebbels, speaks for all true German parents: "Today I speak as the father of a family whose four children are the most precious wealth I possess-as a father who fully understands how parents are shocked to see their most precious treasure delivered to the polluters of youth. In the name of millions of German fathers: these corrupters must be wiped from the face of the earth!"

It is an acknowledged fact that homosexuality is an infection injected into German youth by the international Jewish conspiracy to soften our Fatherland's manhood and to deprive it of new offspring. But the pope-the heir to the throne of the notorious Borgia and Medici heretics -has not condemned this Jewish deviance in the ranks of his own followers.

A police source in Muenster revealed that Priest-Sodomite Werner has escaped to Rome, where he will serve the pope.

Any loyal German with information concerning a Catholic priest or nun who attempts to seduce a German child must, in conscience, bring that information to the authorities so that these poisoners can join the hundreds of priests who are now confined to rehabilitation camps for their perversions. Let the Pope of Rome and his subversive agents be warned!

* * * * *

Saturday, 16 April 1937 - Muenster

Dear Kurt, S.J.,

If I listed alibis for not writing, they'd stretch from here to Pullach. If I'm not mistaken, the last time I wrote you was *Christmas*! I should be drawn and quartered; here I am home for Easter! I'd do penance, but you know how I go overboard on that, right?

When I got back from Labor Service, I had two semesters to do in one, and *one* in one is tough enough! Canon Law, which has me cross-eyed. It must have been easier when there was just the Lord and twelve peasants sitting around the dinner table. Would you know what to do if a Moslem with four wives wanted to become a Catholic? The first thing *I'd* do is to show him how terrific it was to be a Moslem and hope he'd forget the whole thing.

Also, I've had this accursed cold since a month before I even came home from the Labor Camp. I sound like a trained seal: bork, bork, bork, all the time. No sooner did I get home when my mother (who doesn't hear "no" too often!) hauled me off to see some quack. He stuck one of those wooden planks down my throat far enough to see down to Africa. First, he said strep throat; then he said shouting too much. In the seminary, right? So he gave me some red cough syrup. With codeine! Terrific! I stagger for about a half-hour after I take it—*six* times a day! I'd have felt a lot safer going to Doctor Weiss, but Doctor Weiss and his family have just...gone. Maybe to America. But I doubt it, if you know what I mean.

It seems hardly possible a year from now I'll be ordained a deacon. And the Christmas after that, a priest! Do you think they'd let you out of the dungeon for the diaconate? (Maybe I could convince my cousin, Fritz Weider, the Luftwaffe pilot, to *fly* you up. Ha-ha! Fritz would do us a favor just after Karl Marx!) But you've *got* to be at the priesthood ordination, even if I have to send my mother's gypsies. Threaten your Father Master Pfizer with that!

Even though I don't write enough, know that I think of you every day when I say my rosary on the beads you gave me. And a sinner's prayers are always answered, right? I owe a lot to you, my friend. You made me see what loving really means.

Your loving friend,

Paul

P.S. I heard yesterday from his mother that Josef Vogel's joined the Wehrmacht. Vogel? I suspect the fine hand of a judge. Maybe the best thing in the world for him. But I'm not so sure. Pray for him. Sinners' prayers are always answered, and you're a *bigger* sinner.

P.P.S. Do the Jesuits censor your mail? If so, I was only kidding. We're all sinners, right? And Kurt's a larger *person*, you see? I'd better quit while I'm ahead, right?

Paul folded the letter, slipped it into the envelope and sealed it. He tossed it on the desk to mail on his way to Mass tomorrow. He went down the stairs, past the pictures of his incompatible aristocrat and peasant grandparents, uncles, and aunts. His mother turned with a huge grin, looking as if she'd like to eat him up.

"Silly fool," she chortled. "There's no Mass Holy Saturday. Why didn't you sleep in?"

"Force of habit. They electrify the beds at six. You learn to leap at 5:59." Paul laughed and coughed quietly behind his hand.

"Paul, do you smoke? I don't care. I was just wondering."

"It turned me green. So I said, who needs this?"

"Have a cup of coffee and some kuchen. I told you they wouldn't feed you."

"Oh, they feed us plenty, Mama. I'm on the go a lot."

"Why are you so stringy? And that cough."

"Mama, six hours in that library is worse than a full day in that Saxon swamp-including the Nazi bilge they drowned us with at nights."

His father spoke from the door. "I'd be careful of that kind of talk, son."

"Morning, Papa. Just joking." Paul grinned. "Have the Gestapo planted a snoop?"

His father looked over his shoulder, then at his wife. "Is Gretel up yet?"

"I imagine she is." His mother looked annoyed.

"Paul," his father sat next to him. "Your mother and I are worried about Gretel."

"She's not sick is she? I hope I didn't give her this cold."

"Not physically," Elly said, scooping eggs onto a platter.

"Paul," Willi said, "Gretel's had a different education from the kind you had. It's as if...as if there were a teacher sitting in Gretel's room every night while she does her homework."

"Telling her lies," Elly grumbled.

"Elly," Willi said, "we've got to be just as cautious."

"What are you two talking about?"

"Gretel's gotten the notion," his father said, "from reactions of her teachers to what she says we talk about, that...."

"Sweet God in heaven!" Paul gasped. "She's a *child*!"

"These last few days, you've talked about the indoctrination in the Labor Camp."

"Papa, I was joking. It was the way to keep our sanity. Even the Nazis joked about it."

"Well, son," Willi said, "Gretel can't make those kinds of distinctions. She's only fifteen."

"I'll talk to her. Do you think that would help?"

"God knows," his mother sighed as she bought the platter of eggs to the table. "If you can get through to her, you're better than your peasant mother or your diplomat father."

Gretel came into the room, scrubbed and pink and shy. Her long blonde hair shimmered from brushing. "Morning," she said quietly. She'd been listening.

"Good morning, darling," her mother said, too heartily, and got up for the coffee. "Paul, pass those eggs before they get cold. Tomorrow is Easter. We have sausages!"

"Did you sleep well, Paul," Gretel asked, like a talking doll.

"Like a log, beautiful lady. Say, maybe after breakfast the two of us could take a walk through the Schloss. That is, if you don't have some swooning swain...."

There was a knock on the back door.

"Odd," Elly said, carrying the coffee pot to the table and wiping her hands on her apron, "so early on a Saturday morning."

She went to the door and opened it. Aloys Lange stood there flanked by two SS men, one a grinning blond stringbean, the other a dour lump of dough.

"Herr Lange," she said tentatively.

"Frau Reiser, may we come in?"

Willi rose and walked to the door. "Yes, Herr Lange?"

"Just a few questions. Nothing serious. May we come in?"

"Of course," Willi said. "Please. Come in." He looked round apprehensively.

Lange came in, pulling off his leather gloves. The two troopers followed awkwardly. "My!" Lange sighed and looked around. "The kitchen is the heart of the home, and the mother the heart of the heart." He looked at Gretel. "Ah, and this is the lovely Gretel. I'm told you are a very, very bright young lady."

Gretel blushed and nodded once.

"And you are...are you Father Reiser yet?"

Paul stood. "No, I'm only a seminarian, Herr Lange."

"What a loss to the Hitler Youth, eh? But I've been told God's ways are not man's ways."

"I've been told they're often completely incompatible, Herr Lange."

Silence, everyone looking at nothing. Elly cleared her throat. "Coffee, Herr Lange?"

"That would be most kind," Lange gave her a yellowed smile. "And while we are having our coffee, perhaps your son might show my two assistants his room. His diaries."

All four Reisers raised their eyes, wondering if they had heard him correctly.

"I understand there are diaries. Several years. We are interested for historical purposes."

Gretel's mouth pinched. "We were talking in class. About keeping a journal," she sniffed. "I told the class my brother had always...."

"Fine. Seminarian Reiser...I'm sorry, I don't know the proper title. You will accompany my men to your room and return with the diaries, please." It was a statement.

"Herr Lange," Paul said, "those diaries are personal. Nothing in them about the Catholic Youth Movement. I swear it. They're my meditations. Adolescent poems. Nothing subversive. No lists of agents or maps of buried treasure."

"Paul...," his father's voice warned.

"Then if they are perfectly innocent," Lange said mildly, "you'll have no problem in letting us borrow them awhile."

"I swear I haven't been involved in the Muenster youth group for over two years. I've been halfway across Germany, Herr Lange, in Freiburg. Then Labor Service in Saxony. If there even is a group now, I have no idea who the members are. My diaries are *private*, Herr Lange."

"For a good German, nothing is private. The good of the State comes before your girlish modesty. Now get them."

Paul looked helplessly at his father, and Willi shrugged back, helplessly. Paul turned furiously toward the door, and the troopers followed him out of the room.

"Now," Lange said, his face crinkling into a sulphurous grin, "A cup of coffee would take the chill off a brisk April morning."

Elly looked at him, her jaw working grimly. She set a cup and saucer at the place Paul had vacated, her chin fixed, and Lange coiled himself onto the stool next to Gretel.

"Oh, please, Fraulein Gretel," he said, "no tears. Your brother is a fine young man. He's going to be a priest. This is merely a precaution.

Please. No tears, eh? Where is the stiff spine and the upthrust chin of the *Deutsche Jungmaedchen*, eh?"

Gretel sniffed again and raised her chin, eyes downcast. Paul came back into the room, face crimson. The trooper brought the notebooks to Lange with Paul's letter to Kurt Fuehlen.

"This was on the desk, Chief."

Lange riffled through the diaries. "Hm," he said, thoughtfully. "The Jewess."

"Herr Lange, *please*," Paul said, close to tears.

"My knowledge of Catholic...doctrines," he said without looking up, "is inadequate. I will really have to correct some of my false...Well, well! I had forgotten you were once at the same camp with my son. I recall now that...." He looked up, his brow knotted. "Several pages razored out here. Can you explain that?"

Paul took a deep breath. "A time in my life I find too unpleasant to remember."

"Ah, yes. Now I recall. A matter of...."

"*Please*! Will you just take my diaries and *leave*?"

Lange picked up a table knife, slit the envelope, and pulled out the letter to Kurt. The others stood like spectators who had come in too late to understand the play.

"Hm."

"Herr Lange, that's a personal letter," Willi said, his face beginning to sour.

"You are a public official, Herr Reiser. You know the law allows me. This Fuehlen is the one you usually got into trouble with?"

"We were in the Catholic Youth together."

"*He* is now a seminarian, too? Jesuit? Odd. These seminaries havens for subversives."

"Hardly, Herr Lange. Unless the gospel is meant to subvert the values of...'the World.'"

"You mean National Socialism?"

"No, Herr Lange. Materialism, selfishness, disrespect for other people's pr-...."

"*Paul*!" his father snapped.

"Are there many Moslems converting to Catholicism?"

Paul's eyes went to the ceiling. "It was a *joke*, Herr Lange. To show the subject of Canon Law tries to cover every conceivable situation."

"I don't see the point of it."

"I don't see the point any more myself."

"Who is this Doctor Weiss?"

"He used to be our doctor," Elly said quickly.

"You mean the kike, Weiss?"

"He was a Jew, yes."

"And why doubt he has gone to America, Seminarian Reiser?"

"I...I never heard him speak of relatives in America, and I understand one has to be sponsored. I heard him speak of a brother in...Argentina. I naturally assumed...."

"Really? Unwise to assume on such slim evidence."

Willi Reiser shot a quick warning look at his son.

"Why would Leutnant Fritz Weider do a favor for Karl Marx, a Communist, before you and your friend, Jesuit Seminarian Fuehlen?"

"Another weak joke, Herr Lange. As a good National Socialist, my cousin Fritz, detests atheist Communism, as we all do."

"And why would he do a favor...?"

"It was a *joke*, don't you see!"

"What my son means," Willi cut in anxiously, "is that when they were boys, Paul and Kurt were great cut-ups, and my nephew Fritz was a very serious young man. Obviously, he hasn't seen them in a long time. They've matured a great deal, obviously."

"Obviously," Lange smiled, scanning. "What? Frau Reiser is a *gypsy*? Gypsies are...."

"What?" Elly pushed away from the sink.

"It says here...."

Paul came over to the table. "Please, Herr Lange. Another family joke. My mother is one hundred percent Aryan."

"Why do you think that young criminal Vogel would not profit from the Wehrmacht?"

Paul turned, taking deep breaths. His father put his hand on his shoulder.

"We were friends when he was small, Herr Lange. But since the...in the last few years, as you must know, he's become quite toughened. I only hope he can get in with a better class."

"In the Wehrmacht, that goes without saying. They don't go into battle in black dresses."

He looked slowly back at the letter. "'I owe a lot of that to you, my friend! You made me see what loving...really...means.' Well, well. And this *Dreck* at the end about who's the biggest sinner." His face creased into a smirk. "My, my, my."

Paul's mouth worked against the tears. "Please. You just don't understand what *words* mean. You're so...univocal!"

"Maybe," Lange smiled, "but I'm interested in learning a great deal about words." He tucked the letter into his inside pocket. He stood up, moving to the door, his aides behind him, and fluttered the pages of the notebooks. "These might enlarge my sense of words, eh? 1933. An interesting year. Hm. 'Her eyes like sapphires in the night.' How sweet."

He looked back at Paul whose forehead was resting against his father's chest. "I have no ear for words, it's true. Especially for poetry. But I really want to learn. '*Her* eyes' and the words about love to Seminarian Fuehlen are...interesting. What's the word I'm looking for, Seminarian Reiser? 'Ambivalent'? Good day." He bowed. "And thank you, Frau Reiser for the excellent coffee. I only wish I'd had time to drink it. Come, you two."

The skinny trooper shut the door behind them.

Paul leaned against his father's shoulder, his whole body heaving with sobs. Elly moved to them and laid her head against Paul's back.

Gretel rose from the table, her pretty face corroded with confusion and grief, and ran to her brother and her parents. She held onto all three of them and shuddered with tears.

"Oh, Paul, I'm so sorry. I'll never...I swear. I swear."

Willi Reiser looked at his wife, and she looked at him. Everything had such a heavy price.

* * * * *

1939

Saturday, 16 April 1939 - Muenster

Paul awakened in pitch dark. He looked at the clock. Five. Every-thing was in the wrong place. Then he smiled. He was in the Bischof Priester Seminar, not the seminary in Freiburg.

This was to be his home for the next year. It was one week after Easter. This morning, at ten o'clock, he was going to be ordained a deacon. Like Stephen, the first martyr. And in less than eight months, at Christmas, he would be ordained a priest.

He reached down, punched the pillow back under his head, looking up at the light and shadow on the unfamiliar ceiling. Next to his bed, there was a picture of the new pope, Eugenio Pacelli, Pius XII. A spare man, the face almost disappearing around the riveting eyes.

He coughed viscously and reached for his handkerchief. It had stopped raining, and smells of spring drifted through the open window. Outside in the dark wet morning was the bridge over the Aa he and the other subdeacons would cross in white albs to the cathedral. A block beyond was the Kaiser Friederich Halle, where he had washed dishes and printed subversion. Across the Dom Platz the university library, where he had watched boys burn Mark Twain and Thomas Mann at the feet of Felix Mendelsohn. With Lisl.

Too late to get back to sleep, too early to get up. But he was edgy, so, despite his infernal cold, he went for a long run around the Promenade.

At five minutes to ten, the seven subdeacons stood in their white albs on the steps of Saint Paul's. Inside, the organ filled the enormous church and spilled out into the square, expanding the soft throbbing of their own pulses, standing on the brink of the brink of the priesthood. Behind them, in cassocks and surplices and birettas, priests of the dio-cese chatted quietly, and on the steps of his mansion at the corner of the square, flanked by the Dean of the Seminary and Monsignor Lutz, Bishop von Galen loomed like a prophet, coped and mitred in gold.

The organ gave its first premonitory chords. The choir swelled into the slow insistent thunder, *"Ecce Sacerdos Magnus,"* and the procession began slowly down the long aisle. Ahead, the altar laden with lilies and ablaze with candles. The air heavy with the smell of wax and incense and expectation. "Behold, the High Priest, who in his days was found pleasing to God!"

At the section on the main aisle reserved for his family, he saw his mother and Gretel, grinning and sniffing into their handkerchiefs, his father's arm tightly around the two, beaming. He tried to return their smiles but everything inside was thrumming like a guitar string.

On a throne in front of the tabernacle, flanked by the Dean and Monsignor Lutz, Bishop von Galen raised his resonant voice intoning the opening prayer: "Lord, hear our prayers and guard us with your everlasting protection, so that, without the slightest fear, we may offer you forever our free servitude in the offices for which you have chosen us, through Christ, Our Lord."

The Latin scripture passages rolled on, interrupted by the arabesques of Gregorian chant, and finally the moment had come. The Dean rose and began the Latin formulas which began the rite of diaconate ordination. "Let them come forward!"

The subdeacons rose and answered, "Behold! Here I am. Because You have called me."

Then the bishop intoned, *"Adhuc, liberi estis.* Up to this moment, you are free." Then, as a symbol of their willing submission, the seven prostrated themselves full-length on the floor of the sanctuary, foreheads resting on their hands.

As the choir intoned, "I will go to the altar of God, to God who gives joy to my youth," they rose to climb the altar steps and kneel at the bishop's feet to touch with their fingertips the chalice, the paten, the purificator. The bishop raised the stole of office from their shoulders and arranged it diagonally across their chests: "Let yourselves be clothed in Christ."

Afterwards, when all had hallowed their commitment by receiving the Eucharist, they turned and began their procession back down the aisle. *"Magnificat anima mea Dominum.* My soul magnifies the Lord, and my spirit exults in God, my Savior!"

As Paul Reiser walked down the aisle, swelling with pride and relief. There were no more doubts. None. The die had been cast, freely, surely. There was no turning back. Never.

*   *   *   *   *

But that was in April. In August, Fuehrer Adolf Hitler was to make an unexpected speech in a beerhall in Munich, to celebrate with his veteran comrades their attempted putsch of 1923. Ostensibly because of his concern to prolong Sitzkrieg and prevent all-out war, he would leave the meeting after an uncharacteristically brief talk. Allegedly, a communist cabinetmaker, knowing of the Fuehrer's speech but not of its brevity, would set off a bomb that would kill seven and wound twenty-three of his old comrades.

And miles away, in a Black Forest sanatorium, Paul Reiser, recently ordained deacon of the Catholic Church, would make an incautious remark that would change the rest of his life.

II

DACHAU

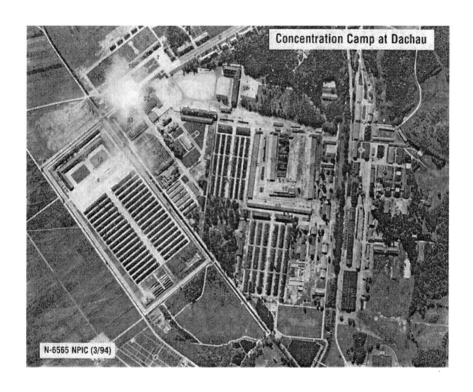

Concentration Camp at Dachau

N-6565 NPIC (3/94)

1940

Sunday, 7 April 1940 - Sachsenhausen

It was nearly 8:30 in the evening, almost time for "All to barracks!" Paul still hadn't found a morsel for old Father Czudek. Usually, in the hour after evening roll, he could scrounge a wad of bread, even a pair of pants. In his three months in Sachsen, he'd made good connections.

Even the trustee Kapos liked Paul, many against their own firm resolve. A persnickety buoyancy about him they somehow envied, like the uneasy mix of hatred and adoration they'd felt for gifted boys at school. A few thought him an arrogant son of a bitch, but even the flintiest took reluctant pleasure in his being around, a hazy reminder of hope. He stopped to chat them up, give them a butt, ask after their chilblains. Hard to remember when anyone cared.

So, he delegated himself moocher for the old men who had no money, or couldn't get around, or had simply lost the courage or humility to beg for their lives. Paul had covered for many a man who couldn't work fast enough in the quarry or who had to creep to the shadows with diarrhea, so he could often bring a bit of sly pressure to bear on someone who'd had a windfall. Sometimes it meant bare-faced charm. With hoarders, his ploy was wounded moral rectitude, which ultimately found his victims forcing him to turn his back while they grumblingly pawed through their caches.

Father Czudek would die by midweek, but after forty years a priest in a Warsaw slum, he deserved not to die raving. Since the occupation of Poland, more than three hundred Polish priests had died in Sachsen alone. Stahl had said Slavs were meant to be slaves, priests or not. Any pretense at learning defied Providence. Starvation of belly, heart, mind, soul. Paul had once faced that soul-starvation that craves death and vowed to face it down wherever he found it.

The Gestapo had come to Saint Blasien and taken him to Freiburg, a cell nine by eight. No beatings, no interrogations. Just desolating loneliness. The guard handed in his watery soup three times a day, grimly. As if whatever he'd done was contagious. Leprous. Lisl. Herschel.

After a week, he had been allowed to write and receive letters-the cruelest kindness. On one of those rare letter-days, after he had read a letter from his mother eight or ten times, weeping, the Voice began. At first he thought the Voice might be coming through the toilet, from the next cell. Paul answered. No reply. Then he realized the Voice was in his own head. Aloys Lange's voice, familiar, sneering.

The Voice kept whispering out of the ringing silence, "Chose a hard road, didn't you, aristocrat Reiser? A hard, hard road. My, my. Looked for love, didn't you, and found bitterness. So sad. You mouthed all that pious crap about a wife and family not being enough. Ah, large-hearted, open-handed love!" A dark, deep snigger. "You goddamned moron!

"Feel the old stirrings down there between the thighs, my friend? Perfectly natural, of course. Isn't that what you preached to all those little boys in their short pants? Ah! You honestly believe that's *natural*? Just doesn't make *sense*! Here you are in this hellhole. Noble! Righteous! *Alone*. Clinging to your great commitment to be miserable, and lonely, and *used*...for the rest of your life. My, isn't that im*press*ive?"

The Voice chortled. "Who's impressed, Reiser? Read between the lines in that letter. Your own mother! Always a wise lady, wasn't she? She knew from the beginning you were a goddamn fool. You can tell what she's asking. Throw the whole thing over and come out." The Voice slowly became his mother's voice, soft, filled with pain, pleading. "'Wait till all this blows over, dear. Oh, *please*, Paul. Then if you want to try this priest-business again, you can. But now, Paul, come out. It's just sheer, stubborn pride, Paul. Arrogance. Just doesn't make sense!'"

"You're *not*...my *mother*!" Paul screamed.

"It really doesn't, you know," it whispered. "Make sense?"

For awhile the Voice went silent. And then it began again. "Think of Lisl, Reiser. Same mistake. Think of the two of you. *Conjoined*. Then up on your pious soapbox, badgered that lovely girl for loving someone besides you. Hah! So much for the big heart and open hands, eh?"

Silence. Then just the faintest whisper: "Why not hammer on that door? Say you made a stupid mistake. Needed time to think it all through, the way Von Schleich asked you to, back at the camp. Tell them you love the Fuehrer. And it'll all be *over*, won't it? And you can find Lisl. Think of Lisl. You can still feel the sweet curve of her waist against your palm, can't you? And...the rest?" The Voice paused. "Ah, yes! I thought you could."

And so it had gone, hour after hour, day and night, until finally he was hammering his head with the heels of both fists to make the Voice be silent at least for awhile.

At the end of November, as Christmas drew near-the time he was to be ordained-the Voice had almost driven him mad. "You gave up your whole *life* for this rathole. Merry Christmas, Reiser! No first Mass on Christmas! Or New Year's! Or Easter! Or anytime. Stupid. Stupid. Stupid. You rather disgust even yourself now, don't you, Little Paulli Asshole?"

Sometimes he had to hold onto the shelf-bed, sobbing, on his knees, to keep from running to the door, and hammering on it, and shouting he'd be a good Nazi, leave the Church, join the Gestapo, father a litter of children if that's what they wanted. If they'd stop the Voice. If they'd only open the door and let him go free.

Then on November 30, the day before his trial, when he had resolved to confess anything they chose to accuse him of, to recant all he ever believed, all he foolishly surrendered his life to, the guard hurled in a few letters and a package and clanged out again.

Dumbly, he clawed open the package. A priest's stole his mother had embroidered for his ordination. White. Letters pricked out carefully in red stitches, course and nubbly under his thumbs. *In vinculis Christi.* In the chains of Christ.

He looked blindly up through his tears at the dirty grey square of window high up in the wall, his fingers wandering roughly over the knotted letters like a blind man's at his book.

He had no idea how long he had sat there on the floor, reeking, stubbled, in the litter of letters and rags of wrapping paper, fingering the message from Elly Reiser, who from the first instant of his life had known him better than he'd known himself.

His cell had not filled with light. No angel tapped him and said, "Get up! Hurry!" The chains did not drop from his wrists. But he felt the chains around his guts melting into nothing, the infuriating whining Voice wisping away like candle smoke. And finally, there was only peace.

Aloud he said, "I don't know what I believe anymore, God. Do you know that? I'll think about that later. Later. But one thing I believe. By *God*, I *won't* be broken! I will *not!*"

The following day, after an hour's trial, the judge had condemned him to five years of penal servitude. Aloys Lange who had testified took a certificate from his briefcase. "Warrant for Protective Custody." Prepared in advance.

Next morning the big prison van had been ready in the courtyard. Each prisoner was given a slice of bread, a potato, and a bit of cheese. The van took them to the railroad station. They were pushed through the curious onlookers to the prison train with barred windows. After a week, they had no idea where they were or any clear recollection of where they had been, sitting in freezing sheds for days on end when their trains had been commandeered for essential war duty.

And here he was now, at a correctional facility for incorrigibles. But since Christmas his spirits had been irrepressible. He had hit rock bottom and found he did not like it there.

By now it was close to 8:40. Paul had tried all the usual Sachsen sources and come up empty. He guessed he had less than five minutes to get to his bunk before the voice brayed over the loudspeaker, "All to barracks." Then he spied Katze.

Katze had been a pimp in Duesseldorf. Very little available in camp for which he did not have right of first refusal. He was returning to his barrack now after what looked like a fair-to- average night's work, a guitar over his shoulder and a greasy bag under his arm. A final chance. Katze had taken a shine to Paul.

"Katze!" Paul called after him, and the pimp turned, arching an eyebrow over dark wary eyes. He was smooth-skinned, recently shaved, probably with a real razor. Katze never wore the same prison uniform more than a few days.

"Ah, Reiser," Katze grinned, "after this vision, may I go blind!"

"Katze, there's an old Polish priest in my block. Over eighty. Dying, Katze. What can you spare? You've got a heart in there somewhere. I just know it."

"Look, Beauty," Katze opened a gold-flecked smile and laid his long hand appreciatively on the mound of Paul's shoulder, "I'll get the old bastard pheasant under glass-feathers and all-if you take my offer: Give you *twenty* per cent. *Twice* what I give any other *Pueppchen* I got. A body like that, you could make enough in a week to buy your way out of this shithouse."

Paul smiled. He'd heard the pitch three times a week at least. "Why not fifty-fifty?"

Katze squinted. "You mean that? Will you at least *think* about it? If I make it fifty-fifty?"

"What's in the bag?"

"A chicken."

"Yes-for the chicken."

"Done! Take it!"

"And the guitar."

"Fuck you. The guitar's promised. Some pimply rich kid come in yesterday. He'll go down on Goebbels for a guitar."

"Get another guitar."

"Like guitars grow on trees in this shithole?"

"Katze, if a cutthroat came in tomorrow with a guitar, you'd have it before morning soup."

The loudspeakers crackled on. "All to barracks!"

Katze sneered down at the guitar, cocking his head back and forth. "Weeeeell, what the hell. Don't even know if the spotty shit's worth a guitar. You on the other hand are worth a whole goddamn village band. Take the goddam guitar." Paul reached for it, but Katze pulled it away. "*If* you'll think about it."

"I *said* I'd think about it. Katze, I knew there was a heart in there. Big as the moon and just as cold." He took the bag and the guitar and started to walk away. Over his shoulder he winked at Katze, "I didn't say *what* I'd think about it."

Katze stood in the middle of the broad camp street with his mouth open. Then he started to laugh. "You sonuvabitch, I take that back! You're worth the whole Beyreuth goddam Festival! Think about it, you goddam gold *shit*!"

* * * * *

Tuesday, 30 April 1940 - Muenster

A week ago, Monsignor Johann Lutz had been sitting in his cathedral study paging slowly through a fine book of reproductions of ninth-century Chinese porcelains, stroking the silvery tuft of hair at his temple, when he was interrupted by a discreet tap at his door. Frau Vogelsanger, the housekeeper, said there was a young lady in the parlor. No, she would not see a curate. She'd already spoken to one of the curates in her own parish. A matter, she said, which the young woman claimed could be handled only by "the Boss," and he surely couldn't expect her to show some woman off the streets in to see Bishop Von Galen himself.

Lutz huffed, laid his book reluctantly on the table by his easy chair, and rose, smoothing the elegant lines of his magenta-piped soutane. He was "a fine figure of a man," ruddy and trim, except for a faint hint of paunch which many took to be the first symptom of purple piping.

"Yes, yes, Frau Vogelsanger," he sighed, "tell the young woman I shall be right there." Frau Vogelsanger disappeared down the hallway, rolling her eyes at the litany of grumbles behind her. If Our Lord Jesus came back to Muenster this night, she thought, he'd whip that per-fumed goat from the Temple like the Pharisee he was. She had no edu-cation, but she had eyes.

Lutz entered the smallish parlor with a floor-walker's smile and asked the young woman to be seated. About eighteen and vaguely familiar, under a thick patina of paint. She looked like a child made up to play Carmen, and he dreaded the unwelcome burden she was about to share with him. And she was nervously grinding her jaws on a disgusting wad of chewing gum.

"Forgive my keeping you waiting, my child," he said, taking a chair behind the tiny desk. "Ordinarily those who come to the cathedral seeking advice are greeted by one of the younger priests. I myself am involved in matters of much more...."

"You Von Galen?"

The Monsignor's fine hand fluttered to his hair. "Why, no, Bishop von Galen is...occupied at the moment. But I am the chancellor. Bishop Von Galen's surrogate."

The young woman's jaws stopped it mid-stroke.

"His, uh, his chief assistant," Lutz smiled with a sour indulgence. "Chief of staff, as it were."

"What the hell's 'at mean?"

"To put it *far* too simply, when Bishop von Galen is engaged, I am, to all intents and purposes, the Bishop of Muenster."

"Good. That's close enough. The rest of that military crap's too damn confusing. It's all this military rigmarole 'at's at the bottom of this whole damn thing in the first place."

Lutz winced at the coarseness but decided, out of charity, that it might best be attributed to nervousness. For the moment.

"And how may I help you?"

"We wanna get married."

"Oh?"

"Yeah. Me and Karl. In a church."

"Our housekeeper said you've already spoken to the priest in your parish. Why would you want to see his Grace, the bishop?"

"Yeah, I saw the priest at Heart of Jesus. Harz. Just a kid. An idiot. Then I saw this Jesuit. New guy. Pfizer. Only there maybe a year. Doesn't know what it's all about yet."

"And both priests said you couldn't be married in a church?"

"Yeah. 'Cause of Karl. But they don't know what it's all about yet, ya know? Karl's got influence now. Just made officer, good as any aristocrat now, with the war on and all, and I know plenty aristocrats don't gotta go through this red tape crap."

"And what is the problem? Your age?"

"Eighteen, and anyways my parents think it's fine, us married in church and all. See, Karl had to take this oath new officers in the SS gotta take. Just a stupid new rule. Don't mean nothin'."

"Oath?"

"That he won't go to church no more, but that don't cause no problem 'cause Karl don't go to church much anyway, except maybe Christmas and Easter, and, like Karl says, I can do the goin' t' church for both of us till this all blows over and we can have kids. And Karl's a nice man. Very clean. And he knows how bad I want a church for my wedding. I was the one in my class crowned the Madonna in the May procession. My religion means a lot to me."

"Do you go to church?"

"Sure. Except when I gotta work. An' once in awhile I oversleep, ya know? But, yeah, I go ta church a lotta times."

"And...," he winced at a crack from her gum and smoothed first one side of his hair, then the other, "forgive me, but if I'm to be of any help, I must know the situation. What...uh, precisely is the...uh, arrangement between you and this...Karl?"

"Whaddya mean? We're engaged."

"I mean...I don't wish to be intrusive, but...."

"You mean do we sleep together?"

"Well...yes."

"Course we do. Nothin' wrong with that. My parents know. They don't mind. They don't mind the age difference, neither."

"Age difference?"

"Karl's forty."

"And he's left the Church."

"Well now, ya *see*? That's what got this snotty Pfizer at the *Jesuit* church all screwed up. Ya *can't* really *leave* the Church, now can ya? I mean, it's like family. I mean, you don't have dinner every Sunday with your family, right? Ya go special times. Christmas, Easter, and like that. An' I thought Jesuits was supposed to be the brains! Karl says Jesuits're practically the SS of the whole Church. Right!" She popped her gum for disdainful emphasis.

"Young lady, we could perhaps explore the possibility of a dispensation, from disparity of cult, since your fiancé has obviously left the Catholic Church for another religion."

"Karl don't go to no other church."

"Well, uh, in a sense, he does."

"You mean the SS is a church?"

"Well, not precisely. But...."

"Oh," she said, a glint of realization flickering under the green eye-shadow. "Oh, yeah. I see. Yeah. I can see that. The banners and the uniforms and the ceremonies and all that. It *is* like a religion, when ya stop and think about it."

"So you see, the best you can hope for is a dispensation."

"Well, that's all right. Where do we go?"

"And the wedding will have to take place in the rectory."

The young woman looked at Lutz as if she'd just caught him with his thumb on the scales. "*Oh*, no. Oh, no you don't. My parents got no money, not like the aristocrats that could come in here and get their annulments and their divorces and walk down the aisle like the Virgin Mary an' Saint Joseph. But they by God worked hard for the Church. They scrubbed the damn floors and the pews, for God's sake! An' they're gonna get better'n some *rectory*."

"I'm sorry, young lady, but it's not a matter of your parents. It's a matter of you and Karl."

The tears began to run in alluvial streaks through the thick make-up. She clasped her big purse under her small bosom and stood. "Yeah," she choked. "Well! Well, is that right? Well, maybe I just may have to see what me and Karl can *do* about that, eh?" And she left the small room, chin fixed firm, muttering, "Goddamn fairy phony. You an' Harz an' Pfizer. Right. We'll just *see*."

The following morning, at the customs desk in the station at Weil, two Gestapo agents stopped Monsignor Johann Lutz as he was about to board for a visit to his sister and her family and returned him to Muenster under protective custody for questioning.

* * * * *

The cell of the Muenster jail was too small for the two bunkbeds, and it was very cold. Johann Lutz could not stop shivering. While he had been processed, a guard had admired his black velour jacket and said, "You won't be needing this."

In the bunk above him, Father Franz Harz, a young Jesuit curate, lay in his torn soutane, staring at the ceiling, motionless as a figure in a mausoleum. Father Otto Pfizer, once Jesuit Master of Novices at Emmerich, was now pastor of Sacred Heart in Muenster. He sat next to Lutz and wrapped a blanket around his quivering shoulders and held him tightly, trying to warm him.

Pfizer had the posture and physique of a drill instructor, raw-boned, lined and tanned from years of outdoor afternoons clearing woods with his novices. He was mostly bald, and a sharp nose beaked between shrewd pale-blue eyes.

"I only did what was right, Otto, no?" Lutz whimpered. "What else could I say to the girl?"

"Nothing, Johann," Pfizer answered. "You said the same thing Father Harz and I had already said to her. Don't go over it all again. It does no good."

"And what's going to become of us now?"

"I think it's best not to imagine."

"Will there be a trial, do you think?"

"I don't see how there could be. We've broken no civil laws. This is merely vindictive."

"But nearly a week. They have to charge us with something, don't they? That's the law."

"Whim is law now, Johann."

"But that's not poss-...."

The door banged open, and a policeman beckoned to them.

"*Raus!*"

Otto Pfizer stood. He turned to Father Harz staring at the ceiling and jostled his arm. "Come, Franz. We're wanted."

The younger man eased up and looked uncomprehendingly at him, as if a stranger had suddenly materialized in his room. Pfizer took his elbow and helped the young priest down. He leaned down to Lutz. "We have to go, Johann. Whatever it is, we must face it."

"I'm afraid, Otto."

"Of course. We're all afraid."

"Will you hear my confession, Otto?"

"I heard your confession yesterday, Johann. Now come."

The guard snarled. "Will you for Christ's sake *move!*"

"May I...the blanket?" Lutz whined. "That guard took my...."

"Take the goddamn blanket, but for Christ's sake move. Jesus," he muttered, "sendin' up goddamn priests!"

Pfizer shepherded Franz Harz like a mannequin to the doorway. He stopped and looked at the guard, who chewed the inside of his cheeks and tried to avoid the priest's eyes. "You said 'sending up.' Do you know where they're sending us? Dachau?"

"Dachau's closing. Temporary training camp. SS."

Pfizer looked at him and waited. The policeman muttered and looked away. "Some place in Austria. Mauthausen. Now move."

He turned and they followed along the cells to the stairway, Pfizer trying to steer the glaring young priest and Lutz following, hooded in his blanket and mewing like a bereft grandmother.

In the courtyard they were loaded on a truck with other men with fish-belly faces and darting eyes. The tailgate clanged up. The truck moved over the cobbles toward the railroad station.

The trip took nearly two weeks. They were off-loaded for two days in Giessen in a shed with a group of prisoners who had been there ten days. Then they were herded into slatted cars, rank with the smell of manure, and hauled further to the southeast and across the Austrian border. On Monday, May 13, they arrived in Linz, where their train was shunted onto a spur to Mauthausen.

Line by line, they filed into the administration building to be processed. SS men asked endless questions and filled in cards, red for politicals, green for criminals, black for "anti-socials," pink for homosexuals, violet for Jehovah's Witnesses. The priests were reds.

Each was photographed, full-face and side view, then booted in front of a doorway and told to wait, like a queue for a bus. Pfizer held Franz Harz's elbows, obedient as a blindman. Behind him he heard Lutz take a deep breath. Cautiously, he turned. Lutz had pulled himself full height, chin fixed firmly. His hand drifted up to caress the snowy hair above his ear.

"I've behaved badly, Otto," Lutz whispered. "I'm going to be all right now."

A tired smile slowly creased Pfizer's face. "We'll be just fine, Johann. Just...."

"You there! Priest!"

Pfizer froze.

"Shut your goddamn mouth, or I'll break your goddamn jaw!"

The line began to file into the next room. The first four men entered and the line halted. In a moment or two, it jerked forward again and stopped. Finally, only two men stood at the open doorway in front of Franz Harz and Pfizer.

"Next four!"

Pfizer followed the two men in front of him and steered Harz toward a chair.

A club struck Lutz in the belly, and he doubled over the pain.

"Wait your goddamn turn!"

Painfully, Lutz straightened and tried to fix a determined look back onto his face.

Then he saw what was being done in this room. Four men with clippers were shaving the prisoners' heads to the scalp. His eyes widened. Both his hands rose unbidden to cover his ears, the fingers moving, touching the silver tufts of his hair.

* * * * *

Sunday, 8 December 1940 - KZ Sachsenhausen

Paul Reiser tried to shiver some warmth into his ropy body without drawing the Kapo's attention. He could discover the burlap bag Paul had purloined from the kitchen and made into a scratchy undershirt. He wiggled his stiffened toes within the wooden clogs.

Around him in the Sachsen morning roll call, men stared torpidly at the puffs of their own warm breath, wishing it back inside them. Some whispered to one another in the ventriloquist speech most had mastered. The loudspeaker crackled:

"Priests and pastors return to barracks and gather belongings. Report back before the end of work assignments. Any priest who is late will receive twenty-five of the best! *Schnell!*"

Minds racing through the blur of possibilities, the priests fell out of their lines and picked their way quickly through the ranks of ragged prisoners swaying dazedly in the freezing morning air and bustled back to their barracks. They opened their locker boxes and quickly scooped out their belongings: a splayed tooth-brush, a razor or a piece of glass, a sliver of soap. No need or use for combs or nail clippers. A few had rosaries; one or two new priests had been foolish enough to hide their bread ration in the locker. The dormitory Kapo had already confiscated it.

"Reiser," a toothless lay brother whispered, "you know what's going on. What is this?"

"Transfer, probably."

"Home?"

"Not likely, Hermann. We know too much."

"One of the Poles told me the Pope twisted their arms. About the priests and religious."

"No one twists the Fuhrer's arm, brother."

"Into monasteries, he said. Out of the way. So we can't tell anybody what they did to us."

"*Raus*, you dried-up old pansies!" the Kapo hollered.

They hurried back to the square. But work assignments dragged on another half-hour.

Their nerves jangled with hope, apprehension, confusion, terror, elation. They clutched their pitiful sacks protectively to bony chests. Some tried to hide the fact their belongings were wrapped in an illegal second pair of underpants. Others had more serious worries. When they had arrived at the camp, they had denied being priests, since second-offenders had told them on the march priests and Jews received the worst treatment. There would be an uproar, questions, lies dreamt up on the spot. But if this were a reprieve, it seemed worth the risk, even the risk of the Bock.

"Paul?" Hermann, the brother, whispered.

"Yes? Careful."

"They don't understand what a lay brother means."

"I know, Hermann."

"But they said priests and pastors."

"Then tell them you're a priest. I'm not a priest, either, am I?"

"But what if something's happened outside? What if the pope condemned the Nazis? What if they're taking us out to shoot us?"

Paul hadn't thought of that.

"Maybe it'd be better if we *didn't* pretend we were priests, Paul."

"We are what we are, Hermann. No time for fine distinctions. We're in it together."

"Well," Hermann sniffed, "one suicide or the other, eh?"

When the last work detail slouched out through the gate, the Kapos thumped the clergymen into a line and led them toward the administration building. The Lady or the Tiger: to the left was execution, to the right, freedom—or something else.

The line turned right. The prisoners' hearts clenched. Then they were led to the storeroom and issued civilian clothes! Years of evaporated hopes had made even the most optimistic skeptical, but this was too obvious a hope to be denied. Then they were marched out of the camp, bagged in ill-fitting suits and shoes, and walked the road to the station. Chins began to rise; spines stiffened with hope. It was over! Sweet Jesus in heaven, it was over!

"Fine comedy team we'd make, Hermann," Paul grinned. "My God, I don't believe it."

Hermann's toothless mouth opened like a padded purse. "I feel like skipping!" he chortled.

Paul giggled. "They'll skip you back the way you came."

At the siding, an engine waited with two cars. Not cattle cars. Passenger cars. They climbed the iron stairs, filed apprehensively along the narrow passageways, and were counted off by sixes   into the third-class compartments!. No one spoke, as if to speak would shatter the dream. The engine ground into motion, and the cars moved slowly out of the yards. As they moved westward, mile after mile toward the German border, they sat warily, afraid to break something or cause a fuss that would draw attention or give a trooper an excuse to haul them off the train. But secretly, Paul Reiser's lizard-skin hands fingered the silk sheen of the wooden benches. There was no feeling at all.

By evening, they were in *Konzentrationslager* Dachau.

* * * * *

For the next week priests came to Dachau nearly every day. From Mauthausen, Groess- Rosen, Auschwitz, and a hundred other camps all over Europe which only those who had been interned there had ever known existed. Seven hundred, eight hundred, finally nine hundred of them. Even longtime guards were a bit disconcerted by the fact this horde of spindleshanks in mismatched clothes were priests and pastors like the clerics they had known as boys. They were used to perhaps twenty priests, and never together in the same work gang; easier to rationalize. Every guard had known at least some priests outside he'd suspected were crooks, or fairies, or fakes. The press said whole monasteries were closed down as brothels. But nine hundred. The largest religious community in the world. In a camp. Hard for a man's mind to accommodate that.

Also, for the first time, most of the prisoners in KZ Dachau were not Germans. And the camp population was now four times the five thousand men it had been built for. It was certainly going to crap up the routine for awhile. But they'd learn.

The newcomers filed uncertainly through the maw of the *Jourhaus*, past the wrought-iron lie "Work Makes Free,"out into the hard-packed square, from which every trace of snow had been scrupulously removed. They stood in sullen lines, like derelicts outside a soup kitchen, looking cautiously around. Then they were herded to the office of the Political Section where young SS men filled out new cards for each and assigned new identity numbers and colored triangles to be sewn on the left breast of the jacket and right thigh of the trousers before the day was out. Polish priests received a red triangle with a black "P."

They paraded in front of the *Rapportfuehrer* to be counted again, then marched off to be shorn to the skin. The clippers were ancient, and most of the prisoners came from the chairs with their heads cross-hatched with driblets of blood like ill-shorn sheep. They stripped off their civilian clothes and threw them into hampers, trooping downstairs to the showers, clutching only their number patches. As they entered, they were sprayed with disinfectant which turned their scored scalps into caps of fire. The showers were operated by an SS man in a booth who delighted in switching from scalding to freezing and back, like an upper-year boy hazing newcomers.

"Tempo! Tempo! Raus!

Naked and dripping, they were prodded to the clothes room where an inmate issued each one at least part of a striped uniform. The war had left the camp hard-pressed. Some priests had a full uniform, patched and stained, but cleaner than what they had left back in previous camps. Others were in motley, bits and pieces of other men's clothes, but always, however ill-fitting, either a striped jacket or trousers. Risky business, facilitating the possibility of escape, but it couldn't be helped. Any prisoners rented out for work as slaves in the many new auxiliary camps such as the SS ceramics company in Allach, however, were given full uniforms-and a razored "path," like a tonsure, down the middle of their heads-for the duration of their assignment.

With each pile was a pair of clogs, wooden soles with a strip of canvas across the instep, or shoes or galoshes, an enamel bowl, mug, spoon. No legitimate need for knives and forks.

They were hurried shivering out of the administration building and across the square to the first of the odd-numbered barracks on the right side of the main camp street, where they were paraded past a line of men who appeared to be genuine doctors. The examination was cursory, except for the anal inspection—since many prisoners hid valuables such as diamonds, and for the scrupulous cataloguing of the gold fillings in the prisoners' teeth.

Finally, they were assigned to a barrack-either 26, 28, or 30-at the far left end of the two rows of barracks, reserved for priests, and told to sew on their patches immediately. The Kapo had needles for them. They had never been billeted together. Something very strange was happening.

Gradually, they began to sift the rumors and piece together a story, aided by two Catholic prisoner clerks in the Political Office with access to correspondence. Since the late thirties and arrests of priests and religious on charges of immorality and currency fraud, Berlin had been under insistent pressure from German bishops to do something about clergy in German camps. What's more, the regular citizenry were beginning to hear stories of priests tortured and dying in the camps. Urns of ashes had been returned to their parishes by mistake. Finally, after frequent appeals from the Vatican, negotiations had begun in Berlin between the Gestapo and Bishop Heinrich Wienken of *Caritas*, representing the German episcopate.

As far as the two clerks could discover, the bishops had a whole list of demands: All clergy in one camp for the least dangerous prisoners; a chapel, breviaries, and permission to assist at Mass; separate priests' blocks; lighter forms of work to conserve their strength and allow more time for spiritual and intellectual work; Christian burial rather than cremation.

Unwilling to risk further unrest among the Catholics and cries of barbarity from the rest of the world, Berlin agreed in part. The High Command could afford complacency: France and Norway had capitulated; the relentless blitzkrieg against Britain would soon result in the emasculation of the Reich's only remaining serious challenge; the Americans were bloated with self-interest and cowardice. Reichsfuehrer SS Himmler, director of the whole camp web, had acquiesced to all the bishops' demands, except the completely unreasonable one about burial.

During those first euphoric days, the clergy had been on their best manners, getting to know one another in the crowded barracks, deferring to one another with all the sensitivity of Ministers of Protocol or first-year novices. Then, under pressure of close quarters and no further signs that the bishops' other requests would be fulfilled, the veneer of politeness quickly cracked. The cheerless charity beneath it melted away almost as quickly. Before the end of the week, there was grumbling unrest, hostile looks, caustic remarks sometimes made in a language the speaker believed only his friends understood.

Polish priests glared at anyone who spoke German, even Austrians, and jerked chins at any German priest who began acting as if he had been reinstated as potentate of his parish. Even Germans found it had been easier, disseminated through the vast camp system in twos and threes. Merely men who happened to be priests. Lost in an anonymous proletariat who judged a man more by his decency and kindness, priests had forgotten the deference due them *ex officio*.

* * * * *

In Apartment A, Barrack 30, Monsignor Manfred Herzog, #21306, a big-boned bear, sat on the lowest of three bunk shelves cursing the needle which refused the orders he was sending to his thick fingers. "My God," he growled, "I can carry two-hundred-pound rocks up two hundred stairs two hundred times a day at Mauthau and can't keep a goddamn needle between my damn fingers!"

Monsignor Johann Lutz, #21292, who squatted opposite him across the three-foot aisle, looked up from his own unimpressive stitching and lanced a look of scorn at Herzog, thick neck bent over the red patch, muttering curses. Really, Lutz thought. Even priests had picked up the appalling vulgarity of the criminals and communists who infested the camps.

Herzog had been a chesty, athletic man, but now little more than a matrix of bones bagged in a sheath of translucent skin. He held the needle up and snorted at it, like a thorn in his paw. Then he let the air from his lungs and looked helplessly over at Lutz.

"Father," Herzog began, "are...?"

"'Mon*sign*or,'" Lutz smiled up with sweet tolerance, trying to make the edges of his number patch stay under the thread.

Herzog gritted into a sour smile. "Mon*sign*or," he said, "are you better at this than I am?"

"I'm afraid not," Lutz smiled benignly. "We were all spoiled by doting nuns and housekeepers. I was thinking of asking one of those Polish seminarians if he would do it for me. The Kapo will make a raving case over it if it's wrong, and the Order priests seem to have a knack for these things. Different backgrounds, perhaps."

Herzog scowled at the prim figure sitting like a shorn old nun. "No housekeepers."

"Ah, that's it, then, isn't it?" Lutz sighed and looked scornfully at the patch, stitched on crooked. He liked things neat and squared off. "The Kapo will make a stew." Suddenly he looked up, face wreathed in a smile. "Whatever am I thinking of? That's all behind us now, isn't it, thanks to Our Holy Father?"

Herzog's salt-and-pepper brows curved around his dark skeptical eyes, as if Lutz had expressed belief in bottled genies.

"I mean, now that the Holy Father knows we're in these awful places," Lutz went on, "the Kapos will watch their step, won't they? Only a matter of time now before we're released, and we certainly have a lot of stories to tell already, eh?"

"Lutz," Herzog began slowly, "if the Holy Father knows we're here, why the *hell* didn't he just make Himmler haul our pious asses out of the camps we were in and send us directly home?"

Lutz smiled charitably against the coarse language. "Oh, I imagine it's some administrative thing. Our masters *do* love their paperwork."

"You actually believe they're going to let us *out* of here, with our 'little stories to tell'?"

"Of course. Matter of processing. A few weeks. Meanwhile, lighter tasks to allow us time for spiritual and intellectual work. And a chapel." He plucked out the stitches, careful to save his one piece of thread, and began again on his number patch.

"Jesus wept," Herzog gasped, "and I could, too. Chapel? I'll believe it when I see it. And 'intellectual work'? You going to start a damn doctoral dissertation or something in this shithole?"

Monsignor Lutz looked up disapprovingly. "Father...."

"'*Monsignor*,'" Herzog said acidly.

Lutz's elegant brows arched in an uneasy mixture of surprise and dismay. "Monsignor. I realize we've all been coarsened by this barbaric life, but your language. It sets a bad example."

Herzog grinned. "I doubt I can sully your character, Monsignor. If you knew a word for this place more elegant and just as accurate as 'shithole,' I'd use it. '*Excretorium*'? '*Stercorarium*'? Damn," he chuckled, "you may be right. Could get an article for *Stimmen der Zeit* out of that."

"Scoff if you wish," Lutz huffed, "but we priests have an obligation to enrich our minds and souls by study and meditation. Especially returning to our flocks after these places."

"Monsignor Lutz, my biggest job right now is getting enough food to keep my sanity."

"But don't you see, that will soon be over. Meanwhile...."

"Meanwhile, who do we minister to? I didn't do much, but in Mauthausen I could at least help *some* poor bastards die in some sort of peace. We were little pockets of us all over the system, Lutz! That's *why* these Nazi bastards backed down so easily! Now there are *no* priests to 'pollute' any other camps! Except here, and we're locked away in the same barracks and we'll be on the same work details. Light labor. Like that goddamn ten-ton street roller!"

"Then we minister to one another."

"Mother of God, you're really serious."

"Of course, I'm serious. The Evil One goes about *sicut leo rugiens, quaerens quem devoret*, and no one the lion's more eager to devour than God's priests. 'Strike the shepherd, and the sheep are scattered.' Especially in a hellish place like this where Satan's agents are everywhere."

"And the rest of the time we sit in our chapel and mumble our breviaries. While all around us thousands of men gasp for water, bash their brains out in the quarry, throw themselves on the electric wire because they have no hope? Dying without a priest? And we're in our chapel like nine hundred cloistered nuns! Just the Church our Fuehrer'd like to see all over the world."

Lutz's patrician face was a mask of disdain. "Do you mean you disregard the power of prayer, Monsignor Herzog?"

"I think a good swift kick in the ass is pretty effective. Maybe a nice blood-and-guts encyclical from the pope, spiked with an anathema after every paragraph like the good old days, when the popes and the princes squared off against one another like men with balls. I'd *like* that. But prayer? Let's say in the last three years behind the wire I haven't found it as effective as I used to preach it was. Maybe a few hours in our new chapel'll exorcize my cynicism."

"I sincerely pray it will." Lutz's face slowly clouded over. "There's only one problem with the chapel," he whispered.

"And what's that," Herzog whispered back, trying to suppress a giggle, "inferior linen?"

"Father Schelling, an Austrian who knows his way around this place, told me there are at least fifty Protestant pastors with us, mostly Lutherans, but several Orthodox, er, clergymen from conquered countries. Will they let them hold heretical and schismatical services in our chapel?"

"*What?*"

"After all, it was *our* bishops and *our* Holy Father who got the chapel for us."

"I don't think they'd contaminate the place with their prayers, Lutz. And I think all those rumors about human sacrifice are grossly exaggerated."

"Perhaps. But one is ready to die for one's beliefs."

Herzog rose and pinned his red badge to his striped jacket with his needle.

"You've given me one excellent idea, Monsignor," he said.

"Well, I'm quite pleased. And what is that?"

"I'm going to go look for some Polish canon law professor."

"You mean about the Protestants using our chapel?"

"No. About sewing my patches on for me in exchange for not wringing your sanctimonious neck. I want to find out if the excommunication would be worth it." He smiled wickedly and walked down the alley of rough shelves to the doorway.

* * * * *

In Barrack 26, Father Otto Pfizer sat back across the stiff straw mattress of his bunk, hands laced on his chest, bald-eagle head wedged against the wall. He turned to Paul Reiser on the lower bunk next to him, his blond-furzed head nearly touching the raw boards of the shelf above. Around them in the crowded room, priests, pastors, scholastics and brothers, without distinctions now in their striped prison issue, sat chatting quietly, waiting for the dorm senior, Father Schelling, to start his meeting. Czechs scowled at Austrians and Poles scowled at Germans, quite sure each had just been insulted, or completely misunderstood, or both.

Further down the row from Paul and Pfizer, Father Stanislaw Bednarski, a bull-chested young Polish Jesuit from Cracow sat between old Father Szopinski and Father Richard Schneider, wiping perspiration from their faces. The two men trembled violently inside the thin blankets they clutched to their shoulders. Their eyes glared. Both the old Pole and the young German had heavy fever. Useless to take them to the infirmary. In camp, every man was in perfect health or dead. The two priests would not suffer much longer.

"You know, Paul," Pfizer said, "I suspect that, in all the years I was a master of novices, your friend, Kurt Fuehlen, was one of the best I ever had. Bit of a tendency to flare. But that's not all bad. Heart of a stallion. He told me a great deal about you. A young man of quite devious skills, he said. I also met a Polish priest with you in Sachsenhausen. Paul Something. Priblewski? Like that. God forgive me, all those K's and Z's and -ski's get snarled in my brains."

"Kap Prabutski. 'Kap' because he was chaplain in the Polish Army, for as long as it lasted. In the first war, he was chaplain in the *German* Army. Think about that," Paul said. "Kap's a good man. Solid as an oak. Just as quiet."

"Well," Pfizer said happily, "he told me at Sachsen you were something of a scrounge. I may not be as limber, but I'm not a total failure scrounging myself. The Jesuit in me. I like to sniff out chinks in the armor, hidden passageways, closeted skeletons. And food. It keeps my mind from drowning in a salt sea of self-pity. Perhaps you might consider a merger of talents."

"Pfizer and Reiser. Like a pair of aerialists."

"And so we are!" They shook hands, grinning.

"Kurt told me you'd had tuberculosis."

Paul's eyes rolled upward toward the rough pine boards over his head and he blessed himself. "Thank God, it was just about gone when I dug my grave with my own mouth."

Pfizer's brows contracted. "No problems?"

"I bark once in awhile, when the weather's heavy."

"Perfect spot," Pfizer grimaced. "Bogs. Snow to your hips from October through May."

"Better than Monaco. And plenty of outdoor exercise."

Father Georg Schelling entered the room, a bit out of breath. So he could be heard by the priests in both rooms, he stood in the latrine between the dormitory section of Barrack 26, IV, and what had been its dayroom, now converted into another dormitory. Schelling had been editor of the Vienna archdiocesan newspaper, early forties but looked older. His gentle face webbed into lines around eyes and mouth, etched there by his indomitable need to grin.

"I'm sorry, fathers-and brothers, and scholastics, and pastors....My goodness, we're certainly going to have to simplify that. I'm sorry, *brothers*, that I was late. We don't have much time before 'All to barracks.' I hope you've gotten to know one another a bit better. I was delayed trying to convince Kapo Becher it would be better if he did not visit the barrack just yet, since delay would increase his own fearsomeness. Being fearsome is quite important to him. He's a very small man with a very small amount of power, and the combination is quite dangerous.

"I don't mean to be facetious. Kapo Becher has every right to his reputation. Former SA, arrested in the Roehm purge. Quite without conscience. I'd recommend seminarians especially be careful to avoid Becher as much as possible. He's a homosexual with a penchant for big young men. Too small to use physical strength for his purposes, but villainously shrewd.

"Some of you have been in the camps longer than I. Some only a few months. I've been in KZ Dachau two years now. So I thought I might be able to fill you in on the place. The accommodations are not ideal." Schelling grinned. "But many of you have known far worse. Father Bednarski told me Auschwitz makes Dachau look like a sanatorium. Since the dayrooms became dormitories, things are much less crowded. We have only about fifty men in each room, which is what the place was built for. But unfortunately we also still have toilet facilities for four hundred which were intended for about two hundred. It'll mean some crowding, and Becher-like many morally filthy men-is fanatic for cleanliness. If you can't get right at the sink, have someone wet your towel and pass it back so you can have evidence you've washed.

"But I have to agree with the Kapo there. Keep as physically clean as possible. Only one sign in camp tells the truth: 'One Louse Means Death.' Every night, be *sure* to delouse your clothing, no matter how exhausted you are. I can't emphasize that too strongly.

"Since we've lost the dayrooms, we've also lost the lockers and tables some of you were used to. We're allowed to wear nothing-including underclothing-except a shirt at night, so I'd suggest you roll up your belongings in your jacket and trousers and use them as a pillow. We're all brothers here, but there's not a single one of us who hasn't degraded himself out of despair.

"Well now, the camp. The commandant is Alex Piorkowski. Here nearly a year, hardly ever comes inside. Busies himself with the extensive SS manufacturing plants in the area next door, and from scuttlebutt it seems he's scooping a bit of cream for himself. He leaves control of the guards to his adjutant, Suttropp, and the camp to the Camp Leaders. Three of them work in rotation of eight-hour shifts: Zill, Hoffmann, and Jarolin, but the kingpin is Egon Zill. A devil out of hell.

"The rest, you know-Gestapo run the Political Office; usual SS Report Leaders, Labor Coordinators, and so forth, with a prisoner Kapo attached to each. Each barrack has a prisoner Kapo and an SS non-com assigned to cover all four-now eight-dormitories. Ours is Unterscharfuehrer Heinrich Holler. Former barber and something of a dandy. Completely venal, which is to our advantage. But I suggest we use Holler only for major acquisitions. A sort of ace in the hole. Also find ways, within reason, to do him various favors whenever we can-to make him beholden to us. Here, 'Love thine enemies' has a very self-serving purpose.

"I'd advise that same principle with all guards. Tomorrow you'll report for assignments. If you have *any* skill-even a rudimentary skill, say, for baking or carving meat or art-don't hesitate to claim you're a master craftsman. Immense value to yourself and to the rest of us. Next door, in the SS compound, is an enormous industrial complex, probably four times bigger than the barracks camp: porcelain shop, carpenter shop employing six hundred men to make furniture for camps and offices. Slaughterhouse-not that we'll see one shred of gristle. Bakery making eight thousand loaves a day. Plantation that grows flowers and medicinal plants and packages seeds. *Anything* is better than the street-roller or carrying thermoses. One of the worst is the Moor Express, a five-ton delivery wagon, named for the train that runs through The Devil's Moor from Stade to Worpswede and back.. Little likelihood any clergyman will get a job in offices or the infirmary. They don't trust anyone with more education than they've had, which is almost always very little.

"The SS guards-and even more so the Green and Red Kapos—haven't been happy that most clergy have been concentrated in this one camp. We're a threat to their longstanding control of the infrastruc-ture. They're dreading the day the Camp Leader has the bright idea it would be nice to have thirty doctorates filing his papers rather than toughs who never finished secondary school.

"So. We're going to get on one another's nerves. Sometimes, I'm afraid, even to the point of open confrontation. I want to be forthright from the outset. We've all seen it happen, and there's nothing in any of our ordinations or vows which exempted us from human weakness–especially in this inhuman place. If we all face that fact, I think we'll have a better chance of lessening those occurrences and learn-ing-despite our differences-that we're brothers, that we have more uniting us than we have separating us.

"The work skills I mentioned will be very important to each of us as individuals and to us as a community. Well, most of us. I myself was an over-zealous editor of a diocesan paper, and I doubt that will give me any purchase in here." There were very few polite chuckles.

"But almost all of us have studied and been ordained priests, gifts many of you have used in other camps to help your fellow prisoners, hearing confessions, consoling the dying, perhaps even saying Mass. Those particular ministerial skills will be severely curtailed by our hosts. As a result, we'll all be forced to rediscover what 'priest' really means. But also what it means to be a Christian believer. The thou-sands of times we've said 'thy will be done,' we really thought we knew what we were saying. In here, that will be tested in ways we never imagined. Or could have. What does each of us hold onto when there's nothing left for the soul to feed on? Nothing but faith and hope.

"Therefore, I'd strongly advise–very strongly advise–each man to look around during this first period of, uh, adjustment and discover someone you'd feel comfortable with as a spiritual father. We males have a lot stronger resistance to self-revelation than most of our women friends and relatives. But it's essential we have regular times when someone else *forces* us to remember what's truly important. Most of you know already that food becomes a more intense focus of your attention than even fear. Our hosts are trying to punish not just our bodies but our souls. The Jews here couldn't uncircumcize their bodies, but we could have surrendered what we claim to hold most important in life. We could have kept silent. Gone along. But our God-given task in life is not merely to survive. This place will wear away...*tear* out...anything in you that isn't true, isn't genuine. Nourishing your spirit is probably even more important than keeping your body going. If they break your spirit, your body will quickly follow. We must cling to the reasons *why* we should keep going. Each once of us needs someone to *goad* him to keep his soul alive.

"Within the first three months, the true man emerges-when we cross the bridge from what seemed reality to the truth about ourselves. No reason each of us has to cross that bridge alone."

"All to barracks!" The steely voice of the loudspeakers rasped. "All to barracks!"

Georg Schelling looked at the parchment faces. He smiled and nodded this way and that.

"So. Brothers, could I ask you to reach out on either side of you and take the hands of your comrades. Let us say together, each in his own language, the prayer Our Lord gave to all of us who claim Jesus Christ as our Lord and our brother. Our Father, who art in heaven...."

The harsh whispers joined one another as the barracks lights dimmed. Polish and Czech, German and Lithuanian, Catholic and Protestant. A Babel of voices. Yet beneath the guttural surface something more profound was beginning to heal, a little.

* * * * *

Sunday, 10 December 1940 – KZ Dachau

Free time was at a premium. Reveille was four-thirty a.m. in summer, five in winter. A quick wash where 300 men had to at least dampen their towels at sinks designed for fifty. Slurp the ersatz coffee, then roll call at five or five-thirty for forty-five minutes. As war work became more pressing, that was streamlined. Then a nearly twelve-hour work day, with evening roll-call around six p.m. or later, the thin soup and knot of bread, and finally a sort of reprieve before "All to Barracks" at 8:45, when everybody had to be asleep by nine–or pretend to be.

Sunday afternoons were free, and there was sometimes football on the roll call square. Only the "strong" ones who got extra rations for taxing jobs tried to play. Most just watched, if the fuss drew anyone at all. At times, there was an improvised concert, nearly all professionals, but with no time to practice and each had his own "right" way. The library held fifteen thousand confiscated volumes but for the most part served only to impress important visitors from Berlin.

During the precious moments between evening soup and the summons to barracks, many lay inert on their bunks, praying that the nightmares would not be worse than the day had been. But most prisoners were able to stroll the wide camp street, lined with tall poplars on either side like a town walk, to the *Appelplatz* and back, chatting in small groups, but no more than three.

Paul Reiser and Otto Pies sat with their backs against the street wall of 26, undistracted by the lines of scarecrows passing in front of them.

"All right, then Father Master of Novices," Paul grinned. "'You have not chosen me, but I have chosen you.' Rescue my soul."

"Before we start, remember I've already enlisted your soul in what we hope will be many successfully larcenous endeavors. So you have to realize that in here stealing is no longer a sin–as long as it is from our hosts and not from one another."

"I've been doing my best. But seriously, Otto. I really do get tempted. Just to collapse. To 'go Moslem' and die inside. Surrender."

"You don't really mean that. Not seriously."

"Well...no. I'm not suicidal. But it's always there. Like a dirty thought."

"When I was a kid, the nuns had a great way to head off libidinous thoughts. Just *sing*! In your head. Sort of like jamming the incoming radio signals with better ones. Temptations to give up are worse than sexual temptations. Much, much worse. I jam the despair with praying."

"I try. But somehow it's impossible. How do you keep praying?"

"You mean, how can I keep talking to someone who never answers?"

"No," Paul said. "I mean what do you do when you pray?"

"Funny. I never thought about it until you asked. About what I actually do. I guess I'm praying most of the time. When I'm not talking to anyone else. Which is most of the time. When I first started, all those years in the seminary, it was mostly fake. No, that's harsh. It was sincere. But sort of like punching a bag is to actually getting in the ring. St. Ignatius has a way to get started. You rev up all your senses and really put yourself into the scene. Feel the dust between your toes, smell the sweat. That really worked for a long time. But it was mostly focused on me. I mean, I remember I'd be praying about Jesus washing my feet, feeling, well, more humbled, more embarrassed than Jesus felt. But then...I don't remember how...I switched the focus. And *I* was Jesus on my knees. And the disciples at table were the men in my own Jesuit community." He grinned. "*That* certainly upped the intensity! I said to myself, 'Of course, I'll wash your feet. It's a privilege.' And then I scrunched over to the next one, and looked up, and I said, right from my gut, 'I'll be *damned* if I wash *your* feet!' It brings me down to earth. Which is what humility means. So that's what I do when we're slurping our so-called soup and nibbling our bread. It really helps."

"Probably better than just bitching about how God treats Job."

"And when you're on the Moor Express, imagine the pole is a cross, and you're Simon of Cyrene who's been forced by the guards to share it. And Jesus is on the other side. Your shoulder keeps you from being distracted!"

"Do you say anything? Words?"

"Just 'Jesus,' over and over." He grinned. "Just to keep a focus. What can I tell him he doesn't already know? The reason I pray is to keep remembering I'm not alone."

"So praying's the way to salvation, to sanity."

"Just in the short run, day to day. But deep, deep down the reason is that I vowed myself to accept whatever comes. As the will of God. I married him. I gave him my word."

"Simple as that?"

"Not easy. Just uncomplicated."

* * * * *

Wednesday, 25 December 1940 - KZ Dachau

A week before Christmas, Father Pfanzelt, the parish priest of Dachau Town, had managed an appointment with Commandant Piorkowski, whom he had caught actually in the commandant's office inside the wire.

Pfanzelt was a genial little snowman: surprised little brown eyes and apple cheeks, plumped jauntily atop a pot-bellied body. The commandant yielded willingly to the offer of Pfanzelt's parishioners to erect and decorate a large Christmas tree in the roll call square. To give credit to the commandant's unalloyed utilitarianism, his decision was motivated by the rumor that a commission from Berlin might be on its way to investigate flagrant allegations the commandant was profiteering off the profiteering of his superiors.

For two days, men and women of the town set up and decorated the tree with lights, colored bows, and strings of berries. In the process, they couldn't help see the activities of the camp. They marveled at the streets and square; not a snowflake-even on the roofs. They saw few prisoners–since the villagers had been allowed into the camp only after morning roll call, then corralled quickly out before the men returned. But even in the distance, they heard them coming home, singing! Not a bad sort of place; like the army. An encampment with comrades.

The Lagerfuehrer, Egon Zill, was highly displeased that the commandant had, uncharac-teristically, intruded on the workings of a concentration camp he neither understood nor cared for. But there was no way he could countermand the orders. Instead, at the foot of the tree, where many German families placed a slatted wooden hut with the figures of the Holy Family and the shepherds, Hauptsturmfuehrer Zill had his troopers set up the Bock.

The Bock was not Zill's punishment of choice. Far too lenient and less effective than the Tree, in which a prisoner's thumbs were wired together behind his back and he was hauled up over the pipes in the shower room in the administration basement. The Bock was a concave slatted table onto which a prisoner was strapped, face down, and given "Twenty-Five," or, in many cases, "Twice Twenty-Five" with ox whips across the bare buttocks, and forced to keep the count himself in a loud voice. Still, the Bock struck Zill as having a certain "rightness" as a substitute for the creche.

The slats reminded him of the cribs of Bethlehem he had seen as a boy, and the Bock also reminded him of the Scourging at the Pillar, which was one of the Stations of the Cross. Hauptsturmfuehrer Zill had been trained by nuns, and the whole set-up between the wide white wings of the administration building seemed somehow to bring together the whole message of Christmas and Good Friday and all the other occasions that had radiated a kind of power to him when he was a boy. Egon Zill could not have explained it, but he was certain that he had, once again, made something "right" out of the commandant's mistakes.

The two hundred dormitories in the barracks, each with men stabled uneasily together, were cold-except for the welcome animal heat of men on either side.

The only promise to the priest-prisoners that had been kept was that the clergy would all be gathered together in one camp. Their food was no better. Their work kommandos no less cruel. No chapel. Some felt a reluctant fellow-feeling for the Jews of the camp. The Messiah would not come this year for them either.

In Apartment IV, Barrack 26, they lay awake as floodlights beamed randomly in the windows from both sides of the hut, like legions of alien presences in the cold night sky outside.

Father Josef Hornauer from Marburg had told a class of school-children they should love their enemies, even Poles and French and British. One child had told her parents.

Pastor Adolf von Hoffenburg, who taught introductory science in a public school, had insisted on beginning each class with the Lord's Prayer. One child had told his parents.

Father Bronislaus Popek had heard the confessions of Polish prisoners of war and had refused to divulge what he had heard.

Others were interned on charges less specific: "troublesome," "resistance," "hostile to government," "Catholic action," "critical of the present situation." Like most of the recent laws which justified their arrests, the words carried no real meaning.

Each sat cribbed on the stiff straw tick of his bunk, watching the play of light across the walls and ceiling, half-hoping for the sudden trumpets that would signal the end of it all.

In a corner, shielding the beam of a stolen flashlight with a blanket over his head, Father Stanislaus Kubsky, the oldest, was reading aloud from a page which a Kapo had been about to use in the latrine. Kap Prabutzki, who had been sitting next to him, had promised three-day's ration of bread in return for that page and for the rest of the book.

The old priest read haltingly. It was a privilege to be chosen, but his eyes were no longer good, and he knew his Polish accented Latin was difficult for the Germans and Austrians, and the pastors and brothers might not know what he was saying at all.

But they all knew. His voice was merely an old man humming in the dark a tune they all remembered since boyhood. The language didn't matter. Each knew it, by heart.

"*Exiit edictum a Caesare Augusto, ut describeretur universus orbis. Haec descriptio prima facta est a praeside Syriae Cyrino, et ibant omnes ut profiterentur singuli in suam civitatem.*" And they all went up to their own towns, each to be registered. To their own towns. Marburg. Katowice. Warsaw. Muenster. Vienna. Prague. Czestochowa. Oswiecim.

"*Ascendit autem et Joseph a Galilea de civitate Nazareth, in Judaeam in civitatem David, quae vocatur Bethlehem...*because he was of the house and family of David." A Jew. Obedient to Caesar, to come when he was called. Not knowing the king lay in wait to slaughter all the sons.

"To be counted with Mary, his espoused wife, who was with child. But it happened, while they were there, that the days were fulfilled that she should give birth. And she brought forth a Son, her first-born, and she wrapped him in swaddling clothes and laid him in a manger, because there was no room for them in the inn."

As the old priest's voice coughed on, they could hear echoing down the long camp street, sounds from the roll call square. Like tree branches cracking under ice. Under the brightly lit tree in the roll call square, Death's Head SS were lashing a prisoner on the Bock with ox whips.

"And the Angel said, 'Do not be afraid. For I bring to you good news, of great joy, which will be for all the people! Because today is born to you a Savior, who is Christ, the Lord!'"

The bulb in Father Kubsky's stolen flashlight flickered. It beamed weakly again. And then the darkness swallowed the light.

* * * * *

1941

Friday, 10 January 1941 - KZ Dachau

Because of winter order, reveille had been at five instead of four-thirty-less a concession to the prisoners' softness than precaution against escapes in full dark. It had snowed heavily, and it would be a bitter morning. The barracks were coifed in snow. The broad camp street was pillowed in white all the way down to the silent savannah of the roll call square. And yet, because of the heaviness of the snow on the pitched roof of the administration building, the lesson they learned daily still loomed through in three-foot white letters on the shingles: "There is one road to freedom. Its milestones are: Obedience, Diligence, Honesty, Orderliness, Cleanliness, Sobriety, Truthfulness, Self-Sacrifice, and Love of the Fatherland." Obedience and diligence were a matter of life and death. The rest were negotiable.

From each barrack ragged prisoners filed out of Apartment I, then II, then III, then IV, waiting their turns in the cold shadows between the buildings to move out into the street and form up, eight abreast. While they waited, they clomped rag-wrapped hands on their spindly shoulders, breaths pluming in the air. Most had light overcoats or raincoats of thin rubberized fiber; some were fortunate to have galoshes, brutal penances in summer but gifts from God in winter. Most wore sabots wrapped with rags scavenged from the dead, who no longer minded the cold.

The snow was sodden. Heavier to move-especially on the street and the square, where thousands of men's feet packed it to iron. The young and agile were lucky; they would be sent to the roofs in the first Kommandos to broom down the snow from the blocks. Gravity was their comrade; for everyone else, it was one more enemy.

When the signal came, they moved toward the floodlit square in the cold haze of dawn and silent snow, like prisoners on the moon.

It would be a long roll call. In this cold, more than usual would have died. Such a struggle to drag the stiff corpses out of the latrines and off

108

the top bunks, into the alleyways, then the length of the long street to the square where the living men waited like thousands of grey corn-shocks, stiff and silent and swaying.

Often on days like this Kapos were irritable, paying off old grudges and unpaid debts, and couldn't agree on the count. So it would start all over from the beginning. "Counted like gold," Monsignor Herzog grunted hoarsely to Georg Schelling, "and treated like shit." If morning roll call ran more than an hour, and some men had not provided beforehand, they were not allowed to fall out for the latrine but fouled themselves where they stood.

Since the Snow Kommando was considered light duty, it was given to the aged and the priests. Shovels were boards nailed to wooden stakes which shoved the snow into huge heaps. Then other crews lifted the snow from the piles into small barrows and large carts, which still others trundled off through the gatehouse, past the intermittent guards, to the nearby Amper River and dumped it in, to float down and flood the root cellars of the people of Dachau Town.

Since there were not enough tools, some lugged snow on upended tables, four men carrying it on their shoulders. Those too weak had to put their prison jackets on backwards to use as scoops. Later, in the small heat from the apartment stove, the jackets would never dry, and the old men would be forced to sleep and probably die in them. It hardly mattered.

"Tempo! Backs into it, faggots! You think I want to freeze my ass out here the rest of the morning? Tempo!"

Otto Pfizer and Paul Reiser were at the front of a table, carrying it to the river. They could talk only in side mouthed whispers, and then only between guards.

"I wish *my* ass," Paul whispered, "was as warm as *his* ass."

Pfizer chuckled. "Training for soccer at the university, we carried railroad ties up the mountain and down, up and down. What had we done? Moved a railroad tie five miles to get it back where we started."

"Little did you know it'd be your life's work!"

"Guard, left!"

They moved along in silence, heads submissively downcast.

"Kuntz," Pfizer whispered. "Not a bad sort."

"Who's at the back end?"

"I can't remember."

"Know how big this place is?" Paul asked. "The dimensions?"

"Georg says a thousand feet wide, two thousand feet long. Why?"

"Guard, right."

They lugged the table in silence, trying to keep their balance with the wooden clogs on the hard-packed snow.

"Two more."

They trudged, snuffling moisture from the ends of their noses.

They came to the river, and the guard shouted, "One, two, *three!*" and they lowered the front end and tipped the snow into the swollen stream. "All right, back. Double time!"

The two at the back were Kap Prabutski and Stan Bednarski.

At the order from the trooper, the four broke into a trot with their table on their shoulders. A few feet away from the river and still a few yards from the first pair of guards cowering in the lee of the guardhouse gate, Pfizer whispered back over his shoulder to Kap and Stan, "All right. No need for heroics." Imperceptibly, from intensive practice, they slowed until they were nearly at a walk, like mimes in a circus. They were still puffing, gradually getting their breath.

"I was thinking," Paul panted. "That's about two million square feet of snow."

"Not quite big as the Matterhorn. Are you losing your mind?"

"Keeping body and mind in shape. Two million square feet. Bet that's a world record."

"And still nearly four years to the Olympics!" Pfizer became suddenly serious. "If there are any more Olympics."

"Otto, if you go serious on me, I'll sit right down and cry."

They arrived at their snowbank, and the older men began to pile the snow from the jacket-bags on their ropy bellies onto the belly of the table. The four men stopped and bent over, hands on their knees, reaching deeply into their guts for breath. Prabutski and Bednarski whispered side-mouthed in Polish. Pfizer coughed into his hand in Paul's direction, "No guard?"

Paul rasped, "Inside. Cigarette. Idiot, but no fool."

Some had finished and were scuttling quickly along to their barracks for their ten o'clock break and a little warmth. The square was scraped to the iron-hard clay, and little puddles were beginning to stiffen into panes of ice.

Paul bent over to retie his footrags but suddenly leaped erect. "Good *God*, Whisper! If you sneak up like that again, I'll fry your skinny ass on that electric fence, so help me!"

Like a wraith out of mist, a little man had materialized next to him. His face and body were like a Deadly Sin from a medieval painting, all sharp angles, nearly humpbacked, cackling at Paul's surprise. Whisper liked the priests. More interesting than the ordinary moaning of the camp. And sometimes he picked up tidbits to trade. He liked big, strong ones like Paul. He drew strength from them, basking in their tolerant distaste.

"The priests are going to have a chapel, Reiser."

"I know." He coughed once, and Pfizer shot him a concerned look. "And nothing but light work, Whisper."

"No. It's true. I heard Doktor Gisela talking about it in the infirmary. She's as mad as a bitch with a burr up her ass."

"Well, even if the chapel part's a rumor, Doktor Gisela's burr gladdens my heart. But God help anybody she 'ministers' to today."

"I swear...."

From the broad camp street a Kapo with a yellow armband strutted toward them. He was about five-foot-five, chested like a bantam rooster, walking splay-footed with his hands clasped behind his squatty back and his whip tucked under his arm like a swagger stick. Kapo Becher from Barrack 26.

"Pfizer!" He planted his stubby legs wide and thrust out his pursy chin. His voice was glass scraped against glass. "Bring Blondi. Let the Polacks finish. On the double, turds! All men from 26 *except* the Polacks, on the double! Work."

Otto and Paul fell in behind the bandy-legged Kapo, like two lions in tow of a cockerel.

"Herr Kapo Becher, we just heard...." Otto Pfizer began.

"Si-*lence*!" Becher squealed from the upper reaches of his short throat, and continued up the long street to the far end where the priests' blocks squatted. As they drew closer, they saw priests gleefully carrying pieces of board and scantling from the alleyway between 24 and 26, piling them neatly at the side of the wide road under the naked poplars.

"Watch where you're going, *Arschlochen*!" Becher chittered. "That's government property! And *I* am responsible for it! You Polacks, get back to the snow. You're used to it."

He turned toward Pfizer, eyes lingering a moment on Paul. "Pfizer! Help Schelling direct those brainless professors and abbots and *Schiessepfaffen*! They're trying to saw apart the bunks, and the morons are going to cut off their goddamn hands. Christ! Aristocrats! Wonder they can wipe their own arses!"

For three days and nights they worked, pulling down the walls between the dormitory and what had long ago been the dayroom of Apartment I of Barrack 26, closest to the central camp street. No one minded the work, or even the fact that the two hundred priests of those apartments would have to be crammed into the bunks in the other rooms. They were going to have a chapel! Some of the nine hundred priests and brothers had not been to Mass in years. And, to be honest, most of this work was indoors.

Prisoners bustled about their work, humming snatches of nearly-forgotten hymns. Becher strode up and down, twapping his whip against his short thighs: "*Schnell*, idiots! If I had my way, we'd turn this into another whorehouse. *Schnell*! Himmler himself will be here in *two days* to inspect this priest-sty! *Schnell*!"

After the first day, laymen began to join the work during the short time between roll call and lights out, some recovering from illnesses and on light duty, some through the connivance of clerks in the Labor Office. They sawed bed shelves into sections and set them up where they could in the dormitories of 28 and 30. They swept, washed, pumiced the floor. A Polish lay brother named Wasko had managed to purloin a gallon of oil from a prisoner in the motor pool, and the raw pine now shone like amber. On Monday, a bright clear day, a line of triumphant young Polish seminarians, like medieval heralds in motley rags, trooped from the carpenter shop carrying twelve new windows with green glass and red crosses.

"Better than the stained glass windows in a cathedral, eh?" Becher sneered as he watched from the doorway, like the master of works at a basilica. "*And* no one can peep in from outside and get any free salvation, eh? Move your pious shit-holes!"

On the morning of January 15th, they were finished. The room, sixty by thirty feet, was absolutely bare, but shining. Two of the former dayroom tables put together, about a yard square, made do for an altar, draped with two checked bedsheets. The small crucifix, the tiny chalice, and two candleholders from Kap Prabutski's Mass kit sat in forlorn splendor on top of the altar.

Prabutski, Georg Schelling, and Otto Pfizer stood with Kapo Becher surveying the room. "Good," Becher squealed. "Now, do your Mass." And he walked to the door.

"But Kapo Becher," Prabutski smiled. "We have no wine. We can't have Mass without bread and wine."

Becher turned at the door. "I was ordered to turn a monkey cage into a chapel, Big Polack. You're the ones who turn water into wine. Don't just stand there gawking. Get to it."

That afternoon Reichsfuehrer SS Heinrich Himmler arrived to inspect the chapel. Chinless under a toothbrush moustache, peering with ferret eyes through wire-rimmed glasses, his hair shaved up to the crown. It was hard to realize this was the most dreaded man in Germany, not an undertaker's assistant. Why, Georg Schelling wondered, are so many of their leaders grotesques?

Prabutski and Schelling waited at the door while the Reichsfuehrer SS strode around the empty room, Becher hustling, cap in hand, at his glistening heels. Himmler stopped and turned to the little martinet grinning shyly up through his brows like a puppy caught wetting the rug. The Reichsfuehrer looked at Becher's stockinged feet, his beady eyes moving slowly up to the kewpie-doll face, as if puzzled at the presence of an outsized cockroach. Becher was immobilized by the basilisk eyes under the tall peaked cap.

Reichsfuehrer SS Himmler did a tour, ending at the doorway with the priests, leaving the confused Becher visibly sweating in the center of the room like a pig stranded on a frozen pond.

"Yes," Himmler smirked. "This will satisfy their meddlesome Graces. We shall need someone in charge. Who is the senior priest? What German priest has been here longest?"

"Father Franz Seitz, Herr Reichsfuehrer," Schelling answered.

"Why isn't he here?"

"At work, Herr Reichsfuehrer. In the BMW factory."

"Your name?"

"Georg Schelling, Herr Reichsfuehrer, Number 0-0-9-...."

"Yes, yes. Very low number. How long have you been here?"

"Since May 29th, 1938, Herr Reichsfuehrer."

"You are German?"

"Austrian, Herr Reichsfuehrer."

"Fine. You are the chaplain, then."

"Forgive me, Reichsfuehrer, but, of the thousand or so clergy here, more than half are Poles. Father Prabutski here has been chaplain already at Sachsenhausen."

"You are Prabutski? You speak German?"

"I was a chaplain in the German Army in the 1914 War. Uh, Herr Reichsfuehrer."

Himmler's browless eyes rose. "Indeed? How interesting. But you don't know your way around yet. You don't know the personnel."

"I would be most happy to help out in that regard, Herr Reichsfuehrer," Schelling said.

"Fine. Then everybody is happy. You are the chaplain; you are the assistant chaplain."

Prabutski cleared his throat. "There is one thing, Herr Himmler...Herr Reichsfuehrer. We have no access to altar breads or wine. The chapel is not of much use without...."

"Of course." He turned to Becher, still frozen in the center of the shiny floor. "See to it."

"At *once*, Herr Reichsfuehrer!"

"You," Himmler looked toward Schelling. "Before the day is over, write a letter to his Eminence Cardinal Faulhaber in Munich and Bishop Galen in Muenster that their demands have been carried out. To the full. You will express your *delight* at your chapel"

Schelling nodded. "That I can do in all sincerity, Herr Reichsfuehrer."

"Ha," Himmler sniffed, "sincerity for a priest is rare."

Schelling shrugged awkwardly. "It's not a cathedral, but...."

"No. But if I know the wily clergy, it soon will be. Anything else?"

Prabutski shifted. "The Snow Kommando, sir. Difficult work for old men and the sick."

"I will tell the commandant. No such work for the sick or those over seventy."

"If you could make it sixty-five, Herr...."

Himmler smiled sourly. "We are not the benign God and the kikey Abraham dickering over the number to be incinerated in Sodom and Gomorrah, Herr Chaplain. Seventy."

"Thank you, Herr Reichsfuehrer."

"Well," he said, smoothing his gloves, "that might shut up their episcopal majesties a bit."

He turned on his heel and walked out.

Schelling and Prabutski turned to one another. Grins began to seep across their faces. They locked arms around one another and began to hoot and howl, circling round and round.

That evening, the room was packed with priests, brothers, seminarians and the laymen who had helped with the renovations. Nearly a thousand men in a room nine hundred feet square.

Prabutski was about to say Mass. No alb, only one chasuble, green and white on one side, black and purple on the other. Tonight, in celebration, he wore the white side out, the faded vestment cinched over his grey and blue striped prison uniform like a shabby aproned butcher. But, to the equally shabby men in the silent room, he did not look at all ludicrous.

There was a smile on his long farmer's face as he began to speak, in Polish then in German. "As you know, for reasons none of us understand, I am the only priest allowed to say Mass. And we are allowed only one Mass a day. If...anything happens to me, Father Schelling will offer the Mass. The Mass each day will be at four-thirty, just before roll call. Bit of a hardship, but it will be something, for once, to wake up for, eh?

"Each man has drawn a lot with the day he will be allowed to attend. As soon as Father Schelling and I can get organized, we'll find ways to include laymen....although some not entirely reliable sources have said that Zill will not allow that. Also, in fairness to the fifty non-Catholic pastors, we will work out a schedule when they can have their own time in the chapel."

There were negative murmurs here and there, but they were hushed up.

"We must be brief, starting from the Offertory and ending with Communion. But I think it would be good to allow ourselves a hymn at Communion. Abbot Schwacke will lead it.

"Now, if the priests can take their pieces of bread, we can begin. Then at Communion, if you would share the consecrated bread with the unordained men around you, please.

"*In nomine Patris et Filii et Spiritus Sancti....Suscipe, sancte Pater, omnipotens aeterne Deus, hanc immaculatam hostiam, quam ego indignus famulus tuus offero tibi Deo meo vivo....*"

As the Mass went on, tears ran down the haggard faces. Prabutski intoned the words of consecration, and the whole group said the Lord's Prayer. Then nearly a thousand voices began: "*Agnus Dei, qui tollis peccata mundi....*" It was what they had given their lives for.

Suddenly, at the back door of the room there was the sound of scuffling. Two SS guards pushed through the packed bodies. As the troopers passed, the priests instinctively, like mothers, turned their backs and covered the bread in their hands. The guards shoved to the altar table, elbowing men roughly out of their way, trying to pry through the densely packed crowd.

One was a handsome boy about twenty, a cigarette lolling from his lips. He sat on the front of the table and surveyed the open-mouthed faces around him. He leaned his hands back on the table, his left hand inches from the gilded cup with its teaspoonful of consecrated wine.

Prabutski eyed the cup. "Reichsfuehrer SS Himmler himself," Kap said quietly, "promised we would not be disturbed."

"The Reichsfuehrer isn't here right now, is he?" The boy smiled arrogantly. "We're a couple of old altar boys, *Father*. We want to see if the Baby Jesus does the old Jack-in-the-box."

Prabutski's horse jaw was working slowly. He took a deep breath and exhaled. "Get out."

"Tch-tch-tch. That is *no* way to talk to the jailers, priest."

"I will write to Reichsfuehrer Himmler myself."

"Not with ten broken fingers."

"A thousand men here. You cannot break all their fingers."

The young man looked slowly at the tall priest, smiling sourly, fingers edging toward the aluminum cup. For a moment, the priest and soldier were frozen, like two grim statues.

At last, the young guard stood up and said to his friend, "Come on. Enough hocus pocus for one night. I hated this shit even when I *had* to come. Let's get out of here before I puke."

He turned and found a solid wall of priests all around him. For a moment, fear froze his fine face. Then, impassively, he brought his knee up hard into the groin of the priest in front of him. The old man doubled over, moaning, his hands firmly cupped around the bread in his hands.

"Now, out of our way."

The priests pressed back. A jagged path opened to the door. Behind the wall of bodies, the door slammed shut. In a moment, the men at the back called out quietly, "They're gone."

Kap resumed. "*Corpus Domini nostri Jesu Christi custodiat animam meam in vitam aeternam. Amen.*"

He waited as the priests all over the room bent over the tiny crusts of black bread in their hands, breaking off pieces to share with the non-priests nearest them. Silently, they raised their cupped hands to their mouths and received the sacred Host. Their eyes closed and the room was a crowded sea of silence.

After a few moments, Prabutski nodded to a tall man in a green plastic raincoat to his left, Dom Gregor Schwacke, abbot of a Benedictine monastery in Westphalia. The clear baritone voice intoned the Communion hymn: "*Christus vincit! Christus regnat! Christus imperat!*"

A thousand voices blended into the hymn-reedy old men off key, young men flat but strong, voices trained or raw.

The music swelled in the room. It seeped through the walls, welling out along the icy street under the cold bright moon. It took root in other barracks. Men lying on shelves sung it softly, over and over: "Christ has conquered! Christ reigns! Christ is our Fuehrer! Listen, Lord Christ! Hear us, Lord Christ!"

Paul Reiser stood in the press of bodies, his heart swelling. He thought of Friederich Nietzsche, the spiritual godfather of the insanity Germany had become. Yes, he said to himself. He who has a 'why' can endure almost any 'how.' "*Christus vincit!*" he sang with all his heart. "*Christus regnat! Christus imperat!*"

116

No matter what, I'll live to be ordained a priest. No matter what. So help me God.

* * * * *

Tuesday, 25 March 1941 - KZ Dachau

Although a sharp northeast wind blew across the backs of the men standing at evening roll call, the Spring thaw was just about to begin. But three men had escaped. Twenty-five thousand men shivered in long parallel lines on the roll call square until they were found.

Desperation and loneliness gnawed every man's spine, slowly paring away resistance to the living suicide of apathy. The never-silent mewing of their bellies spawned envy and greed, suppressing scruples to the point few had not stolen bread even from friends. Anyone with money on account had ten marks in camp scrip a week. Sometimes tobacco for those still addicted, low-grade but better than dried leaves in toilet paper. Sometimes there was a salty fish paste that caused a devastating thirst. The little food in the canteen was exorbitant and usually maggot-ridden or moldy. But when a man opened a can of food, there was no way he could throw it away. Instead, either his system immediately rejected it, or he died with a full stomach.

In the first three months of 1941, nine hundred sixty-nine men had died in KZ Dachau. About twelve a day. But so many new prisoners came each week it hardly made a difference, except perhaps to one or two—if any—who cared for a particular prisoner.

Whatever the secret inner core of a man, it emerged within the first few months like a cancer, malignant or benign, and gradually devoured whatever had been his surface personality. Optimists fell victim to total credulousness, grasping at rumors. World-beaters grew quixotic, engaging in hapless schemes which ended in the Bunker or, as often, the crematorium. Cowards became slaves. The hearts of the skeptical became hard and scarred like the pits of peaches.

Since March 15, on orders from Berlin, the men of the Priests' Blocks had been put on easy labor. For old men over seventy, a godsend. They spent the dreary days huddled around lukewarm stoves on the plantation pasting together bags for seeds or clumsily trying to repair mattress ticking. But the priests who had the misfortune to be younger had a hard day at easy labor.

Monsignor Lutz had been on the Plantation Kommando prising the roots of last years' plants from the iron grip of the yellow soil. A claw of pain spread across his back and shoulders. The SS stayed inside the warm hothouse, with a languid eye watching through field glasses. All the prisoners were too frail to outrun a bullet.

As he swayed in the roll call line, Lutz yearned to put his palms to the small of his back and lever himself against the pain, but the Kapo was watching. Instead, he finished his second rosary, pressing his fingertips against his thighs for each Hail Mary.

To Lutz's right, Paul Reiser's mind tried to calm the rage of pain in his shoulders and biceps. His light duty that day had been on the Thermos Kommando, now the exclusive prerogative of the thousand priests. An hour before reveille, he had reported to the kitchens where there stood thirty-five shining cauldrons holding a thousand liters each. Two carriers were assigned to each metal thermos, about a hundred and sixty pounds, loaded with the fifty liters of whatever. In the morning, black ersatz coffee; at midday, thin soup; and in the evening, soup or tea. At the moment, all thermoses sat cooling in apartments while the hungry prisoners awaited the escapees. More than once evening roll call had lasted until noon the next day.

The first secret meeting of the Barracks Committee was to have been tonight. Flattered to have been elected, Paul was happy he wouldn't have to face it.

To his left, Father Pascal Bernard, a Luxembourger, found his pain encasing his legs. His easy labor had been on the Moor Express, a heavy four-wheeled wagon pulled by harnassed prisoners at the front and pushed with four projecting poles by two pairs of prisoners on either side. Otto Pfizer was on his other side, and Bernard whispered to him so loudly Paul could hear.

"Otto?"

"Yes," Pfizer answered.

"I want to pray they'll be caught. I want to pray they'll be put into solitary, not whipped. I just want to get inside."

"We all do, Pascal."

"But I couldn't pray, Otto."

Pfizer's hawk face was impassive. He wished Bernard would be quiet. In his imagination he was trying to drain the ache up from his shoulders and arms, into the top of his skull so he could release it into the cold evening air like an evil spirit.

"I believe in God, Otto. But I hate God, Otto."

"You're tired, Pascal. Wait until you've had some rest."

"It's easier for the atheists, you know. They don't have to defend God. Why has God put me in this place?"

Pfizer chuckled bitterly. "I imagine that's the first question Adam asked God, Pascal. And he was in paradise."

"You were a novice master, Otto. Am I condemned forever for despising a God who'd create a world like this?"

Pfizer paused. "Only if you despise him forever."

"What could he do now to make me forgive him for this?"

"Pascal," he whispered, "did you ever hate your father? Did you ever want to strike back at him and get revenge on him? For being so unreasonable? For being an autocrat and arbitrary?"

"Yes."

"And did you finally forgive him?"

"Of course."

"Why?"

"Because...."

Bernard fell silent.

Paul Reiser heard Johann Lutz muttering on the other side. Something about his "wounded priestly hands." My God, hadn't the man ever looked at a crucifix?

"Paul?"

Oh, my sweet Jesus, Paul prayed, make him be silent. Paul remembered him that awful Christmas, stroking his hair and longing for Paul to finish disgorging his eviscerating secret. Lisl.

"Paul?"

"Yes, Monsignor."

"I've had a lot of time to think, Paul."

"Yes, Johann. We all have."

"I've developed seven principles on which to base my life."

Paul kept silent.

"Seven props to my sanity. I have them now by heart."

Please, God, Paul prayed. Let him keep them there.

"One: Prayer and deepening spiritual life. Two: Intellectual study as far possible."

Let some Kapo, for Christ's sake, see us. Let them put me into solitary where there is nothing but silence.

"Four: Good example to foster respect for the priesthood."

But Paul had been in solitary. Then he had yearned for any voice, even Monsignor Johann Lutz, a torturer whose thick-headedness proved the infinite inventiveness of God.

"Six: No more work than that to which one is compelled."

"Johann, does that mean, if I were to faint, picking me up would interfere with fulfilling your seven points?"

"Seven: No work should interfere with our spiritual life."

Oh, my good Jesus, you lost your temper. There's proof. But only at clerics. I don't ask you to strike him dead. Just let him raise his fingertips to touch what once was his lovely white fringe of hair. Perhaps the shot will hit me.

"You've been elected to the Committee, Paul," Lutz whispered, "I wonder if there might be some way to get these seven rules...."

Some turmoil off to their far right, near the gatehouse. A sigh from twenty-five thousand men. The shit-licks had been found.

A faint sound of thumping, like children playing Red Indians. Hollow as it moved under the tunnel of the *Jourhaus*. Faint, raw voices. Then they appeared. Three men crusted with brown blood, shouting almost soundlessly in the silent square: "Hurrah! We're back! Hurrah! We're back!" Over and over.

They paraded down the west side of the assembled prisoners, across the back of their lines near the first and second barracks, up the east side and back to the platform at the front. Around each neck was a placard scrawled in grease pencil: "HOMO!"

"Hurrah! We're back!" they wheezed. "Hurrah! We're...."

At the front lines, they were ushered onto the platform where nearly all the prisoners could see them. Hauptsturmfuehrer Zill, Camp Leader, shot each of them in the back of the neck, and the other prisoners were finally allowed to return to their barracks and their cold soup.

The priests' barracks were always last released from evening roll call. When they finally plodded up the long camp street, they shuffled to a stop, in groups of twos and threes, staring stupidly at Barrack 26.

Becher was standing bandy-legged in the middle of the street, his small fists akimbo on his fat hips. "So! You see it, eh?"

In the hours they had been at work and roll call, the barracks containing the chapel had been surrounded by raw wooden poles and barbed wire. The clergy prisoners billeted in that barrack were now also quarantined off from the rest of the camp, pariahs to the pariahs.

"Priests are worse for the camp than the Communists, eh?" Becher cackled. "Communists are diarrhea; priests are *typhus*!"

The clergymen stood like scrawny cattle before the fence.

"Priests will now have the same bedding as SS! Oh, *yes*!" Becher shouted, so all the other barracks nearby could hear and report it through the camp. "Priests will have two hours *rest* period after noon work break to study and *pray*! Priests are not to be treated like the *rest* of the enemies of the Fatherland! One *third* of a loaf a *day*! Newspapers and the library are now available to the *priests*! The priests will have *wine*! Every *day*!"

Becher lowered his voice so only those nearest could hear. Paul Reiser was close enough to catch Becher's spittle on his chest. "But you're now twice behind wire, priests!" Becher hissed. "After evening roll call, no wandering the streets. All doors locked. Your chapel locked during the day. The non-priest fairies who've been sneaking to your Mass will be *shot* if they try again!"

Kapo Becher opened the barbed wire gate, and the clergymen filed past him into Barracks 26. As they brushed against one another just beyond the gate, Pastor Langer, an intense man with crooked teeth and crooked glasses, whispered to Otto Pfizer, "We will not be meeting, then, tonight, Father Pfizer?"

"Perhaps tomorrow," Pfizer whispered. "See what happens."

They parted into the darkness like strangers.

Later, just before "All to Barracks," Georg Schelling, Kap Prabutski, and Otto Pfizer stood, arms folded, looking from the open doorway of Apartment III-IV of 26 at the wire glinting like silvered cobwebs in the occasional passes of the searchlights.

"Clever," Schelling sighed. "Camp within a camp. We can't get out, laymen can't get in."

Pfizer chuckled. "Lutz says it's God's punishment for letting Lutherans use the chapel."

"Ha," Schelling grunted. "Things aren't as simple as they told little Johnni back at the Germanicum. Our hosts don't play fair."

"I think we can find ways around the fence," Pfizer said. "They can't use us and still keep us out of all contact with other prisoners. We'll run into them at the Plantation, in the kitchens, at stops on the Moor Express. If they can't get in for Communion, we'll bring it to them."

"Our men'll go mad," Shelling sighed. "Fighting over scraps of bread. We've got to get their minds focused on something, Kap."

"We'll talk about it at the meeting tomorrow. Oh, I arranged with Brother Potempa to switch jackets with Herzog. Brother'll stay in 28, and Herzog can stay here that one night. Pospisil is Kapo in 28 now. He's a decent man. He steals pig swill for their soup. He punishes only bread thieves. If he notices, he'll ignore it."

At that moment, Father Heinrich Steiner came up to them. He was an officious little man with his bent glasses' bows tied with a string around his head. "Father Prabutski. Father Schelling. Father Pfizer," he said, bowing politely at each name. "I have a real surprise. Prince Alban was able to bribe the canteen Kapo into selling him half a *box* of candle stubs from the officers' ratskeller! But please blow the candles out as *soon* as Communion is over, Father Prabutski. They must last."

"Count on it, Father," Kap smiled down at him. "All right with hosts? Wine? Nobody's nipping into the wine?"

Steiner grew a full three inches before their very eyes. "Just let anyone *try*. The two men in my bunk are Polish scholastics. Hulking lads. No one will trouble the three of *us*."

Steiner rose almost to his normal size. "Father Pfanzelt comes with hosts and wine every month from the town, prompt as actual grace. A fine little priest, cheerful as a cherub– though, I confess, I wish he were more careful caring for his clerical clothing. Well, I'll be off, Fathers."

Schelling shook his head, grinning at the little priest scurrying off to his chapel, striped jacket in tatters, brown stain bisecting the seat of his trousers. "Did you see that little man *grow* when he talked about *his* chapel? Proudest little man in this whole camp. You'd think he was back in...." Suddenly Schelling's eyes went wide. "Come on outside. I have an idea."

Prabutski looked at Pfizer and shrugged his oaken shoulders. They turned toward the door but it suddenly heaved shut. An old priest had been sitting behind it and fallen aside, closing the door and lying across the sill like a blind watchdog.

A Jesuit named Lienhard from Saxony, no more than fifty, but the ravaged face could have been twenty years older. He'd been on the mission band, going from parish to parish giving retreats and novenas. A lonely life, living out of a suitcase. Alcoholic. The first months had been more than the usual agony for him.

Pfizer and Prabutski bent down and lifted the staring priest to a sitting position against the wall. The man's sick-sweetish smell made their gorges rise.

"Gone Moslem, I think," Schelling said and waved his hand in front of the priest's face. He snapped his fingers. The eyes didn't blink. "Father, can you tell me what year this is?" No response. "Can you tell us your name?" Nothing.

"No use," Schelling sighed. He saw a young scholastic trying to read a book on his shelf, tilting it to catch the spill of the lights. "Son, could you try to find this father's bed, please?"

"Yes, Father."

The boy leaped down and squatted next to the staring priest, talking softly The three others opened the door and stepped into the narrow yard, along the wire between 26 and 24.

A large padlock hooked over the hasp on the chapel door. Only when they were directly in front of it they saw the lock was open but turned back to look secure from a few paces away.

"Well, well!" Pfizer chuckled. "Faster than I thought. I'll have to find out who that talented gentleman was. Good seminary training."

Schelling looked around quickly and unlatched the door. He stepped up into the chapel with the two other priests in tow. At the far end, Steiner puttered around the altar. In the shadows in the corners, priests and brothers knelt or squatted on their heels praying. Their shoes had all been tucked neatly into the boxes by the door. Schelling stopped and gestured around the big room. "There you have it, gentlemen. Our grip on sanity!"

The two others continued to look befuddled.

"Kap, I'm under direct orders from Himmler himself to give you the best advice I can. Then use this chapel to keep every possible man focused on a common task. We have our two-hour rest period, but only one hour in the bunks, then why not an hour of classes, in here? Get the professors' minds working again, and at the same time give the seminarians at least some philosophy and theology. And a *casus conscientiae*. And Lenten lectures. A retreat. And...."

His crinkled grin became contagious. The other two priests' eyes narrowed as they considered the possibilities.

"Lutz will be in seventh heaven," Otto Pfizer grinned.

"Otto," Schelling began to bubble again, "you were Master of Novices. Every seminary had a chap who was a kind of...dabbler. Auto mechanics, gardening, fix an illicit radio and keep his mouth shut. Anybody here with that kind of kink?"

"Karl Schmidt. Taught physics. Very clever with his hands."

"What if we got him to organize a group to make a decent chalice. Get another group to 'liberate' some paint. Drapes. And vestments! Out of a thousand men there must be a tailor. And brothers who can sew. Probably a dozen. Get their imaginations perking. Let them lie awake at night dreaming of underhanded ploys instead of knockwurst. And a *long-range* goal."

"Wonderful idea," Prabutski said.

"Got it from Himmler himself," Schelling grinned. "You were there. 'A cathedral,' right?"

"Christmas?" Pfizer said, "Maybe even Easter?"

"And a choir. Perfect. No language problems there." Prabutski clapped his hands. "Georg, you should have my job."

Schelling winked. "In the Mystical Body we all have our talents. You're our leader. Our wily Jesuit here is our secret police. And I agree to serve as *eminence grise.*"

* * * * *

The following evening, the first session of the Priests' Barracks Council met in the chapel in Block 26. Nine, proportional representation scrupulously worked out by Father Karl Schmidt.

It was almost impossible to keep watch on anyone approaching the chapel from the camp street, although two seminarians were deputed to keep their eyes peeled, standing outside the latrine door ready to knock on the wall. Highly unlikely anyone would investigate inside the wire-within-the-wire. The only ones aware of the postponed meeting were those present.

There were four Poles: Father Paul Prabutski, the chaplain, a diocesan priest; Father Stanislaw Bednarski, a Jesuit; Fathers Ceslaus Nowicki, a former professor of moral theology from the University of Cracow; and Julian Bronek, former rector of the diocesan seminary in Warsaw. Nowicki was a tall, spare man with hollowed cheeks who carried himself with an elegance which many read as hauteur. Bronek was squat and swarthy and, despite his nearly two years' incarceration, had still not lost all of what must have been a considerable girth.

Prabutski and Bednarski had been elected, many said, by the younger members of the Polish community, because of their activities in the camp. Nowicki and Bronek had been elected, it was said, by older men-who surely predominated-for attributes which were valued outside the camp but not necessarily within it.

There were three *Alt-Germans*: Otto Pfizer, a former Jesuit master of novices, Paul Reiser, representing unordained seminarians, and Manfred Herzog, a diocesan priest who had, it seemed, been elected by a concerted spur. While many more traditional priests had backers, some-like Monsignor Johann Lutz-had declined to serve on such a committee. And since backing for other candidates was fragmented, Herzog found support among a group of priests who had a lower tolerance for protocol and, as they said, bullshit.

Herzog was the only member not resident in Barrack 26, and so, as a precaution, he had exchanged jackets with a big Pole, Brother Potempa, and Herzog would sleep tonight in Barrack 26 and the brother in Barrack 28. Little likelihood, among a thousand clergymen, that a guard would notice the switch in one night. On the way to the morning roll call, it could all be rectified.

Georg Schelling, an Austrian, represented all smaller nationalities of priests. The fact he was German-speaking caused some difficulties, but he had, after all, been longer in the camp than any priest. Pastor Langer's presence was also something of a thorn to the predominantly Catholic clergy, but Kap Prabutski's quiet persuasiveness calmed the troubled waters. Surely the fifty non-Catholic inmates of the clergy barracks deserved some voice in their common decisions.

There were no chairs or benches. So the nine men squatted Indian-style on the shining floor in the northwest corner of the room, where they would be furthest from the door yet still able to hear any rappings from the alleyway which would signal the approach of Becher or a trooper. Otto Pfizer had just been elected, six to three, to chair. He himself had voted for Stan Bednarski, which suggested the only two who felt negatively about his presidency were Fathers Nowicki and Bronek.

"I feel," he began, "like a character in a Kafka novel. I know I have a mandate, but no one seems to be coming forward to tell me what it is. I suppose it's...everything. We've agreed it would be unwise to jeopardize Kap Probutski's position as chaplain to have him in charge of this... somewhat illicit group. So, if someone has to be 'the secular arm,' *fiat voluntas tua*.

"We've spoken already among ourselves about the need for unity in our barracks. The SS policy is obviously to divide and conquer. To be honest, there were already divisions among us before we came here, resentments that go back perhaps even centuries."

The momentary sweep of searchlights caught their faces. Some genially expectant; the two older Poles openly skeptical.

"Each of us in this room has a kind of 'authority' in the clergy barracks, or we wouldn't have been elected. The most fundamental task we face is to heal those cracks between us that-in this place-widen into chasms. That's precisely what the SS want. I beg you to convince your friends that, for that reason alone, we must exercise supernatural forbearance with one another."

He looked around again at the pale faces materializing periodically out of the darkness.

"Would anyone like to say anything about that?"

The men who had been expectant seemed pleased. The men who had been skeptical seemed even less malleable.

"We've been contacted by a representative of other underground committees." He could see brows furrowing, even among those on his side. "They would like us to help them."

"Communists?" Julian Bronek snorted.

"And criminals," Ceslaus Nowicki agreed.

"No doubt," Pfizer said. "But, again, in battle one doesn't check the party affiliations of the men on his own side."

"I would think one should," Bronek sniffed.

Pfizer cleared his throat and went on. "There's one enemy here, despair. If a Communist or a pimp will help us ward off despair, I'll take his hand."

"Perhaps this whole committee was a mistake," Bronek said and turned his squat neck to Nowicki. The grimness of Nowicki's lean face seemed to show he was of the same mind.

"The national groups have their own organizations," Pfizer went on. "They're decent human beings. Their aim is to distribute tasks throughout the camp. Like a government in hiding. Solicit food and clothing from barracks with a relative excess and share with those with less, especially newcomers. Because the SS was forced to allow us to receive packages from home at times, we now have more than anyone else. They're trying to enlist our help. Father Jasinski has already begun a Caritas in 28 to share out of our excess."

"Preposterous," Bronek growled. "We have young men going out of their minds with hunger. We are in conscience bound to save them, no matter what anyone else might think. Would you sacrifice a future priest to save the life of a homosexual or a Communist?"

"They're human beings, Julian," Kap Prabutski said quietly. "'If you have two coats, and your brother has none....'"

"Really," Bronek sneered, "a deviant or a man resolved to overthrow Christianity?"

Paul Reiser grinned sourly. "Or a whore or a tax collector?"

Pfizer continued. "They would also like to enlist our help in radio listening. I've asked Karl Schmidt, who's good at those things, to try to liberate the parts for a crystal radio set....."

"Out of the question!" Father Nowicki snapped. "At least not in these barracks. They could take away the chapel."

Herzog, who had been uncharacteristically silent, said, "So?"

"Surely, Herzog," Nowicki said, "you have some priorities."

"Yes. I do." And he lapsed again into observant silence.

"Thirteen hundred Polish boys," Pfizer said, "from the Jesuit school at Lodz arrived this week. The representative would like to enlist our active help, especially the help of the Polish scholastics, in protecting these boys from the pederasts."

"Well," Father Bronek said with conviction, "now there is something we all must agree to, wholeheartedly."

A smile broke over Otto Pfizer's lean face. "Excellent."

"I'll take that job, Otto," Paul Reiser said.

"Thank you, Paul. And get the Polish priests and scholastics who have taught high school. I think perhaps the best...."

Suddenly, there were three heavy thumps on the wall next to them. The nine men tensed and began to struggle to their feet. But before they could, the door slammed open. One of the searchlights had stopped its random sweeps and froze on the doorway, but the men who entered flicked on the overhead lights. Steiner, the sacristan, slipped deftly behind the altar and under the overhanging sheets. The men who had been praying in the other corners huddled together, blinking against the unexpected light like men who had lost their glasses. But Hauptsturmfuehrer Zill and the four troopers with rifles did not seem at all interested in them.

Zill was a darkly handsome young man, chiseled cheekbones and resolute chin. He wore a leather overcoat over his black uniform, sidearm belted over it. Kapo Becher stood smugly at his left shoulder like a ragged cur he had somehow picked up on the way.

Zill strode toward the corner where the committee squatted. He looked down at them, his tall black cap with its skull and crossbones making him more formidable, half-silhouetted against the overhead lights. The four troopers pummeled the other priests from around the room toward the door with the butts of their rifles.

"Let me guess." Zill showed a white smile. "An illegal gambling operation. No? Of course not. Not in the holy house of God. Which also rules out opium, too, I suppose."

He did not look at Pfizer or Schelling or the Pastor or the Poles. His ice-blue eyes were riveted on Manfred Herzog.

"Ah," he said, "current affairs. International trade. That sort of thing. I remember from school with the moron democrats in charge. Big thing with the limp-wristed boys then, too."

The men looked up at him, humiliated by his polite condescension, like boys caught smoking by the new young headmaster.

"Real mix, eh?" Zill checked their triangles. "Germans. Polacks. No kike? Why, even a Polack *lay* brother, 19446? I thought laybrothers were priests' doormats. Potempa, yes?"

Herzog glared back from under his thick brows. He had been imprisoned for calling the Gauleiter of his district an "arrogant asshole" once too often.

"Say something in Polack for the Camp Leader, 19446."

Herzog hesitated only for a moment and then said, very slowly, *"Potes lingere nates meas, te spurca...situla...stercori."*

Zill's mouth twisted. "I don't take insults easily, Brother *Potempa*. I'm an educated man. I've read Sanskrit, the Hindu Bible. I know Italian when I hear it, *Herzog!*" He jerked his head at his men. "Bunker tonight. Standing stalls. The rest at morning roll call. Becher!"

"*Yes*, Hauptsturmfuehrer," Becher shouted, doffing his cap. "Truly, I knew nothing of...."

"You *should* have. From now on I want a dog loose in this inner compound every night. Understand? Rabid, if you can find one." He turned to the door but stopped. "Get these Bible thumpers back to their bunks." He looked from one to the other. "There'll be no next time, understand?" And he disappeared out into the darkness.

"*Raus*, you *Durckfall* bastards! *Raus*," Becher screeched, flailing around with his whip, thrashing the priests more fiercely than usual, driving them toward the doorway and back along the barbed alleyway to the darkened apartments.

Paul ran with his arms over his head, trying to keep the lash from his face. But a thought blazed in his mind.

Someone betrayed us. A priest.

* * * * *

It was a morning of shredded clouds. Grey ashes and dark blue embers rimmed red. The rising sun was never quite visible, aureoled in feathered caverns of cloud. The kind of sky against which painters captured souls descending to hell.

The priests of 26 and 28 were lined in the front of morning roll call, for a better view.

Spraddled on the Bock was Monsignor Manfred Herzog, Protective Prisoner 21306. His jacket was pulled up over his head, and his bound hands gripped the front legs. His legs were strapped to a kind of step at the back, and his broad, withered buttocks humped naked over the edge of the slatted Bock.

Kapo Cristl had been chosen to administer the flogging as a reward for his having eliminated his one hundred and twenty-fifth Jew the previous day. At Christmas he had secured a full-course meal when he had killed his hundredth, a twenty-year-old rabbinical student from Danzig. Kapo Becher would assist.

Aware of the prestige among the prisoners which such a moment conferred on them, the two Kapos approached their task with the slow and patient ritual the moment deserved. Like fencers they lifted their whips from the wooden bucket of water where they had been soaking to make them more pliable. They nodded almost ceremonially to one another and set to their task.

Kapo Cristl raised his whip over his head and brought it singing down onto the prisoner's buttocks. The prisoner kept the count, shouting the number after each stroke.

"One!" Monsignor Herzog growled gutturally, a shiver of agony in his angry, bitter voice.

Cristl stepped back and nodded politely to Becher who nodded in return and stepped forward to lash the prisoner again.

"Two!"

The priests in the front rows looked at the hard earth at their feet. Most prayed, some audibly. There was little fear of guards or Kapos, who were as fascinated by the performance on the platform as they had been at the traveling puppet shows which had occasionally passed through their villages when they'd been boys.

At the nineteenth stroke, Monsignor Herzog was silent. The chief infirmary Kapo, Heiden, who stood by at all floggings in case of just such emergencies, picked up the bucket in which the whips had been soaked and upended it over Herzog's head.

"*Count!*" Cristl shouted.

The prisoner seemed too dazed to remember, so it began again afresh from the start.

When it was finally over, Cristl and Becher nodded to the Report Leader and stepped aside, tossing their whips into the empty bucket. They were sweating in the mild morning air.

Kapo Heiden stepped forward again with a fistful of cotton and a bottle of iodine and began to swab the prisoner's raw buttocks. When he had finished, he jerked the prisoner to his feet and disgustedly hauled his underwear and trousers up and fastened them at his waist. Then he led the prisoner forward so the assembled inmates could see the conclusion.

Monsignor Herzog swayed like a man who had lost his way, head shifting slowly back and forth, tongue lolling out of his mouth.

"Saxon salute!" Kapo Heiden cried.

Herzog's eyes closed and his brow knotted like a blind man's, trying to comprehend. Then he nodded once, as he finally remembered, and he slowly cupped his hands at the back of his head. Trembling like a tightrope walker, he began to sink into the obligatory ten knee bends to prove no significant muscular damage.

After the sixth, he fainted again. No matter how many times the infirmary Kapo battered him across the face, he was unable to revive him. In disgust, he called the two nearest prisoners in the front row to carry the son of a bitch to the infirmary, where he could be brought around at least enough to be sent back to the standing cells in the Bunker.

* * * * *

Wednesday, 24 May 1941 – KZ Dachau

Paul and Otto sat on a bottom bed shelf, the day's pain aching out of them, waiting for "All to Barracks" to sound.

"When it came up in the council," Paul said, "about us seminarians taking courses from the theology professors, it made good sense."

"When the Americans arrive, you'll have a brain buffed and shiny as a new pfennig."

"But today Monsignor Feuerstein was in seventh heaven! Doktor Schumacher in the library found six–count them, *six*–copies of *The Summa Theologica*. Confiscated from some monastery. In *Latin*. One for each of us and one for him. Like Schumacher had given him the keys to the Kingdom! In Latin."

"For him, it was like a shipwreck survivor finding a box of dry matches."

"Today, right after soup, we hadn't even stopped licking our bowls when he ushered us all into the chapel and started yammering away. I thought he'd wet his pants. He was going on about the 'circumincession' of the Trinity. You're a smart Jesuit. You know what that means?"

Otto's face wrinkled into a grin. "I must have dozed through that one. The Trinity course was in the afternoon, after we came in from games or chopping down trees."

"It means the Father is in the Son, the Son is in the Father, the Holy Spirit is in the Son and in the Father, and the Son and Father are in the Holy Spirit. Like John's gospel...'I in him and him, and he in me, and we in they.' Does that warm your soul? It's like some kind of celestial calculus! In Mandarin!"

"To Feuerstein it *has* to be important, Paul. It rejuvenates him! He spent so much time and effort in Rome getting a degree in it. From people even more boring than he is!"

"Do you think a single one of the original apostles could explain the Apostles' Creed?"

"Probably not."

"But all I want to know is what I need to be a good priest! Is anybody ever going to ask me how the Trinity carry on conversations? Why, for God's sake?"

"Because the rules were made up by guys who'd rather die in agony than be 'just' good parish priests, Paul."

"I'd rather hitch myself to the Moor Express. Or shovel snow."

"I suspect that's hyperbole."

"It's exaggerated so you'll have more empathy with my pain."

"My heart weeps bitter tears."

"I assumed it would." Paul huffed. "Sometimes I feel like I'd rather spend my free time daydreaming about potato pancakes in dark brown gravy."

"That's frustrating, though. Like thinking of sex."

"Funny. Here I am in the prime of my young manhood," Paul said, thumping his chest, "and I never think of sex. Never. Only about food. And this celestial calculus stuff seems even more frustrating. Pretending we can grab a cloud."

Otto patted Paul's bony shoulder. "Look, I confess I don't remember any of that...'stuff.' And I don't feel impoverished for forgetting a lot of it." He chuckled. "Probably most of it. For a lot of men, the dogmatic stuff becomes petrified, crammed with pedantic terminology, no life or warmth in it. But I know it did do something to me. To my mind. It made it nimbler. The same way our soccer coach made us run with our feet pumping down into old automobile tires. It was a specific skill we were never going to use on the field, but we got something useful from it. Something that wasn't obvious while we did it."

"Like the longer you hang in a noose the more skillful you get at it."

"Right. Something like that. In a way, I think it makes it easier in here. For people who've learned to think. We get used to settling for less than perfect answers." He shrugged his shoulders. "Wait. Maybe I don't mean that. I don't know. Is it easier to face this insanity if you're uneducated? To face it dumbly, like an animal in a laboratory, not to have all these questions like 'How could a good God...?'"

"But they do, Otto. Even the Polish boys. It's like their kindly Father has turned devil and screwed them."

"The only alternative to a God with unreadable motives is a God who *likes* to screw his own kids. Like Chronos eating his own children. Or no God at all. Then there's *no* reason. For anything. Getting screwed is 'just the way things are.' And that'd be more obscene, wouldn't it?"

"All right, Father Master. I've thought about what you said before. So Pascal is right? One option's appealing; the other's appalling, and you don't know which. So you might as well pick the appealing one. Because you'll never find out you were wrong? Nietzsche's not going to be on the other side thumbing his nose, because he's hit the toilet, too?"

"You know, sometimes, Paul, in this place, when I want to cry, Pascal makes sense when there's nothing left to hold onto."

"So," Paul's face got serious again. "Like Parsifal. We're *dummlings*. We cling to the hope that there *is* a grail. I do accept everything coming right in the end. I do. But between then and now, Otto...."

"One time, way long ago, in the middle of the Jesuit course, we were set free to teach for three years. I taught secondary-school boys in our school in Bad Godesburg, St. Aloysius. There was a kid's father I talked to once. Well-to-do. Something in insurance, I think. Four boys. All of them athletic, handsome, popular. In class, dull as ditchwater. The father said, 'When I was a kid, I swore to God my kids would never have to fight through the *Quatsch* I had to put up with as a kid. And, by God, I did it. I gave them everything I didn't have when I was their age, except...except what I *got* from wading through all that *Quatsch*,' he said, 'spine.' It may not be the best motive to keep going, but it's not bad."

"So between now and the Second Coming–or death, whichever comes first–all this *Quatsch* is just building my damn *character*?"

"Yes. Your character's *you*, Paul. Who you are, your soul, what you're truly worth. The great accomplishment of your life isn't going to be all the souls you 'save' or all the books you write. The great accomplishment of your life is you."

Paul was silent, buttoning and unbuttoning the one button left on his jacket.

Finally Otto said, "Like pursuing happiness. You never find it. Part of the reason's that most people don't know what the hell 'happiness' even means. They could have it right in their fists and never realize it. And part of it is that most people think happiness means feeling cheerful, giddy, unbothered. Which would make drunkards the happiest people on earth. Or people in cemeteries. Or like finally capturing a butterfly and mounting it on a pin in a glass case so you can enjoy it forever. Dead. Or keeping pictures from a vacation. To prove you once had it. So they just endure life. Tread water, and tread water and tread water. And then they die."

* * * * *

Tuesday, 24 June 1941 - KZ Dachau

In the winter, only 400 prisoners worked each day on the Plantation, mostly old men and pals of the Kapos, since all work was inside the six warm greenhouses. But in summer, the 160 acres swarmed with 1300 inmates, nearly half of them priests, under the Argus eyes of 12 Kapos, 25 under-Kapos, and armed SS guards. The plantation, drained from the Bavarian swamps, supplied not only the potatoes and beets for the prisoners' soups, but all sorts of spices once available only from the East, flowers for the housewives of Munich, and acres of medicinal plants. Twelve acres bloomed with sword lilies, grown as a source of Vitamin C. All were serviced mostly by priests hitched six each to the plows and harrows. The enterprise yielded a profit to the SS of three quarters of a million Reichsmarks annually.

The long lines of Plantation Kommandos trudged out the gate-house tunnel and turned left onto the road toward the farms, singing, after a fashion, "Oh, You Dark-Eyed Gypsy." Those who knew no German were compelled at least to sing "la-la-la." On the way home, they would sing "The End of a Perfect Day."

Otto Pfizer shouldered his way into the center of the column and doubled over with a violent cough. He braced his hand against the picket ribs of the man to his right, and, as he did, managed to slip the aspirin tin of Host fragments into the man's pocket. During the day, Communion would spread from aspirin tins and envelopes and thumb-tack boxes throughout the Plantation to laymen who had been barred from the chapel in 26. On the way back to evening roll call, the other man would have the coughing spell, and the "pyx" would be back in Pfizer's pocket.

Under the dreary singing, the column hummed like a swarm of bees, as the dormitories had the previous night. The news was too enormous to contain. At three-thirty the previous Sunday morning, 129 years to the day Napoleon had crossed the Niemen in 1812, the armies of the Third Reich had turned their blazing blitzkrieg against the largest expanse in the world, Mother Russia.

There had been no need to discover the news through the complex clandestine camp system. Commandant Piorkowski had himself announced it triumphally at evening roll call.

Reactions clashed among the prisoners. Some who were, beyond any logic, still loyal to the regime worried the Fuehrer had waited too long, losing valuable Spring weather stopping to gobble up Yugoslavia and Greece. Others who cordially detested the regime, among them Monsignor Lutz, were disconcerted by the news for different reasons.

No matter what flagrant injustices the Fuehrer had allowed, he was at last turning the might of the greatest war machine in history against the true and ultimate enemy of humanity: godless Communism. Still others rejoiced both at the news and at the lateness of the year and spun visions of Hitler slogging home from Moscow through hip-deep snow with his Mephisto tail up his ass.

Many, however, had withdrawn from all concern with the outside world, as the outside had withdrawn from all concern for them. To live now meant no more than not-to-die.

"Let him attack the Vatican if he wants," one muttered as they slogged along, "or Mars. What the *Verflucht* difference to us?"

"What we need is somebody who can invade hell."

"Like Orpheus," an old professor smiled wanly.

"Or Jesus."

"Maybe Jesus went to hell, but the bastard'd never come here."

"Watch your mouth."

"My ass flies into yours!"

Otto Pfizer withdrew into his own thoughts. For three months he had been trying to find who had betrayed their first meeting and sent Herzog to solitary, from which he had yet to return.

Why only Herzog? Out of nine, not counting Steiner and the ones praying. Herzog spoke his mind, and therefore was abrasive to many, especially the more fastidious. But it just couldn't have been Lutz. The two older Poles, Bronek and Nowicki, found Herzog unpleasant, but hardly enough they would revenge it so cruelly. Priests, for God's sake! And yet, ugly as it was, it had been some priest, brother, scholastic, pastor. But why? And who else even knew?

Pfizer had carefully observed as many as he could of the five hundred men crammed into his barrack. He watched the two young seminarians who had stood guard that evening for approaching trouble, not knowing what the meeting was for. He tried to see if anyone's face was filling out, or if anyone looked smug, or if anyone made any remarks about Herzog. No one mentioned him at all. He was merely one more of thousands who had ceased to exist.

The obvious one was Whisper. His lot in life was to spy. Yet every man at the meeting had sworn he never mentioned the switching of jackets in Whisper's presence. Which led Pfizer back to the eight other men at the meeting- himself, Paul, Schelling, the pastor, and the four Poles. He thought of Oedipus, who condemned himself for refusing to accept the unthinkable.

He tried to wrench his mind from the squirrel cage. He looked at the scenery, brightening in the early sunshine, and tried to absorb himself in every detail, one by one. Far in the distance, the dragon humps of the Alps were still mantled in snow. Bees buzzed in the roadside clover. The old wooden wayside cross hulked up ahead under a thin edge of weathered rooftop.

The cross was older than Pfizer, leaning crookedly toward the plantation like a promise to meet them there. Every day as they passed, Kapo Becher almost absently gave it a boot, making bets with the young trooper, Fischl, about when it would finally topple. It enraged Paul Reiser a bit more each day, but Pfizer calmed him, convincing him crosses could be replaced; men couldn't.

The line suddenly lurched to a stop, and Pfizer, wrapped in his own thoughts, collided with the back of the man ahead of him, who muttered a curse and went silent. Whispers skittered up and down the line: "Reiser." "Stupid bastard." "Oh, hell."

Pfizer edged toward the right side of the line, and each man moved to the left and took his place without protest, glad for the physical insulation from the truncheons. Pfizer edged out a touch and strained to get a look. Up ahead, he could see Paul's striped shoulders crouched at the foot of the tottering crucifix. My God, what's the idiot doing, pulling out of line to *pray*!

He checked for the guard, then tapped the man ahead on the shoulder. The man stepped back, and Pfizer moved up on his left. He did it again and again until he was about ten feet from the cross, too close to move further without Becher or Fischl seeing.

When he peered out again, he saw Paul squatting at the foot of the cross with his arms clasped protectively behind him. The cross was nearly erect again. Somehow, Paul had picked up a couple of sharp-edged rocks along the way and jammed them into the ground like spikes on the side the cross had been leaning. The grim line of his mouth said he was not about to move.

"Back in line, 22356," Fischl said affably. "Come on! And we'll forget it. Waste of a good three-pfennig bullet, no?"

Fischl was a farmboy, doing what he was told. He just wanted to do a job and go home. Breaking ranks was automatically an escape. Shooting an escapee meant three days' leave, twenty marks, and extra cigarettes. But Fischl wasn't a mean sort. Yet he didn't want trouble, either from the other prisoners or from his superiors. And Kapo Becher was a troublemaker.

Becher wasn't as calm. He skittered back and forth on his short legs in front of the cross like a bantam fighter. "Get back into line!" Becher squealed. "I'll have you *shot* on the spot!"

Becher lifted his foot to boot Paul in the face, but Paul took the ankle firmly in one big hand and pressed it back onto the road, almost forcing Becher to lose his balance. On his knees, Paul steadied the little man with his other hand. Then he slumped down and put his arms back behind him around the foot of the cross.

"This is open *mutiny!*" Becher screamed. "Fischl! *Shoot* him!"

Pfizer's heart clutched like a fist. "Paul! Give it up! Get back in line!"

Becher turned his empurpled face back at him. "Shut *up*, Pfizer! I can handle this, goddammit! Back in the line, Pfizer, or die!"

Paul's face glistened with perspiration, but his big jaw was set. "You're not going to do it again, Becher. You're not doing it to insult the cross. You're doing it to humiliate *us!*"

"Paul," Pfizer shouted. "Don't be a *fool!*"

"I told you to shut up, priest!" Becher cried back at Pfizer.

Everyone was looking at the big farmboy trooper, and he knew it. He'd never shot anything in his life except squirrels and rabbits. His father had never let him shoot a deer.

Becher hollered, "It's your *duty* to shoot a prisoner who disobeys an order! If you don't shoot, Sturmmann Fischl, I will *report* you to Sturmbannfuehrer Piorkowski himself!"

The boy looked nervously down at the little Kapo, then at the big-boned young man on the cross. Fischl felt all the prisoners' eyes on him. They would know he was a coward. He would be sent to Russia. Or shot. At the rifle range. Near the crematorium. He had been there. He always fired into the ground. Even with those Polack professors. Always into the ground.

Fischl unslung his rifle. He looked at the ground, balancing the options. No way he could look into that other boy's eyes. He raised the muzzle to Paul's temple. Paul closed his eyes.

Fischl slipped the safety. Then he stopped to wipe the sweat off his right hand on the hip of his uniform. As he did, Paul turned his face up to him so that, when the young trooper looked back, the muzzle of the carbine was right at the base of Paul's forehead, between the light brows and the hazel eyes. For a moment, the two young men simply looked at one another along the immeasurable distance of the blue-black barrel.

Then Fischl lowered the gun, flicking the safety back on, raking his left sleeve across his face. "Get up," he growled, not looking at Paul. "I'm taking you to the commandant myself."

"I'm not going to let...." Paul began.

"Get *up*," the boy screamed. "Nobody's going to touch your precious cross!" Then his voice sank to a harsh whisper. "You've shamed *me*. That's *enough*, isn't it? Now get up."

Fischl jerked his thumb back toward the gatehouse, and Paul turned to move, but Fischl reached out his hand and laid it on Paul's shoulder to stop him. He turned to Kapo Becher. "Listen to me, you roach," Fischl said, voice dry as sand, "if anything happens to that cross, I'll kill you with my hands. God *damn* you!"

Becher thrust out his stubby chin, but his eyes knew.

In the silent side-mouthed whisper of the camp, Paul spoke to Pfizer. "I don't mind, Otto. Someone had to do something. Sometime. Didn't they, Otto? About *something*?"

Fischl put his hand on Paul's back and pushed him forward.

When they were nearly out of earshot, Becher shouted. "Tonight, Blondi!" he screamed. "Tonight we'll see all those muscles turn to dead meat! Do you...hear...*meeeeeee*!"

* * * * *

At the end of the evening roll call, they hadn't hanged Paul. If Zill was on, Paul was probably hanging by his thumbs, wired behind his back, in the shower room. Sometimes Zill pressed the prisoner beyond the usual hour. Nothing left of a man after that.

Pfizer left the roll call, following the line. He had never had a son. The hardest surrender of all. "Iron Man," his novices had called him behind his back. My God, the simple, cretinous bastards. Did they know what it cost? Sweet Jesus!

Benediction tonight, with the new monstrance an ingenious Austrian communist had made from the gold-tinted inner sides of fish cans liberated from the officers' garbage. Pfizer had drawn one of the lucky numbers. The first Benediction of the Blessed Sacrament.

Hurrah.

Oh, Jesus! He's overcome TB. He's kept that shit-eating grin. For a rotting cross! Oh, God, you've done it again!

Kap Prabutski began the benediction. The room was wall-to-wall bodies. There were even a few laymen, God knows how they'd gotten in. The guard dogs had been pacified every night by Stan Bednarski, who loved dogs and could have turned Cerberus into a pup. They take strength from this solemn rite, Otto Pfizer thought. Well, more power to them. His soul was corroded with a loneliness so pestilent no God could find a place within it.

The voices droned the "*O Salutaris Hostia*" and the "*Tantum Ergo Sacramentum*". Ah, yes. Our enemies press their attack on us. Give us help. If only it were an enemy I could face with my fists. But You give them directions to my guts.

Mercifully, the benediction was over, and Kap put the host into the iron-safe tabernacle someone had liberated somewhere.

Otto was not a man for tears. The rock. *Cephas.* Rocks don't weep. The storm-tossed to cling to. Enough to make you sick.

And, without any warning, there was Paul at the door.

Prabutski stopped, big hands flat on the two tables that were the altar. Heads turned. From the kneeling figures, Otto rose unsteadily and threaded his way back to the door. He couldn't do anything but look at the big grinning boy, alive.

"Piorkowski himself," Paul whispered, tears puddling his eyes. "I couldn't believe it. I told him, Otto. I told him it wasn't just that crucifix. I told him it was...I told him it was...."

"Your self."

Paul looked at his friend, and his friend looked at him. No words left for either of them. Otto enfolded the big young man in his arms. The two of them were shaking so much that, if they hadn't been holding one another, they would have fallen.

* * * * *

Pfizer climbed wearily to the top tier of bunks. Three rows of three tiers, each thirty feet long, all of a piece, shelves in a warehouse. Each shelf was thirty-two inches wide where, at least for now, two men slept faces to feet. The upper bunks were coveted, out of Becher's reach, although they had to be made up first in the morning, while the lower occupants stood grumbling and bitching. Otto couldn't remember when he'd felt such joy. Surely never at all in this place. "Quick! Bring out the best robe and put it on him. My son was dead, and now he is alive!"

He turned on his side, watching the erratic light in the windows. The man in the next shelf had been a pale Polish scholastic. Dead yesterday. The place had, of course, been taken.

Pfizer leaned up to see who the newcomer was. It mattered. Some were careless about delousing. Lienhard, the alcoholic gone Moslem. Moslems never got uppers. No Moslem could organize his thoughts to climb up, much less inveigle the place. The searchlight swung again into the window and held there. Otto saw Lienhard's eyes. Looking at him. Sad. But not deadened.

Pfizer leaned over to whisper to him but stopped. As he took a breath to speak, he smelled it. Schnaps.

All the joy that had filled his chest went out like a lamp.

Lienhard whispered, "I saved him, you know."

"Who, Gerd?" Otto said.

"The boy. Reiser."

"How?"

"I told them. The commandant. Things."

"What things, Gerd?"

"Things."

"About someone in our barracks?"

"About Becher. With the Polish boys."

All the loathing Otto had thought he had exorcized flooded back into him. Suddenly he remembered that day the wire had been put around their barrack, when he and Kap and Schelling had stood by the door. Kap had said Brother Potempa would change jackets with Herzog for one night. Lienhard had fallen from behind the door.

"You remember now, don't you, Otto? I was hoping you would."

"But why Herzog, Gerd? What did you have against him?"

"Nothing."

"Nothing!"

The men below told them to keep quiet for God's sake.

"Nothing?" Pfizer whispered. "You saw what they did to him!"

"He's still as strong as an ox, Otto."

"My God, Gerd, how could you have done such a thing?"

"You know why, Otto. They gave me schnaps. Chits for the brothel, too. Oh, I didn't use those. I traded them."

"For more schnaps. Gerd, would the brothel have been worse than what you did to Herzog?"

"I don't know. In here, it hardly matters, does it? God can't send us to hell after he's already sent us here, can he?"

Otto fell back and stared at the ceiling.

"I'm not like you, Otto. You expect everyone to be like you. Strong. Confident. What did I ever have to make me confident? When I taught, the boys made a fool of me. In the parish, the community found me embarrassing. Even the parishioners found me embarrassing. So they sent me on the road. So I wouldn't have to live too long in any community. No parish would have to put up with me more than a week. So I drank. It helped forget. Then it...something I couldn't do without. You don't know what that's like, Otto. You could stand tall without a crutch." He snorted bitterly. "I couldn't even get up the confidence to kill myself."

Otto hiked himself up on his elbow, feeling rage growing. "But you had the confidence to betray Herzog."

"Not confidence. Need. Like an animal. The priesthood has dregs."

Otto fell back on his straw mattress.

"I did save the boy, Otto," Lienhard whispered.

"Yes." Pfizer laced his fingers across his chest and stared at the dark ceiling. "What are we to do with you now, Gerd?"

"Kill me." He said it simply.

So simple in the scriptures. Madmen and lepers were simply cured and went their way. Whores repented. Sons returned. Or not. But Judas didn't come back to the Supper.

Otto heard him weeping. Slowly, everyone in the big room let go the nightmares of the day and slipped into nightmares they prayed wouldn't be worse.

The following morning, they found the corpse of Protective Prisoner Number 21935, Father Gerd Lienhard, kneeling at the fence at the northwest corner of the camp, by the gate to the crematorium. He burnt hands were spread wide, fused to the electric wire, his head thrown back and his mouth rictused wide, as if imploring mercy of the leaden sky.

* * * * *

Monday, 7 July 1941 – KZ Dachau

Tonight Paul and Otto sat at the short street-end wall of Barrack 26, watching through the barbed wire prisoners taking their evening shuffle along the poplared main camp street. Most of them must have had sitting jobs in the plantation, trying to remind their legs how to move.

"I've been thinking of what you were saying a couple days ago," Paul said, "about keeping my sanity by forcing my mind off myself. So I was yoked today with a young guy from Breslau. Almost finished gymnasium, wanted to go to university, but he changed his mind. Then he got arrested at an underground meeting of would-be communists. In here, he's more sure than ever that he wants to be a red. That there's got to be some reason besides God–what he called the sonofabitch God. Really smart kid. Hasn't read that much, but he really kept undermining my defenses. And all I had was seminary answers. We just took God for granted. And we just assumed we'd go out to parishes and serve people who took God for granted, too. But this kid was coming from his guts. And I was helpless. He thinks everybody is a stupid *Scheiss* anyway."

"He's got a point."

"Especially people who get a quote, phony-goddamn education, unquote."

"That's why all the Polish priests are here. Because they defied the Slav nature and got educated. Don't you realize that kid's most of the world, Paul? They don't really *like* 'book people.' We make them feel...inadequate. Most of the human race works with their hands, not with their minds. By far most of them can't read or spell or make a budget. But they instinctively want to *feel* like they're not worthless. Not just 'there'–and then suddenly disposable."

Otto chuckled. "Now there's an irony, right? This place can make us better priests! People like your friend never read Nietzsche, but their minds are saturated with his ideas. And in here, we priests are brought down to the bare essentials, too! The barest! It's a chance to force ourselves to learn the way they do. The best of them are just trying to stay human. Without the slightest notion of what Christianity really means. Except that, somehow, it's good for their children. And it gives them the feeling of belonging to something really big. But now the Nazis satisfy that. They have the vestments and the parades and the hymns. And the commies do, too. What do we have to offer that they don't? Surely not the *Ipsum Esse Subsistens*."

"All right. What then?"

"You offer them who you are. Just by the way you 'carry yourself,' how you react to unexpected challenges, the things you don't let get to you. Making them suspect you just might know something they don't. Your sense of peace. Despite this hell. Having a center. A soul. That's much more important to them than what you know. Augustine said, '*Fac tibi aequalem.*'"

"Make him my equal?"

"And vice versa. Which may be much more important. And more difficult."

"You think I have a chance with this kid?

"Making him smile might be a good place to start. Real commies are too serious. So are true Nazis, yes?" He giggled. "And more than a few professional Catholics!"

"But how can I win over all that passion, Otto? He's so enthusiastic. So genuine."

"If anyone could, you could. But I don't know whether you should, Paul."

"What? Isn't that what we're *for*?"

"Paul, that boy's conviction's been building for years now. And right now he's got *hold* of it. Or, again, maybe vice versa. But that fierce *anger* against the rich and the know-it-alls is what galvanizes that boy's soul! It's not very likely you're going to gradually work him round so he completely replaces the *Manifesto* with the Sermon on the Mount, true? Not in a few chance encounters on the Moor Express."

Paul didn't answer.

"No matter what you or I think about communism, it's what keeps that boy living, Paul. Even if it happens to be dead wrong, do you want to take that away from him?"

"You're going to drive me crazy."

"Or in the other direction."

* * * * *

Sunday, 21 September 1941 - Dachau

Paul Reiser had a cold. The weather had taken a quick turn in a couple of days, like a magic lantern snapping from balmy green mornings to brisk flame-colored days edged in frost. The clothes stores had not yet issued overcoats, since there had been no snowfall, and prisoners would wear them out too quickly. Warm clothing was needed far more by the brave men who, in a mere three months, had pushed 400 miles into the Soviet Union on a 1000-mile front from the Baltic to the Black Sea and were about to overwhelm both Leningrad and Moscow.

Paul followed the line of thermos carriers into the camp kitchens, enormous caverns of steam from shining, bubbling vats of turnip soup and rows of billowing sinks. The tile floors were slick with moisture, and carriers had to learn to glide along on their hard wooden clogs as if ice skating in some surreal swamp.

Paul shivered in the heavy heat, the iron cold in his body repelling the welcome warmth. He waited in line with the rest of the Thermos Kommando, which was now reserved for priests and homosexuals. He was relieved to pair with Teddy Kolocek, a young Bohemian priest nearly his size. The slippery floors were a menace. If he fell, he was not only scalded, but the spilled soup had to be made up from the thermoses intended for his own barrack.

A long row of boilers divided the groups, and while they advanced up the line, Paul angled his head to read the barrack numbers chalked on the dark sides. Block 10-IIA. Fairly close, around the square and only a third of the way up the street.

Paul and Teddy snatched off their striped caps and wrapped them around the sharp handles and picked up the thermos. Their arm muscles went taut as cables at a weight either one of them could have lifted alone without much difficulty outside.

Suddenly, the feet of the man behind Kolocek rocketed out from under him and he fell, shooting his wooden-clogged feet up, sending Kolocek reeling sideways. Instinctively, Paul wrapped his arms around the thermos, feeling the weight down into his guts, and lowered it with a thud. The lid held, and no soup spilled. On his knees, Paul leaned over it trying to get his breath.

"Teddy, are you all right?"

Kolocek's face was vised in pain. "My elbow," he grunted.

Boetger, the Thermos Kapo, pushed from the back and booted the man who had fallen back to his feet. Boetger was a big man with a mashed nose and a thicket of hair frothing from the scoop of his singlet across his shoulders. Sweat dripped from his crumpled nose.

"Can't you goddamn priests stand on your two goddamn feet?" He looked down at Kolocek. "What the hell's wrong?"

"My elbow."

"Goddammit! 'Zit broken?"

"I...I don't think so."

"Well, get over t' the goddamn infirmary and find out."

"No, please, Kapo Boetger," Kolocek winced. "I'm fine. I don't need the infirmary."

"Right. Get your ass over to the goddamn infirmary."

Kolocek got up, gritting his teeth against the pain in his arm yet obviously more terrified of the nursing Kapo, Heiden, than of a broken arm. Hunching his shoulders over the elbow cupped in his hand, he moved reluctantly toward the door.

Boetger looked around for a replacement. He whistled through his splayed teeth at a prisoner bent over the steaming dishtubs. "Hey, you!" he barked. "Fairy! Over here and pick up this goddamn thermos with Blondi."

Paul grunted to his feet, his head heavy with congestion and steam. He sighed resignedly. The prisoner from the dishtubs was young, but at least three inches shorter than he.

The dishwasher was most likely some Kapo's favorite. Dark hair curled unshaven under the edges of his cap. On his uniform jacket, two overlapped triangles, one pink and one black, formed a star with an imprinted "J." Poor bastard. Homosexual, criminal, and Jew. The boy said in a quiet, frightened voice, "I was told I'd work only in the kitchen, Herr Kapo Boetger."

Paul jerked his head at the young man's voice. Herschel Gruenwald.

"Well," Boetger sneered and pursed his boxer jaw close to the sallow face with its ferny lashes. "Your 'Daddy' ain't here, now, *Pueppschen*," he minced sourly. "Pick up the goddamn thermos, eh? Before I bury my boot up the goddamn tool o' your trade?"

Obediently, Herschel walked over next to Paul and removed his cap. He looked steadily at Paul and said, "Ready?"

"Yes," Paul said.

They lifted the heavy thermos and moved cautiously toward the door. The two steps outside were always a danger. They had to strain their ropy muscles to lift the container so the bottom didn't catch on the stairs. Their bodies were sheened in sweat, and the wind encased them in cold. Their hair steamed in the open air.

"Herschel," Paul began.

"Wait," Herschel hissed back at him.

When they got to the edge of the roll call square, Herschel began to speak in the camp whisper, looking straight ahead.

"I wasn't afraid of the work, you know. I've been...I've been lucky. I've kept up my strength. I...I was afraid of you. Of you...knowing. You're a priest now."

"Deacon. Supposed to be last Christmas. But I was arrested."

"Ah," Herschel snorted, "weren't we all?" He turned to peer at Paul's chest. "Political."

"And you?"

Herschel turned his head and looked almost pityingly at Paul under his fine dark brows.

"I'm sorry, Herschel," Paul whispered.

"Don't be. At least I've got a marketable skill. For as long as it lasts." His small mouth arced down. "I hear the priests have it fairly easy."

"Most comfortable part of hell all to ourselves."

"Odd, isn't it?" Herschel chuckled. "Nietzsche was right all along. In the end, we all get the same reward in this shithole life. Saint and sinner, priest and faggot. We all get screwed in the end." He looked grimly over at Paul. "Sorry. Tasteless."

The Kapo of 10 IIA waited at the doorway. He jerked his head at two pals and they took the thermos inside. Paul and Herschel put their caps back on and shivered in the alley between barracks, their arms wrapped around themselves, waiting for the thermos to be emptied.

They looked uneasily at one another, unsure of what to say.

"I'm grateful," Herschel said quietly.

"For what, Herschel?"

"No 'Poor Herschel, how could you sink so low?'"

Paul smiled sadly over at him. "Am I any better? Accomplished thief, myself. Also as adept at charming lies as the best traveling salesman in Germany." He coughed heavily and spat.

"Not quite the same, is it?"

Paul looked away. "No. I don't suppose it is."

"Pays very well," Herschel said, "food, schnaps, tobacco. Protection. And the guarantee– for awhile-you won't get shipped off someplace else."

"For awhile."

"On *The Titanic*, why go steerage?" His breath hazed the air around his sleek face. "My family got to Palestine, you know." He scowled. "I thought they'd been killed. If I'd known.... But they're safe. That's worth it. I think. Sometimes. I've paid their passage by offering myself on the bloody altars of the vindictive old *El Shaddai*. One takes the absurdity he's dealt."

"You said, 'For awhile.'"

The Kapo's two pals delivered the empty thermos, and they doffed their caps to pick it up. They lugged the heavy container toward the street and turned right, back toward the kitchens.

"My God, Paul," Herschel whispered indulgently, "for as long as it lasts. How long have you been in the camps?"

"Nearly two years."

"And you don't know the life of a camp faggot?"

"Well, in a way...."

"There's only one way out, Paulli. For all of us. Up the chimney. But it's an enviable life for awhile—relatively. Once you accept the madness. Like those men in the Greek myths who were king for a year and then sacrificed to the fertility gods. Gods like old *El Shaddai*."

They got to the roll call square and, by force of habit, crossed to the left and around it, making themselves less tempting to the bored guards at the tower machine guns.

"I didn't ask to be bent, you know, Paul-any more than I asked to be a Jew. Ask your God about that sometime, would you?"

"You still haven't told me how long 'awhile' can last, Herschel."

"Well, I'm quite lucky at the moment, you see. Nice old Kapo with a conscience problem about using the Polack kids. But he's got to have it, you see? And I'm only making my living in here the way I did outside, eh? But I see him looking over the newcomers like an old peasant mama checking chickens in a market. If he finds somebody a little less...'used'? *Auf Wiedersehen*, Herschel. Hand me off to somebody he lost to in a card game."

"Oh, my God, Herschel."

"Then, it's 'awhile' with the new one. Then the rocker. That's when 'awhile' stops."

"'The rocker'?"

They got into the line at the door, and Herschel looked over at Paul's handsome, sad face.

"'The rocker,' my priest. You really travel in nicer circles. The patron comes back when he's found a new *Pueppel*, takes the old doll into his cubicle, does what he wants, then the rocker. Lays the miserable fucker on the floor, puts his billy club across the poor bastard's throat, and puts his two feet on either side. And then he does a seesaw." They were nearly up to the door. "Standard practice, Paulli. When they don't want to see their protegés pampered by anyone else."

"Hersch-...," Paul said, "I'm sorry."

"I'm not bitter, Paulli," Herschel grinned. "You can only be bitter when you think things could be better. Goodbye, Paul."

* * * * *

Sunday, 5 October 1941 – KZ Dachau

Paul lay stretched out on the lower bunk, exhausted, and Pfizer sat on the floor, his back against the upright. On Sunday afternoon, there was no work. The others either lay on a shelf, staring at nothing, or walked in a circle within the inner wire around the barrack. Alone or with a trusted friend or two.

"I think I could kill Shütze Waldek. If I had the strength. A lousy private who thinks he's Napoleon because he's got a uniform. He's a sadist. "

"There's been a rash of that. You just noticed?"

"That new French priest. I don't remember his name. Skinny. The one with the taped bombsight glasses. Some kind of scholar. I don't know in what. But whatever it is, he doesn't know any down-to-earth German. So he's at the back of the wagon. And he falls. And Waldek starts screaming orders, and the Frenchman has no idea what he's telling him to do. So Waldek starts banging this French priest's head with his club. And the man's glasses fall off. And Waldek —grinning, mind you—stomps his boot heel on the glasses. Purposely. And breaks them. Where's he going to get another pair of glasses like that in here? Waldek is out-and-out wicked."

"Not wicked, Paul. Just dumb."

"Because he's uneducated?"

"No, no. You've surely known men...friends of your father maybe...who have doctoral degrees but thicker skins than bulls. Professionals who treat their secretaries like slaves and their wives like brood mares and their daughters like investments." Otto chuckled. "I had a few learned seminary professors who used to treat the annual oral exams like sadistic games. People who sneer at shopgirls and tram conductors. How could Waldek intend you evil when you're not really real to him? Not like his mother. Or his dog. He's too dumb to qualify for evil, Paul, just utterly self-absorbed. No perspective. Listen to me ramble! I'm the novice master again!"

"That's why I pay your exorbitant fees." He knitted his brow. "But he's just a kid. How can he be so inhuman? He must have some kind of a conscience."

"Did you ever realize we're the only animals who feel the need to apologize. No tiger gets guilt feelings about being cruel. Humans do. At least good humans do. Bad humans never confess. That's how you tell the difference. Conscience isn't inborn, Paul. Just the potential."

"And we have to choose to turn it on?"

"Like your own potential to have children. You chose not to activate it."

"But they *must* know right from wrong. Even little children know that."

"They've been *told* right from wrong. I assume Hitler memorized his catechism. He probably rattled it off to get confirmed. Didn't do much good, did it?

"So it's original sin."

"That's one clumsy way to explain why. The devil's another way. But neither one's quite good enough, is it? The Adam-and-Eve story depends on a God who holds grudges longer than he allows us to. And the devil's just a scapegoat. Freud, too, in a way. Laying the guilt off on your parents and your weaning. Potty training? Did you ever read Darwin?"

"I stood with Lisl in the square outside the Muenster library and watched him burn. That's the closest I got. We were forbidden to read it."

"In the seminary we had that, too. Darwin was there in the library, but surrounded by a wall of chicken wire with all the other dangerous books, just like we priests are here. To keep poison from the unwary. The faculty could get in there, if the rector gave permission. It was called 'Hell.'"

"What about Darwin? Wasn't he in the Index? With Voltaire. And Descartes?"

"I don't think the Index ever got to Darwin. So after ordination, the Society sent me to the university for a year to study psychology. So I wouldn't twist the psyches of my novices too much. Well, it was like a reprieve into 'Hell.' I devoured all the forbidden fruit–Darwin, Freud, Nietzsche. The lot. Wondrous! But," he chuckled, "quite disappointing in a way. They were nowhere near as corrupting as we'd been told. I was a bit disappointed."

"And what has Darwin and your university sins got to do with Schütze Waldek?"

"Suppose...just suppose that what we call original sin wasn't caused by two dimwit nudists who fell for a fast-talking snake. What if God gave a cortex and freedom to a tribe of apes that wasn't really ready for it. On *purpose*. Like giving a pistol to a chimpanzee. Sin was absolutely inevitable. It makes for much more interesting stories."

"But," Paul took a deep breath and blew it out. "But *why?*"

"Ah, my young friend, you've just hit on *the* question of all questions! That's where every thinker from Buddha to Karl Marx started. If you haven't started there, you haven't started."

"It scrambles my brains. They never asked questions like this in the seminary. It was all just...there. True. Unquestionable."

"Because they simply accepted–even the very brightest–that it was the nudists and the snake. And if it baffles you now, with all your learning, think what it would do to Schütze Woldek's brains. If he was capable of even allowing it through his defenses."

"So our problem is worse because we were taught to *think?*"

"Exactly. Like Job. He wasn't bitching his boils or his dead children or the wife who told him to curse God and die! The instinct to survive in any other animal could drag itself through that. But not the human animal. Job was cursing God for betraying their *friendship*."

"So, it's easier if you don't believe."

"If you don't mind feeling meaningless. I think most people settle for meaningless. Sad. As I said, I suspect they just tread water, and tread water, and then they die.

"Since Waldek was an infant, Paul, everybody in his life told him to shut up and obey. His papa. His teacher. His pastor. His pope. His *Wandervogel* leader. His boss. His wife! So now the government says,

'You're *drafted*!' He comes, obedient. He's sent to a place like this and told to herd men like cattle. What happens to the schoolyard bully when the headmaster's a bully, too? He obeys. <u>What else can anybody expect?</u>"

"You Jesuits are supposed to be the obedient ones."

Pfizer grinned impishly. "We're supposed to be. Ignatius wanted us docile as an old man's cane. Or a corpse. Did you hear the story that Himmler laid out the S.S. modeled on the Jesuits? We take vows; they make a cast-iron oath to the Fuehrer. Even for someone who despises them, their rallies are as moving as midnight Mass–and a hundred times bigger. You could probably make the case that National Socialism is Catholicism without the Christianity."

"You're giving me something to busy my head with at work tomorrow, aren't you?"

"And that's what bothered me about obedience–even with Father Ignatius. Maybe it was that year of eating forbidden fruit in the university library. I could never find a place in the scriptures where Jesus told us to be sheep. To him, but no one else. Be shepherds, like him. So I always had trouble when I came to explain that vow to my novices. I just couldn't bring myself to make a virtue of being brain-dead. So when I came to obedience I rambled and flubbed long enough that I could move on to poverty, which is a lot easier to feel guilty about. You can only feel rebellious when you're absolutely convinced the one giving the order is wrong."

"So you're saying I don't have to obey Jesus when he says to love my enemies. I don't have to force myself to wish the very best for Waldek instead of wanting to strangle him?"

"Ah, you're a devious one! Look, Paul. What would happen if you could challenge Waldek. Man to man. Mind to mind. You ask how the hell can he treat human beings worse than he'd treat his neighbor's nasty cat. At first, he gives you this blank stare. Just like an ox. Then–if he can even find the words for it–he says, 'Look! I don't have your fancy goddamn university degrees! I didn't learn all your fancy goddam ways of thinking! I do my best with what I got, see! And what I got is a bitch of a wife and three hungry kids. And besides, if I didn't do it, somebody else by-God *would*! So piss off!' If there's no connection inside, to a God who *must* have reasons, then he's got no real motive at all, for *any* choice, except to keep from getting hurt, to take care of his own, and the rest of the world be damned."

"Okay. Then how could a good God...?

149

"Right. God must have thought giving freedom was worth the awful risk. What works for me is that, without freedom, there'd be no stories. Just wild beasts tearing at one another. We take hold of our souls by climbing over obstacles. Or, at the other end, without freedom you'd have automatons smiling at one another all day long, helplessly. Wouldn't that drive you mad? And without freedom...could there be real loving, if we had no choice?"

"You're saying putting up with evil is worth it to have love?"

"Father Ecke gives half his bread to Stoffels, who's seventy-five and not likely to last the month. I can't explain wickedness very well. But I can't explain that very well either."

"So in order to have love, I have to accept everything Waldek is."

"Or go mad. That's the other choice."

* * * * *

Wednesday, 24 December 1941 - KZ Dachau

Kap Prabutski was doing jumping jacks in his underwear on the frozen roll call square, trying to keep from freezing himself. The seven hundred Polish priests of Barrack 28 were now segregated like contaminants from their German and Austrian fellow clergy in 26. They were forbidden the chapel and forced to a kind of Mass in secret with wine and hosts slipped to them from 26. At the moment, the others were also jumping or skipping or beating their shoulders with their fists when the cold began to get to them again. Except the old ones. Some were lying on the ground–most likely freed.

Kap had counted about twenty here and there, sprawled at the feet of men sagging or skipping awkwardly in place in the lines, nearly as dead-faced, trying to concentrate only on living. No one was allowed to pick up the dead until delousing was over. It was probably about noon. They had begun at six a.m.

One of the worst days was delousing. In the winter, for many, it was the last day of all. It was essential, of course. The only sign in KZ Dachau that told the truth said: "One Louse Means Death." In the evening just before they fell exhausted into their places, men found as many as a hundred lice on their bodies. But some were careless. Or resigned. In the night, pressed together three to a bunk-shelf now, the men shared their body heat, their breaths, and their vermin.

Also, the inmates now worked in far greater numbers in factories essential to the war effort. Some were trucked out each day; others had been transferred to satellite camps. BMW employed 4,000 Dachau prisoners. Four Messerschmidt factories accounted for 5,600 more. With so many men in the services, manpower was essential to the war effort.

Manpower meant money. A prisoner-bookkeeper in the Labor Office had found a record showing just how valuable in Reichsmarks each of these worthless men was to the Third Reich.

Daily rental of prisoner	+ RM 6.00
Deduction for food	- RM .60
Deduction for use of clothes	- RM .10
	————
Value of prisoner per day	+ RM 5.30
x Usual lifespan (270 days) =	+ RM 1,431.00
Average proceeds from rational disposal of corpse (fillings, clothes, bones, valuables held by bursar)	+ RM 200.00
	————
	+ RM 1,631.00
Cost of cremation	- RM 2.00
	————
Total value of prisoner	+ RM 1,629.00 [2010: $651.60]

A paltry sum, but multiplied by 15 million, considerable. Some prisoners, of course, had little staying power and thus were not as valuable as others. Those from Eastern occupied territories, because they were racially closer to beasts, had more stamina than cultivated prisoners from Western Europe. On October 29, however, five hundred thirty more Polish priests had arrived, most older, and as a result of a hunger cure prescribed for The Itch, eighty had died within a week. It was further proof, many said, that unlike their hardier fellow countrymen priests were softened by their parasitic lives.

In 1941, 2,576 men had died in KZ Dachau, which was a ludicrous waste of manpower. This, coupled with the wartime shortage of food and the enormous cost of feeding the inmates persuaded the camp authorities to allow prisoners to receive food and clothing from home so camp expenditures could be further curtailed. Workers needed to keep up their strength.

The previous week, however, an appeal had come directly from the Fuehrer himself that prisoners donate their excess warm underwear from their families for the brave young men who were struggling under such harsh conditions on the Eastern Front. Block Senior Gehrke had admonished his charges, "We must outdo the other barracks in this voluntary effort. Those who donate generously will have their patriotism noted in their permanent files. Those who don't will get a taste of my billy club." The prisoners had been most generous.

The exercises Kap Prabutski was forcing on himself now were not punishment. They were a matter of life and death. Six hours ago they had left their clothing, shoes, and blankets in the barrack to be picked up by Kapo Pfeifer and his Delousing Kommando and taken to the delousing barrack at the northeast corner of the enclosure. Then the priests were herded, double-time, down the wide camp street barefoot and in their underwear to the shower room in the basement of the administration building. Once inside, they began to tremble in the warmth as they shed their underwear. Then they were driven under the showers which scalded their skin, unless the Kapo at the controls was feeling playful, and told to scour their skinny bodies, especially armpits, crotches, and rectums, where the vermin were most likely to nest.

Then, without being allowed to dry themselves, they put on fresh underwear and trotted up the stairs and out onto the parade ground to wait. The temperature was thirty-six degrees.

All the priests of 28 had long since finished their showers. The delay was caused by the fact their uniforms were not yet dry. Long ago, prisoners suggested they might wait in the relative warmth of the barrack, but the authorities were convinced that would encourage malingering. Besides, the chemicals used to fumigate the rooms might be hazardous to their health.

Finally, one of Kapo Pfeifer's men came sauntering along the street, across the square, and up the walk to the administration building where Kapo Gehrke was watching the priests of his barrack from inside the warm vestibule. He came out, dismissed them, and sent a priest in his underwear to get a Moor Express wagon for the corpses. It would take several trips. As Kap hurried as quickly as he could down the street, trying to support an old priest whose name he couldn't even remember, the thought struck him that this was Christmas Eve.

As he got to the gate of the enclosure around the priests' barracks, he was stopped by a young SS corporal. Kap handed the old priest to someone else and turned to the boy. He had a bland round face with frightened slits of blue eyes.

"Father?" the boy said, looking quickly to right and left.

"Yes, Herr Sturmmann?"

"A German father told me I should see you.

Kap shifted from one foot to another, shivers rippling across his back and down his spine.

"Yes."

"Tomorrow is Christmas, Father."

"Yes, I know, Herr Sturmmann."

"I'm on duty all day, Father. I can't get into town. What will I do about Mass?"

Kap shook his head wearily and looked into the boy's anxious eyes. "I can dispense you, my son. Be at peace. Now, if you don't...."

"That German father I spoke with said the Poles have a secret Mass."

Kap's eyes narrowed. "What priest told you that?"

"He was a very nice looking priest. That's why I asked him. He had white hair like pictures of God. He said it would be too unsafe to come into the German priests' Mass. They might lose their chapel."

Kap's long face sagged with fatigue. God! Lutz! It was too risky. More than a few SS promotions came from luring priests into giving them instructions or hearing their confessions.

"I'm sorry, son," Kap sighed. "You know the rules. The German priests might lose their chapel, but I'd lose my life. Please. Understand. I don't mean to be ungenerous. I can dispense you from your obligation to attend Mass on the holy day."

"But I wouldn't feel right."

"I'm sorry. Please. I'm...I'm nearly frozen, Herr Sturmmann."

The boy turned and walked away.

Kap hurried to the doorway of 1-A and scurried along the aisles of bunks to his clothes. He got into them as quickly as he could and wrapped his damp blanket around his quaking shoulders. All over the room, men huddled, chafing their arms and legs, stamping their feet in their damp bindings. The fortunate ones were shrouded in their thin overcoats.

There was a hammering on the door. Pray God the noon soup would still be warm.

It was not the noon meal. An SS sergeant banged open the door and stood in the latrine, glaring into the two apartments to the right and then into the two to the left of it. "Where's the head Polack priest?" he shouted.

Prabutski pushed through the shivering bodies to the latrine. "I am Protective Prisoner 22319, Herr Scharfuehrer," he said. "Prabutski, Paul. I am chaplain of the Polish priest prisoners."

"You're wanted for questioning in the *Jourhaus*." He turned on his heel and went out into the frozen alleyway. With his blanket still around his shoulders, Kap followed him.

They walked quickly down the Street, Prabutski following the regulation six feet behind. They crossed the square to the gatehouse and mounted the stairs to the Political Section, the Gestapo. The sergeant pointed to a door and turned back down the stairs. Kap knocked and entered.

The office was warm, and the tension in Kap's muscles began to relax. His skin burned. Behind the desk was a young man in an elegantly tailored, double-breasted grey pinstripe suit. His close-cropped hair was blond, his face was ruddy and lean, and his wolf's eyes glanced up.

"If you tell me where your weapons are hidden," the young Gestapo man said, "we can get this over quickly."

Kap's long jaw lolled, and he stared at the stern face. "I..." He had no idea what to say.

"I can see you're surprised you've been found out."

"I don't know what to say, Herr...."

"'Herr Inspector' will do."

"Herr Inspector, my astonishment is about the charges. I swear to you, we have no weapons whatever in our barrack."

"I didn't suspect you did. Where are they hidden?"

"Herr Inspector," Kap said, his mind in a whirl, "there are no weapons. I know of no weapons whatever. I swear to you."

The smoke-blue eyes narrowed under the pale brows. "We are very well informed here, priest. There is to be a Polish uprising."

Kap tried to get a deep breath but couldn't. "Herr Inspector, you must believe me. I know nothing of any uprising."

The young man pushed his chair back. "Metz!" he shouted, and rose to his feet. A uniformed SS corporal opened the door and snapped to attention, "Yes, Herr Oberleutnant!"

The slim young lieutenant came around the desk and went to a fur-collared coat on the clothes tree by the door. "He claims to know nothing. Take him to the shower room. And be quick about it. I have a luncheon engagement in town."

The bottom fell out of Prabutski's stomach. The shower room meant the *Pfahl*.

The corporal pushed him down the stairs and out into the square, prodding him with his truncheon. Kap heard another pair of boots fall in behind them. They crossed the parade ground and into a side door of the administration building, down to the basement, past the storerooms and into the shower room. Prabutski's head was reeling and his empty stomach was a bag of acid.

The enormous cinderblock room which Kap had left hours before, soaked and shivering, was steaming and silent. Down the center, arches stretched from pillar to pillar. Overhead, perforated water pipes snaked back and forth, suspended from the ceiling. Only one light was burning, like a single lamp on a darkened street. Behind him, Kap could hear the metal guards on the inspector's heels echoing through the puddles.

"All right," the young inspector snapped at the corporal and looked irritably at his watch, "I said be quick about it."

Kap, tall and rangy, began to tremble. The man who had joined them was the bland-faced boy who had stopped him at the enclosure and asked him about Mass. Kap's eyes pleaded with him, but the boy stood impassively, his eyes dull as grapes, waiting for his orders.

Sturmmann Metz slipped behind the tall priest. Kap could feel the man's hands as they pulled his arms behind him. They were soft, like his mother's. The piano wire the corporal wound between the knuckles of Kap's thumbs broke the skin. Then, deftly, he threw the coil of wire up over the shower pipes. He and the other boy pulled with all their might.

Kap screamed.

In horrific jerks, the two young men hauled him up until his feet were a foot off the floor. His wooden clogs dropped off, and the lieutenant kicked them irritably out of the way. The two non-coms tied off the end of the wire on the iron wheel valve which turned on the showers.

Kap hung in agony, his arms high above him behind his back, like some bird paralyzed in flight. His long stringy biceps seemed to be ripping apart, sinew by sinew. His shoulder joints wrenched convulsively, and suddenly everything went black, even though he knew he was ferociously conscious. The blood thrummed hotly in his temples. His vision cleared, and his bulging eyes glared down at the fine lean face of the young Gestapo agent. Kap's scrawny chest felt as if it were banded in steel, and he couldn't get enough breath to scream again.

"I will be back in one half-hour," the lieutenant said. "Your recollection will improve."

Their footsteps echoed out along the puddled floor. Kap dangled in agony, turning slowly, dizzily. His thumbs and shoulders were being torn from the sockets. He vomited thin streams of bile, and it spattered down the chest of his cleaned uniform. Each retch was like a lash.

"God!" he gasped. "God!"

He hovered at the edge of unconsciousness. He prayed to die. Pain shrieked across his whole upper body. After a few moments, he heard boots echoing softly along the cement floor. He tried to angle his savaged neck muscles in the direction of the noise, but he could see only a few feet away. Then he saw the long dark sheaths of boots. They had changed their minds!

But no. It was the round-faced corporal.

"Thank God," Kap gasped. "Son, please. Get me down."

The face looked dumbly up at him. "Father," he said, almost reproachfully, "I couldn't."

"Son, I beg you," Kap pleaded. He didn't want to weep. "I beg you."

The boy stood taller. "I have to follow my orders, Father. I'm a soldier."

Oh, Jesus, Kap prayed. Oh, Jesus! He began to weep quietly, the pain consuming him. "Then why...," he croaked, "why have you come back?"

"It's Christmas Eve, Father. I was so worried about Mass."

Oh, my God, my God, the voice inside Kap screamed. What have we done to them? He looked through his tears at the earnest young face looking worriedly up at him. Prabutski almost wanted to laugh at the boy. No more awareness of another human being than an ape. But all Kap could do was whimper. "Son," he rasped, "only one Person ever said Mass in this position."

The boy's face was like a child's whose mother has just said she no longer loved him. "I thought," he said tentatively, "you might please say some prayers from Mass. I'd feel better."

All the pain had coalesced into one pain, vising his head and his shoulders and his arms and his back. Kap gritted his teeth against it. He tried to relax. He forced himself to stop crying. Either the pain would end, or he would die.

"Could...," he choked. "Could you wipe my face, please, son? Then I'll ... I'll try."

The boy pulled out a grey handkerchief from his back pocket and, straining on his tiptoes, wiped the priest's eyes. Then his mouth. The boy's face soured at the smell of the vomit, and, when he finished, he hurled the fetid handkerchief away from him. Each time the boy touched him, Kap swung, sending the pain torpedoing along every nerve of his body. He tried to calm himself. He tried to distance the pain from him.

"*Intro—....*"He gasped. "*Introibo ad...altare Dei.*" The boy's face beamed up at him. And he responded proudly, in his altar boy's Latin, "*Ad Deum, qui laetificat juventutem meam.*"

"Judge me, O God," Kap whispered, continuing the Latin prayers. "Take up my cause against pitiless people. From the treacherous and the cunning, rescue me!"

And the boy quickly gave the Latin response to the psalm, "Because you, O God, are my shelter. Why do you abandon me? Why must I walk so mournfully, oppressed by the enemy?"

The boy looked expectantly up at the priest, dangling in his grey striped rags, waiting for the next part of the prayers at the foot of the altar he remembered so well and fondly.

But Kap had fainted.

He drifted in some nowhere place, his ears echoing with the plaintive voices of the psalms he had read nearly every day of his adult life. It was the voice of the Jews, blundering across the vastnesses of the wilderness. The voice of David.

"Lay aside your scourge," the voice inside him moaned. "I am worn out with the blows you deal me. You punish men with the penalties of sin. Like a moth you eat away all that gives men pleasure! A man is no more than a puff of wind to You! O God! Hear my prayer! I am your guest, and only for a time, a nomad like all my ancestors. Take your eyes off of me! Let me draw a breath! Before I go away and am no more!"

Somewhere in the distance, he heard another voice. It sounded like the young soldier's voice. "I'm sorry, Father." Then Kap sank down into the black broth and everything was peace.

When he came to, he realized from the musty odor and the sounds of sleep he was back in his corner of the barrack, and someone, in kindness, had given him a whole space on the rough shelving for himself, on a lower bunk near the door to the latrine. Stan Bednarski. As he lay there, aching in every joint and shivering against the cold, he was sorry they had. He would have welcomed the warmth of other men's bodies and breath. He had no idea how long he'd been unconscious. But it was night. It was Christmas.

Suddenly, he was aware of someone standing next to the shelves in the darkness. He tried to crane his neck upward, but the pain was too much. There was a creak and the smell of leather as a man squatted down next to the shelf. The SS boy..

"Father," he whispered, and even in the dark, even with his head paralyzed at an angle where he could see only the boy's eyes, Kap knew that he was smiling proudly. "The *greatest* luck! I have some wine in a cup," he said. "And some bread."

"I'm sorry," Kap wheezed. "I can't even sit up."

"I'll hold you," the boy said, and reached his strong young hands around Kap's shoulders.

The pain rocketed up through his brain and, for a moment, he passed out again, but the boy patted his cheeks lightly, and Kap reentered the pain.

So, there in the darkness and the gibbering silence, in that dead end of lost hope, Kap Prabutski, chaplain to the German Army and to the Polish Army, cradled in the strong arms of a young SS trooper who a few hours before—or yesterday?–had helped to string him up like a sheep for shearing, began again to mutter the prayers of the Mass.

There were no readings from the scripture, but it took nearly an hour. Sometimes, the corporal had to stop him and remind Kap he was repeating himself. Several times, the boy had to keep patting the priest's face back to consciousness.

Finally, it was done. Kap gasped, "*Ite. Missa est.*"

The boy whispered, "Thank you, Father."

Kap strained his neck and looked at the boy's stupid, beaming face, streaked with tears.

"Happy Christmas, Father," the boy said. He lowered the priest slowly back onto the hard straw tick, and he blended away into the darkness.

Kap lay still, looking at the raw boards of the bunk above him. Suddenly, his body began to shudder with silent, quaking sobs. He so desperately yearned to be home.

The sobs gentled. His arms ached too much even to reach up and wipe his own face. He lay with the tears puddled in the sockets of his eyes.

Oh, God, he prayed. There's so much pain. Help me remember when there was joy.

It was a silent night. There were no angel voices. There were no voices at all.

* * * * *

1942

Sunday, 29 March 1942 - KZ Dachau

Paul Reiser had begun to cough blood again.

In January, Hauptsturmfuehrer Hoffmann, the new Camp Leader, in an inspection of his new fief, had paid a visit to the chapel in Barrack 26. When he saw the polished floor, the prisoners' art work decorating the walls, greenhouse flowers on the altar, he became enraged. He grasped the green felt antependium which one of the prisoners had liberated from confiscated stores and embroidered with the letters IHS, and pulled it off, sending flowers and candlesticks smashing to the floor. He tried to rip it and, when he was unable to, became even more furious and hurled it at Georg Schelling who had been forced to accompany him on the tour.

Schelling tried, diplomatically, to remind the new Lagerfuehrer that the chapel had been commissioned by Reichsfuehrer SS Himmler himself and was now a high spot on the tour given to distinguished visitors-between their visit to the museum and their inspection of the camp brothel.

Once he realized the Austrian priest was right and he was wrong, Hoffmann backhanded him across the face. All German priests went back on full work details, all extra rations canceled.

For the next two months, Paul had lumbered out with the others on the Snow Kommando and the Moor Express, from six in the morning until seven at night, ill clad, in icy winds. No matter what, he still insisted on giving half his rations to the Polish boys. Of the 1,300 from Lodz, 500 were still alive. Paul had grown paler. His cold rattled more deeply into his chest.

Today was Palm Sunday. Otto Pfizer leaned his back against a post in the barbed wire fence which separated his barrack from 28, talking in the camp whisper to Stan Bednarski, another Jesuit, from Cracow, his opposite number among the Polish priests.

"We had no choice but the infirmary, Stan."

"God help the poor lad in there," Bednarski said, shaking his head ruefully. "Did Heiden give him a rough time?"

Pfizer rubbed his deepset eyes with sinewy fingers. "Bloody godawful," he sighed. "Paul was so weak Schelling and I had to carry him. Heiden looked him over, said he was no worse than anybody else, and started battering his face. He kept saying, 'You sick, Blondi? You sick?' Then Paul hemorrhaged, and Heiden said, 'That's more like it,' and we got him into the ward."

"You couldn't keep him. It would spread like fleas."

"With the Dutch and Belgians coming in now, we're three in a bunk and men sleeping all over the chapel floor. Then Hoffmann found out and stopped it. He said we weren't going to turn Himmler's goddamn chapel into the goddamn stable at Bethlehem. If you follow the logic."

Bednarski folded his arms across his broad scrawny chest and put back his head against the pillar with a sigh. "You've heard they've been 'thinning us out,'" he asked.

"Only talk from Whisper."

"Have you lost any to the *Selektionen?*" Bednarski asked.

"Four, last time," Pfizer answered. "Three priests and a pastor. But weeks ago."

"We've lost a hundred and five."

"My God!" Pfizer gasped.

"There's a man in the Records Office who was a lay teacher in our school in Lublin, where Stefan Wielgoz was rector. He told Wielgoz that, since the second of January, they've taken nearly two thousand off from here–the weak ones—to Schloss Hartheim to be gassed."

"But none in weeks," Pfizer said, with a dubious flicker of hope in his voice.

"Probably just a shortage of trains. When things settle down in Russia, they'll be back for more. They won't feed men who can't work. Can you get in to see Reiser?"

"We have an infirmary orderly. Distributes Communion. French."

"See if he can get you in. Get Paul all the food you can round up. Tell him about the *Selektion* process. If they come around, tell him to pinch his face red. Stand straight. Tighten the buttocks. That's the giveaway. When the buttocks go slack."

"Peuleve-our Frenchman-says they may leave TB patients here. They're experimenting with drugs and placebos. That boy's not going to die, Stan."

"Reiser's been good to the boys from Lodz. If we can help, let me know. When can you get in to see him?"

"Peuleve says end of the week. Things will slacken because so many SS have Easter leave. Not many risk the TB ward anyway, even on orders."

"Ask him to find out what he can about the experiments."

"The Doktor Rascher business? A Top Secret barrack. Something to do with the war."

"Rascher's got twenty of ours. The young ones. The healthiest. Three days."

"They're experimenting on human...," Pfizer cocked his head around the post.

"Finding ways to save airmen when their cabins are breached at high altitudes. Pressure drops. No oxygen. He has a kind of box. They put a man in a flying suit in the box, with an oxygen mask. Pump all the air out. Turn off the oxygen. Record the results. Minute by minute."

"My God, they could do that with animals!"

Bednarski faced Barrack 28 again. "Polacks are cheaper. Slavs are meant to be slaves. Simple as original sin. There's a malaria trial, too, where they cover the men's crotches with infected mosquitos. And they also inject some with pus, to make boils, to test a new Bayer drug called sulfa. And that doctor is a Pole, too! Fialkovski. The infirmary Kapo said priests ought to be pleased to volunteer. For the health of human- ity."

He pushed away from the post and paced, hands on his skinny hips, thick lips pressed furiously together. Finally, he put his folded hands against the post and laid his forehead on them.

"Did you ever want to kill, Otto?" he whispered.

"Yes."

For a moment neither spoke.

"But we both know, Stan. The experiments will go on. With one less to sabotage them."

Bednarski snorted. "Well, there's a bright side to these experiments, you know. If a man survives for a half-hour, they revive him. And he gets a reprieve."

"They release him?"

"No. His sentence is commuted from death to life imprisonment."

They began to chuckle. But Bednarski's eyes slowly filled with tears. "Keep making me laugh, Otto," he whispered. "For the love of God, make me laugh."

Suddenly there was a tapping on the window facing Bednarski. He turned and looked up at a young seminarian there, jerking his thumb to his left, toward the street.

"Trouble," Bednarski said and pushed away from the post.

He and Pfizer ambled toward the end of the alleyway and pressed cautiously against the fence, peering to their right, down the wide street toward the administration building.

An SS lieutenant was leading a platoon of twenty guards the length of the street. A few respectful paces behind the lieutenant, Kapo Schreiber strode proudly. Schreiber was a kind of Kapo-at-Large, squat, powerfully muscled, to ferret out information either with his network of spies or through his skills at causing pain. At the time of the Russian invasion, Schreiber had been reprieved to train for a tank division, but he was found incapable of passing the intelligence tests. Besides, he told his few cronies among the Black-patch criminals, he had really missed the work in the camps. Whatever fulfillment most men got from the act of love, Kapo Schreiber got from hurting people.

The two priests silently prayed the platoon would stop at some other block.

They kept coming.

"It can't be the feebles in 30," Pfizer whispered. "It's you or us."

The platoon halted outside 28. The soldiers marched down the Polish priests' alley, five or six into each doorway.

The lieutenant strode up to the first door. He was nearly as tall as Bednarski. Eyes too hooded for a German. Czech, perhaps, or Rumanian. He had a kind of surly good looks, but the nose was too heavy and the dark green eyes were dulled. His breath told Bednarski the young man had to swallow more than a bit of conviction before this job. This was no ordinary roust.

"What you staring at?" the lieutenant snarled at Pfizer peering at them through the German priests' wire. "Get back in your block 'fore I rearrange your buzzard face, priest."

Pfizer looked apprehensively at Bednarski and turned back, crossing the short, windowless street-wall of Barrack 26, and disappeared around the corner.

The lieutenant looked into Bednarski's impassive face. "'Body ever tell you, priest, you got eyes like a cow? Well, you do. An' big soft lips like a cow." He half-turned to the beefy Kapo. "Doesn't he look like a cow, Schreiber?"

Schreiber's dark eyes surveyed Bednarski's body from his feet to his crotch to his chest, like an insolent butcher. "A priest, Herr Untersturmfuhrer." His voice was a boxer's high-pitched wheeze. "They cut off their balls. A steer, Herr Untersturmfuhrer."

The lieutenant found that very amusing and laughed heartily, jerking off balance, but Schreiber's hand shot out and caught him by the elbow to steady him. The lieutenant's face took on a look of importance, and he jerked his head toward the barrack.

"Inside, priest. Strip. Two minutes to get back out here. Promp'ly. 'Cause if they're not lopped off already, I'll have Schreiber wring 'em off onna spot with 'is hands. Move!"

Bednarski turned and made his way to the door to his apartment. Lines of pale naked men were already on their way out the four doors. Little more than stickmen, with coathanger shoulders, birdcage chests, spindle limbs. As they passed, hunched against the sharp air, many clutching their genitals in shame, he saw the bones standing out from their backs like wings. It suddenly struck him, stupidly, that their bodies were as hairless as boys'. Their pubic hair remained and their beards. And yet there was no longer any hair on their bodies. Why was that?

Schreiber's boot caught him square in the buttocks and hurled him into the line of naked bodies coming through the doorway. They edged to the side and let Bednarski crawl on his hands and knees into the latrine, where he could finally stand erect and strip.

In the dormitory, he could see three SS troopers pawing disgustedly through pockets, hurling straw mattresses every which way, piling what they found on a soiled bedsheet spread on the floor. Rosaries, holy cards, letters. Again, foolishly, Stan wondered why they were riffling so carefully through the breviaries.

He turned and walked naked out the door. Chills goose-bumped across his back and up his thighs. He walked gingerly along the hard-packed alleyway to the street.

They stood fifteen rows deep, two feet apart in each direction. The lines stretched from beyond 29 and 30 at the north end all the way along the street to 23 and 24. Eight hundred naked men. Bednarski quickly took a place Prabutski opened for him directly across from their barrack.

"Stand at attention!" a sergeant bawled.

The priests pulled back their scrawny shoulders and set their chins, their index fingers aligned with their thighbones.

"I said *attention*, you goddam fairy," the sergeant hollered again. "We're all men here, for Chrissakes! Nobody wants to look at your numb old shriveled nuts. Attention!"

Troopers came out of the barrack doorways, bent over like ragpickers under their bedsheet sacks. They squeezed through the gate and dumped the contents onto the roadway. Bibles and prayerbooks. Breviaries. The breeze picked up holycards and flittered them along the road. One fell against the bare toes of a young scholastic and he foolishly covered it with his foot. A trooper came over and hammered his instep, once, with the butt of his rifle, and the boy fell to the ground. A gust picked up the card and cartwheeled it away down the street.

The SS lieutenant looked blearily up and down the lines, his lips pulled back from his strong teeth in disgust at these skeletons who probably still considered themselves men.

Schreiber came through the gate and stood next to the lieutenant, his face wrapped in a smug smile. He opened the breviary in his hand ceremoniously, like a magician preparing an illusion. With his stubby thumb and forefinger, he pinched out several pieces of folded paper and handed them to the lieutenant and bowed humbly, as if to applause.

The lieutenant peered. "How the hell did they get those?" he asked himself aloud.

Schreiber opened the breviary to the front-papers, and pointed. The lieutenant squinted at the page and looked up.

"Stefan Wielgoz?" he shouted. "Protective Prisoner Wielgoz, front and center! *Now!*"

Schreiber leaned over to the lieutenant and whispered in his ear. The lieutenant nodded and called over one of his troopers. He spoke quietly to him for a moment, and the trooper took off on the double in the direction of the Delousing Barrack.

A priest had pushed his way from a back line near 23 and moved like an automaton along the lines toward the pile at the gate of 28. The former rector of the Jesuit college in Lublin was a squat man with a furze of iron-grey hair. The sack that had been his belly hung limply, nearly covering his genitals. His square jaw trembled, but he carried himself as manfully as he was able. As he passed them, the eyes of each of the naked priests followed in helpless compassion.

"Protective Prisoner 22402!" he shouted in thickly accented German. "Wielgoz, Stefan. I have not too good German, sir."

"I'm a Czech, goddammit, and *I* can speak German, you illiterate *Arschloch!*" the lieutenant roared. "Where the hell did you get a hundred and twenty Reichsmarks, *priest?*"

Wielgoz looked at him helplessly, his mind trying to decipher, his lips trying to find the words. "I not have too good German, sir!" he repeated, like a lost child.

The lieutenant pumped his fists against his hips. He looked up past the short priest's shorn head. His eyes locked on Stan Bednarski. "You," he hollered. "Cow Eyes! Come here!"

Bednarski walked slowly around the pile of books. "Yes, Herr Untersturmfuhrer," he said, straining back at attention.

"Ask this ignorant son of a bitch where the hell he got a hundred and twenty marks from. Anybody with more than ten marks means planning an escape."

Bednarski rattled the question in Polish and listened to the answer, his eyes locked on the terrified eyes of the older priest. He turned back to the lieutenant. "It is not his money, Herr Untersturmfuhrer. He was holding it in safekeeping for a friend. A layman. Not a priest."

"If that's the truth, what's this friend's name?"

Bednarski took a deep breath. He looked helplessly at Wielgoz and asked the question. Wielgoz looked surprised, almost insulted, and snarled an answer. Bednarski looked back at the lieutenant. "He says he cannot betray that trust, Herr Untersturmfuhrer."

"Back off," the lieutenant barked, and Bednarski walked past the pile and waited.

The lieutenant looked nervously at Wielgoz, then at Schreiber. It was obvious he had thought this would be easier than it was becoming, and the schnaps had lost its effect. At that moment, the trooper who had run off returned with a jerry can and set it down by the pile of religious articles. The lieutenant looked at him, then again at Schreiber, then at Wielgoz.

"Schreiber," the lieutenant snapped.

"Yes, Herr Untersturmfuhrer."

"Did you find any more money in those other books?"

For a moment Schreiber's dark brows knitted in hesitation. "Only a few marks here and there, Herr Untersturmfuhrer. No more than fifty together. I took them to give to you later."

The lieutenant bit his lower lip reflectively. Finally, he nodded to the trooper standing next to the jerry can. The guard opened the can and upended it on the pile, sloshing the books with benzine. The stink came rankly to the men's noses. The lieutenant nodded, and the sergeant squatted down and ripped a handful of pages from a hand missal. He pulled a lighter from his pocket, snapped it and set the pages on fire. He waited a moment to be sure they had caught, then threw them on the pile.

The flames whooshed up. The lieutenant's eyes narrowed, watching the anguish in the eyes of the eight hundred naked men.

"I knew it," he said quietly, edging away from the raw heat of the blaze. "There was *more* in there. You can see it in their eyes. Probably in the bindings."

He turned to two of the guards. "You and you," he pointed, and two men hustled into the street. "Hold this prisoner while Schreiber reasons with him. I want to find out who his pals are and when they plan their escape. Schreiber!" he snapped.

The heavy-shouldered Kapo sized up the Polish priest's sagging face and bulging eyes. Wielgoz screamed something Polish. Then in German, "No escape! No escape! Do for friend!"

"Pin his arms," Schreiber said to the two troopers. "Lock your legs around his legs."

The two SS men looked at him, puzzled.

"You heard him," the lieutenant growled. "Do what he says."

The two young troopers obeyed, grasping the lolling muscles of the priest's upper arms and pinioning his spread ankles between the black sheaths of their boots. Schreiber looked at Wielgosz, nodding his head from side to side like an artist assessing a subject, then walked a few feet away where Stan Bednarski stood at the edge of the fire. Schreiber looked Bednarski up and down, studying the sharp musculature, his eyes coming to rest on Bednarski's crotch.

"Hm," he said. Then he turned, appraising the distance, like a high jumper focusing his concentration. With three strides he leaped, lancing his foot square into Wielgosz's genitals.

The long, agonizing scream echoed along the silent street.

An instant later there came the audible intake of breath from eight hundred naked men. The lieutenant jerked his head away from the whimpering priest, wincing himself.

"When is the escape?" Schreiber shouted at Wielgoz, sagged between the ashen troopers.

The squat priest's eyes rolled and his mouth yawned with a scream that found no release. Schreiber turned to walk back for another try, but the lieutenant laid his hand on his shoulder.

"Wait," the lieutenant said, trying to stiffen the muscles of his face. Then he raised his voice. "If any of you know anything about this escape, step forward and save your comrade!"

Men stood at attention, eyes fixed on nowhere. Some tried to numb their minds. Others rummaged frantically through impossibilities. Vicious prisoners they could implicate. Insane thoughts of running forward and claiming blame. No one moved.

The lieutenant grabbed his fists angrily behind his back and stomped along the lines, glaring. "Listen!" he shouted. "If I don't get an answer right *now*, you'll all pay for this!" He reached the end of the lines and stopped. He turned and waited, breathing heavily. No one moved. "All right, then! Saxon salute!"

Eight hundred men put their hands behind their heads.

"By the numbers! Count! Out loud!"

Erratically, the lines fell into a squat and rose, the old men tottering, the young men almost relieved to take on themselves some of their comrade's pain, to surrender thinking, to keep warm. They shouted the numbers in a babel of Polish and German. Those directly in front of the fire, like Bednarski, began quickly to sweat.

"Nine!...ten!...eleven...."

The lieutenant paced back toward the fire. He turned and looked at the appalling bodies jackknifing up and down.

"Fourteen!..fifteen...."

Schreiber stepped up next to him. The lieutenant clenched his teeth for a moment, then nodded. Schreiber set to work again on Wielgoz's face and head with his fists. At each blow, the priest's face became bloodier, and the two troopers recoiled from the spattering blood.

The lieutenant paced behind the dying fire, head down, fists still clutched behind his back. His face was ashen, defeated. Finally, he stopped and raised his voice. "*Enough!*"

The lines raised themselves agonizingly to stand. They swayed dizzily, trying to lock their quivering joints in place. Some bent over the bodies of those who had fallen and tried to help them to their feet. Schreiber turned his sweaty face toward the lieutenant. His thick chest heaved and his eyes blazed, like a rapist's driven from his task too soon.

One trooper supporting the priest lurched toward the wire fence and was sick.

The lieutenant stalked over in front of Wielgoz and shoved the priest's gelid chin back with his gloved fist. His voice was a soft growl from between his teeth. "You fucking asshole, give me a *name*, for Christ's sake. *Any* name. Think of somebody you *hate!*"

The priest's eyes flared up under their swollen lids like a terrified horse's, his lolling mouth gargling and whinnying.

The lieutenant turned to Bednarski. "You! Here! Now!"

Along the lines, thin rib cages surged, eyes riveted on the bloody mess by the road.

"Listen, priest," the lieutenant whispered to Bednarski, "get him to tell me a fucking *name*. I don't give a shit *what* fucking name it is. Even somebody *dead!* Just get a *name!*"

Away from the fire, Bednarski's wet skin was like an icy casing. He leaned to Wielgoz's savaged face, whispering, pleading with him in Polish to say the name of someone he could remember from Poland, someone who was not even in the camp. But the older priest merely stared contemptuously back at him.

Bednarski looked deeply into the other priest's eyes for a moment. Then he stepped back a pace and, raising his right hand, made a sign of the cross. *"In Paradisum deducant te Angeli. In tuo adventu, suscipiant te Martyres et perducant te in civitatem sanctam Jerusalem."*

The lieutenant shoved Bednarski's shoulder, spinning him halfway around. "What was that? That wasn't Polish. What did you just say to him?"

Bednarski's arms hung leadenly. "It was a hymn. Of commendation," he sighed.

"You mean you're commending him for keeping silent? After what those men...."

"No," Bednarski whispered hoarsely. "He's dead."

He turned to go back to his place in the line. As he passed Schreiber, the Kapo's lips curled back from his teeth, and he growled ferally, deep in his thick chest, "I'll get to you."

* * * * *

Friday, 3 April 1942 - KZ Dachau

On Good Friday, Peuleve, an infirmary orderly, agreed to let Otto Pfizer into the TB wards and even find a way to get Stan Bednarski in to see the Poles in the experimental ward. From what Peuleve could gather, they were pampered like fighting cocks to be comparable to healthy young fliers of the Luftwaffe. Experiments on already weakened men would be useless.

At first, the infirmary had been only three of the odd-numbered blocks, but over the years it spread to the first five odd blocks, one to nine, linked by a long enclosed corridor. One block was restricted to offices, and several others were reserved for medical experiments. There were two well-equipped operating rooms, a full laboratory, electrocardiograph, and the latest Siemans x-ray being tested. As the war worsened, the regular SS professional staff began to be replaced by prisoner-doctorsin order to serve on the Russian front. One of the best was Franz Blaha, a Czech. Recently, Blocks 11 and 13 had been cleared for the hundreds of tuberculosis patients. Drug companies used them as guinea pigs.

Little chance of the two priests getting caught. It was the beginning of the Easter weekend, and the SS had never shown much enthusiasm for checking on the TB patients. For that reason, more than a few inmates condemned to a *Selektion* had been hidden there till the danger had passed. Also, with the toughest SS shanghaied to Russia, and the influx of new inmates from occupied countries, there had been a noticeable easement in at least the most brutal reprisals. All this week, for instance, evening roll call lasted only a half-hour, unheard of even six weeks ago. Pfizer and Bednarski had almost an hour before "All to Barracks."

Otto had connections and had spent the previous evening shopping for Paul Reiser. Franz Banska, a wealthy pawnbroker from Bratislava before the annexation, was Kapo in the warehouses which stored all properties confiscated from prisoners and from homes of wealthy Jews in the Dachau area. If the price were right, Banska could procure nearly anything an SS man or inmate might desire—from Bechstein pianos, to gold lamé gowns, to scarcely worn trusses.

Banska had a remarkable head for figures but was illiterate in German, and for the sake of proper censorship each twice-monthly outgoing letter could be written only in German for the sake of the censors and on forms purchased from the canteen, printed legibly, no longer than fifteen lines. Pfizer and Paul had written Banska's letters to his aged mother. They had continued even after discovering the letters were in code, not to Banska's mother but to his mistress, Ilona, who was keeping his various pots at a healthy boil back home. For that reason, Banska was happy to supply Pfizer a wool vest and long underwear for Paul, since after the night sweats, he had to wear his damp clothing the rest of the day.

Doktor Kurt Schumacher, former Chairman of the German Socialist Party, worked in the library cataloguing thousands of confiscated books. The week after his arrival, he was assigned to a Moor Express with the priests, despite having only one arm. Each day, when he had appeared near collapse, Otto and Paul heaved him up among the potato sacks in the cart and took his place.

Schumacher loaded Otto with *Mein Kampf*, Rosenberg's *Myth of the Twentieth Century*, several detective novels, and Sainte Therese's *Story of a Soul*, rebound in the jacket of Nietzsche's *Beyond Good and Evil*. He asked only that the novels be returned, since the library had hundreds of the Hitler and Rosenberg books from SS who received them as wedding presents.

Three weeks ago, Pfizer had written his sister, Mother Superior of the Poor Clares in Freising, fifteen miles to the northeast. After brief inquiries about relatives, most deceased, Pfizer continued in a crude code: "I surely pray for our dear Sister Paul. In this time of her sickness, I recommend an open-hearted meditation on the words of Dt. 28:22, combined with Jer. 30:13." The quotation from Deuteronomy read, "The Lord will strike you with consumption," and the verse from Jeremiah, "There is no medicine to make you well again."

Within a week, he received a letter telling him: "Our Sister Paul is well enough now to make you calves-foot jelly, which we are sending separately. Say a prayer for Doktor Muenthe who sent his new discovery, Sanocrysin, in ampules all the way from Copenhagen. As long as our dear Paul has her injection once a week, her illness should be kept at least in check."

Two days later, he got a box with a hand-knitted scarf, some biscuits, and a jar of calves-foot jelly, in which was embedded twelve small vials of clear fluid, enough injections for three months. And now they had quite a few friends in the infirmary like Peuleve: Doctor Blaha, a Polish doctor named Ali, Edi Pesendorfer, Father Alois Theissen.

The previous night after lights out, Pfizer had hollowed out Rosenberg's immense tome and stuffed the vest into it. The pages became latrine paper. The long underwear, of course, would not fit. He would just have to wear it and take it off in the infirmary. Then he'd hollowed out *Mein Kampf* and put in the jelly with the Sanocrysin, and packed it with bits of bread from all the priests with whom he knew Paul had shared his. Some gave willingly, some reluctantly. Some refused outright- knowing it would be just like Reiser to give it away.

Tonight, after roll call, Otto and Stan walked the street toward Barrack 11. Bednarski carried the novels and Nietzsche, Pfizer the two larger books. Suddenly, from between 12 and 14 on the opposite side, Kapo Schreiber stepped out onto the road.

"Halt!" he shouted. His shoulders bulged on either side of his chin, pulleying his elbows outward so his fists seemed immovably suspended just below the bulges of his pectorals. "Over here, you two."

Their hearts beating like triphammers, the priests crossed the wide roadway to where the Kapo stood under the light shining down from the street wall of Barrack Twelve. "And just where the *Scheiss* do you think you two are going?" he said, cocking one eye at them.

"The hospital Kapo said we could visit some patients, Herr Kapo Schreiber," Pfizer said, standing stock-still, but shifting the books to his left hip out of sight. "To give them a bit of encouragement. Because it's Good Friday."

"Let me see the books, Cow Eyes."

Stan handed him the novels and the disguised autobiography of Sainte Therese. Schreiber flipped the pages, disdainfully.

"What's this shit?" he sneered.

"Just a couple of novels, Herr Kapo Schreiber."

Schreiber cocked his eye again at Bednarski, without looking again at the books, waiting.

"Stories, Herr Kapo," Bednarski said. "To pass the time."

"Lying on their asses reading storybooks," Schreiber spat. "That's work for a man? They got no balls. Now, *you*, Cow Eyes," he said, nodding reluctantly, "you got balls. I seen 'em." His eyes snapped over at Pfizer. "Gimme them books."

The two books in Otto Pfizer's hand seemed loaded with shot. He reached them over, pinching them on the open end so they wouldn't spill their contents onto the roadway.

Schreiber gripped them in the vise of his fist and spied along their spines as if he had forgotten his reading glasses.

"As you can see, one is the Fuehrer's book, Herr Kapo," Pfizer said quickly, running his finger along the title on the spine. "*Mein Kampf*. I know you've read it, as we all have."

"Of course I have, Chrissakes!"

Schreiber was about to flip through the next book, but Pfizer coughed. "Please, Herr Kapo Schreiber. Forgive me. That other book is nearly as...well, as holy as our Fuehrer's book. You've read your own copy, but this...this one is...well, it's...it's nearly sanctified. It was sent to one of the patients in the infirmary directly from the author, His Excellency, Herr Rosenberg himself, the Governor General of all the conquered territories in the former Soviet Union."

Pfizer lowered his chin to his chest in a desolation of humility. "I was sorely tempted, Herr Kapo Schreiber, to read it myself. Just as you must be. But the Governor General has expressly forbidden anyone to open it...except Reichsfuehrer SS Himmler, himself, of course, who had to approve it. He sent it personally, dedicated...I'm told...to a relative in the infirmary. Reiser. A young man he's hoping to convince, by reading this masterpiece, to mend his ways."

Schreiber's brows knotted, as if he was facing two snake oil salesmen.

"Open it, if you like, Herr Kapo Schreiber," Pfizer said, coughing again. "But...."

"But what?"

"But...."

"Books are bullshit," Schreiber spat, shoving them back at Pfizer. "Get movin'."

Pfizer and Bednarski turned to walk down the alley into eleven.

"*Wait* a minute!" Schreiber bawled.

The two priests turned, their breathing suspended.

"It don't take two men to deliver five goddam books," Schreiber said with a sour smile. "You. The old bastard. Take the books. Cow Eyes stays here."

There was a distant rattling down the street, from the roll call square. A group was coming home late from a Kommando. Pushing barrows.

"You heard me, old man," Schreiber sneered patiently. "Move! Cow Eyes stays here."

A look shot between Pfizer and Bednarski. Stan nodded.

"Go ahead, Otto," Bednarski said, "it doesn't matter who delivers the Governor General's book. As long as his relative, Reiser, receives it."

Otto moved off into the shadows between the barracks.

Schreiber's eyes lingered up and down Bednarski's body. "Big, Cow Eyes," he said, his lip curled against his reluctant admiration. "I mean, I could punch your brains outta your asshole, but you're...big." He squinted up at Bednarski's face. "You didn't shave this morning!" he rasped in his high boxer's wail.

Bednarski winced. "I'm sorry, Herr Kapo. I have a very heavy beard. By dinner time...."

"Who the fuck you think you are, *Jesus*?"

The late Kommando was closer. Jews going to 17. Hands dirty and bloodied.

"Hey, you *Jews*," Schreiber bawled. "Doesn't he.... Will you for Chrissakes halt!"

The Jews halted. Mostly old men. Their eyes sagged with the weight of too much pain. They looked dully at the husky Kapo, like dogs beaten too often and no longer caring.

"All right! Tell me! Does this big, hairy ape look like Jesus, or doesn't he?"

The men looked impersonally at the Kapo, then slowly at Bednarski, their eyes sending him mute fraternal empathy.

"Why the fuck you so late?" Schreiber demanded, kicking the barrows and rattling them.

A thin, ascetic man stepped forward. "Forgive me, Herr Kapo," he said softly. "Our Kapo was...was sick. He sent us on ahead. We were repairing the barbed wire."

Schreiber kicked the barrow again. "What this shit?"

"Our tools, Herr Kapo."

"*Tools*?" Schreiber spat. "Your *tools*? What moron son of a bitch let a bunch of goddamn kikes take *tools* into their goddamn barracks?" He kicked the barrow again, almost spilling the tools and wire. "Jesus! You goddamn kikes'll be cuttin' our *balls* off with those goddamn tools! Well? Doesn't this guy look like Jesus?" he asked, hopefully.

The thin Jew cast his eyes to the ground and kept silent.

"Don't you recognize *Jesus* when you see him, sheenie?"

"Please, Kapo Schreiber," Bednarski whispered.

"The Jews have *got* to recognize Jesus!" Schreiber screamed.

The old Jew and the Polish priest looked at one another helplessly. They knew there was no smell on this Kapo. He wasn't drunk. There was a fever in him no alcohol could induce. They could only wait and grind their teeth till whatever it was had run its course.

In his frustration, Schreiber kicked the barrow once again and this time tipped it over, spilling tools and wire onto the street.

Something was moving behind Schreiber's eyes. Slowly, he turned and looked at Stan Bednarski's handsome face.

"What did you say tonight is, Polack Cow Eyes priest?"

Bednarski looked down at him, his face slack. "Good Friday, Herr Kapo Schreiber."

The Jew nodded. A fraction of an inch. But Bednarski heard a harsh whisper from somewhere in the clot of Jews. "'*Mah nishtanah, ha-lay-lah ha-zeh, mi-kol ha-leylot?*'"

"What did you say?" Schreiber shouted.

The Jew's soft eyes moved slowly to the Kapo. "That man said...." He paused to swallow. "He said...'How is this night unlike any other night.' Herr Kapo. A prayer."

"Well," Schreiber said sourly, "I'm going to show you goddamn kikes things have been different for a *long* goddam time." He bent over and picked up a pair of wire cutters. "Get that goddamn wire. Make a circle of that wire," he said," arcing his fingers, "*that* big."

The old Jew stood impassively, waiting. Then his eyes swung slowly back up again into Stan Bednarski's eyes. "You are a Catholic priest?" he asked.

Bednarski nodded.

The old Jew's eyes shifted quietly to Schreiber. "No, Herr Kapo. I will not."

The wire cutters came from nowhere and struck the old man on the side of his head. He collapsed. Schreiber skewered a young Jewish boy with his furious dark eyes. "You. Kike. Braid me a circle of that stuff. Or I'll use this goddamn cutter on your goddamn half-prick!"

The doe-eyed boy came forward, trying not to look either at the old man unconscious next to the toppled barrow or the tall priest standing by the wall under the overhead light, like a mannikin in a window. He squatted and began to braid wire with two pairs of pliers. His torn hands were rusty with blood. He had done this kind of thing since dawn. The other Jews gazed unseeing at the road. Bednarski tried to empty his mind, to think of people he had loved.

Finally, the boy finished. Slack-faced, he held out the coiled circlet to Kapo Schreiber.

"Put it on Jesus's head," Schreiber said, his huge chest beginning to swell in short heaves.

The boy looked at him with his wounded eyes.

"Did you hear me?" Schreiber wheezed, scowling directly into the boy's face.

"I can't," the boy whispered.

Schreiber brought the cutters up cleanly into the boy's testicles. The boy grunted over.

"Do what you're told, Jewboy."

His hand shaking, the Jewish boy hunched to his feet and raised the circlet of wire and set it gently on Bednarski's brow.

"Goddammit, can't you kikes do anything *right*?" Schreiber whinnied. He took the wire cutters and hammered the wire onto Bednarski's head. Pain bellowed from the priest's lungs and he fell to his knees.

His face impassive, but his eyes blazing, Schreiber set to hammering down the wire on the priest's head, like a farmer securing the cap on a milk can. At each blow, a cough of anguish hacked from Bednarski's gaping mouth.

Schreiber stepped back, breathing heavily. "There now. You see?" he said. He turned to the Jews but they had averted their faces. "*Look* at him, goddammit! See! There's your *man!*"

The infection of the priest's pain invaded the Jews' haggard faces as they slowly turned toward him, and their eyes reached helplessly toward him, sharing his burden.

"Down on your knees!" Schreiber shrieked.

The Jews' eyes turned questioningly toward him. Dully, they sank to their knees on the hard roadway, their eyes locked on this madman, knowing it was not yet over.

"Now," he said, his breath huffing, "here's the one you been waiting for. Show him you're glad he come. Worship."

The thin old men and the boy couldn't comprehend. Their open-mouthed faces moved slowly back and forth in disbelief.

"Say it! Hail, King of the Jews!"

The priest and the Jews knelt to one another. They could speak only with their eyes, imploring and bestowing forgiveness.

"Say it! *Hail*, King of the Jews!"

Silence.

Schreiber walked to and fro outside the circle of kneeling men, huffing, walled out by their resistance, by the way they were looking at the priest and he at them. He didn't want to tell them again. So he laid about him with the cutters, hitting flesh or bone with an unsatisfying thud.

"To barracks!" Schreiber shouted in his high-pitched wail.

The Jews groaned up, nursing elbows and heads. Two picked up the unconscious old man and began to drag him toward 17. The rest lurched after, not wanting to look back. The man who had been pushing the barrow got back between the handles and squatted to pick it up.

"Where you think you're going with that?" Schreiber shouted.

"To...."

"Leave it there! You're not taking tools into a *barrack*!"

The man shrugged and limped off after his comrades.

Schreiber moved toward the barrack wall and stood above Stan Bednarski, who swayed on his knees in the pool of light, his breath coming in short guttural gasps through his clenched teeth. Schreiber took the priest's square jaw and lifted it into the light. The long-lashed eyes wet with tears. Blood trickled in tendrils down his face from his forehead. But he was silent.

Schreiber's other hand swung down and cracked across the dark-stubbled jaw. Bednarski crumpled at his feet and lay face down with his jaw against the dirt road. The Kapo's face was twisted into a knot of frustration.

"It wasn't right, goddammit," he whispered aloud. "It just didn't go right."

* * * * *

Peuleve led Otto to the doorway of Apartment IV-D at the far end of the TB barrack from the camp street. He whispered nervously in the priest's ear. "Shelf Three, that wall. Slot 20, middle row. If you hear me talk loud at the door, get down and crawl back against the wall."

There were over a hundred men shelved in the ward. The air was fetid and close. Men moaned, coughed, stared. But only one man to each bunk. The sheets looked grey but clean. Pfizer moved along the shelving to the bunk Peuleve had indicated.

Empty. He checked the chart on a string at the foot. "22356: Reiser, Paul; Stable."

Otto looked around worriedly. The man on the other side of Paul's shelf turned his face languidly toward the visitor.

"Have you seen Reiser?" Otto whispered.

The big eyes merely looked across the room, then back at Pzifer. Otto moved around the intervening bunks and looked down the line on the opposite wall. Paul was kneeling next to one of the bottom bunks, talking quietly to a broad-faced boy on the bunk and holding the boy's first three fingers pinched in his own. Paul moved the hand up to the boy's forehead.

"*Ottza*," Pfizer heard him say. Then Paul moved the boy's fingers down to his broad chest, "*Syna*." Then first to his right shoulder, then his left: "*Svyatovo...Dukha*."

The boy smiled weakly and made the movements himself. "*Ottza...syna....*" The young man's body was constricted by a deep, liquid cough. A trickle of red dribbled from the corner of his mouth. Paul pulled a rag from beneath the pillow and dabbed the bloody spittle from his chin and the sweat from his brow.

"Just do it in your mind, Sergei," Paul said, overarticulating each Russian word and pointing to his own temple. "Then," he said, and arced his right hand high over his left arm, "tomorrow, we try again. All right?" The boy nodded back with another weak smile.

Paul patted the boy's forehead and struggled to his feet, holding the top bunk a moment till the dizziness passed. He turned and caught sight of Pfizer. His mouth dropped open. Then he looked to right and left. He came and wrapped his arms around the older priest, patting his back.

"Otto," he whispered in Pfizer's ear, "for God's sake, I haven't passed this damn thing on to you, have I?"

"No, no, you dunce," Pfizer chuckled. "Peuleve let me in. He didn't tell you in case I didn't make it." He held out the books.

"Ah, thank God! I was going crazy. Come back to my bunk. We'll have to whisper. The brothers need their rest."

Otto followed the gaunt young man to his bunk. When they got there, Paul laid his hands on the shelf and stopped to get his breath. "Do you mind if I lie down while we talk, Otto?"

Paul hooked his foot on a brace and lifted himself with a wheeze onto the bed and stretched out on the clean sheet. He was breathing heavily and a sheen of sweat covered his forehead. He wiped it off non-chalantly with the cuff of his grey-striped sleeve.

"There," he whispered. "Stowed away. Oh, Otto, it's so good to see a familiar face!"

Pfizer plumped the books up onto the bedshelf, and Paul cocked his eye at their spines.

"My God," he whispered.

"No, no," Pfizer grinned. "The two novels are real. The rest are fake. The life of Sainte Therese inside this one. And inside this...." He opened the Hitler book and poked through wads of bread for the jelly. He opened the jar and probed his fingers into the goo, pulling out a slicked ampule. He looked for something to wipe his fingers. Then he thrust them at Paul's face. "Lick," he said. "No use wasting it."

With a snicker, Paul licked most of the jelly off Otto's sandpaper fingers. "Mmm," he smiled. "Rich. I'm not used to such delicacies. Tell you the truth, I don't have much appetite."

"This was made by my sister, a Poor Clare, and those nuns must've all gone hungry for a week to get it, so you eat every gobbet. Share the bread, *not* this jelly. *Intentio dantis.*"

"Yes, Father," Paul smirked and nodded his head.

"The ampules. Once a week. Hide them in your pillow and give them to Blaha or Ali or someone you trust totally. Understand?"

"Yes, Nurse."

Pfizer opened the Rosenberg book and pulled out the vest. Then the older priest began to take off his clothes.

"My God, Otto, what are you doing?"

"Taking off my clothes."

"Oh, I didn't think of that."

Pfizer got out of his uniform and turned around, displaying the long underwear. "Direct from Paris," he said, and began peeling it off until he was in his own underwear. "Put it on. Leave your own underwear for the daytime. This is for the sweats."

With some amazement, Paul pulled off his own clothes and awkwardly began to shimmy into the long underwear.

"My God, you're thinner than a meridian of longitude."

"Call it svelte," Paul said and rolled up his own clothes, stuffing them under his pillow.

"Well, then," Pfizer smiled, "anything else you need?"

"Food, Otto. These boys are so starved, and so confused. A lot of them are Russians, and they get no food packages. They're sure they're here to be killed. A lot have been. A few of us are trying to make a kind of dictionary. To help them be less afraid. Paper, that would help."

"Let me check with Schumacher. Maybe he can get a Russian dictionary. I doubt it, but I'll try. Anything else?"

"God, Otto," Paul whispered, "in this infirmary I'm actually a *priest*! Oh, I don't hear confessions, but I let them talk. Even when I don't understand the words, I can tell by their faces, and I make the right faces back. That boy I was with? His grandmother used to make the sign of the cross, and he never knew what it meant. He's never heard anything else about God, Otto. I got the words from a Russian sergeant. He called me *dolboeb*, when he was telling me, which I suspect doesn't mean "pal," but he was giggling. Russians do it backwards, and I think I got that part right."

"Damien among the lepers," Otto smiled fondly at this unreasonably happy young man.

"I'm learning a bit of Polish, too. I thought I knew Greek, but I make a terrible botch of it. Everything I say to the Greeks sends them into hoots. But that's all to the good, right?"

"And how do *you* feel?"

"Bit woozy right now, but it passes. The doctor said I'm in good condition. Considering. I've got a good attitude. And, of course," he winked, "all this bracing mountain air!"

"Those shots from my sister won't conflict with your other medicine, will they?"

"Not possible."

"How come?"

"He's not giving me anything."

"What?"

"An experiment. The ones in the first ward get some unpronounceable drug. In the second they get another. And the ones in the third get another. And we get nothing."

"That's insane."

"He calls it 'homeopathy.' I think we're the control group. If we do as well as the others, then the drugs are no good."

Off in the distance overhead, the loudspeakers blared: "All to barracks! All to barracks!"

"Do you want to make a quick confession?" Pfizer whispered.

"Not much I can do in here, right? I'd take a blessing."

Pfizer raised his hands and made the sign of the cross, his mouth forming the words. As he did, Paul grinned and said, "*Ottza, Syn*a, *Svyatovo Dukh*a." Pfizer grasped his hands and they smiled at one another, not needing words.

"I'll try to get back Sunday. With a Russian dictionary," he smiled, and went toward the doorway where Peuleve waited to click out the lights. "Thanks, Peuleve. You're a good friend."

"Ah, Father, that boy is the only medicine in this ward. You will bring Communion tomorrow, or Father Schelling?"

"I'll slip it to you on the way to roll call."

"More good medicine. Sleep well, Father. Quick home."

Pfizer slipped out and felt his way along the dark alleyway to the street. He was about to turn right toward the German priests' barrack at the far end of the camp, but he froze.

Across the wide street, under the overhead light from the peak of the barrack, Bednarski hung spread-eagled on the wall. His wrists and insteps had been nailed to the siding. His head, circled with barbed wire, was flung back. His mouth was open wide and his eyes were gaping, dead.

There was a rustle in the darkness at the other corner of the TB barrack, and Schreiber stepped out of the shadows. His face was flat, like a man spent. His voice was a reedy whisper.

"I waited for you. You say nothing."

Everything inside Otto Pfizer froze.

"Do you hear me? Nothing. One word and your TB *Pueppchen's* on his way to Poland. Understand? I know his name. Reiser. You told me yourself. One word, and he's gone."

The squat man melted into the darkness.

Otto stood helplessly by the wall of the infirmary, transfixed by the image of the priest crucified on the wall across the road from him. There were no tears. Only a total inner emptiness. Like a man drugged, he began to walk slowly across the street. He stopped and began to raise his arm to commend this fine soul to a so-distant God.

* * * * *

Saturday, 19 December 1942 - KZ Dachau

In mid-November, the chief infirmary orderly, Heiden, had met a mysterious but unlamented death. Doktor Blaha, inmate physician in charge of autopsies, gave the cause as careless handling of lethal injections. In fact, as Doktor Blaha well knew, the Kapo's death had been caused by one of Heiden's own assistants, Heinrich Stoehr, who had pressed a hypodermic loaded with ten cc's of hydrogen cyanide deep into the Kapo's spleen as Heiden stood over a man he had just battered to death with his fists.

Heinrich Stoehr was promoted to the office of the man he killed, and the perquisites the infirmary Kapo commanded in return for favors were considerable. Actually, the motive was of little concern to anyone. No one criticizes a man for disposing of a malignancy.

Unlike Kapo Heiden, who had been a locksmith and safe cracker before internment, Kapo Heinrich Stoehr had been a medic for two years in the First War and had later settled in Breslau as a policeman, arrested in an after-hours raid by the Gestapo on a bar catering to homosexuals.

The charge on which a man was arrested was as important in a camp as his nationality and former occupation, since those factors could make him either friend or foe. Stoehr seemed to have neither friend nor foe. He neither consorted with the other pink triangles nor did he make any overtures even to the most attractive patients over whom he had utter control.

He was a squat man, whose heavy face was swarthy, even in winter, and he had the sleek skin and hooded eyelids of his Polish mother. As the head infirmary Kapo, he needed few verbs. He snapped "Bedpan" or "Syringe" or "Dead," with the assurance something immediate would be done about it.

This evening, he sat pouring the last of a bottle of schnaps for Scharfuehrer Wilhelm, the SS staff sergeant who vaguely oversaw SS interests in the infirmary complex. Wilhelm didn't enjoy drinking with a man who hardly spoke, but schnaps was schnaps.

"By the way," Kapo Stoehr said, his jaw hardly moving. "Injection. TB ward. 22356. Priest. Paul Reiser."

"Angh, *Scheisse*, I'm off duty," the sergeant said muzzily and stood. "Knock off the bastard, and I'll sign the book tomorrow."

"Not on your ass," Stoehr grunted. "Authorization."

Wilhelm waited for his head to clear. "All right. Lemme take a look and I'll sign the goddamn chit. Fuckin' red tape."

Stoehr led the staff sergeant along the corridor which had been built to connect the multiple infirmary barracks. He turned into the third block and led Wilhelm between the racks and stopped. He pointed to the gaunt patient stretched out on the middle shelf.

Wilhelm squinted at the tag at the end of the shelf. "22356. Reiser, Paul. Political. TB."

Stoehr raised a stubby forefinger to his lips and jerked his head. "Not too close."

Wilhelm looked at the prisoner's face and whispered. "He looks already dead, fer Chrissakes. Why's he gotta get a shot?"

Stoehr crooked his finger for Wilhelm to follow. Back in the Kapo's cubicle, the sergeant sat at the desk and opened a ledger. He uncapped his pen and waited.

"Well?"

"Typhus."

Wilhelm leaped to his feet. "*Jesus!*"

"One case. Don't want it to spread."

"Why the fuck didn't you tell me? I woulda took your fuckin' *word* for it, fer Chrissakes!"

"Rules."

Wilhelm sat heavily and picked up his pen. "Number?"

"22356."

Wilhelm wrote the number, his hand shaking. "Name?"

"R-e-i-s-e-r. Paul. Seminarian. RC. German. Age 27. Typhus."

Wilhelm finished, blotted the page, and slammed the book shut. "Jesus," he wheezed, rising. "You're a worse fuckin' sadist than Heiden was, Stoehr."

Stoehr shrugged.

"What the fuck can I wash myself with so I don't get that shit?"

"Lysol water. You won't."

"*Jesus!*" Wilhelm said and slammed out the door.

"Peuleve!" Stoehr shouted.

The spindly Frenchman entered from the next room.

"Cart," Stoehr snapped. "22356. To Blaha. Stat."

The little man nodded and disappeared down the corridor.

An hour later, Peuleve returned with a sealed glass bottle and set it on the Kapo's desk and left. On the bottle was a label: "22356. Reiser, Paul. Specimens from spleen, liver, heart, brain: typhus. Dr. F. Blaha. 19:35. 12/19/42."

Kapo Stoehr rose from his desk and took the bottle to a refrigerator, opened the door and put the bottle into a carton with the shipping label: "Institute of Hygiene, Berlin. Refrigerate."

He went back to his desk and pulled out a set of files he had requested for the weekend from the Political Office, the Labor Records Office, and the Property Room. The files were labeled: "40304. Vandermark, Kristof. Age 27. Dutch."

Outside, the loudspeakers began their evening bray: "All to barracks." Stoehr uncapped his pen and, in each of the folders, wrote the date and "Dismissed from infirmary. No work: two weeks. Consult infirmarian." As he finished, two men knocked hesitantly at the open door. Georg Schelling and Otto Pfizer.

Kapo Stoehr looked up at them from under his dark brows and handed them the folders. "Barrack 11," he said. "Row three, bunk two. Vandermark."

Georg Schelling's face crinkled into a grin. "There's no way we can thank you, Heinrich. We'll offer the high Mass for you."

Something nearly like a smile touched the corners of the Kapo's grim mouth. "Fine."

The two priests crept quietly down the corridor to Barrack 11 and made their way along the rows of bunks to where Paul lay, hands folded on his broad thin chest, eyes wide open and sparkling. The number patches on the chest of his jacket and the thigh of his trousers said 40304.

Schelling and Pfizer helped him quietly off the shelf. He put his thin arms around their shoulders, hugging them gratefully, and they led him along the corridor, into Kapo Stoehr's office.

"Thank you, Herr Kapo Stoehr," Paul said quietly, the heaviness in his chest wheezing. "For saving me from the *Selektion*."

Stoehr growled inaudibly and handed Otto the folders. "Memorize. Back Monday."

He flapped his hand toward the door, and the two older men helped Paul through it, out into the cold street leading to Barrack 26.

* * * * *

Reichsfuehrer SS Heinrich Himmler, on his inaugural tour of inspection of the chapel in 26, had made a very shrewd prophecy. Not quite a cathedral, but no longer a stable.

Gifts from friends had found their way through the plantation store and thence, hidden in carts and sacks, into the compound. When food parcels were allowed, Otto Pfizer and his artful dodgers had been able to trade food and cigarettes for raw materials-at times even labor. The storehouses of confiscated goods in the camp were stuffed from floor to rafters with goods no longer obtainable even in the outside wartime austerity.

The two altar tables had been encased in inlaid rosewood, and the antependium, decorated with symbols cut from foil by a Salvatorian named Steinbock, changed color with the liturgical seasons. One antependium, reserved for special occasions, was made of grey parachute silk. Karl Schmidt had made the first tabernacle, with two adoring angels cut with several pairs of nail scissors from the yellow tin of old fish cans. Flanking the altar were two candelabra fashioned by two Communists in the metal shop. Next to the altar was a lectern and a harmonium which Father Pfanzelt, the priest of Dachau Town, had loaned to the priests.

Each Sunday, the first Mass was at four-thirty a.m. After roll call came a High Mass, at the end of which Georg Schelling addressed four hundred priests of the barrack, in "The News of the Week," informing them of ways to give practical assistance to those in special need, pointing out dangers, and offering "points for good will." Schelling was a gentle man who gave good advice with good humor, but he never hesitated to state his opinion, severely if need be.

At the end of this Sunday's High Mass, he stood at the lectern ready to begin the "News."

"You have gotten to know," Schelling began, "our first human Kapo, Willi Bader. Once a transport worker in Ludwigsburg. Willi has the lowest number in camp: 00009! Since 1933. He says the first nine years are the hardest."

There was a polite riffle of laughter through the haggard crowd. Men looked down at the hands folded in their laps, which had at one time never been soiled by anything more than a newspaper, hands that now could have hung from the arms of miners or stevedores.

"But I believe-I hope-after this worst hunger year, the fact we *have* survived this long is some miracle, surely. And we may hope the war has crested, and the tide has turned against...." He paused to pick his word. "Against the villains who have usurped this country."

Several looked up. Schelling was treading dangerous ground.

"Since the Allies invaded Africa last month, the...Axis forces are stalemated there and falling back in Russia. No matter what our feeling, we must remember in our prayers the young men surrounded at Stalingrad, not only by the Russian armies but by infernal wind and cold."

He shuffled his notes, glad to move on to something else.

"The second item concerns Barrack X. You all know that, in order not to tie up trains by moving 'unproductive' prisoners to Mauthausen and the East, plans have been drawn up for a gas chamber here, just on the other side of the crematorium.

"So far, with cooperation of all the comrades in the camp, we've managed to sabotage its progress. I mention it here so that, if you stumble on anything that looks like a small part of a piece of equipment-hidden under a barrack, buried on the Plantation-try to conceal it better than it was. If you handle anything in the shops you know is for the gas chamber, damage it in the least obvious way, so it will have to be brought back.

"Item three. Obersturmbannfuehrer Weiss is taking a far greater personal interest in the inmates than his lamentable predecessor. As you know, he's forbidden all arbitrary beating and slapping by the Kapos. The dead need no longer be brought to roll call. Three priests have been put in charge of all incoming packages so prisoners can be sure they won't be stolen.

"Commandant Weiss isn't doing all this for humane reasons. Manpower is critical. He can't get the maximum work out of men badly fed and dazed with constant fear of punishment.

"Item four. This coming Friday is Christmas, and Dom Albert has asked me to say any of you who don't share my tin ear are still welcome at choir rehearsals. But also Christmas is a time for sharing. We must be generous with comrades in the camp who are in need. Every evening Otto Pfizer has a watchman at our gate and a courier to come in and request food. Some have been inordinately generous and I've had to reprimand you. Others...."

Schelling stared directly into the floor so he would not find himself, against his will, looking directly into the faces of the men he was about to chastize.

"Others have hidden their packages, sometimes even letting them go bad rather than sharing. That simply has to stop. We're all brothers in pain here. Last week, for instance, a transport came from Stutthof with three hundred men and boys, most of them Russians. One Russian officer in the infirmary told one of our men two of the corpses had been cannibalized on route. They aren't Communists anymore. Or enemies. Just frightened, starving boys."

"Item four. There have been two cases of typhus."

All the heads jerked up this time, eyes flaring.

"Both men have died, and I will have something further to say about that at the end, but I have to exhort you again, no matter how exhausted you are at bedtime, *delouse* yourself.

"Let us continue to pray for the souls of the twenty-five hundred of our comrades in this camp who died this year, not counting three thousand sent to Mauthausen for...elimination-three hundred of our Polish priests and sixty from this barrack. At the same time, let's say a prayer of thanks that there have been no Invalids Transports for two months.

"Let's remember, too, the twelve priests who have died in the gangrene experiments. The victims were all Catholic clerics, all under fifty. But thanks to the antidote Otto's sister has been able to send secretly to us, only twelve of the forty have died; the others are recovering. If you are chosen, you know we'll do our best for you.

"Finally...." Schelling paused an inordinately long time, waiting till all eyes had risen to meet his. "Finally, I hold everyone in this room—priest or seminarian or lay brother—to *confessional* secrecy in regard to what I am about to say now.

"Some of you have been puzzled this morning by a young man who has a striking resemblance to a young deacon you used to know as Paul Reiser, who had been suffering from tuberculosis and, according to our sources in the infirmary, was slated to be chosen in the next *Selektion* for disposal. But...but the man you knew as Paul Reiser...was one of the two typhus victims I mentioned before. This new young man is a Dutch citizen named Kristof Vandermark. I know we will all welcome and accept Kristof. As Kapo Bader generously has.

"The boy you remember as Paul Reiser was self-destructively generous. You've all witnessed that. Many of you owe your very lives to him. I know you will sacrifice all you can and offer the gift of your prayers and your silence to keep alive Paul's memory in our new brother, Kristof Vandermark."

Somewhere near the back of the room, Otto Pfizer rose to his feet and looked down at the gaunt young man at his feet. Softly, he began to applaud. One by one, the four hundred chosen for that Mass struggled to their feet, grinning, and offering their affection and willing connivance.

Slowly, the room began to empty so that Father Steiner and his helpers could ready the room for the next service. Georg Schelling pulled the alb over his shoulders, set it on the altar and walked to where Paul was leaning heavily against Otto Pfizer.

"You looked pretty exhausted, lad," Schelling said.

Paul smiled, his cheekbones white against the feverish skin. "I was always the last one to leave the party."

Pfizer hiked Paul's arm around his own neck and took most of his weight. "Willi Bader says we can use the Kapo's cubicle," Pfizer said. "That way we don't have to sneak Kristof back into the infirmary at night."

Paul looked at him, frowning. "Where's Bader going to sleep?"

"On the floor."

"What?" Paul screwed up his face. "He can't do that. Not in the same room."

"He says he not only can, but he will."

"But Otto, that's too dangerous. I'm contagious."

"Bader says by now he's got a resistance to diseases they haven't invented."

As Schelling reached to open the door for them, it flew open seemingly of its own accord. The three men jumped back. At the altar, Steiner and Loebenstein looked up, afraid of the worst.

Framed in the doorway was a middle-aged woman, broad in the beam but tightly corseted, her heavily made-up face framed by raspberry ringlets. She stood with one hand on her cocked hip and spread a broad grin of remarkably bad teeth. She looked like a poster of Mary Pickford defaced by mischievous boys.

Behind her, his dark eyes disappearing up into his head, stood the new Camp Leader, Michael Redwitz. The five clergymen stood bug-eyed, their mouths agape. None of them had seen a woman in years. None of them had seen a woman like this one in their entire lives.

"Howdy, boys," she clapped Georg Schelling on the shoulder. "I'm Sister Pia."

Schelling tried to get his breath. For a moment he thought it might be a transvestite inmate gone round the bend. But not with the new Lagerfuehrer standing in torment behind her.

"No, no, no," the woman snorted, "not a *nun* sister! Hoo-boy! Not by a *long* shot! Just a *nurse* sister. They used to call me that way back, when the Fuehrer was just a slip of a veteran from the war. Right here in Munich. Didn't have a pot to piss in. I took care of him when he got out of the army hospital. So he used to call me his 'Little Sister Pia.'"

She looked at Paul. "You could use a little nursin' yourself right now, *Liebschen*."

"I...I just got out of the infirmary, uh, Sister," Paul tried to smile. "I guess I overdid it too soon. The crowd, you know?"

"Whatcher name, honey?"

"Prisoner Number...."

"No, not that number crap," she said and moved her hands expertly around his bony chest. "Whatcher Mama call you?"

"Kristof, Fraulein...Sister Pia."

The blowzy woman turned to Von Redwitz. "Mikki, I'm gonna have my driver bring some thick chicken soup over here *every* day, hear? We're gonna fatten this gorgeous boy up. An' you make sure he *gets* it. He's got a wheeze in there sounds damn near like TB."

She turned from the steaming Camp Leader and winked at the three priests. "Anything I want, the Fuehrer says. Never forgets a favor, that man! Soon's he got t' the top, he says to me I never have to work another day in my life. An' ya know what? I haven't. Three husbands. All of 'em industrialists, lookin' for an in with my old pal. Greatest man ever lived. Give me the Order of the Blood. You're lookin' at a lady here holds the rank of SS *General*. No bullshit. So Mikki here gets out-ranked, right, Mikki?"

"Yes, Frau General," Von Redwitz hissed through his teeth.

"So, don't let me hold you up, honey," she said to Pfizer as she patted Paul's cheek. "You get to bed, you handsome devil, and plenty of rest. Sister Pia'll take care of ya."

Pfizer and Paul edged past the Camp Leader through the latrine to the next apartment.

"So!" she said, walking around like a prospective buyer. "Whaddya want? Christmas. Used to be a good Catholic girl, just like my Big Pal who just now happens to own half the world and an option on the other half. I owe a lot to the nuns, ya know? From when I was a kid. And if *you* guys'd bend a bit on divorce, I might think of parkin' my broad backside back into the pews. God, you guys *do* put on a show! Specially Christmas. I'd give a fortune to park my unrighteous ass in a church at Christmas. Midnight Mass. Ah well," she sighed, "who's the big cheese?"

Schelling took a step forward, a bit dazed. "Frau General."

"Just Sister Pia, honey. Whatchername?"

"Father Georg Schelling, Sister Pia."

"Well, Georgi, you could use a few vestments, right? These things are a disgrace," she said, picking up the reversible chasuble like a leprous bandage. "Got a couple monks over Ettal Abbey that's my pals. Gentle as churchmice, just as poor. So, I get 'em t' do me things. That supposed to be the Mass cup?"

"It's the best we could do, Sister Pia."

"Well, *hell*, Georgi. I'll send couple real ones. Gold. *Nothin'* too good for You-Know- Who, right? Specially at Christmas. Make a note, Mikki. Let's see. Soup for Kristof. Gold cup. Vestments. I'll have the Sisters o' Charity send Christmas cookies. Share 'em with all the Frenchies and Belgies and Dutchies. But not one *crumb* to the Polacks, right? Polacks is like dogs that'd eat their own puke if they was hungry enough."

She looked around, like an interior decorator. "Gotta hit the road, jailbirds. Think of anythin' else, just tell my driver when he comes with the soup. Those cups and vestments aren't here by Friday, just tell Von Redwitz there, an' I'll raise a little hell. I want you to have a pretty Mass for Christmas. Wouldn't mind comin' myself if I wouldn't have to go to confession first."

She put her hands on her hips and rocketed her laughter at the ceiling. "God!" she chuckled. "If I started confession right *now* I wouldn't even be halfway *finished* by Christmas!"

She turned on her high heels toward the doorway. "C'mon, Mikki. Number Four's coolin' his faggoty ass in the car. So long, boys!" she shouted. And she was gone.

For a moment, none of the three men moved.

"My God," Georg Schelling finally gasped.

He looked at Steiner and Loebenstein, their jaws ajar. "You don't think...she'd actually show up for Mass on Christmas Eve?"

Little Father Steiner pulled himself up at least six inches and set his jaw like a Viking prow. "Let...her...*dare*!"

* * * * *

1943

Wednesday, 10 March 1943 - KZ Dachau

"*Memento homo quia pulvis es, et in pulverem reverteris*," Otto Pfizer said, making the sign of the cross with ashes on Paul's forehead as he lay unmoving on his shelf back in the TB wards. Not ashes from burnt palm. From the crematorium, ashes perhaps of men they had known. Some felt the practice immoral, if not sacrilegious; others argued that the ashes were merely going to be scattered from their huge piles to the winds, and, unlike burnt palm fronds, these ashes had been hallowed by the human spirit.

"We have 20 priests and brothers working in the typhus wards, Paul," Pfizer whispered, capping the tin. "A quarter of the camp is infirmary now. There've been 600 prisoners and 290 guards dead of it. So the SS refused to go in anymore. So they asked us. Shelling's stock with the Commandant is very high. Good, isn't it?"

Paul merely lay in the infirmary rack. Remember, man, you are dust, and into dust you shall return. For two months, the thick soups Sister Pia sent had a remarkable effect on him, but then she or her cook or her chauffeur had lost interest. When Paul began coughing blood again, Schelling had no other choice but to ask Pfizer to get Paul back into the infirmary.

"You remember Johann Lutz, Paul?"

Paul turned his pale face to Pfizer. "Insufferable prig," he said in a viscous rasp. Lutz. Manicured fingers caressing the frothy curve of white hair. Hearing his confession after that painful summer of Lisl. Lutz who fought so strenuously to keep the Protestants from profaning the chapel with their "heretical and schismatical services." He didn't want to think of Johann Lutz. Or Lisl, either. He even wished Otto would leave.

"Johnni caught typhus, Paul," Otto went on, relentlessly. "I hope you'll pray for him. Oh, he's recovering, thank God."

Paul's eyes turned limply again on Pfizer. Why thank God? What difference would Johann Lutz's prolonged life mean to anyone but himself?

"But his bunk was next to Monsignor Herzog's. You remember him, don't you? Great one for swearing, but a big-hearted man. In the bunker a long time. You remember him?"

Paul remembered. Bow-legged bull. Didn't take any crap.

"Well," Pfizer went on, "Herzog was dying. So Johnni asked Herzog if he'd like to go to confession. And Herzog said....Herzog said to Lutz he'd rather face God's wrath than Lutz's mercy. And then...and then Herzog died. Right then. His last words."

Bravo, Herzog, Paul thought. But the thought tasted bitter. He wanted to regret it.

"Terrible shock for Lutz. He's been a good priest...in his way. For a long time, all he did was weep. Guilt. But now he just lies there. Pray for him, Paul."

"Why?"

Pfizer had been leaning with his elbow on the bunk, numb with fatigue, merely trying to get some response from Paul. Slowly, he raised his eyes to the boy staring at the slats above.

"I have no tears to spare for Johann Lutz, Otto," Paul said. "Why should I pray for a man who never had a single thought for any other human being but himself in sixty years?"

"Paul," Pfizer whispered, "that's not like you."

"No, I suppose not. What *is* like me anymore, Otto?"

"You're...you're a fine man who's worn himself out taking care of his brothers. You're...."

"I'm a goddamn fool, Otto. Why did I give up so much to lie in this filth? I have time to think, you know, lying here? To do the math. Did you know I've been in this hellhole going on three whole years now? And did you know I've been lying here in this goddamn Magic Mountain shithouse, coughing my lungs out in little bits for twelve months and twenty-one days. I figured that out. All by myself, I figured it out. I'm just so much *Dreck* that doesn't know enough to get picked up and hauled to the village dump."

"No, you're *not*," Otto said, bunching the blanket in his fist. "You're going to be a priest."

Paul turned to Pfizer. The tears spilled down his cheek. "No, Otto. I'm not."

"I won't have you...."

Paul's hand closed on his. "Otto, you're the only one I can tell. Sometimes I just pull the blanket over my head and cry, and cry, and die inside."

"I'll try to come more often. You need someone to talk to. Would you like me to pray with you for awhile?"

"No." The answer was like a fist hitting a table.

Pfizer looked at him, combing his mind for a way through the bitterness to the boy he knew was still hiding inside it.

"Why is all this happening, Otto? If God is love, where did the love get lost, Otto? Even if he's playing a game with us, like a treasure hunt, why does it take so long to find the love, Otto? I've given him everything. Where's the hundredfold, Otto? I sure haven't seen a fart's worth of hundredfold in a long, long time. Maybe God's a sadist after all, Otto. Maybe he enjoys this."

Pfizer reached his stringy arms around Paul, holding him against the cage of his chest. "No, no, boy," he said, "it makes him proud. He trusts you enough to ask you to bear it."

The boy sobbed and sobbed against his friend's shoulder. "Oh, Otto, I want God to leave me alone. I want God to keep his hands off me. I want to die."

"You will not, *damn* you!" Otto's knuckle flew into his mouth. "I...I didn't mean that." He blew out a big breath. "No. No, I *did* mean it, Paul. You damn *yourself*. Don't you see? You damn yourself to a hell worse than a Dante hell. If you quit. If you give in to it all."

"But I want to, Otto. Everything down to the bottom of my guts wants to let go. To be rid of it all. To unclench my goddamn teeth. Please. Please let me go!"

"No, I *won't*! We need you," he said fiercely. "Dammit, *I* need you. To keep going."

Paul wept against Otto's shoulder. "Oh, Otto," he sighed. "You're so good. You're... harder to resist than the diehard God." He took a breath. "All right. I can't. But I'll...I'll try."

Suddenly, there was a rustling in the darkness. Pfizer laid the trembling young man back onto the bunk and turned, warily.

Whisper coalesced out of the darkness.

"Ah, Pfizer. I'm glad it's you. There's to be a *Selektion* tomorrow. Reiser-this one, Vandervelt-is on the list."

The twisted little man turned to go.

"Whisper, stay," Pfizer growled in the dark. "I want you to get word to Father Schelling. Do you hear me? Right *now*! I want two volunteers here as soon as he can get them. *Quick!*."

"Why should I?"

"Because Father Schelling will tell the commandant you seduce Polish boys for food."

"I do *not*!"

"That doesn't make any difference. Father Schelling will tell the commandant, and he believes everything Father Schelling says."

Whisper melted into the dark.

Paul pulled up on his elbow and looked at Otto. He began slowly to shake his head. "Pfizer," he said, "you're unprincipled." He tried to sit up and began to cough.

"Easy," Pfizer said, pressing the thin body back onto the straw tick. He wiped the pink trickle at the side of Paul's mouth with the blanket. "We're getting you out of here."

"No, Otto," Paul said, breathlessly. "I'll infect everybody. Leave me here, Otto."

"Like *hell* I will," Pfizer growled, pulling off the blanket. "Wrap that blanket around your shoulders, and stop your bitching. Only a day. You'll be back in this paradise tomorrow night after the *Selektion*. I'm *not* going to let you die in here, do you hear me? Or let them transport you to a goddamn gas chamber. Or let you drown in your own goddamn self-pity, goddammit."

The boy hung on the edge of the bunk, his skin grey. A smile smudged the tear-streaked face. "Otto, you're such a good man."

"*Quatsch*," Pfizer said, fumbling the bindings around Paul's feet. "Somebody's got to take care of you, you young fool."

"Otto," Paul sniveled back the tears, "maybe that's why God put me here. To bring out the heart in an old troll like you."

* * * * *

Saturday, September 1943 - KZ Dachau

With the same twinge of resentment he felt every morning, Georg Schelling pitched a scoopful of peacoal into the rusty pot-bellied stove. Coal to keep Herr Himmler's personal angora rabbits cozy warm, even when there was no more than a faint hint of Autumn.

He dropped the scoop in the bin and ambled over to the first hutch. Nested in the straw, Sieglind and Uta looked at him suspiciously, like fat houris at an intruder in the harem. They weren't made for this indolent life. Their long legs were meant to streak across meadows and nose out warrens for the young they phlegmatically begat month after month. Instead, they lolled in chicken-wire cells, nibbling bruised lettuce leaves, daydreaming like all good Hitler mothers, of the next visitations of Hagen and Etzel.

"Ah, my fat beauties," he chuckled to himself, "your lovely locks are nearly three inches long. Nearly time for the palace eunuch to get the nasty buzzer and shear them off."

The priests in his charge were working, before dawn to dark, out on the Plantation and in the SS factories west of the camp, and here he was playing pander and handmaid to rabbits. But Commandant Weiss had insisted Schelling be available if needed at the Kommandantur.

Things had changed for the better since Weiss had taken over. No more humane than the others, merely more pragmatic. The typhus epidemic had claimed a fourth of the 30,000-prisoner work-force and, since the defeats in Stalingrad and North Africa, Weiss was under orders to exploit the prisoners to the utmost. To do that he needed competent managers. The priests, he realized, were educated, disciplined, accustomed to authority and responsibility-less susceptible than the Blacks and Greens to corruption. As a result, Schelling had achieved a great deal of prestige with the Commandant because of his calm ability to handle things.

The shed door rattled. A young man leaned in. Karl Schmidt, the priests' jack-of-all -trades. Under his round glasses a grin was strung like a hammock from one jug ear to the other.

"Wonderful news on the radio, Georg!" he hollered. "The Allies have invaded *Italy*!"

And away he flew to spread the news, leaving the door wide open and allowing the heat of the Reichsfuehrer SS's leporidum to leak out into the brisk Autumn morning.

"Well, now." Schelling's comfortable face crinkled into a grin. "That is good news. What do you think of that, ladies? Maybe before the winter's over, you'll be a sweater walking down Fifth Avenue in New York. If I don't eat you first."

He turned to close the door, but an SS corporal stood there. Hundreds of rabbits began to chatter and huddle at the far ends of their hutches, away from the intruder.

"Ah, good morning, Herr Sturmmann," Schelling smiled. "I was hoping the Commandant would have time to...."

"He was called to Berlin," the young man snapped and handed him a pass. "You may bring Mass wine to the Bunker priests."

"May I visit the standing cells, too, Herr Sturmmann?"

"Only the 'Specials.'" He handed him the pass. "And only Monsignor Neuhausler. He can take care of the others. Heil Hitler!" He handed him the pass and disappeared.

For months, Schelling had tried to prevail on the Commandant to allow him into the camp prison to see to the needs of the men in solitary and to the "Specials," prisoners considered too dangerous or too eminent to mingle in the general population. The Benedictine abbot of Metten, Pastor Niemoeller, Kurt von Schussnigg, the Austrian Chancellor, Prince Frederick Leopold of Prussia, several Russian generals, one of them a nephew of Molotov, Thyssen, the German industrialist, Miklos Kallay, the Hungarian ex-president. Even, Whisper assured him, Elser, who had tried to blow Hitler back home to hell in the Burgerbrauekeller blast and the two British secret agents who had recruited him..

Schelling crossed the hard-rolled north square and into the gate at 26. He slipped quickly into the chapel, genuflected, and asked Steiner for an aspirin bottle of wine. The little priest poured it without question, but cautious as an apothecary, and Schelling went out the door, then through the gate and turned right, down the central street toward the roll call square.

At the end of the bunkers, he cut left along the wall of the infirmary, rather than cross directly across the square. The guards had eased up; some even addressed him with the familiar "*Du*," but it was best not to offer oneself as a target and have his pass found later. He went along the east end of the administration building and stopped. A line of five soldiers stood directly in front of him, holding rifles diagonally across their chests, awaiting orders from their sergeant.

Tangles of barbed wire stretched along the eaves of the one-story Bunker ahead, but at the end of the long yard, against the brown-stained cinderblock wall, three prisoners stood with their hands bound behind their backs. Civilian clothes. Signs around their necks which Schelling couldn't read at that distance. Why do they always try to escape in threes, he wondered.

The sergeant was a grizzled Wehrmacht veteran, not SS. "Where you going?" he snapped at Schelling, who stood not knowing whether to go back or cross to the Bunker.

"I am a priest, Herr Feldwebel. 009025. Georg Schelling. Interned by the Reich for...."

"Forget that shit," the sergeant said, his tense face softening. This was obviously not a task to his liking. "I mean... what are you doing here, Father?"

"I have a pass to the Bunker. From the Commandant."

"Oh," the sergeant said, "I thought they'd sent you to...to pray with these men before...."

"I'd be glad to, Herr Feldwebel. May I also...?" Schelling paused, wondering whether to risk telling him. But the man had the decency to hope these three might find some peace before they died. "I have the Eucharist, Herr Feldwebel. May I...?"

"Of course. But be quick, Father. I don't want my ass on a spit." Regular army men hated this infernal job, especially old-timers who had taken pride in being German soldiers.

Schelling began to walk down the long yard. As he approached he could see the men had been beaten after they'd been caught. The one on the left whimpered. The one in the center stood with his chin thrust out. The one on the right stood listlessly, looking as if he would be glad to have the whole damn thing over. The signs around their necks said "Homo." Whether they were or not, made no difference. They had tried to escape.

Schelling stopped in front of them. "I'm a Catholic priest," he said. "I don't know whether you're Catholics or not, but it hardly matters, does it?"

"I'm a Catholic, Father," the weeping boy on the left said.

"Let me give you all general absolution, and the Feldwebel has said I can give you Holy Communion, but I have to be quick." He raised his hand: "*Ego te absolvo ab omnibus peccatis tuis, in nomine Patris, et Filii, et Spiritus Sancti. Amen.*"

He fished out the ointment tin and opened it as he crossed to the weeping boy. The boy put out his tongue, and Schelling said, "*Corpus Domini nostri, Jesu Christi, custodiat animam tuam in vitam aeternam. Amen,*" and laid a tiny piece of the wafer on the boy's tongue.

The boy murmured, "Thank you. Oh, thank you."

Schelling went to the young man in the middle. "Are you a Catholic, son?" he asked.

The boy looked at him down his sharp nose. "Used to be."

"Would you like to receive Holy Communion, son?"

"I'd rather have a cigarette."

Schilling had a butt he was saving for old Father Stegmeier. He pulled it out and put it between the young man's lips. His face fell. "I'm...I'm sorry," he said, "I have no matches."

"That's all right. It tastes good," the boy winked. "You're all right, too. For a priest."

"Thanks."

"Father?" the sergeant called from the other end of the yard.

Schelling nodded and moved to the last young man. He had a mass of dark curly hair and pale olive skin. He wasn't gaunt like the other two. Probably new to the camp to be so well fed.

"Would you like to go to Communion, son?"

"I'm a Jew," the boy mumbled sourly.

"I'll pray for you anyway, son."

The boy's eyes were so swollen from his beating that he had to cock his head to see. "Oh," he said, "Schelling."

"Yes. Do I know you?"

"No. I know one of your priests. Paul Reiser. We went to school together in Muenster. I've seen you around camp."

"Father?" The sergeant's voice was becoming insistent.

"What's today?" the young man asked.

"Saturday. September fourth."

"Ah. Sabbath. Rosh Hashanah." He chuckled bitterly. "The beginning of the fast. For me, the end of the fast. I've always done things ass-backwards. Tell Paul to survive, Schelling."

"What's your name, son?"

"Herschel Gruenwald. Tell Paul...I went like a man."

"I'll tell him. Courage. Go with God, son."

"I'd like to. But this sign tells the truth, Schelling."

The priest touched the boy's swollen cheek. "What does that matter to God now?" He turned and walked slowly back toward the firing squad. The sergeant looked relieved.

"Thanks, Father. You made it easier. For all of us. That was a nice thing you did for that kid. With the cigarette. If you want to get to your business in the Bunker, we'll wait."

"No," Schelling said quietly. "I'll wait with them."

He looked down the yard at the figures posed against the splotched grey wall, like three crosses on a hill.

"If you want. All right, boys. Let's get to it. Ready?"

The men raised their rifles and sighted along them.

"Aim. And for Chrissake put the poor bastards out of their fuckin' misery. *Fire!*"

The five guns cracked, and the bodies slumped to the ground.

The sergeant unholstered his pistol and started toward them but stopped and came back to Schelling. He reached into his pocket and pulled out a pack of cigarettes and thrust them into the priest's hand. Then he turned and began to walk toward the heaps waiting for him by the wall.

* * * * *

Sunday, 19 December 1943 - Dachau

"Seven barracks already in quarantine," Georg Schelling said as he came to the end of his "News of the Week" after High Mass, "but the quarantine is next to useless. Over a hundred dying of typhus every day. The crematorium can't cope, and you've seen the poor wretches stacked in the alleyways. It's criminal, but Sturmbannfuehrer Schwartz has told me nothing can be done for now. I've assured him we'll do anything we can. Otto has written to his sister's Poor Clares, and they're bound to come up with medicine.

"But I'm also asking for volunteer nurses. Several Polish fathers from 28 are working in quarantine now, but they've suffered worse from hunger than we have. Kap tells me conditions are beyond words. But you can't catch typhus from the victim, only from his vermin, so if you take the precautions, you'll be safe. Still, if you volunteer, you'll be subject to quarantine yourself the full fourteen days. For the moment, Doktor Blaha says they can take three."

He looked around the double room at the 500 German-speaking clergy, raw-boned, eyes enormous in their sunken faces. What in God's name am I asking them, he thought.

"I want no feelings of guilt if you're simply unable to volunteer. For many, just filling packets of seeds has become exhausting work. You'd only be in the way. Others are in jobs too important to all of us, especially for labor assignments. If they volunteer, I will have to refuse. Each man must weigh the cost in his own heart.

"I think that will be all. Go with God, brothers."

They began to shuffle out. Several hung back to help the sacristans tidy up and air out the chapel for the French Mass. Schelling lifted the chasuble over his head and handed it to Father Steiner. Sister Pia's vestments. If Sister Pia could read the signs of the times, she was probably on extended vacation in Argentina right now. And Sister Pia was no one's fool.

"Father Schelling?"

He turned. It was Berthold Posch, a priest from Bavaria. The poor man was ravaged with scruples to the point where he hadn't even been able to say a public Mass for two years before he was arrested. A Gestapo agent had tried to question him, and Posch had simply been too terrified to speak, so he had been imprisoned for refusal to cooperate with the authorities.

"Yes, Berthold?"

"About the quarantine?"

Schelling handed the alb to Steiner and laid his hand on Posch's meatless shoulder. A man terrified of the germs on door handles. A great heart, imprisoned in the thickets of Canon Law.

"I'm grateful, Berthold. But your health is much too poor." He smiled softly down at the imploring, spaniel face. "But you can do something for us, Berthold. Build up your health. Then you will be most valuable. But that means you can't be so cautious about what you eat, yes? Even if the bread you're given is a bit moldy, you must nourish yourself. For our sake, all right?"

Posch's face crumpled toward tears. "I'll try, Father."

The little man turned and walked toward the door. Behind him, Schelling saw Reinhold Friederichs and Karl Schmidt, standing like two men waiting for the other to enter a door. Friederichs had been Bishop von Galen's canon lawyer for the Muenster diocese before he was arrested to punish the bishop's criticisms. Now he was in charge of distributing unclaimable parcels to the neediest prisoners. Schmidt was their radio man, their factotum.

Schelling smiled his gratitude but shook his head. The two priests turned to leave, still not speaking, each trying perhaps to sort out the feelings of disappointment and relief.

Schelling crossed to the door. When he stepped down into the snowless alleyway, he was surprised to see Monsignor Lutz standing there, huddled into a suitcoat, his prisoner's cap tied to his head by a moth-pitted scarf. The handsome patrician face had corroded as all of their faces had. The glistening white hair of which he had once been so proud was now a snowy stubble. Since he had come from the typhus wards nearly a year ago, he had hardly spoken, and there were times Schelling worried he might go Moslem. But he went about his work resolutely and without complaint, avoiding conversation as much as possible, wrestling with his own demons.

"Georg?" Lutz said.

"Yes, Johann?"

"Georg...you can count on me for the typhus blocks."

It was almost as if Lutz had struck him. "But you've had typhus yourself, Johnni."

"I could well be immune, then, no? And I did take courses in East European languages at the Germanicum. I'm rusty, of course. But I might be of some help with...with the Russians and Poles. It's just that last year, when I was there, when I had the typhus, and Herzog...."

"I understand, Johnni. And I'm grateful. At noon tomorrow? By the gate into the road. I'll walk over with you."

"Thank you, Georg. Truly. Perhaps this time, I might...I might hear confessions."

Lutz turned away and walked back down the barrack toward Apartment Four. Schelling watched him, shaking his head at the wonders of God and man. The pugnacious spirit of Manfred Herzog was calling Johann Lutz back to the infirmary to be healed.

* * * * *

Monday, 20 December 1943 - KZ Dachau

After the noon soup, Schelling stood at the barrack gate. With him were two other priests, Kamil Kos, a young Czech, and Emile Gleton, from Dijon. Kos had not been ordained a year when a platoon had pulled him from his pulpit in Nitra and taken him off, fully-vested, for "violation of the currency laws" with a sermon on the missions. Gleton was also young. He had a shy, boyish grin one didn't associate with a Frenchman, and surely not with a Biblical scholar.

The door to the chapel opened and Lutz stepped out, hustling with a cloth sack. He was smiling nervously. "Georg," he said, "I hope it is all right. There was a small crucifix. At the foot of the statue of Our Lady. It was just lying there. No one could see it. I thought perhaps the patients might find it consoling."

"Of course, Johnni. Of course. I'll tell Father Steiner."

Schelling swung open the gate, and the four began to cross the road to the quarantine barracks. As they passed 19 and 17, they tried not to look down the alleys at the piles of corpses, like stacks of grey driftwood, open-mouthed and staring. They turned in at fifteen, and a prisoner, 22494, was waiting for them at the first doorway.

"Fathers," Schelling said, "this is Father Felix Caminski, the head nurse of this block. Felix, this is Father Kos, Father Gleton, Monsignor Lutz."

"How happy we are to have you!" Caminski beamed like a genial host greeting late arrivals. A round-faced little man, his merry eyes struggling manfully against weariness. The sleeves of his jacket and long underwear were rolled up above his elbows, and he reeked of Lysol. "Georg," he smiled, "I'm afraid you can't stay any longer, or we'll have to quarantine you, too."

"Of course." Schelling turned to the three men, his gentle face heavy. "You are truly brave, selfless men. I...."

"No need," Gleton grinned. "We're happy to be chosen."

"Yes. Well. Is there anything we can do for you, Felix?"

"Just food, Georg."

"I'll put a sign on the door of the chapel. Well. Go with God, then, brothers," he said, and turned back to the street.

"Come out of the cold, Fathers," Caminski said as they passed into the cold latrine. He closed the door and turned smilingly. "Now. Ward One is patients in quarantine merely because they have been exposed. No headache. No rash. Monsignor Lutz will be in Ward One.

"Ward Two's suffer no more than severe dysentery, but their block-mates wanted to get rid of them, so they brought them and said it was typhus. Father Gleton will be in Ward Two.

"Ward Three is serious typhus but quite hopeful. Patients are in agony, raging fever, spots of gangrene, mild pneumonia or renal failure, but none as severe as those in Four. All mostly conscious. We already have two priests serving in Three. Father Kos will be in Ward Four, I'm afraid. The dying, almost surely. Terrible delirium...."

"Excuse me," Monsignor Lutz said.

"Yes, Monsignor."

"Please. Johann. Am I in the Ward One because I am oldest?"

"Well, it did...."

"Please. I would like to change places with Father Kos."

"But...."

"I had the disease last year. I could be immune."

"Well, yes, that's quite...."

"Thank you. I'm sorry to have interrupted."

"Two things to be absolutely certain of, brothers. First, even if you haven't been actually cleaning the patients, wash your hands in Lysol water once every fifteen minutes. Second, check for lice at least five times each shift. You'll find at least ten each time. Examine every stitch of clothing scrupulously before sleep. Even one bite could mean death. We all sleep in Ward One, by the way. On the floor, I'm afraid, but at least there are mattresses in Ward One. The mattresses in Three and Four had to be burned.

"Other than that, you don't have to be careful here. No SS man will set foot in here." He gestured to the apartment on his left. "Now, Father Kos, if you would go right in to Ward One, Brother Zajac will get you situated. And Father Gleton, right through there to Ward Two. The nurse in charge is a scholastic, Anton Ludwik. And Johann. If you would follow me?"

Caminski opened the door and led Lutz along the alley to the other door. "I'm very grateful you volunteered Johann. You know from experience how wretched the poor men are."

"Yes," Lutz said quietly.

"It was most generous of you to spare the two younger men."

"No," Lutz said. "It's a debt to a friend."

"A friend?"

"Herzog. Monsignor Manfred Herzog. From Frankfurt. He died next to me. Last year. Just at this time."

"How good that he had a friend to console him at his passing."

Johann Lutz said nothing.

"Well," Caminski said. "Here we are. Father Prerja will show you round. Don't forget the Lysol water, every fifteen minutes, and the delousing. No matter how busy or how tired you are." The little Polish priest laid his hand on Lutz's arm. "We thank you."

Lutz put his own hand on Caminski's and smiled. "No, Father," he said. "It is I who am in debt to you."

Lutz opened the door and stepped up into the latrine. The moaning and remembered stench assaulted him. His chest and back were instantly soaked in sweat, his heart thundering against his ribs. He turned into Ward Four.

A house of horrors. Lengths of skin and bone lay naked on each of the bare wooden shelves, not packed together as in the regular barracks, but without blankets or mattresses or pillows, for fear of absorbing contagion. Their bodies were wrapped only in scarlet rash and an amber stain of Lysol water, shellacked in sweat, shivering with fever. Some moaned for water. Some cried out against whatever was flying in their isolated deliriums.

A ferocious question focused in Lenz's mind: They shoot Russians. They send incurables to be gassed. Why do the monsters leave these wretches in such agony? Of course, it was unthinkable to want them euthanized. Did some of those "in charge" find this hell in some way justified?

"Mother of Jesus! Mercy!" someone screamed, scratching madly at the rash on his body.

"The Mother of Jesus wants you to stop scratching, Anton," a weary voice said from somewhere along the line of bunks. "Please. You're making it worse. Let me put some of this on. It will help. Ah, well. Live and scratch. When you're dead, it will stop."

"Hello?" Lutz called, fighting down his gorge.

From between the bunks, a squat-bodied man emerged. A dark furze of hair, dark-green eyes heavy-lidded, as if the greatest effort of his day went into keeping them propped open. Beneath them, grey gouges underlined his weariness. He had a trumpet player's thick lower lip, and he spoke German like a klaxon.

"Ah! Welcome! You must be Father Kos!"

"No, Father Lutz. Please, call me Johann."

The other priest put out his hand and gave him a welcoming grin. One of his upper teeth was missing. Lutz felt an instant's hesitation but took the man's horny hand.

"Ah, no fear, Johann. I've been soaking in Lysol so long lice drop dead when I walk in a room. My name is Prerja. Which is hard for a German. Tad. That's my name. Thaddeus."

"Like the apostle. Jude. Patron of the hopeless."

The squat little man gestured around him. "And what better place for me, eh?"

"You seem to be so...," Lutz began.

"Too light-hearted? Ah, when I was a boy, my mother told me my bladder was too close to my eyes. But now I live in the graveyard, I've run out of tears. Let me show you around."

Suddenly a man right next to Lutz sat up and screamed. Lutz clutched his chest and fell back against the iron bunkframe.

"Ah, not to worry, my friend, Johann. Our *tovarich* here is having fever dreams."

Prerja laid the naked man back onto the boards and whispered in Russian. Lutz could almost make out the words. "Think of your wife, my friend. Her glorious breasts."

He remembered his own tormented delirium. Voices zooming at him from out of the black, satin ooze. Things coiled, crouching, ready to spring. Succubi with great gourd breasts risen from the hidden depths of himself, scarlet rubberous lips like smiles constructed by an undertaker, muttering obscenities and touching the shameful parts of his body. Gargoyle faces looming into his vision, with hulking shoulders, gargling glossolalia, blasphemies about whether he felt like receiving Holy Communion now.

Lutz wiped his forehead. "I've been here," he muttered. "Not here. Another ward. Last year. We were all together."

"Ah," Prerja smiled, "an expert. We can get right to work."

"Not really an expert," Lutz said, dragging the sleeve of his jacket across his lips. "I was mostly delirious then."

"Well," the squat priest said, "you can usually tell their chances by the spread and color of the rash. Most of it depends on age. And condition before they were bitten. Usually the younger they are, the better. Will you give me a hand here?"

"Of course."

Prerja bent over to the shoulders of a naked, staring man on a lower bunk. "Get the feet, would you? He's dead."

"Shouldn't we...?"

"No chance. Sauer. Austrian, I think. Damn. Should have kept better watch. Suicide."

"What?"

"Today is the nineteenth, yes? December?"

"I think so."

"His anniversary. He told me that on his fifth anniversary in this place he was going to escape. He drank Lysol."

"God in heaven!"

"Yes, poor bastard. Face God on his own now, without *carte blanche* from us. Pity. But he had plenty of stock with Our Great Friend. He gave God praise with his suffering."

The two men carried the almost weightless body to the door, and Prerja and Lutz angled it through the latrine, as if they were moving a prop offstage. The Polish priest hipped open the door, and they clumped down into the alley. They heaved the mortal remains of Protective Prisoner Sauer onto the stack of corpses awaiting the Moor Express. Prerja pulled off his cap, and Johann Lutz did the same, not knowing what to expect.

"Father," Prerja said, "Sauer here was in great haste to come to you. If you find no place for him, with the burden of pain he brings to you, you cannot even hear this prayer. Amen."

Prerja put back his cap and moved back to the door to the latrine which joined Wards Three and Four. Lutz followed him.

"We bathe them with alcohol. Actually, expensive French perfume from the canteen. Confiscated, and who's going to buy it here, right? It fights the stink and sometimes sweetens their dreams toward wives or sweethearts. Sometimes it even lowers the fever. Not often in this ward. By the tenth or twelfth day, fever plummets and they get better, or it doesn't and they die."

Prerja handed Lutz a chipped basin of tobacco-colored fluid. "Lysol water. We'll start again. Once we get them washed down, you can take over. I've got to sleep or walk into a wall. I've learned a great deal about these crawly things that love our underwear. He sets his teeth into our thighs and sucks blood. Eats and shits at the same time, did you know that?"

"No, I, er, I didn't."

"But if he's just emigrated to you from a man who has typhus, then he *shits* typhus. And you scratch the bite. And you give *yourself* typhus."

Hard to blame the poor dumb louse. We bring it on ourselves. All the louse is doing is what God made him to do. Eat and shit. One consolation. Soon as the bastard becomes a carrier, he's dying, too. Daub it all over the body. They like the cool feeling. They don't know it, but they like it."

"So, there's no danger in the corpses."

"Only in their clothes. The louse shit turns to powder. If you strip the corpse, it gets into the mucous of your eyes. Or your lungs. Don't be too fastidious, Johann. Paint his balls, too. If he lives, he'll be grateful. If he dies, he'll die smiling."

When they finished, Prerja lurched off to bed, and Lutz began again, dousing with alcohol the men who screamed the most in flight from their dreams. Between two and midnight, he baptized two men and heard six confessions.

At midnight, Tad Prerja came back, digging sleep out of his eyes. "Ah, Johann," he yawned. "Morpheus awaits."

In a rush, Lutz suddenly remembered he was tired.

"Father?" a voice at his hip whispered.

A boy. There was no way Lutz could make out his name on the chart. Lutz squatted, pain shooting up his thighs to his buttocks.

"Yes, son."

"I have no good German, Father," the boy rasped. "Lithuanian."

"Yes, son."

He had obviously been a big peasant boy. Now he was a great skeleton, feverish eyes full of fear. "I want Jesus, Father."

"Yes, son. What is in the way of Jesus?"

"Many sin, Father. Too big for Jesus get round."

"No, no. No sin so big," Lutz said, unconsciously falling into the pidgin and using gestures where words failed him. He pointed to his own chest, "I," he said, "I *big* sinner, too."

"Oh, no. Not a Father."

"Yes, son. Yes."

"Women?"

"No, son. Worse."

"Boys?"

"Worse," he said, pointing again to his chest. "No heart."

"No heart?"

"Yes," Lutz beat his breast, "deep, deep sorry. I tell God. And God...." He choked for a moment. "And God said..." He pointed to the boy. "You...." He pointed upward again. "You are my...." He cradled his arms, rocking. "You are my son." Lutz sat on the floor, leaning his back against the wall. "So. Tell me."

The boy began, in stumbling German, all mixed together, as if all the sins were merely facets of the one sin. Masturbation. Killing Germans. Many Germans. Whores. Killing what Lutz could only guess was his sergeant who had raped a nun. It made no difference to Lutz. The boy had turned for home.

"No more," the boy smiled, then wheezed. "No more."

"*Deinde, ego te absolvo ab omnibus peccatis tuis, in nomine Patris, et Filii, et Spiritus Sancti. Amen.*"

The boy's big brown eyes were swimming, smiling at him. Lutz whirled his hands in the air and wiped them out flat, palms downward. "Gone," he said, shaking his head "God no remember."

He brought out the aspirin tin with the Eucharist. "You know what this is, son?"

"Jesus," the boy said.

Lutz put a particle of a Host on the boy's tongue, and the brown eyes closed, but the smile did not. "Thank you," he whispered.

"I go sleep now," Lutz said. "You talk to Jesus. And I bring Jesus again tomorrow."

The boy shook his head slowly back and forth, his eyes still closed, but still smiling. "I no more there tomorrow, Father."

In a stupor of fatigue and dull joy, Lutz dragged himself upright and said good night to Tad, lurching out into the latrine and into the black cold night. He moved almost unseeing along the alleyway, heedless of the nightmare faces glaring at their first and last encounter with death.

He pushed through the door at the other end of the building and threw himself on the nearest mattress. He stretched and yawned, trying to ease the dead cramp in his back, knowing he had forgotten something. His prayers. God would understand. He knew now for the first time in sixty years God could understand anything.

It seemed seconds later he was shaken awake. Felix. "Morning, Johann," the gingerbread priest smiled. "You slept the sleep of the just. Nearly ten. I saved hot water for you."

"Ah, thank you, Felix."

Lutz sat up, instantly aware of his protesting sexagenarian muscles. He looked around the room, bathed in winter light. The men under observation were chatting and reading, like men in a charity ward. Lutz found himself scratching under his arm.

He sat bolt upright, in a sudden cold sweat.

Last night, he had forgotten to check himself for lice. He tugged his sweater and his shirt and his undershirt over his head all together, as if they were pustulant bandages. There were at least five bites near each armpit. Suddenly, his whole body felt itchy. He crawled to his knees and got to his feet, blundering into the latrine, stripping off all his clothes as he went.

On a shelf above the big round wash basin there was a bottle of Lysol solution. He unscrewed the cap and poured it over his head. It ran down his body, and he wiped it all over himself wildly with his hands, especially all the hairy crevices where the lice loved to nest. He was back in the fever dreams again, imagining the tiny vermin, eyeless, groping his skin, affixing their lines of teeth to his body. He poured the last of the solution over his head and set to work again with his hands till his body was almost dry, except for the sheath of sweat.

He leaned his withered buttocks against the chipped porcelain sink, trying to get his breath. His vision began to clear, and he slid slowly to the floor, his bony shoulders against the cold grey bowl. He reached slowly for the pile of his clothes and began, inch by inch, to explore them-armpits, crotches, seams.

When he finished, he had found six. He crushed them between his thumbnails. Each no bigger than an "O" in a book. All the power of a bomb in that tiny casing. Finally, after the second search, he sat back against the cold sink again.

"Well," he whispered. "Nothing more to be done. In five days we'll know." He looked the length of his flaccid muscles, tanned by the solution as if he had just returned from a week at Capri. He put his splayed fingertips against his bony chest.

"I...," he said, "trust...." He looked slowly to the bare beams of the ceiling. "You."

* * * * *

1944

Monday, 15 May 1944 - Freising, near Munich

Mother Antonia Pfizer was glad some warmth was finally coming back into the stone floors. She had to force two aspirants to the Poor Clares to wear sandals because they were unused to the cold and chilblains. Penance was one thing, endurance of needless pain was sheer foolishness. Besides, who could pray and work when her whole mind was focused on her feet?

Mother Antonia sat at her desk, poring over tasks for the day. The blue of her eyes was edged in black that made them seem opalescent. Since she had not looked into a mirror in thirty years, she had no idea her brows were turning grey. Even had she known, it would hardly have been important. Her face was serene, framed in its dun-grey veil, of which she was by now also never aware, once she had put it on each morning. Her habit fell to her bare feet, cinched by a thick white cord with four knots-for her vows of poverty, chastity, obedience, and enclosure.

She had been twenty when she had finally realized the vocation she had been resisting was irresistible, a girl fresh from a degree in German literature and longing to teach. Now she was a Martha in charge of twenty-seven Marys-twenty nuns, three novices, and four out-sisters allowed to deal with externs. She was also in charge of novices, as her Jesuit brother, Otto Pfizer, had been, and four postulants preparing to enter: Josefa, Katrin, Elizabeth, and Madi.

And now there were the Jewish children. Herr Hanselmeyer, their most generous benefactor, had said it was surely the safest place. And, of course, he had been right. Only once had an SS officer demanded to inspect. She had met him in her office, fearful of entrusting him even to the redoubtable Sister Boniface. He had been the first man other than her brother and the doctor she'd seen in nearly thirty years. Lucky he was so unpleasant.

When she refused to open cloister to satisfy his ignorant curiosity, and he sneeringly suggested force, she showed him the Concordat. He sniffed, calling it "quite temporary." Then she walked to the rope hanging in the corner of her office, attached to a bell in the roof tower.

"We are totally dependent on the providence of God and the good will of our neighbors," she said. "When our food runs low, we tell our neighbors by means of this bell. We ring it only once, and they bring us what they can. If we were to ring it more than once, you would see half of the people of Freising outside our wall. Bavaria is quite Catholic, Herr Untersturmfuehrer. The father of one of our sisters commands one of the Wehrmacht units in Munich. We find it consoling." She smiled. "I shall pull this rope for as long as it takes you to shoot me."

"Sister," he said, looking at the rope, "there is hardly need for a woman to threaten a man with a gun. No matter. In a few years, you also will be wearing the Nazi uniform."

"When the Fuehrer rises from the dead," she said.

The officer had gone away and hadn't returned.

At least in regard to food, the war had been easier on the Poor Clares than most. The nuns fasted every day except Christmas and were used to getting along on little. At first Mother Antonia thought it was good for the Jewish children that the nuns also ate no meat. No problem if the older children suspected some flesh might not be kosher. But the children had to have some kind of meat. She'd have to talk to Herr Hanselmeyer about that. Or, rather, she'd have to have Sister Boniface talk to Herr Hanselmeyer about that on the Braunsdorfs' telephone.

Then, too, she had the priests at Dachau. Her brother, Otto, was tireless in offering her briars to flavor her gruel, offering her "matter for her pious meditations." How she'd love to heave the pious fraud into a pond, as she had so often when they were children, when he was a wiry colt and she a Brunhilde, too broad and brainy to attract any iron worker in Duesseldorf.

"My seraphic sister," he had written, and she had nearly gagged, "I know you will petition our Father in your many prayers for our needs here in this Vale of Tears."

Surely there was a censor with brains enough to see. "For your progress in the way of perfection, ponder the Holy Scriptures: (A) Gen. 18:18; (B) Job 39:44; (C) Mt. 26: 26-29; (D) Cant. 7:2; and, finally, (E) Ezek. 47:12. And remember in those prayers, as we do, Sister Paul."

She hauled the big Bible onto her desk and flipped through for the texts. (A) meant "Abraham took butter and milk." (B) was one of the silliest of all: "The ostrich leaves her eggs in the earth." If she could find an ostrich, she would send him one. (C) she didn't even have to look up. They were the words of Institution at the Last Supper. He needed more hosts and wine. She had to puzzle over (D), and finally looked at *The Song of Songs* for the first time since she had become a nun: "Your navel is a goblet, well-rounded and with no lack of liquor." She began to wonder about her brother and the God she served, who always chose to send his burdensome messages through the imaginations of males.

The last was always the same: "Their fruit will be good to eat and their leaves medicinal." The Sanocrysin from Doktor Menthe.

The cognac was on her desk, the ampules in their icebox. All that the parcel needed, other than the perishables, was the crock of calf's foot jelly to hide the Sanocrysin. Sister Boniface knocked and looked in. "Madi, Reverend Mother," she said, and withdrew.

Mother Antonia wished Madi were prettier. It would have made her freer to ask for entrance to the community. Undersized and shy, like a boy never chosen for games. She was long-necked, her skin pitted by some childhood disease, but she was so eager to please. How could she be truly free to renounce the world if she felt the world had already renounced her? If she felt no man could find her desirable? Or at least passable. But she herself had been at least partly motivated by that, and she had no question about her own vocation. Not now anyway.

Madi stood in the doorway in her lank black dress and stockings, frizzy red hair leaking out from under the veil. Her skin was as pale as pitted parchment, her eyes like a baby seal's.

"You sent for me, Reverend Mother?"

"Come in, child," Antonia smiled and gestured to the chair next to her desk. "Sit. Please."

The girl perched like a frightened heron.

"Madi," Mother Antonia said, smiling, "Sister Boniface tells me you've been doing a wonderful job with the Jewish children."

The girl's pale skin flushed. "I love them, Reverend Mother."

"Well, we have to find some way to feed the children, don't we? Herr Hanselmeyer has been very generous, but there is just not that much he can find for so many. I've been thinking of digging up the lawns and extending the gardens. I wonder if you would take over a new plot of vegetables. Perhaps use the older children? They get so nervous when they're idle. And we do need the food."

"Oh, Reverend Mother, I'd love to. If you think I'm able."

"Of course you are able, child. You're a very intelligent, resourceful girl. Do you know about growing things?"

"Nothing, Reverend Mother," she said, grasping the edge of the desk with both hands. "But I could read. I will work very, very hard to learn. And the children, too. We really will."

Antonia patted her hands. "Well, we are late for seeds. You know the priests we pray for in the camp run a plantation. They have seedlings, at a roadside stall. You could take the train early tomorrow through Munich to Dachau. Only a half-hour's walk from the station, but I thought that you might take Braunsdorf's bicycle. With the small front wheel and the large basket. Sister Boniface will have a package for you to take. For the priests. But...." She looked at the girl and wondered if she were doing the right thing. She'd be safer, though, than any of the other three girls who were prettier. "But you'll have to be very cautious with the package, do you understand, Madi?"

The girl's face shone like Christmas morning. She had never thought of herself as a Mata Hari. "Oh, Reverend Mother," she gasped. "I'd be so proud."

"Ask for Prisoner Schowalder. He's in charge. If not, ask for Father Bloedkopf."

Suddenly, Madi snorted and put her hand up to cover her embarrassed smile. Mother Antonia looked at her and loved her for that.

"Yes," she smiled, "'Father Booby' is a code. If my brother is not there, the prisoner at the stall will laugh and say something like, 'All priests are boobies.' Or worse. Then you will blush and say you made a mistake. Talk to the prisoner and explain that you have been put in charge of our vegetable garden and need his advice. Men love to give advice, especially to women."

"Reverend Mother, if I see one of the prisoners I think might be trusted, may I ask him if he knows Father Bloedkopf? If he does, then I can slip him the package."

Antonia smiled. Yes. You'll do, my Madi, she thought. "But never ask for Father Pfizer, do you understand?"

"Yes, Mother. I can be very vague."

Mother Antonia smiled at the girl. "Ah, Madi," she sighed.

"Yes, Reverend Mother?"

"Nothing, child. I'm just very proud of you."

Madi's face closed like a flower around her blush.

At just short of noon the following day, Madi pedaled her bicycle and its package up the dirt road toward the roadside produce stall. She had been surprised at the well-kept lawns and the large industrial complex along the way. They somehow made the great gate and barbed wire less awesome, like a farm for breeding dangerous dogs to protect children.

Then she saw a line of men filing down the paths toward the road. She braked to a stop and stood, aghast, the cool spring breeze drying the dampness on her back and shoulders. The men were like phantoms from a nightmare, gaunt, hollow-eyed, slouching along. None of them so much as looked up at the thin girl, open-mouthed and shivering in the sun.

When they had gone by, she still looked after them, as if graves had opened up in the farm and the dead had walked silently past. After a few moments, she hitched herself back on the bicycle and pedaled to the produce stand, shaken, unable to acknowledge what she had just seen.

At the counter was another gaunt prisoner in striped uniform, his brows notched against the sun. His cheekbones loomed over hollow cheeks, and the stubble on his shaved head looked as if he would be nearly bald even if his hair had not been shorn.

"May I help you, Sister?" he said. He had a hawk nose that beaked between pale blue eyes, edged in black.

"Yes," she stammered, "I'm...looking for Father Bloedkopf."

The priest fought against a smile. "Father Bloedkopf isn't here. Perhaps I might help. My name is Father Otto Pfizer." He frowned and jerked his head toward the guard reading a newspaper across the stand. The girl's head turned slowly toward the guard and nodded ever so slightly.

"From Freising?" Otto Pfizer asked. "Mother Antonia is one of our best customers."

The girl handed him a limp sheet, and he scanned it.

"Yes, I think we can take care of this. Maybe it would be easier to wheel your bicycle through into the greenhouse. We'll put the seedlings into that big basket." He turned to the guard. "Sturmmann Bredekamp, all right if Sister wheels her bicycle into the greenhouse? It would save double-handling. The nuns at Freising are among our best customers."

At "Sister" the paper crackled down. He was handsome in a coarse way, a toothpick idling from the side of his thick lips. He took a quick scan of Madi's body up to her face and winced. He grunted something inaudible and went back to his paper.

"Right through here, Sister. Let me wheel it for you."

"No, really, Father," Madi smiled weakly. "I can do it."

Madi followed, concentrating on not looking back to see if the SS man were paying any attention. The room was airless and steamy, spiked with the smell of loam. Pfizer led her to a table halfway down the glassed building and took the bicycle, poking down the triangular kickstand and rocking the bicycle back onto it.

He lifted out her package, crossed to a worktable, then reached up to remove an identical parcel from a shelf. He brought his own parcel back and lowered it into the basket.

"Fertilizer," he said, "concentrated. A cup in a liter of water. Tell Antonia," he whispered, "Sister Paul does so well. He almost gave up on us for awhile, but he's slowly coming back to us. She should be proud." He winked. "Not *too* proud."

He lifted a flat into the basket. "Tomatoes. Sturdy. Only a quarter of a cup of fertilizer per liter, till they've found their feet."

"Father," Madi whispered. "Those men I just saw marching by. They looked like dead men. Are they being punished?"

A sad smile came over Pfizer's lean face. "No more than the rest of us, Sister. I'm sorry but I forgot to ask your name."

"Madi Mack, Father. I'm not really a sister. A postulant."

"Well, you're a brave girl, Madi. Tell my sister I know I put burdens on her, and I'm sorry. The Polish priests have rejoined us, and there are eight hundred of them."

Her eyes went wide. "Eight hundred priests in prison?"

"There are closer to two thousand, Madi," he said, and went to pick up two small burlap sacks. "Plant the corn in rows," Pfizer said, raising his voice, "crossways to the prevailing wind, so the plants can pollinate one another. And I'll have those other plants for you next week, Sister. You can pick them up next Tuesday."

Bredekamp leaned in the doorway. The top of his open tunic was tufted with dark hair. He worked the toothpick in his side teeth. "Pick up her plants, eh? Pick up her skirts, too?"

"Herr Sturmmann, the girl is a nun."

"Hungh!" he smirked. "Ain't that what they're for? Get the pocky little bitch outta here, Pfizer. Even *you* ain't that hard up. C'mon, Sissy, get your bicycle and peddle your skinny ass somewheres else. Next time wear the veil over your face."

He leaned across the doorway, and Madi pushed the bicycle off the kickstand and pinched the stand back up. Her eyes were rimmed with tears and her cheeks burning, but her trembling chin was fixed. "Thank you, Father Pfizer," she said, and wheeled the bicycle along the duckboards. She stood there a moment, thin shoulders unwavering as an ironing board, waiting for the private to lower his arm. When he refused to move, she simply curtseyed under his arm and pushed the bicycle past the counter where two sad-faced women stood eyeing her, and out onto the road.

Behind her, she could hear the young man's sneer, "Hah! You couldn't get nothin' but puffs of talcum powder from that shriveled up old thing, Pfizer. Get out there. Two old grannies wanta feel up your last fall's turnips."

Madi got onto her bicycle and began to pump against the weight, down the road past the camp. She had a whole week to think up a way to bring that young pig down a peg or two.

* * * * *

Tuesday, 26 September 1944 - KZ Dachau

Because of Karl Schmidt's crystal radio, the priests of Dachau knew that, in August, the Allies had entered Paris. Every day, air raid alarms were a reminder that, if they could hold out, scrabble together enough food, they just might survive their sojourn in hell. Men spent their free time engrossed in the grain of the rough pine walls of the barrack, fearful that, if they spoke, they would say something that might be reported, for food.

Rain tack-hammered the roof of 26. The broad road outside was a morass. No evening roll call tonight. Waiting for the end was sapping everyone in the camp.

Suddenly the door between Apartments III and IV banged open and a beet-faced trooper bellowed, "More Frenchies, Padres!"

The men entered like sodden cats and stood in the latrine, not knowing what to do. Under the unshielded bulb, their skin was grey as cement. Otto Pfizer leaped from his bunk. He tried to put on the face of a genial camp counselor on the first day. "*Bonne nuit, mes freres,*" he said. "Don't be afraid. You're among friends. Priests, brothers, scholastics, pastors. Please. Don't be afraid. Brothers," he shouted into the two rooms, "the Kingdom of God has just grown a little!"

Some priests got from their shelves, reaching under pillows for a bit a bread. They came to the two doorways of the latrine and held out what they could. "Please, Fathers," some whispered, "don't be afraid." "*Je parle Francais...un peu.*"

The French and Belgian veterans pushed forward, smiling through the stubble, trying to make the newcomers realize they had reached a place where the agony was more or less predictable. Others hunched on bed-shelves, sullen animals, glaring at the intruders. The French tended to be cleaner. Mostly the typhus came from the east. Slavs. Typhus hadn't begun yet this year. These would not have typhus. But they would stretch the soup further.

Georg Schelling pushed into the harsh light, face crinkling. "*Bienvenu*! Please, Fathers. Find them places, would you?"

The rain thrummed the roof.

Men reached out their towels, and the new men took them hesitantly. Hands came forward to lead them to places less crowded on the shelves. As the arrivals nibbled on the wads of bread, looking over them like squirrels at the inhumanly cadaverous veterans, the story began to trickle out.

When they had begun their journey eight days before, as the Allies threatened their previous camps in France, there had been fifteen hundred, politicals in the cattle cars-professors, officials, students. No food, water, ventilation, or toilet arrangements for over a week. Corpses began to putrefy. They stopped only once for chloride of lime because the smell was sickening the guards. When they begged for water, the SS fired into the car, randomly, not from wickedness but from raw, stupid frustration.. About a third were dead when they arrived. About a third more could hardly live long. And the living were closer to dead than alive.

Otto Pfizer put his hand on a bedraggled little man. A little snowman, like Father Pfanzelt, in a dank grey overcoat, but the same sweet smile and dumpling cheeks.

"Father," he said, "My name is Pfizer. I'll find you space."

"Oh, thank you, Father," the little man said in accented German. "I'm sorry we're so...edgy. We're...unused to kindness."

"I know," Pfizer smiled.

"Piguet," the squat little man said. "Bishop Gabriel Piguet."

As a reflex, Otto's knees bent, and he reached for the bishop's right hand. But Piguet caught him under his elbow. "I'm afraid some SS man is wearing it now, Father," he said softly,

Otto Pfizer stood with his elbow on the shelf. He stared into the fetid room, unaware of the whispering, the smell, the cold.

A bishop, he thought. A bishop!

* * * * *

The following day, Madi was able to take the train only as far as Schleissheim. An air raid had torn the tracks beyond it into a warren of twisted iron and shell holes. The rest of the way she had to pedal the

Braunsdorf's unwieldy bicycle. To make matters worse, just as she turned from Dachau Town toward the camp, it began to rain again. Her legs felt dead as brick, and the rain had found ways inside her slicker. Her black veil hung around her pale cheeks like a sea-hag's hair. As she pushed past the officers' homes to the gates, she tried not to think of the trip back. She was almost there, and let God take care of the rest.

Suddenly a fierce cramp seized in her thigh, and the bicycle veered over and skidded away along the pavement. Madi landed on her shoulder and lay with her head pillowed on the curb, too shocked even to weep.

She saw through the wash of rain a soldier limping toward her from the camp gate. She pulled up to a sitting position, locked between the pain in her shoulder and the knot in her thigh, and looked at the bicycle. It seemed all right. But the box had skidded along the road and broken open, the contents tumbled out. Hosts, the jelly with the seminarian's medecine, a small smoked ham butt Herr Hanselmeyer had found somewhere, which neither the Jewish children nor the nuns could eat. The bottle of wine had broken against the curb and was bubbling pink along the gutter.

She pulled herself up quickly, her shoulder burning, and crabbed her way through the rain to the pile, trying to stuff what she could into the broken box.

"Here, Fraulein," the guard said, "let me help." An older man with a beefy face, rain cascading off his shiny helmet.

"I...." She just stood, kneading the cramp with both thumbs.

The old guard picked up the smaller packages. "Ah," he said, rolling the small ham into the carton, "Now that's a real find." He pulled off the torn brown paper from the box and threw it aside, then closed the flaps. "Perhaps if you give me your kerchief, Fraulein," he said. "And ride with your slicker over your head? I could tie up the box."

Numbly, she untied her long black veil and handed it to him.

"Do you have much farther?" he asked.

"Just...just to the plantation store. Down the road."

"Well," he said, girdling the broken box and cinching it tightly, "you'll be able to dry off there, won't you?"

"Yes," she stammered, suddenly wondering how Father Pfizer would switch the boxes.

The guard righted the bicycle and brought it to her. She grabbed the handlebars with her small white hands to stop them from trembling. Then he bent over with a grunt and picked up the broken box. He lowered it into the big basket.

"There we are. You're sure you're not hurt?"

"Yes. Thank you. My shoulder a bit. But...but I'm fine."

"Here. I'll hold the bicycle. Pull your slicker over your head, or you'll catch your death."

Madi reached back and pulled the collar of her coat up over her wet red hair. "I'm...I'm very grateful to you, sir."

The heavy face smiled fondly at her. She noticed that most of his upper teeth were missing. "Not at all. Hurry on now. It will be warm in the greenhouse. Good day, Fraulein."

He turned and limped back through the rain toward the gate.

Madi hiked herself onto the seat and began to pedal. The slicker, stretched over her head, dug into her armpits, and she bent over the handlebars like a bear in the circus. She just pedaled dumbly, trying to work against the throbbing in her shoulder and thigh, veering from one side of the puddled road to the other.

When she got close to the produce shed, she saw Father Pfizer pushing around the counter and standing under the overhang peering through the rain. When he saw her zig-zagging drunkenly, he ran out, hunching his shoulders against the downpour. She braked to a stop, and he took the bicycle. She was shivering and shaking.

"Quick, Madi," Pfizer said, "inside with you."

They hurried into the shelter. The rain sputtered on the overhang. Bredekamp looked languidly up from *Sturmer*, square jaw swollen with a wad he had just bitten from a fat red apple.

"Magh," he mumbled, mashing the apple in his big white teeth, "now you *really* look like a sewer rat, Sissy. Take her inside, Pfizer, and do whatcha gotta do. I don't wanna gag."

Pfizer angled the bicycle into the greenhouse, and Madi followed, her cheeks hot now, clenching her teeth to keep from weeping, but trying to get between the trooper and the basket.

"To the stove, Madi," Pfizer said and leaned the bike against a table. "What happened?"

"I got a cramp and fell. The box broke. I'm so sorry. I broke the bottle of wine."

"Now, now, don't think of that. Are you hurt?"

"I got a brush burn on my shoulder, but it's all right."

"Stand by the stove. Here," he said, and handed her a burlap bag, "dry your hair or you'll catch cold."

Madi stood next to the hot flanks of the fat stove and began rubbing her steaming red hair with the dank-smelling bag. A shiver shuddered across her thin shoulders.

"Are your clothes wet through?" Pfizer asked, looking uncomfortably toward the door to the stand. "I mean...."

Suddenly, Madi began to bubble with laughter. "No, really, Father," she giggled. "Just the bottom of my skirt. It wouldn't do if that great bully came in and...."

Pfizer startled to chuckle, too. "You must stay here till this lets up," he said, and he went to the sink and filled a tin can with water and set it on the stove. "We have no tea, of course, but hot water will warm you a bit, eh?"

Madi handed the burlap back. Her head was as tangled and shiny as a new scouring pad.

"Sit down," he pushed a wooden box near to the stove, "you look exhausted. How far did you have to come on the bicycle?"

"From Schleissheim. The tracks had been blown up after that."

"Well, you must go to Father Pfanzelt's church in the town. He will call Antonia, and you can go back tomorrow. And I have a message for you for Father Pfanzelt. And one for Antonia."

He went to the stove and picked up the can of steaming water with the burlap bag and handed them to her. "Careful. Hot." He pulled up another box and sat next to her as she sipped decorously. "Madi, *wonderful* news! A *bishop* has been interned. A French bishop. Piguet, from the diocese of Cleremont. In France."

"A bishop? Then you mean...."

"Yes. We will get Paul Reiser ordained! I don't know how yet, but we're going to do it."

"Oh, Father, then our prayers are answered."

"And you are in great part responsible, Madi. Paul is still very weak, but the food and the medicines are doing wonders. He's up and moving around. Slowly, but wonderful progress."

"Does he know yet?"

"Madi, even Bishop Piguet doesn't know yet! But I'm going to see Paul tonight. This will be the best medicine of all. I want you to ask Pfanzelt to contact Cardinal Faulhaber in Munich to get the proper permissions. Ask my sister to do the same with Bishop von Galen in Muenster. And a copy of the Ritual. She'll know what we need."

"Faulhaber. Von Galen. Ritual. And vestments?"

Pfizer pinched his gnarled fingers down his lean chin. "I hadn't thought of that. We really should do it up, shouldn't we?"

"Piece by piece," she said, touching the shiny tin can to her eager smile. "At least some small things. And the oils."

"And we have some very clever people here, too. There's a tailor shop for the SS. There's probably more chance of our liberating the actual things right here. And what we can't find, we'll make. What month is this?"

"September. The twenty-fifth."

"What day does Christmas fall on this year?"

"I don't know."

"Well," he said excitedly, "time enough for that. You just tell Father Pfanzelt and Antonia, and we'll start at this end, too."

He levered himself to his feet and went to the bicycle. "Oh, my," he said, "you did have a spill, didn't you?"

Madi stood, hugging her slicker. "I'm so sorry. It broke. A guard tied it with my veil."

Pfizer looked toward the door. "Do you think Bredekamp saw?"

"I tried to block it so he wouldn't."

Pfizer picked up the broken box and took it to the shelves. Quickly, he reached his box down, ripped the paper from it, broke it open, crushing the box as he did. Deftly, he unknotted the veil from Madi's carton and tied it around his own. Then he shoved the provisions up onto the shelf and carried his own back to Madi's bicycle. He looked at the door, expelling air.

"Small turnips," he said. "All I could liberate this week."

The door banged open and Bredekamp hulked in the doorway, sucking his teeth. "Time's up, Sissy. Hit the road."

"Herr Sturmmann," Pfizer said, "it's raining very heavily."

"She got here, didn't she? Maybe put her up in the 'Sorority House,'" he sneered, what they called the camp brothel, twelve women reprieved from Ravensbruch. It had failed as an incentive to greater work. Almost all the achievers preferred food as a reward instead. "Nagh. Even Whisper'd puke pokin' into little Sissy here. And Whisper'd go down on a goat."

Madi's pocked face flushed, and her little mouth pinched.

"Thank you, Father," she said and handed him the tin can. "May I keep the burlap bag, please, to cover my head? I will return it when I pick up our order next week."

"Certainly, Sister," Pfizer said, trying to smother his own anger with the forced serenity all the prisoners had learned.

She wheeled the bicycle toward the doorway. Bredekamp leaned across it, forcing Madi to curtsy to him again in order to leave. But she stopped and looked up at his self-assured smirk.

"Sturmmann," she said tightly, "what is your first name?"

"Karl, why? Wanna name your next bastard after me, Sissy?"

"No. I would like to mention it to my cousin."

"Yeah? And who's that? Adolf Hitler?"

"Reichsfuehrer SS Heinrich Himmler."

The sneer on Bredekamp's face very slowly began to fade. He cocked a quizzical blue eye at the pale, pitted face, the jutting chin. He couldn't tell if she were bluffing. But slowly his thick arm came down from the doorpost.

Madi pushed past him, out into the downpour.

*   *   *   *   *

Sunday, 12 November 1944 - Dachau

Otto Pfizer pawed through the murk and stink of the wards, looking for Paul. Finally, he spied him on a top bunk, just where Father Theissen said he would be. "They moved you."

"On his shift, Brother Celestine got me onto a top bunk, Otto. It's triage. The ones with a chance get a top bunk because the worst ones have loose bowels. And it all drips down. They put the ones who are sure to get well in the middle, to discourage malingering. Because of the drip. And the ones who're sure to die are on the bottom. And because it's easier to take out the...bodies."

Paul grinned. "I'm a *lot* stronger, Otto. It's driving the lab tech who checks me out crazy. He's a super-doctor from some research institute in Frankfurt. Communist. Headed for a Nobel prize if he lasts, and he will, with all that zeal. And he's damned if he'll let them cart me off on the Invalids Transport till he finds out why I'm doing better than the others when the stuff they're giving me is placebos! Of course, I can't tell him about the shots from your sister, and Brother Celestine won't tell him the ampules are right there in their cooler, so he's pulling his hair out over how I have fewer and fewer jigglies in my urine and my spit. He's vowed he's going to discover what it is, then he's off to Oslo. If not, he'll admit it's a miracle and 'become a goddamn Catholic.' So it's like Ecclesiastes, 'There's a purpose for everything.' Even my jigglies."

"And you've turned our barracks into a beehive, Paul! Thank God they're still letting some food packages through. Better than gold. And there's stuff in the warehouses even the biggest tycoons can't buy anymore! Carl Oestreicher, from Vienna, has charge of the clothing depot now, and Father Bauer–Peter Bauer–he's a tailor in the SS uniform factory. And two Polish brothers. Making albs, amices, two full sets of *violet* vestments! From material they looted in Warsaw."

"What? They told the Kapo these are dresses for a play or something? A cotillion?"

"No. It's a secret induction ceremony for very top bigwigs. Orders from the very top."

"You Jesuits are shameless liars."

"It's called equivocation. We practically invented it. It's the truth! It *is* an initiation, yes? A secret, yes? So we can't say who the bigwigs are. And you can't get more 'very top' than God, can you? And Father Durand, the English oblate from the Channel Islands. He's made a miter for Piguet. Parachute silk. Decorated with pearls! They may even be real, but I doubt it. Some shrewd Kapo would have copped them by now. And a biretta for you!"

"I seem to have caused a whole new industry."

"It's wonderful! Kohlmann, the Benedictine, carved a crozier in the wood shop, and some Russian pal of Lutz's made Piguet a ring! Brass, but who could tell? In the Messerchmidt factory. He switches from making one on the sly for a guard's *schatzie*. She'll think hers is gold, too."

"You're incorrigible! Schwacke's been sneaking in to run me through the rites. He's so damn *eager*. I had to tell him I could maybe put off learning the rites for weddings for awhile."

"And Madi's brought the oils to the plantation store. And the Ritual. And she sewed the white strip that the bishop binds your hands with after the anointing. And young Mossbauer has the choir rehearsing every evening. He's had to remember all the harmonies in his head, but Fr. Pfanzeldt's castoff harmonium helps. And everybody in the choirs already knows the hymns. No matter what language, they're used to the Latin. And the harmony. At least they used to know them. At least they claim to. Mossbauer says at least three of them are tone-deaf as anvils, but he doesn't want to dampen their enthusiasm. He's got them softened down to lip-reading."

"I wish I could tell my parents."

"Taken care of. We needed Bishop Von Galen's permission, but the Muenster chancery was destroyed in an air raid, and he was off in some village some place, but Antonia says they chased him down. He'll tell your family. And a Jesuit I know, Fonz Zawacki, barged right into Cardinal Faulhaber's office in Munich. This ordination's as iron-clad as the Last Supper."

"Otto, you're a prince of thieves!"

"You had moral theology. They didn't teach you about 'occult compensation'?"

* * * * *

Sunday, 17 December 1944 - KZ Dachau

For three weeks, Otto Pfizer had felt like the mother of the bride. The more excitement of the upcoming ordination spread through the priests' barrack, the more the men brought new ideas to him. The choir practiced lustily every evening, with Steiner and a crew of scholastics buffing the chapel floor around them with bricks wrapped in ragged towling, insisting they leave their foul footwear outside in the latrine.

All kinds of items had been liberated from the storehouses, sometimes in exchange for food, sometimes simply pilfered for "the greater good."

The flurry was sweeter because of the need for total secrecy. Like hiding presents from the children before Christmas. Otto hadn't seen so much life in all the time he'd been in prison.

Only at one point had there been a hint of betrayal. One evening Pfizer and Schelling had been returning from the infirmary. The prospect of ordination had put new life into Paul. He was practicing rubrics, carving a chalice for himself out of a block of wood, trying to get strength into his spindly limbs. There was even color in his cheeks. He hadn't coughed blood in over a week.

As Schelling and Pfizer neared Barrack 26, Whisper, the camp snitch, materialized out of the shadows between the barracks. "Pfizer!" he hissed, his sallow face like a sack of doorknobs.

"How much will it cost, Whisper?" Pfizer chuckled.

"A lot of fuss in your place. What's up?"

"Oh, you know," Pfizer said, looking warily at Schelling's worried face. "Christmas, keeping the men's minds occupied."

"Was over in the censor's office awhile ago. Business. Langer sits staring at one of your men's letters, and he says, 'Whisper, what the fuck's a "primessa"? I can't make out the writing." So I tell him it's some devotion. Don't want to get you into trouble, do I? But what is it?"

Pfizer coughed, but Schelling's face wrinkled into a grin. "'*Prima*' in Latin means 'first.' And two weeks ago was the first week of Advent. Somebody was writing home about that."

The corners of Whisper's mouth arced down, but he melted back into the dark alley.

As they turned into the gate and "All to Barracks" blared, Schelling sidemouthed, "If you find out who wrote that, I don't want to know. I'd be tempted to throw him over the deadline."

On Friday, Paul had been spirited out of the infirmary for a run-through of the ordination Mass, and at considerable risk Karl

Schmidt had taken pictures of him for Madi to smuggle out to Paul's parents. But Schmidt had taken only a few pictures before Paul fell forward against the altar, exhausted. They had to sit him in a chair to remove the vestments, and then Schmidt and Pfizer took him back to the infirmary, his whole weight on their shoulders.

All day Saturday, priests took turns kneeling on the bare floor of the chapel, praying strength back into this man who had become the focus of their hope.

This morning was *the* morning! Gaudete Sunday. Pfizer and Schelling met him at the doorway of the Infirmary. He was calm and determined, his hollowed cheeks set firm and slightly flushed, big thin shoulders braced back in his grey-striped jacket.

"*Adsum*," Paul grinned, and took their arms for the walk up the camp street.

They entered the latrine outside the chapel, and Bishop Piguet was already vested, looking like a plump little Infant of Prague, except for the tattered cuffs of his prison trousers dangling under the hem of his alb. They began to vest Paul, making him sit down once the amice and alb were on so he wouldn't tire too quickly, draping the stole across his chest, cinching the cincture.

"A dummy in a store window," Paul said, smiling weakly.

Pfizer smiled at him proudly and biffed his fist softly against the pale chin. A thin sheen of perspiration on the boy's forehead and upper lip. "A snap, Paul. Most of it's lying down."

"What if I pass out again?"

"In the first place, you won't pass out again. And in the second place, if you do, everybody within ten feet of you has a little bottle of ammonia. Bring you back like a shot."

It had been a matter of some debate how to restrict the number of people and lessen the strain on Paul. But in the end Paul insisted they have as many as possible. A month ago, Schelling had convinced the commandant to give Poles one day to attend Mass in the chapel. And the commandant had failed to specify what day. So the chapel was packed to the walls, and those who couldn't get into the room leaned in the cold winter sunshine against the outer walls of the barrack, underneath the painted windows, at least to hear. Those chosen to witness inside the chapel were first the young seminarians, then the priests of Muenster, then the oldest. But room was made for all who had worked on the preparations, the Russian ringmaker, an ardent Communist who said he wouldn't have missed the ceremony for a seven-course meal.

Father Steiner poked his head into the latrine. "Are we ready?" he asked.

"Well, Paul?" Pfizer laid his hand on Paul's thin shoulder.

Paul laid his hand on Pfizer's. "As I'll ever be. It's not as if I'm rushing into this."

Steiner nodded into the crowded chapel, and Pfanzelt's old harmonium began pumping. Then the choir began the entrance hymn: "*Ecce sacerdos magnus, qui in diebus suis placuit Deo,*" and the procession began through the gaunt, hollow-cheeked men standing in tattered uniforms, beaming at the thin young man, his chin high, his cheeks flushed, walking through them in his white alb, his violet chasuble over his left arm, a lighted candle in his right hand. Behind him Friedrichs, Pfizer, Schelling, and the little bishop.

Paul sat, pale and calm, and in the haunting stillness, the choir softly began, "*Veni Creator Spiritus.*" Then the bishop began the Mass with the opening prayer of Gaudete Sunday: "Rejoice always in the Lord! Again I say to you, rejoice. For the Lord is near."

Then, helped by his friends, Paul stretched out on the floor in his white alb, his forehead resting on his hands, while all the priests and seminarians, inside and outside the chapel, chanted the Litany of the Saints over him. When they had finished, the bishop turned and, his voice trembling, chanted three times: "We ask that You deign to bless, sanctify, and consecrate this chosen one," and all the rest responded, "Lord, we beg You hear us."

They helped Paul lift himself to his knees at the bishop's feet, and the little man silently laid hands on his head. A great stillness fell over the room as the priests of the Muenster diocese stepped forward and, one by one, laid their hands on Paul's head and returned to their places, hands upraised. Slowly, around the room, the other priests raised their hands in witness, and Piguet intoned, "*Tu es sacerdos, in aeternum-*You are a priest unto eternity."

And a thousand voices responded, "Amen."

* * * * *

An hour after the chapel cleared, Otto sat next to Paul on the iron-legged cot in the kapo's cubicle, dabbing with a rag at the perspiration on his forehead. The purloined finery was now nested in old valises under the altar in the chapel.

"I feel guilty being here, Otto," Paul pulled deeply for breath. "I'm a walking contagion."

"Nonsense. Bader insisted. I told you, he says he's even immune to death. Only decent kapo we've ever had, son. Don't deny him his goodness! And the blankets will be in de-con before morning roll-call."

Paul angled his chin toward the older man. "You saved my soul, Otto."

"I was just a stand-in. For Someone Else."

"Still. Thank you. For my soul."

"You just keep a firm grip on it from now on." Pfizer stood, and moved in front of Paul. He dropped awkwardly to his knees and looked up at him. "Father, may I have your blessing?"

Paul's mouth pursed together, his teeth digging in against the tears. "Yes."

He pressed his hands together, then slowly circled them over his friend's bowed head and lifted them. *"Benedicat vos, Omnipotens Deus: Pater, et....Filius...et Spiritus Sanct-....."*

His voice choked off and he wrapped his thin arms around his friend's shoulders, his cheek against his cheek. And the two men silently wept. For joy.

* * * * *

1945

Sunday, 11 February 1945 - KZ Dachau

George Schelling stood ready to give his "The News of the Week" and silently prayed the end would come soon. As his eyes roved the dulled faces, he wondered how many would see the Americans arrive, even if they arrived within the week. Kapo Willi Bader, after twelve years, had died that morning. So unfair, to struggle upward for so long only to drown just at the surface.

"My first item is hardly news," Schelling began. "Our best estimate is that there are 32,000 men in the main camp, not counting those who'll be transported here today. And these new prisoners we must take care of. There is simply no shelter for them, even in this terrible cold, and even with the increasing number of deaths opening spaces for them. In all my years here, there were usually about four deaths a day. Now there are over a hundred. You've seen the pitiful bodies stacked between the infirmary barracks. We must pray for them and for those who know they'll join them today. But let those bodies remind you to keep saying, 'I *will* survive!'

"In order to provide at least one more barrack, the Commandant has ordered that we use the chapel for sleeping quarters.

"Item two, Sturmbannfuehrer Weiter wants a list of all priests, by clerical rank. I don't know what that means, and I think it would be foolish to speculate, even though today, thank God, eight more of our German brothers are being released to make space.

"With the war going the way it is, rumors are bound to spread: 'The Russians are at the gates,' 'The Americans are at the gates,' and so on. Let's be practical. At least for the moment, the SS are at the gates. I've heard rumors-you all have-that this list means we're to be marched out with the Jews as the least desirable elements and led into the Alps to die and be covered by snow. Let's not face that until we have to. Wasteful worry.

"We know from the radio the Americans are closing in on the Rhine. Not a rumor. Fact. These could be our last few days in captivity. But who knows how the Allies could be diverted? It could be weeks. We can't let our hopes get too high-or too low. I think that's all."

When the priests had filed out, Schelling put away his vestments, and left the chapel, walking the length of the barrack to 26-IV where the men were already back on their shelves and huddled together for the warmth and the assurance they were not alone.

At his bunk along the back wall, on the side away from the feeble stove, Otto Pfizer was packing a rag with things from under his mattress: his breviary, a few letters, not much else.

"'Neither wallet nor scrip,'" Pfizer grinned. "I still don't believe it, Georg. I still don't understand. Why us?"

"Well," Schelling chortled, "could be they want to get rid of the biggest troublemakers– you, Lutz, Schmidt. I hope they don't probe Karl's underpants. Those pictures could be invaluable if he can get them to the Americans. But don't ask why. Just rejoice!"

"It won't be long, Georg, till you're back in Vienna, waltzing with the matronly President of the Altar Society in one hand and a seidel of beer in the other."

"Pray God the Americans get here before the Reds."

"I went to the infirmary and saw Paul, Georg," Pfizer said. "I know you'll check on him. I'll be at the seminary in Pullach. Only a few miles away. Get a message to Madi, and my sister will get it to me. If they try a *Selektion*, I'm counting on you to hide him again."

Schelling nodded and smiled. "No more *Selektionen*, Otto. But I'm afraid they'll leave the Americans nothing to find."

"Georg, they can't march out 30,000 men. Where would they get the guards? The only way they can handle this number is inside the wire. The only reason they're keeping non-Germans is it would be chaos to release them all, wandering between two battle lines, not understanding a word, not even able to beg."

"They could always bomb the evidence away." For a moment, both men were silent. "Well, then," Schelling said finally, "you'd better get out of here before they change their minds."

Pfizer took his sack and looked around. "You know," he said wistfully, "it reminds me so much of the seminary. Every time I left one of those places, I was straining at the harness. But I always sat in the back seat of the bus, looking back."

"For the good times."

"And there have been good times, Georg," Pfizer said, his eyes drifting toward the window. "Perverse, isn't it? Melancholy leaving hell. But I've never known finer men." He looked back. "You've been here longer than anybody, Georg. They told you to go, didn't they?"

Schelling smiled, looking at his soiled fingers. "I'll miss you, Otto. I just hope you've left a map of all your secret ins and outs. If the Americans don't get here quick, we're going to have to get all of them back to full power again."

There was a silence between them. Pfizer laid his hand on Schelling's arm until the other man was compelled to look up. Their eyes locked for a moment. Then they wrapped their arms around one another, saying what they needed to say without words.

The wrinkles around Schelling's eyes were limned in tears, but he grinned and slapped his friend heartily on the back and they broke apart, looking at one another for the last time. "Send me a bottle of cognac," Schelling smiled, "disguised as a lamp."

Pfizer turned and walked toward the door without turning, but lifted his sack into the air.

* * * * *

They were alert as rabbits to every omen, every rumor, every hint from the guards' body language. It was certain they would be led out into the Alps, all 32,000 of them in huge groups, to die and be covered by snow. No. Not enough guards. Someone had actually seen orders to bomb the camp to oblivion. Signed by Himmler himself, saying no prisoner could fall into the hands of the enemy alive and capable of witness. SS troopers were burning documents. The frequent alerts brought both joy and terror. What if the Americans bombed the factories next door?

The minutes oozed by. But it was impossible to suppress the surge of this new life-wish.

On Thursday, April 19, General Charles Delestraint was taken from the Bunker and executed with eleven other French officers and a group of the former French Resistance. Near the hillocks of corpses waiting next to the crematorium.

On April 23, the 2,300 Jews who still remained in Dachau were lined up in the Appelplatz at 1:00 PM and stayed there drooping all day. They stood all night, and early next morning they were led to the station and loaded in boxcars. The rumor was that they would be taken to an area likely to be bombed by the Allies.

On April 24, dignitaries from the Bunker, like Pastor Niemoeller, Bishop Piguet, officers from Greece and Italy, and Best and Stevens, the two British secret service agents arrested as part of the Munich beerhall bombing, were taken off in busses. As they passed the railroad station, they saw on a siding, at least fifty freight cars with open doors, crammed with corpses, with nowhere else to accommodate them.

Dr. Sigmund Rascher had presided over the freezing and oxygen-deprivation experiments in the camp for years. He had attempted to ingratiate himself even further with Reischfuehrer S.S. Himmler by offering evidence of child-bearing capacities in middle-aged women when his 48-year-old wife delivered three children. However, investigation showed all three had been purchased or kidnaped. The doctor was locked into solitary cell 73 in the Dachau Bunker. On April 26, on direct orders of Himmler, an SS captain enter Rascher's cell, placed his gun against the doctor's neck, and fired. Such an embarrassment had to be eliminated.

At noon on Friday the 27th, 2,000 half-dead and half-naked men appeared at the gate. They had been 6,000 when they had started their 200-mile journey on foot from Buchenwald. The veterans rejoiced in their arrival. The newcomers overwhelmed the system for awhile with distractions from any plans to annihilate the camp. Some were crowded into the infirmary, some were billeted under canvas canopies between barracks, some were Moor-Expressed to wait their turn in the long lines for the crematorium. The shortage of fuel made it impossible any longer to cart the excess corpses to the mass grave at Etzenhausen a half-hour's drive away.

The days were manic-depressive. Terrifying shrieks of sirens. Then sudden silence, immobilized, expectant. A flash of despair. A surge of hope. Waiting.

* * * * *

Saturday, 28 April 1945 - KZ Dachau

KZ Dachau was beginning to look like a gypsy encampment. Weiter had not sent out work Kommandos, fearful even armed men-most no longer SS-could not keep the prisoners from bolting. The majority of the guards were now *Volksturm*, old men and boys, probably too shaky or too cowardly to kill even this scum. The bakery, heating, and crematory were still operating, but SS still in the camp were not bothering with the prisoners. They were trying to loot anything portable and worth the effort.

One SS boy had caught Schelling by the sleeve as he walked toward the leporidum. Under the shadow of his helmet, his black brows pinched between his sea-blue eyes. "Father," he said. "Can you help me? It will be simple for you priests when the Americans come. But what about us? What can we do? If we run away, our own people will shoot us, and if we stay, the enemy will hang us all. I was conscripted, Father. I didn't ask to be here. What can I do now?"

Schelling had no idea what to tell him. The boy walked away, mumbling.

Suddenly, around ten in the morning, sirens began to wail. Not the usual air alert. A one-minute blast, followed by a short pause, then another one-minute blast, for five minutes.

The enemy was in sight.

Everyone stood silently waiting.

Nothing happened.

All day the air was smothering, electric, uncertain. Waiting for the clank of tank treads.

In the afternoon, twenty Jewish women appeared, wandering aimlessly in the fields beyond the camp, calling names no one could hear, like women in a dream. Apparently the train bringing them from the East had been derailed, or blown up, or the crew had simply panicked and ran. The women were in shock. Or insane.

The crematorium had fallen so far behind that the Death Kommando was told simply to dump the bodies in the eight-foot ditch between the camp and the second fence.

Finally, toward dusk, aircraft flew very low over the camp, and the prisoners could hear loud explosions from Dachau Town.

Then, at evening roll call, the distant roar of artillery suddenly silenced.

It must be! The Americans had found them!

With a sudden, huge roar, men at the back of the ranks broke and climbed to the tin roofs of the first infirmary barrack and the canteen, waving caps and shouting, "America! America!"

For a few moments the guards panicked, looking toward the gate. Nothing emerged. The men on the roof fell silent.

Hearing the noise, Sturmbannfuehrer Weiter came stomping from the Kommandantur and ordered the troopers in the towers to fire at the prisoners on the roofs. They fired over their heads. The prisoners climbed down and filtered back into the ranks.

The guns began again, distantly.

That night, there were no searchlights. The men lay wide-eyed in their bunks, staring at the boards above them or at the feet of the men on either side, breathless.

In Apartment III-A of Barrack 26, Father Leo DeConinck prayed aloud, in Latin, so at least most of the motley community could understand, "'Lift up your heads. Your deliverance is at hand.' National Socialism is dead. May it rest in peace."

One of the Italian priests spat onto the floor.

"*Non in pace*," he growled, "*in pece*." He looked sullenly around at the quizzical faces turned to him in the darkness. "Not in peace," he said in German. "In shit."

A day of bits and pieces. Like bracing for a hurricane. Which would not come.

* * * * *

Sunday, 29 April 1945 - KZ Dachau

Sunday morning, Georg Schelling woke from a fitful night's sleep. He lay on the shelf, sandwiched between Peter Van Gestel and Rudi Posch. It was a time of peace, the early morning, the only sounds the heavy breathing, the heartbeats. This was the only moment of solitude one had, even wedged as you were between the warmth of two others, your breathing unknowingly in rhythm with theirs. He wondered what he could say at this morning's Mass, if the Americans didn't come.

Despite frost on the roofs, it would be a beautiful Spring day. Sunshine already streamed through the dirty windows.

Sunshine? His heart spiked in his chest, and Schelling jerked upright with the shock.

They had missed roll call!

Schelling looked around the room. They were all sleeping. He eased himself down off the shelf and went to the window. Judging by the light, it had to be nearly six o'clock.

Then immediately he went to the door, stopping a moment in the latrine, then hurried out into the alleyway. This could be the best time in the world to dispose of the evidence. Of them.

The gate in the priests' inner wire stood open, the lock smashed by a short length of pipe that lay in the dirt.

Men milled up and down the central street, whispering, drifting toward the square. There seemed to be no guards anywhere, but there had to be guards somewhere. Still, Schelling felt an almost terrifying freedom. For the first time in seven years, there was no one to tell him what to do!

When they got to the end of the street, no prisoner ventured out into the square. Then they saw that guards were still at the machine guns in the towers. But, dangling from the mouth of the tunnel under the *Jourhaus*, like a giant flag, was a white bedsheet!

In the distance, there was the growling chatter of machine gun fire and the thump of mortars. The windowpanes of the barracks shivered. Geysers of white smoke drifted over the trees from the direction of the town.

Schelling felt a tug at his sleeve and turned to see the sad face of Arthur Haulot, a Belgian layman who was on the secret International Committee.

"Father Schelling, I wanted to tell you-so you can tell the priests-we have seen the new commandant, Oskar Mueller and I."

"New commandant?"

"Yes," Haulot said with a tiny smile, "Weiter is gone. Schusslich is gone." He spat in the dirt at their feet. "Instead, we have two hundred Viking SS and an Obersturmfuehrer Sagan. The cur wasn't even going to open the kitchens, but Oskar and I assured him that, if he didn't, we wouldn't need the Americans."

"Thank you, Monsieur Haulot. I'll tell them. Survive."

"Survive, Father Schelling."

And the afternoon dragged on.

Then, at three-fifteen: "They're *here*! They're *here*!"

Like rats from thirty sewers they tumbled over one another, anyone who could walk, anyone who could stumble, down the long street to the square. Pushing past one another, falling back, caught in the eddies of bodies. Still wary of the square.

But the press of bodies was too much, and they spilled out into the flattened *Appelplatz*. It was empty. The guns had fallen silent, and the silence was contagious. From each of the watchtowers a white flag hung lank in the freshening afternoon breeze, and the machine gunners were standing with white handkerchiefs in their hands.

The square filled with men peering about, listening.

Then they heard the grinding of a heavy engine, and a long metal pipe poked out of the darkness of the tunnel, slowly swiveling from right to left. The monster gunned slowly into the square and stopped. The engine grunted hugely once, then went silent. An iron door atop its shoulders opened and a head slowly emerged. The soldier's hand reached up to pull off his tight headgear, his mouth sagging as he looked around him.

Then came the clack-clack-clack of boots under the gateway, then a hesitation at the opening, and finally a platoon of helmeted strangers came slowly, warily around the tank into the silent square. They were husky boys, stubbled, open-mouthed. They stopped in silence. One rushed back into the throat of the gateway, and the only sound was the echo of his being sick.

We make them vomit, Georg Schelling thought. For a moment, he felt like Adam, when God found him, naked and ashamed. Please go away, he thought. We are used to conversing with corpses. Let us be liberated by your own—mutants and lepers. Until we heal.

A prisoner near the gate fell to his knees at the boots of one of the soldiers, embracing them, sobbing. The husky American pulled the man to his feet and put his big, rounded arms around the skeleton in sacking, embracing his stink and sharing his tears.

More soldiers came cautiously, curiously from the archway into the silent square. The first men moved in further among the throng of silent, gaunt, ragged men from some other planet.

Then one prisoner reached out, his eyes running tears, and touched a soldier. "Thank you," he whispered.

It triggered a volcano. The prisoners began to embrace the soldiers, fall on their necks, kiss them. The noise grew until it was like the roar of a great army with trumpets and banners. Suddenly, on the roofs of the barracks, men were waving flags hidden for years inside mattresses: a Polish flag, a Czech flag, a French flag, and, atop Barrack 26, someone was sitting waving the yellow and white papal flag on the end of a crutch!

Finally, some soldier had the presence of mind to blow a bugle before the American liberators were stampeded or smothered to death in gratitude, and the tumult slowly subsided.

An American officer climbed the platform. No one could see his rank, but there were gold crosses on the lapels of his jacket. He cleared his throat several times and began to speak. Very few could understand. But the quivering of his voice and the tears in his eyes spoke more eloquently than his words.

"One of your...one of your escaped prisoners managed to penetrate...to get through to our lines," the chaplain said. "The story he told was so...unthinkable that we thought...we thought he must be...insane. Now I see that it was...that God had not given any human language the words to...to describe...this place."

The square was quiet. Here and there, a few who knew English were quickly translating. But for many the translation was merely an irritating interruption.

"I know how...I can guess how disorienting...how confusing this experience must be. But we have to think of the practicalities, or this camp will be worse than when the Germans...when the Nazis were here. It will be an enormous task, but we can take care of you, if you'll just give us some time, if you'll just...be patient. Just a little longer. It would do no good simply to fling open the gates and let you all out. You'd find a world about as devastated as in here.

"Please, if there's anyone who can speak English, you can help us all a great deal if you tell your fellow prisoners we will have to keep you in the camp a while longer. Supplies will arrive this evening-food, doctors, medicine, clothing. An officer will be assigned to each barrack, to find out your needs. So...please... go back to your barracks now, so we can try to begin to bring some order into this...this hell. You've had faith, for so long, that you would be delivered. And...and you have been delivered."

From somewhere in the ranks it began, a single voice intoning the chant. *"Te Deum, laudamus. Te Domini confitemur"*. And slowly it spread until the whole square was filled with it. *"Te Aeternum Patrem, omnis terra veneratur."* Poles, Germans, Yugoslavs, Frenchmen, Czechs. *"Tibi omnes angeli, tibi Caeli et universae potestates."* Professors, carpenters, Communists who had thought they had forgotten the words. *"Tibi Cherubim et Seraphim incessabili voce proclamant: Sanctus! Sanctus! Sanctus!"*

* * * * *

Monday, 30 April 1945 - Berlin

The next afternoon about 2:30 p.m., in the Fuehrerbunker fifty feet below the Reichschancellery in Berlin, ten days after his 56th birthday, Adolf Hitler, the new Siegfried, architect of the Thousand-Year Reich and idol of millions, held a Walther PPK7.65 pistol to his right temple and ended it.

* * * * *

Wednesday, 2 May 1945 - KZ Dachau

The following Wednesday morning, Paul Reiser lay in his bed in the infirmary, caught between vague exultation and focused despair. The soldiers had been like fussy mothers, cleaning the barrack, washing their bodies, feeding them broth with real chicken. But Paul knew his TB was beyond critical. Doctor Blaha lied only to the SS.

He felt a soft touch on his hand and he opened his eyes. At the side of his bunk stood Georg Schelling, his comfortable face crinkling in an impish grin.

"Feel up to a couple of visitors, Father?"

"Yes, Georg." It was little more than a dry hiss.

"Paul, I don't think you've ever met Monsignor Pfanzelt, the pastor of Dachau Town."

A little round doll of a man, with round cheeks like peaches and little round glasses put down a suitcase and reached around Schelling's shoulder to shake hands: one-two.

"Oh, Monsignor, I'm so glad to meet you," Paul rasped, and Schelling offered him a sip of water. "I wanted to thank you for all you did for my ordination."

"It was nothing, my son. A privilege."

"Someone else, too," Schelling grinned and stepped back.

Paul squinted up from the pillow and then his eyes went wide. "Otto! Oh, *Otto*. Oh God, I thought I'd...." Tears choked him.

Pfizer sat on the bunk and took the boy in his arms, rocking him gently. "Ah, my friend, I made you a promise, didn't I? What was the one thing I promised you, again and again?"

"That," the young man mumbled against the black shoulder of Pfizer's cassock, "that you wouldn't let me die in here."

"That's right. Now, even if I can get you out of here, I don't know whether you'll live. But you won't die in here."

Paul pulled back, holding Pfizer's shoulders, suddenly frightened. "What do you mean?"

"The Americans are tied up in their own regulations. No one can go from the camp to a hospital other than a military hospital. But there are obviously no military TB hospitals. So, we're taking you to the sanitarium at Planegg. In Monsignor Pfanzelt's suitcase, we have another cassock. And we've got copies of your papers from Bishop Von Galen. Paul Reiser. And there is no Paul Reiser on their lists here. You remember he died of typhus? We have a car outside the gate. There are so many people going in and out that a couple of foxes like Monsignor and I can probably convince the guard at the gate that he let in three priests and not two."

"Oh, Otto, I *can't*!" His head sagged against Pfizer's arm. "I can't, Otto." he whispered.

Pfanzelt beamed at him around Pfizer's arm. "My son," he said, his eyes twinkling behind his little glasses, "what if the Israelites had been like Paul Reiser, asking Moses for a guarantee, eh? Or if the apostles had stayed in fear back in the Upper Room? Father Schelling, you could help me with his clothes, please?"

A few minutes later, they left Schelling at the door of the infirmary. Slowly, the other two priests gripping his elbows, Paul Reiser tripped 900 feet to the big iron gate which said, *Arbeit Macht Frei,* through which he had walked five years before.

The harried MP took their passes, hardly looking, then did a double-take, looking up at Paul's white face and his flushed cheeks. "Are you all right, Father? I could get a doctor."

"No, no, no," Monsignor Pfanzelt bubbled. "Father was a prisoner here himself, you see, and the visit has unnerved him."

"God, I can understand that. I hope he's feeling better."

"Thank you. Thank you. We hope so, too."

They walked out of the tunnel on the other side, and Otto opened the back door of the car and got in. With little huffs of breath, Pfanzelt reached Paul in to him, and Paul lay with his head cradled on Otto's lap. The Monsignor trundled around and got into the driver's seat, started the engine, and the car moved away.

Paul was trembling under Pfizer's hand.

"It's all right now, Paul," Pfizer said and wiped the perspiration from the young man's face. "You're free, son. Free."

"Oh, Otto. My good friend."

"And that's what friends are for, to keep promises."

"From now on," Paul coughed, "all the days are gifts."

"Like the first one."

The car moved past the officers' stately homes and turned at the corner where three iron SS men ran above the sign toward the SS camp and the fat officer whipped two circus buffoons in the other direction, toward KZ Dachau.

The car turned toward town and moved out through the fields of the first new wheat, filled with light.

ACKNOWLEDGMENTS

I began research for this book in 1980. The stories of the German Catholic underground in the first half, though fictionalized, are all true but not necessarily about the man I have called Paul Reiser. The Paul Reiser stories and all the other happenings in the second half come in large part from *The Victory of Father Karl*, by Otto Pies, S.J., about the seminarian Karl Leisner. He died about one month after his "release." Thirty years ago, I had no way of knowing that in the summer of 1997 Pope John Paul II would publicly beatify the hero of this novel.

Thanks to:

The late Fr. Josef Mitros, S.J., #22416, who was arrested in Lublin, Poland, February 13, 1940, as a seminarian, who suffered in Dachau from December 14, 1940, until the end, and who graciously read and critiqued this manuscript.

Jack Post who believed in the task when few others did.

The Jesuits of LeMoyne College, Syracuse, NY, who for ten summers allowed me space, time, and victuals to write. And rewrite. And rewrite.

Richard and Kathleen Moon, who gave me a cover better than I could have hoped for.

The Rochester Public Library for its fine collection, especially the invaluable 1935 Baedekers with every street and byway of Germany.

Fr. Vincent Lapomarda, S.J., who gathered the excellent Holocaust collection in the Dinand Library at Holy Cross College, Worcester, Ma.

Fr. Michael Nagle, who pushed me to make sure this got published.

Finally, perversely, to the editor who said years ago, "Nobody would go to a camp for the Catholic Church. They would have just shut up." Which kept me from shutting up.

CPSIA information can be obtained at www.ICGtesting.com
Printed in the USA
LVOW12s1355141113

361195LV00005B/273/P